"MY LITTLE RED-HAIRED WITCH! I WANT YOU HERE, FOR MY CONVENIENCE. . . ."

He leaned forward, capturing her face again, imprisoning her head between his hands. His mouth was hard and forceful, demanding a response that she stubbornly withheld. He covered her face and throat with kisses, his hands coaxing, caressing, tantalizing her. His hands grew more urgent, demanding, and she trembled violently, fighting against giving in to the hot pleasure of surrender.

Rufenna willed her treacherous body not to respond. It wasn't fair! "No! No, I won't . . . I can't be used like this," she cried. "Anything you get from me will be by force!"

WINDS OF FURY, WINDS OF FIRE

Rosalind Foxx

A DELL BOOK

Published by
Dell Publishing Co., Inc.
1 Dag Hammarskjold Plaza
New York, New York 10017

Dell ® TM 681510, Dell Publishing Co., Inc.

ISBN: 0-440-19533-0

Printed in Canada

First printing—September 1981

To Judy and June,
without whom this book would not
have been possible

WINDS OF FURY, WINDS OF FIRE

CHAPTER ONE

Rufenna Lyall slipped the catch on the heavy shutters and eased them open. As she pushed them wide, the pale, mid-afternoon sunlight poured in the window, splashing across the gray stones of the Abbey corridor. She had counted on finding this wing of the Abbey deserted at this time of day and, for once, luck seemed to be with her. The nuns would be in other sections of the rambling building, going about their daily chores or meditating in the chapel; the other girls would also be occupied with their assigned tasks; only an ill-chance would bring anyone to the wing housing the sleeping quarters at this time of the afternoon. Rufenna sent another hasty glance up and down the deserted corridor, leaned precariously out the window, and with a happy sigh sat down on the broad sill. In a swift movement she had swung her legs over the rough stone sill and had dropped down onto the dry, brown grass. Rufenna stopped long enough to push the heavy wooden shutters back into place over the window, so her route of escape would not be easily discovered. She ducked quietly behind the clump of tall heather that grew in profusion against the back wall of the Abbey. A loud, shrill voice floated

to her on the slight breeze and Rufenna froze. Sister
Martha! Had she already discovered that one of her
charges had escaped her eye? Rufenna wrapped her
long gray woolen skirt around her and burrowed
lower behind the sheltering bush until the merciless
voice finally faded out and vanished. So intent was
Rufenna on escaping Sister Martha's vigilance for a
time that she did not even notice the pale blue sky,
a rarity at this time of year; she did not see the fleeting clouds that carried a hint of rain. All she saw
was the empty stretch of garden here at the back of
the Abbey, and a chance for a few moments of freedom. It was time for Nones, she knew, since she had
heard the bells ring over ten minutes ago, but she
wasn't in the mood to go meekly to chapel.

A quick dash across the dry grass brought her to
the safety of the tall gray stone wall that encircled
the Abbey like a prison wall. She found a springy
patch of heather and sat down, wrapping her skirt
warmly around her long legs, and relaxed against
the hard stone of the wall. Her eyes wandered over
the garden and to the solid stone of the Abbey buildings. Their grim bulk was softened by the clumps of
heather, by the pale sunlight caressing its walls. Nothing could make them appear a cozy, inviting sight, but
Rufenna had grown up with that rough gray Border
stone and tall, forbidding walls.

The Scottish border, as it moves down from the
North Sea, travels in a vertical sweep for a distance
of twenty or so miles. Then it curves as gently as a
woman's breast before it continues on its journey.
In this curve, and not five miles from the English
border, nestled the Abbey of St. Whitby. St. Whitby's
was one of the last strongholds in Scotland that
maintained the ancient traditions of the Church.
When a girl was sent there for safekeeping, her parents were assured that she would be instructed in
the rules of chastity, abstinence, and, above all, just

plain hard work. The girls were prepared by the nuns for the running of a castle, the management of servants, and the behavior of a lady. Most of the girls took their duties seriously and heeded the caution of the nuns and learned as best they could. Rufenna Lyall was not such a girl. It seemed that she could not, or would not, learn to walk with dignity, to do her needlework properly, to moderate her voice, to concern herself with housewifely chores. Instead she longed to be outside the walls, meeting life halfway. The nuns did their best but she sorely tried their patience; and she was just as anxious to terminate her stay there as they were to see her go. Even in the Abbey, life was trying enough in this late winter of 1544. They did not need the added complications of this wayward girl.

The heather, not yet in bloom, was scratching her legs savagely, so she cautiously stood up, shook the twigs from her skirts, and moved away from the bushes. If she was lucky, she could still enjoy another hour of peace before it would be time to return to the Abbey. The bells for Nones rang just before three and she shouldn't be missed until four. Certainly she must return well before supper, because Sister Martha would scold her terribly if she missed Vespers.

While she contemplated with pleasure what to do with this stolen hour, a soft cough behind her sent her whirling around, her hand flying to her throat. Found out! A tall young man stood there, watching her with blue eyes. It was only Willie! Rufenna gasped in relief as she leaned against the stone wall and regarded the village lad who helped with the heavy work in the garden.

"Willie, you frightened me!"

His smile broadened. "Sister Martha was hunting for ye, Mistress Rufenna. Did ye not hear her?"

"I heard her, Willie, as did everyone else in the

Abbey, but I didn't want to go back yet. You won't tell, will you?"

"Nay, I wunt tell. What mischief are ye brewing now?"

Rufenna smiled up at him, noticing, not for the first time, the width of his shoulders under the coarse woolen shirt. Willie was what her father would call a strapping lad, and she had to agree. The work-hardened muscles rippled as he put aside his hoe and joined her against the wall. Besides the Abbot, Willie was the only man who came to the Abbey regularly. The Abbot was both old and ugly and could scarcely be considered a man, so Rufenna paid little heed to his visits. But she had warily made friends with Willie. She must be careful, for the Abbess would not like any of the young ladies to be friendly with such a husky young man. The Abbess would admonish her that Willie was not of her class and should be treated as a servant. The Abbess would not be doing her duty if she did not impress upon the young ladies in her care that class distinctions should be learned at an early stage and should never be disregarded. Rufenna cared little what the Abbess thought about it but she did not relish the punishment that would be meted out if she were caught. So she had been careful and not one of the nuns was aware that Rufenna had even spoken to the young man.

Willie looked at her, his gaze admiring her unruly red hair, her green eyes, her wondrously white skin that neither summer sun nor winter chill could alter. His eyes slid down her body to her firmly jutting breasts and curving waist. He turned his gaze away from the skirt that clung to her thighs and abdomen before it trailed away nearly to her feet. Willie was an unusually tall boy, but he had also noticed that Rufenna was tall, the tallest young lady in the Abbey. He cleared his throat and searched nervously for something to say.

"What do ye out here, mistress?"

"Oh, Willie, just escaping for a little while. I grow so tired of work and prayers. There is nothing to do here but work and pray and I long to be away from the Abbey."

Willie nodded. They had talked of this before and he knew she chafed at being penned within these cloistered walls and he could understand. The young ladies of good family, sent here by their parents until time to wed, were closely guarded. They were never allowed outside the walls except in the presence of a father or brother when an occasional visiting day permitted them to go for a short ride. His gaze flicked again to her fiery hair as it tumbled in burnished strands around her shoulders and he thought she was not a patient lass. From the time her father had placed her in the care of the nuns when she was twelve, she seemed incapable of settling down happily to Abbey life. She fretted at the restrictions and rules and waited impatiently for the time of her release.

"How old are ye now, Mistress Rufenna?"

"Seventeen, Willie—I will turn eighteen in the spring and pray God I will be home when my birthday comes."

"Seventeen! Your father should be sending for you soon. Did ye not tell me ye were to wed in the winter?"

"November, Alexander said on his last visit."

Rufenna sank down on the dry, brittle grass, and after a moment's pause Willie joined her. Rufenna thought back to her brother's last visit, when he brought her Christmas present from her mother. He said their father was ailing and she was to light a candle for him and pray for his recovery. She begged for other news and he told her she would be coming home by summer to prepare for a winter wedding.

Neville Kerr was her betrothed and she was not

at all sure she wanted to wed him. She had only
seen him once, when they were children. She recalled
that day when she and David Shelby, an orphan and
kinsman of her mother, shyly invited him to join in
their game. For a brief time the three children played
amicably, but when the outcome of the game was not
to his liking, young Neville burst into tears and
threatened to tell his uncle Robert, who was there
on business with Rufenna's father. What manner of
man was he now? she wondered. He was not allowed
to visit her here, but surely she would see him when
she returned home.

An image came to mind of another man: tall, shoulders so broad they had blocked out the sunlight as
he had towered over her in this garden, dark eyes
resting with amusement on her as she had sat cross-
legged under the apple tree. Looking back on it, she
wondered how she had so coolly dared to offer him
an apple. He had as coolly accepted it and stood above
her as he ate it. They had exchanged a few words
about the lingering autumn weather and he introduced himself. Isobel's brother, Lord Hammond.
While she searched frantically for something else to
say, he thanked her for the apple, inquired where his
young sister could be found, and left her. Rufenna
had watched his flat back, his arrogant black head,
as he went in search of Isobel and she admitted to
herself that Isobel had cause to be proud of her
brother. His very dark eyes, nearly black, she recalled,
had crinkled at the corners when he smiled down at
her. She had never seen clothing as fine as the blue
velvet doublet and hose he wore and the fur-lined
cloak he had casually thrown over his shoulders. Besides Willie and her own brother, Alexander, Davon
Hammond was the only man Rufenna had seen for
five years. Sophia, her other good friend, had sighed
over him quite openly and wished she could wed

such a man. Some reticence kept Rufenna from joining her friend in daydreams about this man.

She was betrothed to Neville Kerr and that was
all there was to it. If only Neville would be as tall
and handsome and—what was it?—assured as Davon
Hammond! Rufenna knew she should not indulge in
these dreams. She would have no choice in the matter, since she would wed Neville whether he was
handsome or ugly, tall or short. Betrothals were nearly
as binding as marriages and almost as difficult to
break. It had long been agreed upon by her father
and Neville's uncle, the powerful Sir Robert Kerr
of Cessford. Soon it would be her turn to leave the
Abbey. Sophia had left last year to marry Tim Scott
of Tushielaw. Isobel . . .

Isobel Hammond had left quite suddenly without
waiting to say good-bye. Rufenna was deeply hurt
by such neglect and she asked the nuns what had
happened. Strangely enough, they refused to tell her
anything about it. They merely said that Isobel had
been fetched and would say no more. Rufenna had
wondered about that, for she knew that Isobel was betrothed to Ian Hunter, but they were not to wed
for another year. Young Ian was still completing his
education in France, the last she had heard. Why
then had Lord Hammond taken Isobel away? It had
been so confusing. That last evening Isobel had been
flushed and excited but had said nothing about leaving. She must have known. Now that Isobel had gone
too, the last few months had been worse than ever.

Willie, watching the play of emotion over her
vivid face, voiced the echo of her thoughts. "Ye have
been lonely since the two other lasses went? Aye, I
warrant you have. Ye have no other special friend
here now?"

Rufenna shook her head. "No, it was Sophia, Isobel, and me from the first. Sophia left to wed Tim

Scott and Isobel left so suddenly. She didn't even say good-bye," Rufenna said softly, watching Willie through thick, dark lashes.

Willie shuffled his feet uneasily. He knew how and why Isobel had left and was aware that Rufenna did not know. He cleared his throat and made an effort to shift the conversation to safer ground.

"Ye should write to your father and remind him 'tis time to fetch you away."

"I did that, Willie! I wrote to Papa, Mama, and Alexander. All of them. And not a word have I had back since Christmas. Willie, I want to go home. I'm lonely here and feel shut away. 'Tis like a prison. Except for prayers, all we do is work, eat, and sleep. The other girls are so young; I'm the oldest now that Isobel is gone. I have nobody to talk to. Except you," she added, lightly touching his work-roughened hand.

Willie stirred and pulled away his hand and looked down. Rufenna stared at him in mingled dismay and puzzlement. His cheeks had flushed slightly and he would not look at her. She was not aware of the picture she presented in her too-tight dress. The soft wool of the gray bodice strained across her firm young figure. It flowed away from her long legs and Willie knew just how shapely those legs were. He had found her too often perched in the limbs of the apple tree, bare feet swinging.

In her cloistered surroundings Rufenna had grown into a young woman without realizing it. But Willie knew! She was a startling contrast to the skinny little girl the nuns received nearly six years ago. It would be more than his life was worth to touch her, and he had carefully kept his distance. She regarded him only as a friend, someone to talk to, to laugh with. She had no notion of how her beauty stirred him. She had no idea of his struggles with himself as he avoided looking too closely at her maturing body, at her vivid, expressive face. Rufenna gazed at him now in perplexity, misunderstood his confusion, and realized that she had seen Willie react this way before. What ailed him? Did he not like her? Impulsively she laid her hand on his strong arm, forcing him to look at her.

"Willie, Willie, what is amiss? Do you mind talking to me? Are you not my friend?"

He stammered slightly. "Nay, mistress, nothing is amiss. I am proud to be your friend but the nuns wouldn't like it. Ye'd best be careful, mistress, or they'd send you away. Nay, now!" he cried, seeing the sudden light of hope flaring in her eyes. "No mischief, lass! Your brother would be angry and I be the one to suffer. Think of that, lass."

Rufenna hadn't thought of it before but she knew Willie was right. If their friendship became known, Willie would be blamed and punished. They would dismiss him and he needed the work to provide for his widowed mother and younger brothers and sisters. Even a simple friendship with a youth her own age was denied to her, it appeared. What a hateful place the Abbey was!

Slowly she became aware of the bronzed young arm under her hand and looked up at him wonderingly. His arm was trembling! The muscles rippled smoothly under his skin as he pulled his arm from her touch. Did Willie fear the consequences of their friendship so much that he trembled in fear? Rufenna was sorry, too, that he had withdrawn from her. The feeling of his firm arm under her fingers had been reassuring, warming. It had, in quite another way, been exciting! Other than her brothers and father, she had never touched another man, even casually, and she discovered it was quite different. The restlessness that had beset her for months, the yearning for something she could not name . . . these inexplicable sensations were further roused by the touch of his young strength. She wanted to lean against him, to feel that strong shoulder against her head, to be comforted and warmed by the contact. Such sudden emotions confused her and it was reflected in the clear green gaze raised to him. Willie, more experienced, recognized the danger signals and backed away. She was a mighty temptation in her innocence and he dared not answer the dawning question in her eyes.

"I must go, mistress. 'Tis past time to see Sister Mary about tomorrow's work. Take heart, lass. Your brother will fetch you at the proper time."

"Willie!"

He ignored the outstretched hand and turned away.

"Nay, lass, not now. There is much yet to do before dark. Best get back before you get into more trouble with Sister Martha."

Before Rufenna could protest, Willie was gone, melting into the thick shrubs that bordered the high gray wall. Alone once more, she considered his words. Even so innocent a friendship as this one was doomed to failure. She had noticed this growing uneasiness in Willie, a withdrawal that confused and puzzled her. He once lifted her down from the apple tree, his hard hands easily spanning her slim waist. Now if he found her there, he waited below, gaze averted from her flashing limbs, for her to descend on her own. No longer did he tease her and pull her hair; neither did he pick her up and threaten to drop her into the duck pond. What had come over Willie? Dejectedly Rufenna made her way back to the bleak gray walls of the Abbey buildings. Now there was not even supper, tasteless though it was, to look forward to. Bed without supper was Sister Martha's favorite form of punishment when one of the young ladies broke the rules.

That night, after Compline, the last church service of the day, she lay on her narrow cot in the small stone cell that was her own room. The corridor was lined with little stone cubicles similar to this, holding a cot, chair, and small table. Here the young ladies lived, doing without luxuries, existing in this Spartan life. She was desperately lonely. Could this be the reason for her restlessness, her disaffection for this life? She was bored! Would life with Neville offer more variety? Would she find him a good husband?

The nuns had tried to train them to be good wives. They could grow and dry herbs, make butter and cheese, dry and preserve the fruits of the orchards. They could even sew a fine seam. Rufenna hated needlework instantly and passionately. Too often Sister Martha had enforced her supperless punishment for careless stitching. Rufenna had learned to do it properly, but never ceased loathing it. She much preferred the more active chores such as scrubbing floors and working in the dairy and soon she and Isobel had devised a way to handle this. She would give her needlework to Isobel, who enjoyed it, and do the heavier chores from which Isobel shrank.

What else did she need to know to be a good wife? Her thoughts strayed to the more intimate side of marriage. She knew she would be expected to provide heirs for Neville. She, Isobel, and Sophia had often held whispered conversations late at night, all three crowded on one cot, about that side of marriage. Only the farm animals had shed some light on the mating process but the girls shied away from that in horror. Their conversations were not very productive, as their knowledge was so scanty as to be nonexistent, but they discussed it with great enthusiasm anyway.

Their cherished romantic fantasies filled the gaps of their knowledge. They had all visualized themselves as being swept into the arms of the knight of their dreams, being kissed, and . . . their imaginations stopped there. They had vague, confused, frightened ideas of what happened next and it had no connection with the stray bitch that had been observed with a pack of dogs taking turns mounting her. What happened next must be a pleasure, since it was not discussed. As Sophia shrewdly pointed out, it must be something wickedly fun since the nuns constantly preached against it. They called it, when they were forced to refer to it—"the appetites of the flesh," and that statement was even more confusing.

Rufenna had learned over the years that anything that was enjoyable at all was considered sinful by the Church. They were reproved for laughter, for high spirits, for innocent fun. They were impressed with the beauty of the Virgin Birth but could only hazily understand how it was different from all others. They had all heard enough about childbearing to know it was a painful and serious matter for a woman, but the conception of the child was a mystery to all of them. Rufenna wished she could stop worrying about it, as Sophia vowed to do when she said she would leave it up to Tim. After all, he would be her husband and he would be able to tell her what to do.

Would Neville find her beautiful? Cloistered as she had been, she knew not what a man considered beautiful. Suddenly she remembered the pleasant feel of Willie's arm under her hand and for the first time wondered what it would be like to have Willie kiss her. Would she like it? She thought it might be pleasant, as was the touch of his arm. Perhaps she could persuade Willie to kiss her; then she'd know.

Willie. She wondered again at his manner, his confusion. And, she realized, he had not wanted to discuss Isobel! Did Willie know something she did not? What *had* happened to Isobel? Something out of the ordinary, Rufenna was sure. She had changed so those last few months. She had become secretive, more reticent. She often sat for hours on her narrow cot with a soft smile on her face, a smile that had baffled Rufenna. It had suggested a remembered joy or pleasure. What had brought about this change in Isobel? No longer was she the lighthearted young girl who was eager to share her thoughts and feelings. She had grown dreamy, quiet. She had once talked constantly of her brother Davon, whom she adored. Those last months she had scarcely mentioned him.

The day Davon had found Rufenna under the apple tree had been his last visit to the Abbey. Isobel had told her later that night that he was leaving for a visit to France, on business for Mary of Guise, the Queen Mother. He must have returned almost immediately, Rufenna thought, as it was such a short time later that Isobel had left. Maybe he had sent his men to fetch her. Why did he not take her from the Abbey when he came? Rufenna sighed. Lucky Isobel. She was married, no doubt. Safely away from this bleak, boring life.

Rufenna deliberately turned her thoughts from that strong, dark face with the wickedly smiling brown-black eyes, the firm, well-cut lips. She would never see Isobel or Davon Hammond again. She had better concentrate on her own future.

As Rufenna slid into sleep, she found it difficult to build dreams upon a child's face, barely remembered. Neville had been blond-haired with blue eyes, she recalled dimly. Were they blue? She could not remember. The only eyes she could recall in her drowsy state were dark ones, crinkling with amusement. Rufenna sighed again and slept.

CHAPTER TWO

Tentative gray light had made its way into the small cell-like room when Rufenna was awakened by Sister Martha shortly after dawn. Rufenna stumbled sleepily from the hard cot, shivering in the dawn chill. The stone walls were clammy and damp and she hurried into her woolen clothing after a hasty wash from the bucket of cold water. She had only five more minutes before she must appear for morning prayers. Resolutely she pushed back her heavy hair, tying it with a strip of rawhide given her for that purpose by Willie. She slipped slender feet into the heavy leather shoes. She hated the clothing they had to wear at the Abbey. She had complained bitterly about it to Alexander but he ignored her. In despair she had written to her father and after a long while he had sent her a length of soft gray wool which she and Isobel had fashioned into a high-necked, long-sleeved dress that helped a bit against the chill of the stone walls. It did not chafe and scratch her skin as the coarser wool had done and she was thankful for that.

She glared with distaste at the leather shoes and decided that when she was married to Neville, she would have slippers of the finest satin and the softest kid. An image of her working in the Abbey chicken yard, raking out the droppings and cleaning the hen house, in a dress of silk and dainty satin slippers, sent her off to morning prayers giggling. Her mood was not even dampened by the stern reproof from Sister Sarah about the disrespect of mirth during prayers. Rufenna, escaping to the dairy after breakfast, could not account for her lighthearted mood. After yesterday's strained talk with Willie, she should be in low spirits, but she wasn't. A faint premonition of change had touched her this morning. She saw nothing different in the sisters and the other young girls demurely eating the plain, coarse food at the table, but perhaps it came from within.

Something was in the wind, in the air. Perhaps it was the first real hint of spring! If so, it was unseasonably early! Not a purple bud showed on the heather, and the trees were still gaunt and leafless. Still, she knew spring was coming. With it would come her release. Humming to herself, Rufenna began the daily chore of churning, ignoring the curious stares and whispers of the other girls. Sister Angelica cast an indulgent eye on the happy face and said nothing. She always turned a blind eye to her girls' happier moods. Youth was the time for it, she decided comfortably. So, undisturbed, Rufenna started her morning tasks with a will to work.

At midmorning she paused, finding Sister Martha at her elbow.

"Come, child. The Abbess wishes to see you."

Rufenna stared at the plump face and her heart sank. Had the stern Abbess found out about her friendship with Willie? Rufenna swallowed nervously, took off the sack apron and the linen coif that covered her hair, and went meekly with Sister Martha. They paused at her little cell so she could wash her face and hands and tidy her hair. Sister Martha's punishment for her escapade yesterday would be as nothing compared with what the Abbess would do.

Sister Martha showed her into the Abbess's room and retreated quietly. Rufenna walked to where two people waited. She was astounded and overjoyed to see a tall, lean red-haired man standing beside the Abbess. Alexander! With a little rush she was across the stone floor, flinging herself into her brother's arms.

The Abbess touched her on the shoulder and she looked into steely gray eyes filled with disapproval, and something else that Rufenna didn't understand.

"Mistress Lyall," the Abbess chided. "Do strive for more seemly conduct! As you see, your brother has come to fetch you."

Fetch you! Rufenna turned wondering eyes on her brother and Alexander nodded. His hard face softened slightly into a smile. "I'll take you with me today if you hurry. It is time to come home."

"Oh, Alexander!"

Rufenna ignored the disapproving look on the Abbess's face, almost one of cold contempt, and threw herself back into her brother's arms, hugging him hard. He patted her awkwardly and held her a little away from him.

"Hasten, child. We have far to travel before dark. My men await me outside."

On flying feet Rufenna raced down the deserted corridors. Never again would she be stopped by one of the nuns and cautioned to walk with dignity. She could hardly think of her coming release. It couldn't be true!

Through a tall, narrow window she glimpsed Willie, walking toward the back garden. "Willie!"

He turned, saw her hanging half out of the window, and cautiously came over, his gaze taking in the lovely face, blazing with emotion, the green eyes sparkling with excitement.

"What, lass?"

"Willie, Alexander is here! He's taking me home today!"

Willie, who had seen the troop of men waiting outside the gate and had recognized the fiery red head of Alexander Lyall, nodded.

"I saw him arrive. God go with you, lass, and behave yourself. It is time for you to go," he added, but gruffly, knowing he would miss her.

"Aye, Willie, more than time." She stared straight into her friend's face and impulsively leaned forward. "Thank you for everything."

Before she could have second thoughts, Rufenna leaned farther out the window and pressed a shy kiss on his firm young mouth. For a second his mouth moved convulsively under hers, sending a surprised ripple of response through her; then he stepped back, pulling away his head as if he'd been stung.

"Good-bye, Willie," she choked.

Then she was gone, running down the hall to her little cell. Swiftly her meager belongings were bundled together and her heavy woolen cloak thrown around her shoulders. Rufenna gazed around the small cubicle and felt not the slightest tremor of regret that she was leaving it. She was full of excitement, of joy at her escape from the dreary gray walls and such a restricted life. Then she joined her brother in the courtyard and said a prim and respectful farewell to the Abbess. The old woman entrusted Rufenna's care into the hands of God and stalked back into the Abbey without another word. Rufenna started to comment on it when she noticed the horse Alexander was holding for her.

"Oh, Alexander, must I ride sidesaddle? I have not been in the saddle for months and this is so awkward."

"Sidesaddle it is, unless you stay here. You must remember you are a young lady now, nearly a married woman, and you should behave with dignity. Ladies ride sidesaddle."

Holy Mary, thought Rufenna, I may as well be back in the Abbey! Will people be reminding me all my life that I must behave like a lady?

"Well, what will it be?" asked Alexander. "Come, lass, 'tis not so bad. Father instructed the saddle-maker to make it just for you. Enough of this. Up you go."

Knowing herself beaten in this skirmish, Rufenna allowed herself to be helped into the saddle. She settled herself firmly and hooked her knee around the horn and draped her skirt and cloak modestly about her. It had been months, nay, last autumn, since she had ridden out of these sheltering walls and she knew she would be stiff and sore on the morrow, but it was worth it! She was so anxious to put behind her this part of her life that she would willingly have accepted even more discomfort. Besides, the morrow would bring Mama, Papa, and her young brother, John. Home at last! She shivered in happy anticipation.

As they rode down the rocky track leading down the hill, Rufenna turned to her brother. "Why, Alexander! Why did Papa send for me now?"

Alexander frowned and glanced at her. "Papa did not send for you, Rufenna. I came for you myself. Papa is . . . not well, my dear. He has grown increasingly frail during the last year. I am in charge now at Lyall. Sir Robert Kerr wishes the marriage advanced and he advised me he wishes it to take place during the summer. That will not leave you long to prepare. Mama is very busy caring for Papa so you will have to do much of it yourself."

Rufenna assimilated this and eased the horse around a huge boulder blocking the path. Why did Neville's uncle want the marriage advanced? And Alexander in command at Lyall? She glanced at his face, noting the hard, shuttered expression, and decided not to ask. Mama could tell her when they arrived at Lyall and she felt it would be foolish now to try to question Alexander. He was more than ten years her senior and she had always been a bit afraid of him. He could be hard and ruthless, she knew, and let nothing stand in the way of what he wanted. She shivered slightly, remembering he now commanded Lyall. He had never had the humor or indulgence for her that Papa had. She might cajole her father successfully but such tactics would get her nowhere with Alexander. She had not seen him in months and thought that he, too, had changed. He seemed harder, more grim. Was there trouble that she knew nothing of? Rufenna kept silent, crushing back the many questions that hovered on the tip of her tongue, and was strangely shy to ask them of Alexander. For his part, he ignored her.

They reached the brow of the hill and began the twisting descent down it. St. Whitby's lay not far from Whitton, not over five miles from Sir Robert Kerr's castle of Cessford. Neville had never been allowed to visit her, since only brothers and fathers could come there, but she wondered if he ever gave a thought to her, so near and yet out of reach. She had wondered often enough about him.

As they followed the narrow paths through the rolling hills, bypassing the village of Middlesknowes, and crossing small streams, she thought about Willie and their farewell. Patiently she urged her horse up and down the unmarked paths that twisted through the hills. Had Willie been as startled as she by that brief touch of their lips? She had never been kissed before, much less kissed a man herself, and it had been pleasant, she decided.

She gazed blindly at the trees, still leafless but for the stands of evergreens which were just dark smudges against the hillsides. Prickly gorse blanketed everything, giving way here and there to large patches of heather that were stark and ugly in the wan sunlight. The cold was damp and penetrating. Rufenna wrapped her cloak more closely around her. She wondered at the way the Abbess had behaved. She appeared to disapprove strongly of Alexander and was barely civil to him. What on earth could she know about him to cause her to dislike him? Perhaps the Abbess had heard of her own recent escapade and her annoyance spilled over onto everyone. That must be it, Rufenna thought, and tried to put the puzzling question out of her mind.

When they stopped at midafternoon, she ate the cold meat and cheese offered her with no comment. They still had hours to go before the towers of Lyall would come into view, where it stood above the valley, guarding it as a grim sentinel. She ached in every limb now and was numb with cold. The sun vanished behind a heavy cloud, and the rain which had threatened began to fall. The rocky path grew increasingly slippery and Alexander sent her back into the middle of the troop of men while he remained at their head. He was scanning the rough terrain with alert eyes. She wondered what he was looking for. Anything in particular or just the normal alertness any Borderer needed to stay alive in these rugged hills? Bandits and outlaws used these hills as a refuge, Rufenna knew, and the very air seemed brooding and uneasy.

She was so tired now that it was difficult to follow any train of thought, so her mind whirled with thoughts of Willie, the cold, icy behavior of the Abbess, Alexander, her ill father. The little troop pressed westward toward Stobs. Lyall lay secure in the Teviotdale hills, between Stobs and Riccarton. Not over ten miles or so, as the crow flies, from the border with England. It had need of the rugged hills that ringed it, giving protection from the bands of marauding

English Borderers. Alexander would be alert for any raid now, she realized, remembering all she knew and had heard before being banished from the castle to the Abbey. It was their proximity to the Border that made a safe, cloistered Abbey desirable for sheltering young girls of good birth. So far the Abbey had remained untouched by the raiders, although the village of Whitton had often been plundered.

Thinking of Whitton reminded her of Willie and how she would miss him. He had been more a brother than Alexander would ever be, she realized, gazing ahead at her brother's tall form at the head of the troop. Willie had offered a sympathetic ear, had joined in her fun and laughter, had given her simple but good advice, as a brother usually does. However, that last farewell had not been brotherly, her mind said suddenly. Far from brotherly. She thought about their kiss again, at the sudden burst of warm feeling that had raced through her as his firm young mouth had answered her touch. Rufenna wished there had been time to talk to Willie about it, to get him to explain. So much was happening to her that she didn't understand.

They left the hills and entered a steep-sided valley that eventually widened out. The brown, dried-up grass muffled the hoofbeats of the horses, and the trees that thickly lined either side of the valley were gloomy in their darkness. Rufenna pulled her hood more firmly over her hair and tucked her skirt around her legs. The afternoon chill was growing worse and she wished Alexander would stop for the night and light a campfire. They could never make it to Lyall before dark, she knew, and she was not anxious to ride through the night. She already felt numb with cold and damp. She wondered if she dared suggest they stop.

She did not see the horsemen waiting silently in the woods as they watched their progress down the

valley and patiently held their swift Border ponies
in check. Her first warning that something was wrong
came when, with mighty cries, the horsemen swooped
down the hill upon them. They had cleverly planned
their charge, catching the troop of men strung out
along the narrow valley and skirting a dangerous bog.
She saw Alexander call out to his men as he frantically regrouped them into a tight square, and her
bridle was snatched by one of the troopers and her
horse urged around. The damp reins slipped from
her grasp and she followed helplessly as he tried to
turn her back the way they had come, away from the
fighting that had erupted. The shouting horsemen
poured down the slope and fell upon the troops, hitting them hard as they were caught by surprise. Rufenna, at the back of the troops, could see the battle
clearly.

Hand-to-hand combat raged over the once quiet
valley. Rufenna saw the Lyall men mutilated unmer-
cifully. She heard screams of agony as arms were
cut off, men were disemboweled, swords were driven
deep into unresisting flesh. The ponies, maddened by
the confusion, reared and plunged, occasionally slipping in the slime of blood, intestines, and mud that
covered the little battlefield. The air was filled with
the smell of gore, excrement, fear, and death. Rufenna closed her eyes but she could not close her ears.
The little trooper valiantly guiding her to safety
was forced to release her bridle and turn to face a
horseman rushing at him.

Unrestrained and frightened by the din around
him, her horse bolted. He plunged high and bucked
with insane ferocity, trying to rid himself of his rider.
Rufenna was clinging to him with all of her strength
as he broke into a breakneck run, fleeing from his
terror as fast as he could. She clutched his mane and
the hood of her cloak fell back, exposing her cas-
cade of curling red hair.

Rufenna did not see the leader of the attacking men spot her, or notice her flaming hair glinting in the watery, dying sunlight. He signaled to a nearby horseman and pointed to her just as her horse galloped furiously up the slope and into the bracken and trees. Rufenna clung desperately to her mount, clutching at whatever she found, knowing she could never stay on if he did not slow his headlong pace. The limbs and twigs tore at her hair and scratched painfully at her clothes. Something moved in the gloomy light in the woods and the horse, with a frightened snort, reared. A rabbit dashed under his hooves and Rufenna felt her grip slipping. She was falling, sliding sideways, as the horse danced and bucked. Parting company with her mount, she flew through the air to land in a big clump of gorse. With stunned eyes, half dazed by the fall, she saw the horse race into the dark woods, his mouth flecked with foam and his limbs lathered with sweat. She lay breathless and ensnared in the resilient, prickly gorse. The chilly breeze carried the sounds of battle to her ears and she groped for a way to release herself from this thorny prison. Painfully she dragged herself free and staggered to her feet.

Alexander! What was befalling him and their men? On unsteady legs she rushed to the wood's edge and sank down upon the wet grass. She had a clear view of the valley below, through two clumps of underbrush. She saw the fiery head of her brother and watched in horror as he beat off a big, burly horseman. The leader of the attacking men, separated from her brother by half a dozen fighting men, was trying to cleave his way through to that red-haired figure. Rufenna let out a moan as she stared in disbelief. She knew that dark, crisp hair just showing beneath the steel helmet he wore! She had dreamed about that dark, handsome face! Davon Hammond! It couldn't be! Why would Isobel's brother attack Alexander? But there was no doubt of it now. So indelibly had her memory of him been imprinted on her mind that she felt she would know him in the pitch dark. It was Lord Hammond, and his men were taking a terrible toll of Alexander's troops. One by one they fell, prey to a superior number of men. Some of the horses went down heavily, never to rise again. Those that did survive raced for the far end of the valley away from the battle. In dread and horror she watched a horse stray onto the treacherous bog and she turned her gaze away from his pitiful struggles. When she looked again there was no sign of him; the bog had swallowed him completely.

Davon was still fighting his way toward Alexander, and before he could reach him, before her horror-stricken gaze, Alexander went down, mutilated horribly by the terrible sword wielded by a giant horseman. Alexander slid from his horse, beneath the hooves of the maddened, blood-drenched animal, and she closed her eyes with a moan. Nausea was rising in her throat, and tears stinging her eyes. She opened them in time to see Lord Hammond force his way to the spot, to dismount and kneel by Alexander's trampled body. His hand went to Alexander's throat, feeling for a pulse, and he shook his head. Rufenna, shaking violently at the sight of her brother's torn body, was promptly sick, leaning into the underbrush as the waves of nausea flowed over her. When she turned back to the battle scene, Alexander's body was being lifted, put across a saddle, and secured. The fighting was nearly over. Only one of her brother's men was still mounted, and one, dripping blood, broke for the trees.

Suddenly, as sick and dazed as she was, Rufenna's own instinct for survival came to life. She must hide. The horsemen had seen her, she knew. They would search for her. She dragged her limp, weary body to her feet and fled deeper into the woods, looking for a place of refuge. The clash of steel had stopped and the shouting was faint now. She knew the slaughter was over. Except for her. She forced her stumbling feet to move faster and plunged wildly through the trees, searching frantically for a place to hide. Her gaze fell on a tall, extremely thick clump of under-brush and she turned and ran to it. A fallen log of massive size lay before it. She ignored the scratches and the agony of forcing herself through it and crawled deeper into the underbrush. The log cast a shadow over her. She tucked her cloak tightly around her and pulled up her hood to hide her vivid hair.

Time passed but she had no idea how long she lay there, afraid to move. The unaccustomed position on the hard ground was causing her muscles to ache and she longed to stand up and stretch. But she kept motionless. The Hammond men might have left the area, she thought, relaxing a little. She was begin-ning to consider moving when she heard them en-tering the woods. She could hear Davon's deep voice as he spoke to his men.

"She can't have gone too far. Her horse was out of control. Wat, take some of the men around that way and you three come with me."

Rufenna held her breath as they passed her, un-noticed in her sheltering position. The deepening gloom of the woods helped to conceal her and she waited with bated breath for them to pass. The sounds of the horses faded away and she lay chilled and numb in her hiding place. She was shaking now, from head to foot, with shock and fear, knowing her posi-tion to be disastrous. She was on foot, alone in a dark wood. She did not know where she was, which direction or how far away Lyall was, and these men were searching for her. She shivered violently as she thought of her fate if they found her.

CHAPTER THREE

She could stay here no longer. Instinct drove her from her safe hiding place into the open. Frost crunched underfoot and trimmed the bare brush. She was so numb by now that she could scarcely move but she knew she could not lie there all night. If she didn't start moving, warming her chilled limbs, she would die of exposure. She had lost her cloak and remembered dully that she had had it when she crawled into her hiding place. No doubt the briars and brambles had torn it from her shoulders when she stood up but she had no memory of it. There had been no further sound of the men and she assumed they had given up their search and ridden for home. She had a vague idea that the Hammonds' major stronghold, Torrey Castle, was not too far from here, if she was right in her guess of their approximate location. She had only been this way once, when her father had taken her to the Abbey, but she remembered the valley. Her father had warned his men of the bog, she recalled, and she thought this valley was about halfway from Lyall to the Abbey. Rufenna groaned. That would mean she was nearly twenty twisting, hilly miles from home . . . and safety.

She must do something! She could not stand here
the rest of the night debating with herself what was
best. They were traveling west, if she remembered,
to get to Lyall. In the morning she would put the
sun at her back and strike out in that direction. Perhaps . . . a sudden thought led her to run for the
edge of the woods, to the top of the slope. The valley
lay quiet below her, dimly lit by fitful moonlight.
She scanned the valley with anxious eyes, seeking
movement that could mean a horse remained. Nothing moved. Hesitantly she descended the slope, looking about her warily. There was no sound other than
the sighing of the wind through the treetops as she
reached the floor of the valley.

In the near darkness she stumbled over something.
One of Alexander's men? Her hand flew to her throat
to stifle a cry of horror. She glanced about wildly but
saw nothing else. The body was lying behind a large
boulder and must have gone unnoticed. The other
men had been taken away, as far as she could see.
Hating it more with every moment, her hands trembling with outrage and sheer horror, Rufenna knelt
by the body and gently pried the dagger out of the
cold, stiff hand. She might need it before this night
was finished, her rational mind told her. She was
hardly aware of what she did now, so dazed with
terror and panic was she. She was guided purely by
instinct and relied upon it completely. Still numb
with despair, she found her hands unclasping the
heavy cloak from the body and huddling it around
her. It could not help him now and she had need of
all the warmth and comfort she could find. So di-
vorced from reality had she become, she did not even
shudder as the warm woolen cloak eased some of her
chill. She ignored the sickening odors that emanated
from it. Blindly she turned and began moving down
the valley in the direction they had been riding when
they were attacked.

Rufenna reached the end of the valley and began a stiff climb out, scrambling over the rocky path that was more suitable for goats than a girl afoot. On she went, as the moon appeared and vanished, flirting with heavy clouds that threatened to swallow it up. Then true darkness would descend upon her and she would be forced to stop. She would sit impassively, all sensation and feeling long numbed by the nightmare that stalked her every step. When the moon would reappear and light her path, she would force herself to her feet. Up rocky, boulder-strewn paths she wandered, having no idea where she was going and scarcely caring. Down the steep hillsides, she felt her skirt torn and ripped by the vicious thorns and gorse bushes. Hunger pierced her apathy once and was dismissed. In her trance she continued her journey through the dark hills, following the easier path when presented with a choice.

A flickering light off to her right caught her eye and she stared dully at it. It took precious moments to penetrate into her brain. A fire! Her gaze sharpened with awareness. It *was* a fire! A shepherd? Unthinkingly she turned from the path and headed toward that dancing, beckoning light. Warmth, possibly food? Too late the murmur of voices reached her and she stopped abruptly. No shepherd, then, not with a number of men gathered around the fire. Dimly she could see horses and at that moment one of them whinnied softly. Coming out of her trance, Rufenna backed away, anxious to retreat before she was seen. She turned to run and stumbled over a large rock. It went flying down the slight hillside, rushing and clattering as it fell. Silence fell on the campers and she was aware of a sudden, startled flurry of movement as she ran back up the slope.

"There she be," a man's voice shouted as her tall, full-skirted figure was clearly outlined in the moonlight as she reached the crest of the hill. Fear lent

wings to her feet as she darted around rocks and
through crevices, but it was no use. She was too cold,
too tired. Her weary limbs would not obey her; she
stumbled and faltered. Hard hands caught her shoulders and spun her around. She hit out at the man
but he ignored it, swinging her up in ironlike arms
and clamping her against his solid chest. In the
moonlight he appeared to be a giant of a man and
Rufenna closed her eyes in despair. Were they outlaws, hiding in the hills? Or Lord Hammond's men?
She hardly knew at that moment which would be
worse. She was carried down the hill and back to the
fire and there dumped on her feet. Rufenna staggered and again those hard hands braced her, shor-
ing her up. A tall, wide-shouldered man loomed before her, moving from the shadows into the light of
the campfire.

"Over there," his deep voice said, motioning at a
buttress of rock that offered a sheltered niche from
the wind. The burly man lifted her again and strode
around the edge of rock and set her down by a small
fire tucked back in the deep crevice running into the
rock. A tumbled blanket on the ground told her that
the leader of these men, the man with the deep voice,
had been sleeping there. The burly man released her
and Rufenna sank limply down by the fire, her hands
going out toward it for warmth. She dimly heard the
clatter of the man's feet as he went back around the
rock to the main campfire. She looked up at the
tall, dark man who faced her over the fire.

"So we found you at last," Davon Hammond murmured.

Rufenna was incapable of answering.

He looked her over in the moonlight, not missing
the tangled hair, the torn and battered dress and
cloak, the scratches on her face and hands. Yet there
was a youthful dignity about her as she squared her
shoulders and met that impassive gaze.

"What do you want of me?" she managed to ask, forcing her voice to be firm and unshaken.

He did not answer. Instead he turned to the leather saddlebag lying by his blanket and took out a battered silver flask.

"Drink some of this."

She looked up and away from the hand holding out the flask and shook her head. "No, thank you," she said primly.

He grinned slightly at her politeness and knelt before her. "You either drink it or I'll force it down you."

It was said quietly but beneath the soft voice was a tone full of determination. With trembling fingers she took the flask, being careful not to allow her fingers to brush his, and hesitantly raised it to her lips.

"Drink it."

It was a command. She took a large gulp and then gasped as the fiery liquid coursed down her throat and into her stomach. Tears stung her eyelids and she blinked hard.

"Another swallow."

Obediently she swallowed more, feeling the sudden warmth spreading through her, renewing her strength. Firmly she thrust it back into his hands before he could demand that she drink more of the potent whiskey. She needed her wits about her and not fuddled with drink. He rose and stepped to the edge of the rock and called to one of the men.

"Wat, bring food and water, quickly."

A large chunk of bread, a wedge of cheese and several strips of dried beef were pressed into her hand, and mechanically she ate them. It would do no good to refuse, she thought dully. He would only force her to eat if she rejected them. A cup of icy water was raised to her lips and she gulped it down greedily. While she ate, Davon was appraising her. He had recognized her instantly as the young girl who had given him the apple. What he had not realized until now was that *she* was Alexander Lyall's sister. His mouth hardened suddenly and the angry thought flashed through his mind that it was sheer luck that had placed this girl in his hands. He had been cheated of the satisfaction of squeezing the life from Alexander Lyall's throat with his own hands. The man had been dead when he reached him, trampled by his wounded horse. But this girl . . . she would not escape him so easily.

Rufenna raised her eyes suddenly and saw the glittering fury gazing at her from those brown-black eyes and she swallowed nervously. What had she done that could cause this man to regard her with such bitter hostility? She knew little of men, but if she had ever seen a man consumed by a flaming rage, it was Davon Hammond at that moment. Apprehensively she wiped her hands on the coarse woolen cloak and tilted her chin slightly. Emerald-green eyes, steady and questioning, met those blazing black ones.

For a second time she asked, "What do you want of me?"

His gaze flickered over her like an angry lash as he stated coldly, "An eye for an eye." Mirthlessly he laughed. "Indeed, yes, that is the very answer. What a godsend you are, Mistress Lyall. I had not expected the pleasure of your company. What an opportunity to put into practice our ancient law of the Border."

"Why did you attack us and kill my brother, Lord Hammond? It was a cowardly thing to do, to skulk in the woods and . . ." Her voice died away, stricken by the furious hatred that flared in his face.

"Cowardly? You dare to speak to *me* of cowardly action, Mistress Lyall?" he ground out between clenched teeth. She could not know the struggle he was having to control his temper. He could have torn her to pieces at that moment.

Rufenna shrank back, frightened afresh by the sheer menace in his face. Her hand groped under her cloak, finding and gripping the cold brass hilt of the dagger secured in her pocket.

"Where are my brother and his men? What did you do with their bodies? At least they deserve a Christian burial."

"Such a man as your brother deserves nothing. He and his men have been consigned to the bog." He made a motion toward her. "As to what I plan to do with you, my girl, the answer is simple. I will enjoy you."

The stark statement nearly stopped her heart with fear as she began to grasp what he meant. She knew little of the physical dangers a young woman faced in hostile hands but there was no doubt that he meant her an injury. The girls had whispered at the Abbey about village girls and servant girls who were willing partners to the local knights and lords but none of the young girls there knew any details. She wished passionately that she knew more, that she had some idea of his form of attack, of his meaning. She did not relish the idea of waiting to find out.

His hand moved abruptly and she pressed back against the rock. "Do not touch me," she stammered, gripping the dagger more firmly.

A grim smile touched his mouth and he rose easily to his feet. Panic urged her to stand, to be ready to strike or run, and she scrambled up, pressing against the rock. Over the fire their gazes met and locked and hers was the first to fall. The menace in his was clear and she subdued rising panic. She must try to defend herself and addled wits would not serve her now.

He saw the movement as she flinched from him and nodded.

"You have cause to be afraid, little virgin. If you obey me and make some effort to please me, you might survive this experience. Come here."

Rufenna blenched and recoiled. The rock was digging painfully into her back, its unyielding surface no more rigid than his face. She scarcely sensed his movement and yet, before she could recover, he had gripped her firmly, forcing her farther against the face of the rock.

"I said you would learn obedience and you should take the warning now. It will not pay you to defy me."

She could feel his hard, supple body pressing against hers as he crushed her against the cliff, demonstrating the strength that lay in his grip. Panic assailed her and she began to struggle against him. Merciless hands tightened painfully on her arms and then one hand came up and gripped her hair. She cried out in pain and tears stood on her lashes but she did not cease her struggles. He pinned her firmly and shook her. Rufenna's hand flashed up and she drove the dagger at him with the last of her rapidly fading strength. She clearly heard the ripping of his leather doublet as the dagger sliced through it. He winced with pain. He ground out a curse and the dagger slipped from her nerveless hand, clattering among the stones at her feet.

"You little . . ."

Faintness was overcoming her, dulling her senses, robbing her of her strength. She saw his face, contorted with fury, bending over her and it grew more and more dim. With a sigh she welcomed the darkness, going limp in his hands and sagging against the rock. Her head tumbled forward to rest on his shoulder and as his grip on her slackened in puzzlement, she slid noiselessly to the ground. Her last coherent thought was that she had at least wounded him, and that he would kill her for that. As the darkness closed around her, she found that she didn't care what he did now. She drifted away into oblivion, unaware of the hard hands lifting her.

CHAPTER FOUR

Wan light struck her face and her eyelids fluttered. Confusedly she wondered where she was, forgetting for a brief moment the events of the preceding day and night. Stirring slightly, feeling the hard rock beneath her, she opened her eyes fully in a sudden, fearful question. She was lying in the little crevice, wrapped tightly in a heavy blanket. Of her captor there was no sign and she sat up, removing the blanket and pushing it aside. She still felt weak and shaken and blinked nervously as a tall Borderer came around the outcrop of rock. Silently he placed a wedge of cheese and bread on a flat rock near her and handed her a cup of water.

"We ride soon," he said sullenly, eyeing her with dislike.

He had quite obviously been ordered to bring her the food and he detested the task. Why did Lord Hammond's men show such resentment toward her? She had never done anything to them. Alexander? With a lump in her throat she knew in that instant that whatever it was, it concerned Alexander. He had offended the Hammonds and in the tradition of the Border only an exact revenge would satisfy the

injured party. She took up the bread and cheese and
wolfed it down hungrily. The cold water slid down
her dry throat like a balm and she felt refreshed,
ready to think and plan. She must get away from
Lord Hammond. Whatever he meant to do to her,
she had to prevent it by escaping. There was no
chance of that now, she realized, seeing the big Borderers bringing forward the fleet ponies. She was surrounded. Rufenna turned her head, surveying the
deep crevice with hopeful eyes. There was no escape
that way. The crevice ended a short way back and
a steep cliff faced her.

Davon Hammond came around the outcrop and
stood silently in the opening. Her frightened eyes
saw his cut doublet and the blood-streaked bandage.
He followed her gaze and smiled coldly.

"Daggers are meant for throats, mistress. Remember that."

Too stricken to respond, she choked back the hot
words that flooded her throat.

His hard gaze took in her rumpled hair and pale
face. Something flickered in his dark gaze as she
straightened proudly and met his eyes unflinchingly.
She had no idea how desirable she was, standing there
with pride in every line of her shapely body. The
torn, ragged dress, exposing part of her white shoulder, only served to emphasize her delicate beauty.
The dull gray material threw her burnished hair
into strong relief; her young breasts jutted forward
as she squared her shoulders. His gaze lingered on
them for a long moment and she felt a new, dis-
turbing sensation touching her. Something in the way
he was regarding her brought a faint blush to her
white cheeks and a grim smile just touched his well-
shaped mouth. He plainly read the fear and defiance,
the pride and femininity, and his own pulses quickened. Perhaps this business need not be so distaste-

ful after all, he thought, motioning her to precede
him to the horses.

He was not sure of the extent of her innocence.
Even in an Abbey, he thought grimly, they learned
about love. Then his mouth twisted into scorn at
his unthinking use of the word *love*. They learned
desire, how to use those feminine wiles to ensnare
a man. But some, he thought swiftly and painfully,
did not learn until too late. Until they were taught
too well by . . . He wrenched his thoughts from that
direction and turned his attention to getting his men
mounted and ready to ride. He would deal with his
lovely captive later.

The late-afternoon sun was fading deeper into crimson as they rounded a hill and approached a peel
tower or square stone fortress found on many a Scottish hill. Rufenna was forcing her tired body to stay
upright in the saddle, bounced and jolted as it had
been over the rough trails they had followed. She
thanked the Virgin silently that she wasn't riding
sidesaddle. At least with her knees gripped in the
pony's sides she had some control over her balance.
She was past caring whether or not they had planned
to continue their search for her on the morrow. She
had saved them the trouble, she thought wryly. She
looked up at the tower with indifferent eyes. They
must be on Hammond land or he would not approach
that grim fortress with such confidence. As she expected, a cry was raised from the battlements and
the massive portcullis raised. The party cantered
through into the small courtyard. It was an ancient
tower, with an outer wall built at the front to form
a small, square courtyard. It was the type which stood
pugnaciously on many hills across the Border, nearly
invincible to attack and open only to siege when
starvation would drive the occupants out. There
would be little chance to escape from here, she

thought as she dismounted. She heard the heavy portcullis rumble loudly as it was lowered into place.
She followed her captor up the wooden stairs of the
ramp to the first floor of the solid keep.

A dozen men waited in the Great Hall. As Lord
Hammond spoke to them, Rufenna eyed the great
fireplace on the back wall, with its smoldering logs
and strength-giving warmth. Before she could move
toward it, her arm was grasped firmly and she was
half dragged to the spiral staircase in the corner and
urged up it. His strides were too long for her and
she was half running, half falling as they went up
the twisting stairs to the upper floor. He opened a
heavy door and motioned for her to enter. When
she hesitated, an ungentle hand pushed her in. Without a word the door was closed and she heard a key
grate in the lock. Weary and dispirited, Rufenna sank
down on the narrow bed and looked around her. It
was a small and cheerless room. No effort had been
made to cover the cold stone walls or the high slit
of a window that barely lighted the room. The fire
was laid with wood but unlighted, and she shivered.
Beside the bed there was a rough chest under a window, a table, and a chair. How long she sat there
in a tired stupor she did not know, but she was
roused at last by the grating of a key in the lock.
A man stood there, one she recognized from their
ride today. He beckoned her, led her silently down
the dim hall to another door, and showed her through.
Again the door slammed behind her and a key turned
in the lock.

Confused, her senses dull with fatigue, Rufenna
surveyed her new prison. It was a large chamber.
His chamber, her mind screamed. The large bed was
covered with a warm quilt and heavy hangings. Tapestries hung on the walls, blanking out the chilled
gray stone and stopping some of the drafts. The fire
crackled gaily at her and she rushed to stand in front

of it. A tall chest held a large bowl and pitcher and
she could see the steam rising from the hot water.
Beside it lay a towel. He had already been here; she
saw the second linen towel, still damp, thrown over
the back of a heavy chair. On the table was a covered plate and a cup. The fire brought life into her
and she moved toward the steaming water. She would
feel better once she was clean and fed!

Hastily she stripped off her clothes and washed
the mud and grass from her arms and legs. Becoming
slightly reckless, she bathed herself thoroughly, towel-
ing her body until it tingled. A glance around showed
her a soft wool dressing gown hanging from a peg
by the door. She would not put on those wet rags
again, she decided, taking the dressing gown and
sliding into it. The soft wool caressed her flesh and
she sighed. That was better. She carried her dress and
petticoat to the fire and spread them out on a chair
near the hearth. By the time she needed them again,
she hoped they would be dry.

The food was like nectar to her growling stomach
and she sipped the ale cautiously. She was already
drowsy from the warmth and fatigue and the beverage
would only send her to sleep. Once fed, she settled
down in the chair to wait. For what, she knew not.
As an hour passed and then two, her head nodded
again and again. She could dimly hear the sounds of
laughter from the floor below. She listened at the
keyhole several times and the sounds from below annoyed her. Enjoying himself, was he, while she waited
here like a sheep penned up for slaughter? She tossed
her hair and returned to the fire. She was so tired!
Without another qualm she went to the large bed
and turned back the covers. The linen sheets were
cold to her limbs so she pulled the dressing gown
down and tucked it around her. Then she relaxed
with a tired sigh.

So deep was her sleep that she did not hear the

turn of the key in the door. Only when she felt movement did she awaken, becoming aware of him as he slipped into the bed beside her. His hand touched her waist and she jerked upright, only to have two determined hands pull her down again. She moved away from him, realizing to her horror that he was naked. As she struggled against him, she was aware that she was pitting her strength against a formidable foe. He could break her in half if he chose and her struggles were doing little but tiring her already weakened body.

"Leave me alone! Oh, go away," she cried, turning her face from him,

His hand gripped her hair and forced her head around to him. His dark eyes surveyed her frightened face and grew thoughtful.

"Answer me one question, and I warn you, answer it truthfully. I will soon know if it's a lie and you will regret that. Are you a virgin?"

Dumbly she nodded, knowing only that one was a virgin if one had not been intimate with a man. He searched her face and seemed satisfied with her answer.

"It will go easier on you if you've told me the truth."

"I-it is the truth," she stammered, aware of that hard, naked body so close to her.

"Good," he murmured, tilting her head back and placing his lips against her bared throat. They moved caressingly over her silken flesh, causing her to tremble violently and press away from him. Her hands came up in mute appeal.

He raised his head a fraction, gazing down into her frightened green eyes. "Don't fight me, Rufenna. I will only hurt you if you do."

She gulped and her lip trembled. She gripped it firmly in her teeth to still its quivering and stared hypnotized into that dark gaze. His face descended

and his lips were against hers. She tried to pull away
but the hand deeply entangled in her hair held her
prisoner. His mouth was hard, punishing for a long
moment, then, at her frightened shrinking away from
him, it softened a bit, becoming more persuasive. It
moved, caressed her, forcibly parting her lips until
she lay quivering beside him. Then, leaving a trail
of fire behind them, those firm, sensuous lips moved
across her cheek to her throat, caressing the soft warm
skin. They paused in the shadowed hollow at the
base of her throat and he could feel the hard beating of the pulse there against his mouth. His hand
freed her hair and moved down to her shoulder.
Lightly it touched, coming to rest on her firm, young
breast. He felt her convulsive recoil as his hand slid
across her breast and tightened his hold.

He was beginning to gauge her innocence now and
understood that no man had ever touched her body.
He doubted that she had even been kissed! It excited
him, realizing that she was his for the taking, every
desirable inch of her! She was wholly in his power;
he could be as gentle or as brutal with her as he
pleased. She was defenseless, shrinking helplessly away
from his hands and mouth. His mouth moved down,
caressing her breasts and his hand slid down her
thighs. Passion flared in him, driving out his black
thoughts of revenge. He only knew he wanted her,
wanted to taste the unsullied freshness of her innocence, to sample the beauty that no other man had
ever seen.

Rufenna lay limp and stricken under his hands.
She was so numbed with terror that she scarcely knew
what he did. She bit her lip painfully in an attempt
to stem the frightened tears that trembled on her
lashes. She would not show her fear! She would not
give him cause to scorn her, or laugh at her inexperience. She was helpless in his arms now but he
would not break her spirit. She could not bring her-

self to plead with him, to beseech him to let her go.
For long minutes she lay there, insensible to the
warm embraces.

Then his mouth came up again to claim hers and
he kissed her hungrily, urgently, with a passion being
held firmly in check for the moment. Somewhere, deep
inside her, a response quivered into life. When his
hands began caressing her again, the warmth they
left behind registered in her brain. Struggling out of
her apathetic stupor, she became aware of him, of
the response he was drawing from her body. Helplessly she fought against it, determined to give him
no satisfaction, but she found her mind had little
control over the quivering limbs that were answering
his touch. She forced from her mind the image she
had long carried of him, of the romantic daydreams
she had woven about him. This was reality and she
knew not how to fight it. She began to perceive the
nature of the attraction he held for her, an attraction that had penetrated even the unawakened bar-
rier that surrounded her the first time she met him.
She had felt this urgent attraction even then and
had not understood it. Warmth was spreading through
her, more fiery than the strong drink he had given
her, attacking her limbs and building a growing ache
within her.

Bemused, totally bewildered, she gazed helplessly
at his dark head. He looked up and met that gaze
and read it plainly. She was weakening in her defense against him. He could feel it clearly in the
yielding of her body. His hands grew more urgent,
stroking her breasts, her stomach, her thighs, until
she lay shaking in his arms, her eyes tightly closed.
A low moan forced its way through her lips and she
quivered with weakness. When his hand explored her,
she stiffened away from him in instinctive rejection
but his hands and mouth gentled her, readied her.
Her head was swimming wildly, her body felt on

fire, and she shuddered against him as he entered her. A cry of agony was torn from her but he held her tightly against him and she sobbed into his hard shoulder.

When he left her body, Rufenna lay limply against the pillow, scarcely noticing his hands gently wiping the blood from her lips where she had tried to repress her cries. He wrapped the warm gown around her and eased her into his arms, cradling her head against his shoulder. Her sobs quieted and finally ceased, and she unconsciously turned closer into his arms and slept. For a long time he lay gazing down at the tumbled mass of coppery hair spilling across his arm and chest.

Why had he not made her pay? he wondered angrily. That had been his intention. Why had he let her fear and innocence sway his determination to extract his full revenge from her? He did not understand the effect she was having on *him*. He had wanted to see her weep, to plead for mercy; he wanted her on her knees to him, broken and ashamed. Instead he was holding her to his broad chest, smoothing the silken hair from her brow, comforting her! Putting the problem aside, he turned his head into the pillow and slept.

Rufenna came awake, layer by layer, from a bottomless well of sleep. What had awakened her? She groped for the reason, glancing fearfully around the dark room. Then she knew. Warm hands were touching her, sliding over her soft skin, awakening a surge of feeling that dazed her. Drowsily she turned to him, hardly hearing his soothing words, obeying those firm hands. His urgency reached her finally, stripping from her the shell of sleep, bringing her alive to the hot response her body was giving him. It was different this time. Still drugged with sleep, relaxed and no longer afraid, she let him guide her. He played her body skillfully, as a master musician touches an instrument. His own passion was carefully restrained as he broke down the last of her inhibitions, aided by her drowsy state. He coaxed and fondled her until she was writhing beneath his hands, on fire from his touch, burning with an ache and hunger that she had never dreamed possible.

She couldn't think, only feel. Her hands clutched at him, clung to him, pressing him closer to her. She melted against him, savoring the feel of his chest against her throbbing breasts. His hard body seduced her and enticed her until she was trembling violently beneath him, gasping with mingled pain and rapture, nearly mindless with a fierce raging need of him. When he moved to her, she rose to meet him, following the guiding hands, moving with him until she felt as if she would explode with the searing ecstasy. Her nails were digging wildly into his shoulders but he gave no sign of feeling the pain. For a long moment he was trembling helplessly in her arms, as weak as she, and she realized this with acute astonishment. Then his strength flowed back, wrapping around her its comfort, and, exhausted, she fell against him. The waves of drowsiness and fulfillment swept over her and she sighed. Her soft, pliant body curved to fit his and she burrowed against him, sliding painlessly into sleep. She did not feel his hand gently, tentatively caress her cheek and lightly touch the lips still rosy from his kisses. He gazed down at her in dawning wonder and apprehension. She was snuggled against him like a kitten, curling warmly, trustingly, into his embrace.

A tremor of foreboding touched him and was dismissed. He would enjoy her as long as his desire for her lasted, and that was all, he told himself firmly. He would not be deflected from his purpose by an artful little lass who unknowingly had disarmed him totally tonight. He would not wonder who was the victor in this round. It was only that she was so damned innocent! So unaware of her latent power! He would not give her the opportunity to use it on him! Tomorrow she would dance to the tune of his piping and never know how thoroughly she had conquered him tonight. Pressing closer to her soft, warm body, he sighed. He would do well to remember that even an unweaned kitten has sharp claws!

CHAPTER FIVE

Rufenna awoke to a bright, clear day. The sun poured a golden waterfall through the pair of tall, narrow windows. It struck sparks from the silver-hilted sword carelessly lying across a chair. Recollection returned in a flood of remembering and swiftly she turned her head. He was gone! Only the pillow retained the indent of his head and the tumbled covers betrayed his presence during the night. She stretched leisurely, wincing at the soreness of her body. She ached from the hours in the saddle, the wild flight through the wilderness when she had fallen many times and had been torn by briars. Another ache, an unfamiliar one between her thighs, made itself known. As the events of last night began to return in detail, she sat up, hugging the quilt close to her naked body. When had her woolen dressing gown been removed? She had felt it tucked warmly around her after he had ravished her the first time.

Then drifting memories of waking the second time struck her and a warm, shamed flush rose to her cheeks. With a moan she buried her face in her hands, remembering painfully well her sleepy surrender in the middle of the night. How could she? Why had she given in so easily? Why had she not fought him? Shame flowed over her in burning waves. She tried not to think of the hot, burning ecstasy of his caresses, but to turn her thoughts instead to her response to him. He was, clearly enough, the enemy. He had demonstrated that fact not only by his behavior but his words! He spelled it out for her last night. She did not know why or what she had done to create this hostility between them, but he *was* the enemy! She wondered what he intended to do now, after having reduced her mind and pride to shambles, humbling her, showing her clearly her weakness. Could she fight him when he was caressing her so tenderly? Rufenna threw back the quilt in a fever of rage and shame. She must get away from him! She would not stay here, letting him toy with her, tantalizing her as a cat does a mouse before he moves in for the kill.

The dressing gown lay tumbled on the floor at the foot of the bed where he evidently had carelessly thrown it. She slid into it, wrapping it tightly around her as if buckling on armor. The fire had been lit and a pitcher of warm water awaited on the table. Rufenna bathed her face and hands and looked around for her dress. It was gone! So were her petticoat and shoes and stockings. Did he plan to keep her here, wearing nothing but a dressing gown? She certainly could not escape from the tower dressed in nothing but that! Anger licked through her veins as she considered how she had been used by him. The weakness and fatigue of the night were gone. Rested, again in command of her senses, she felt able to face him, to let him know she was no plaything for his amusement.

The key scraped in the lock and Davon entered, carrying a breakfast tray. Silently he stood and surveyed her, taking in the defiant tilt to her chin and the cold challenge in her eyes. A faint smile touched his lips as he put the tray down on the table and firmly closed the door.

"Good morning," he said quietly, walking across the room toward her.

Rufenna turned her face away from him and did not answer. His hands went to her waist and she jerked herself from his touch. A dark brow shot up in amusement and he reached for her again.

"No morning greeting? Are you still cross and sleepy?"

She whipped around and faced him. They would have this out here and now, she thought.

"What do you intend to do with me?" she demanded.

He studied her face closely. "We leave for Torrey Castle this afternoon. You will accompany us."

"Torrey Castle. Your family home? What will your family say when you ride in with a strange woman? Won't you have to answer questions?"

"I answer to no one but God. You will accompany me."

"I will not go anywhere with you, my lord," she said clearly, enunciating each word distinctly and coldly.

His dark eyes mocked her defiance. "I think you will. I believed, last night, that you had learned obedience. Perhaps I was wrong. Have you forgotten so soon?"

His reference to the night before fanned her rising anger. "Do not speak to me of last night! You have had your revenge, sir, and your pleasure. I demand that you release me."

"Demand? Indeed, you fail to understand your position, Rufenna. You will go with me, whenever and wherever I say, and remain with me until I give you leave to depart. I trust that is sufficiently clear? You will stay at Torrey until I tire of you," he added, seeing the fury glittering in her green eyes. He felt a surge of passion as he looked at her. She was very desirable with her hair tumbling about her shoulders in a riot of flaming curls and her mouth still warm and soft from their night of love.

"You intend to flaunt me before the world as your . . . mistress?" she said in blank astonishment. "You would not dare! My father will ransom me, m'lord, or Sir Robert will."

"Sir Robert?"

"Sir Robert Kerr of Cessford," she said with great satisfaction. He would not *dare* offend that nobleman. "In case you've forgotten, Sir Robert is the Warden of this March and is the uncle and guardian of my betrothed!"

"Indeed?" he drawled lazily, watching her with growing amusement. "Who is the lucky man?"

"Neville Kerr and . . . and Sir Robert will not tolerate this abuse!"

"You terrify me," he murmured, reaching for her again and catching her shoulders in a firm grip. "I tremble with fear over what Sir Robert will think of it."

This made her angrier than ever, to have him mock at her so coolly, and she struck at his hands. With a swift movement he pulled her to him, pinning her against his lean body with arms of iron.

"Let me go! I demand that you—"

Her protest was cut off immediately by his mouth and she struggled to free herself. He lifted her and tossed her onto the bed, catching her effortlessly as she tried to roll away from him and pressing her against the quilt with his body.

"You're very full of spirit this morning," he remarked, pulling away the dressing gown. Deliberately he reached out and ran a careless finger across her soft breast. A treacherous warmth followed the movement of his hand and she stifled her automatic response.

"You are a murderer!" she gasped, trying to evade his lips.

"And your family are blameless? Don't taunt me with *that* charge, for I assure you I am innocent of it. I did not kill your brother. Unfortunately," he added, goading her into action.

Her hand flashed up and she struck him hard across the face, bringing the blood welling to his mouth from the blow. For a long terrified moment she met the blazing fury of his eyes, trembling at the murderous intent she read there. He wiped the blood away with his hand before gripping her painfully.

"Do not ever strike me again, Rufenna, or you will live to regret it," he said evenly.

In the tense silence that lay before them she felt half suffocated by her fear and thundering heartbeats.

"Think you, m'lord, that I have no one to protect me?"

"Your father is ill and helpless, Rufenna; your brother is dead; if you look to Sir Robert, you look in vain. He might very well be the Warden of this March but he would not dare to interfere with me."

With a sinking heart Rufenna realized the truth of his words. She remembered Isobel's talk of Davon's connections. He was highly regarded at court and had the ear of both Arran, the Regent, and the Queen Mother. They would back him against Sir Robert with pleasure. She swallowed painfully.

"I will never forget this, Davon Hammond," she ground out furiously. "I will have *my* revenge someday!"

It was a proud boast but she had no idea how she would ever fulfill it.

"You will pay for what you have done to me," she added for good measure, hoping to see some sign of softening in that dark, grim face.

"You are welcome to tilt your lance against my shield whenever you choose but it will avail you nothing. I will release you when and only when I am tired of you and that moment has not come." He leaned to take her lips again, not tenderly this time, and she began to fight like a frightened cat. She twisted her head back and forth away from him, struggling helplessly under his weight.

Suddenly he laughed. "You wear yourself out to no purpose, mistress. Cease this fighting and resign yourself to your fate."

"Never!" she cried, renewing her struggles. His strong hands held her, imprisoning her face so his mouth could find hers. She quivered under his touch but did not give in to it. As he continued to kiss her, she pulled back a tiny bit and bit his lip savagely.

"You little devil," he muttered, jerking his head back. His hands crushed her against him and she cried out in pain. Waves of agony were shooting down her arms and up her neck as his hands gripped her shoulders mercilessly. Tears filled her eyes and forced themselves from under closed lids to trickle softly down her face. He saw them and his grip loosened slightly. One hand left her shoulder and went to her chin, tipping it up. His gaze rested for a long moment on the angry red imprint of his hand on her white shoulder and a wave of shame washed over him. To use his strength, which was more than twice the strength of hers, to hurt a woman! Furious at himself, detesting the unfamiliar feeling of shame, angry at her for precipitating the scene, he started to speak and broke off when a thunderous banging began on the heavy oaken door. With a swift movement he rolled clear of her and pulled the quilt over her half-naked body before going to the door.

Rufenna, lying spent and aching on the bed, was only dimly aware of his voice at the door, sharply questioning the clansman who stood there. It was enough that he had taken his hands and his force from her for the moment. After a brief time she looked up to see the door closing behind him. Wearily she crawled deeper under the quilt, willing her thundering heart to slow down and her limbs to cease their shaking. She had flicked him on the raw with her taunt about being a murderer, and it had roused a devil in him. It was a dangerous game to play, she thought, wondering what to do now. He could break her if he chose, if he cared to exert the considerable strength of his hands and arms. Rufenna began to weep softly, hopelessly, burying her face in the pillow. Despair overwhelmed her and she held back her fear with considerable effort.

When the door opened to admit him, she stiffened, not moving from her position on the bed. She heard the clatter of his sword as he picked it up and buckled it around his lean hips. Then he came to the side of the bed and looked down at her. She did not look up so she did not see the look of admiration in his eyes.

"Plans have been changed." He forced his voice to be crisp and businesslike. "We ride at dusk. One of my men will bring you some clothes. See that you are ready."

Without another word he left her, casting a last glance at the huddled form on the bed. The door was slammed with furious frustration and the key firmly turned.

After a long time Rufenna dragged herself from the bed and forced herself to eat the cold breakfast that lay forgotten ᴄ the table. It revived her drooping spirits a little and she settled down to wait. A book lay carelessly thrown on the chest and she picked it up curiously. He had brought it back from France with him, she guessed, translating the title from Latin. A war between two Greek armies? Who would have thought he would be interested? Curling up in the big chair by the fire, she began to read it.

Soon she was engrossed in the story of the Trojan War, pagan though it was, and forgot the time. The sun was dropping low into the horizon when she was roused by the unlocking of the door. A young clansman came in, carrying a covered tray. From the open door she could hear voices and a sound of bustle going on below. Something was happening. Rufenna laid aside the book and turned to the silent man.

"What is going on down there?" she asked.

For a long moment she thought he wasn't going to answer her. He looked her over, taking in the slender form and mass of fiery hair, and softened at her unconscious appeal.

"We ride for the Border within the hour, mistress. M'lord sent you these," he added, putting down a folded pile of clothing. "They were the smallest we could find."

"The Border?" She ignored the clothes and fastened on his first remark.

"Aye." He turned toward the door.

"Wait! Are we crossing the Border? A raid?" she gasped.

"Aye," he admitted, standing awkwardly by the open door. "He said you'd go with us," he added in obvious disapproval.

"But . . . why?"

"He said—"

"I know," she interrupted. "Why are we going there instead of Torrey?"

He shuffled his feet a bit and wondered how much to tell her. "Ask him," he said finally, deciding to play it safe.

Rufenna watched the man leave and turned to the pile of clothing. A linen shirt, leather breeches, heavy wool stockings. Her own shoes, cleaned of mud and dry. The dead man's cloak was also cleaned and dry. Why had he not returned her dress? Thoughtfully she seated herself at the table, to eat the meal while

it was warm and to puzzle over this new information. What if she told him she would prefer to remain here at Hammond Tower? To wait for his return? Would he allow her to do that? It might offer
her the best chance of escape. Knowing he was gone,
out of reach, would give her more courage. Deliberately she took her time with the meal and then returned, still wearing the dressing gown, to her chair
and the book.

"Why are you not ready?" Davon demanded, standing in the open door and flicking an angry gaze over
her.

"I am not going," she said firmly, not rising from
the chair. "I will await you here."

His mouth tightened. "You have five minutes to
get into those clothes and come downstairs. You are
riding with me, whether you like it or not."

Rufenna glanced up at him defiantly and sat mute
and motionless.

He slammed the door furiously and advanced to
the table. The pile of clothing was swept up and carried to her. Still she did not stir. A hard hand jerked
her from the chair and ruthlessly ripped the dressing
gown from her. Gasping with shock and anger, she
turned on him, but stopped at the anger glinting in
those dark eyes. The shirt was jerked over her head
and buttoned at the throat.

"Put them on," he said coldly, holding out the
breeches.

With trembling hands she took them and stepped
into them. He brushed away her trembling fingers
and deliberately tied the laces of her breeches. They
were still too loose. Muttering angrily, he crossed to
the chest and opened it and took out a wide leather
belt. For one awful minute she thought he was going
to strike her with it; then he was putting it around
her waist and jerking it tight. She gasped as the hard
leather bit into her flesh and he loosened it slightly.

The woolen stockings were pulled up her legs with ungentle hands and the shoes thrust on her feet. After one look at his face she dared not oppose him. She stood or sat mutely while he dressed her and accepted the heavy cloak in tense silence. At last he was finished.

"You will follow me down the stairs and mount your horse," he said with cold anger. "You will not argue or refuse to do anything I tell you to do or that belt you wear will serve another purpose besides holding up your breeches. Do I make myself clear, mistress?"

For an instant she glared at him and then choked back the rage she felt at the indignation she had suffered at his hands. She nodded meekly and went down the stairs behind him, pondering in her heart the revenge she would seek.

CHAPTER SIX

Dusk was falling as they rode beneath the heavy portcullis and started down the rocky path to the valley.
Rufenna was riding on Davon's left and a burly
Borderer, the one he called Wat, was right behind
her. She knew there was no possibility now to escape.
The best thing to do was to keep her wits about her
and wait for a chance. Perhaps after dark . . .

The lingering dusk faded and darkness fell. The
sky was overcast and the moon nearly obscured by
heavy clouds. Davon moved closer to her and leaned
from the saddle.

"We go single file from here, Rufenna. I will guide
your horse. Just concentrate on staying on him and
leave the rest to me."

She bit her lip in vexation at his reference to her
falling from her horse and nodded curtly. Perhaps it
was just as well if he thought she was an unskilled
horsewoman. She was riding one of his Border ponies
astride like a man and quite enjoying it. How much
easier it was not to be perched uncomfortably on a
sidesaddle, maintaining a precarious balance over
rough terrain. Unhampered by skirts, she could enjoy

the ride in the darkness, reveling in the freedom breeches gave her.

The land was rocky, bleak. They wove their way through hills, cutting down imperceptible paths through gorges and gullies, never placing a foot wrong on the dark rocky slopes. She didn't know how they knew where they were going, for it was pitch black and she could barely see Davon's horse in front of her. Her surefooted pony picked his way daintily through the boulder-strewn path, his hooves rarely slipping on the loose stones. The motion of the horse was soothing her, making her drowsy. She forced her eyes open and listened in the darkness. She could hear the clatter of the hooves of the horses behind her and then she felt the difference as they came out of the gorge onto a grassy plateau. The moon made one of its fitful appearances and she heard Wat move past her and draw rein beside Davon.

"Not far now, Wat. They won't be expecting us this quickly."

"Aye. They'll not think the news reached us today. What about the lass?" Wat asked with clear disapproval.

"Tell Sim and Will to stay close to her. They are to keep her out of the fighting and will answer to me if anything happens to her. Understand?"

"Aye," Wat said dourly, turning his horse to go back down the line. At his signal the men moved forward, regrouping into a solid square. The wide valley lay quietly before them, sleeping peacefully in the flickering moonlight. Two dark shapes moved up on either side of Rufenna, and Davon handed Sim the reins of her horse.

"You're to stay with them at all times, lass. Obey any orders they give you without arguing. They are responsible for your safety."

Rufenna accepted this strictly masculine situation. For the moment her safety depended upon it. The troop filed past, twenty-five men, well armed. They wore light coats of chain mail and protected their heads with steel helmets. Each man carried a long, wickedly pointed lance, either a sword, or in some cases a Jedburgh ax, and, jutting from their belts, a dagger. Rufenna eyed the Jedburgh ax with a shudder, the metal sparkling in the pale wash of moonlight across its distinctive round, sharp edge. She had noticed that Davon carried only a sword and dagger, leaving the thrusting lance for his men. As she waited under an overhanging tree with her personal escort, the men trotted past, silent, grim, ready to go about the night's work. She waited for the men to move past and then leaned over and addressed Sim.

"M'lord said you would tell me . . . where are we?" she asked, pleased at her clever way of phrasing the question, so it would not be refused an answer.

Sim eyed her doubtfully for a moment and then whispered, "Near Bellingham, in England."

"England!" she gasped.

"Aye," he said, surprised that she needed to ask.

"But . . . why? I mean, what are we doing here? His lordship didn't have time to explain to me," she added hastily, seeing his doubtful look.

"The Charltons raided Treelow last night," he muttered unencouragingly.

"Treelow?" She groped about in her memory and came up blank.

" 'Tis one of the Hammond farms. They burnt out the tower and took the cattle."

"Oh, and we've come to get them back?"

This amused him. "Aye, we'll get them back and more! They didn't know his lordship was home, ye ken. They thought he was still in France, else they'd never have tried it. They'll learn," he added complacently, repressing a regretful pang at being assigned to guard the lass instead of being up front with his lordship.

The last horseman passed and Sim urged her into line. Rufenna mulled over this information and understood the change in plans. The Charltons must not have realized the news would reach the Hammonds so soon, which was why they would not be expecting this retaliatory raid. She knew about raiding, of course. It was how many of the Border families made a living, stealing cattle and goods from the other side. Her family had not depended upon such ill-gotten gain for their livelihood and she wondered about Davon Hammond. Then, thinking about the man she was coming to know, she realized that no one would raid and burn his property with impunity. He knew well how to guard his own, she thought ruefully, casting a glance at her two stalwart escorts. Getting away from him was not going to be easy!

They moved silently across the crisp, frosty grass; the only sounds breaking the quiet were the clinks of harness and bridles. No word was spoken now, as they were deep into enemy territory. Davon led his men directly to the Charlton stronghold, lying in a curve of the Tyne River. Spreading farms dotted the plain and he unerringly selected the richest Charlton holding. It was very dark now due to the obscuring clouds.

To her fury, Rufenna was left behind as the farm came into view, sheltered in a thick copse of trees near the river. Sim and Will were silent, watching grimly as the troops moved forward toward their objective. At Davon's signal Wat moved ahead, going in to reconnoiter on foot. He moved like a dark shadow across the meadow, heading for the main pasture. In a few moments he was back, stopping at Davon's side and nodding. Their cattle were there, along with another small herd. Davon waved the men forward and they moved in groups of twos to the pas-

ture. Rufenna, waiting in the trees, couldn't see what
was happening.

"Now what?" she whispered to Will. He ignored
her, straining his eyes and ears to hear what was
happening. Sim, when her question was repeated to
him, answered.

"They'll take the cattle and move them out. Once
they're on the way, we'll attack the farm."

Hardly had he spoken when Rufenna saw dark
massed shapes move past their concealing position.
The cattle! The Borderers were driving them past,
using their steel-tipped lances to hurry them on! Did
not the Charltons realize what was happening? As
the herd jostled out of the way, Sim turned her horse
and led her out of the woods, joining the ring of
men moving toward the Border.

Behind them there was a sudden shout, and a flare
of light. The alarm had been raised and men began
pouring from the buildings, grabbing weapons as
they came. Davon immediately wheeled, barking an
order to his men. Half the troop turned with him
and thundered down on the farm, as the other half,
casting silence aside now that they were discovered,
hurried the cattle toward the hills. Once into the
shelter of the hills they could hide or elude pursuit
at will. Sim was urging her horse into a canter, trying to move her away from the now tumultuous battle raging around the farm. Haystacks burst into
flame as Davon's men hurled torches into them, and
hand-to-hand combat exploded all over the pasture.
Looking back, Rufenna could see the fires roaring
high; acrid smoke blanketed the farm in a dense
cloud.

Now, she thought! While they were occupied with
the fighting and the cattle! Some of the Charltons
had reached their horses and were riding madly to
catch the moving herd of cattle. Sim moved closer

to her as Will turned to engage a horseman who appeared out of the darkness. With a swift movement Rufenna leaned forward and grasped the slack rein and pulled sharply. It slid from Sim's grasp and she wasted not a moment. Before he could recover, she kicked the horse into a gallop and was racing down the line of men who were mercilessly prodding the cattle to a faster pace. They were too occupied to take note of her but she was sure Sim wouldn't be far behind. In the soft, dim light she could see the bulk of the hills before her and she raced for their shelter. Once there it would take more than Sim to find her!

Her heart was beating hard with excitement and exertion and she gasped as a troop of men rode out of the hills directly in front of her. The moonlight gleamed on their helmets and she wondered frantically what to do. They had seen her; she was sure of that. Turning the horse, she drove him toward a cluster of trees, hoping to lose herself there, but they were galloping headlong after her. Behind her she heard Sim's shout of warning but she kept up her pace. Just as she reached the thin, straggly edge of the trees, a horseman pulled alongside and neatly swept her from the saddle. Rufenna struggled wildly in his arms and was roughly thrown over his saddle. She kicked and fought but he held her there with an iron grip. The other troopers, seeing the fleeing horseman taken, turned about and rode hard toward the scene of the fighting. Her captor began to circle the entangled mass of cattle and fighting men and rode for the farm. Rufenna was too breathless now to do much but try to hold on. As she bounced along across the saddle, afraid that she was going to fall off head first, the horsemen disappeared in the other direction.

Davon, unaware of what was taking place, saw his men drive the cattle safely into the hills and rallied his remaining men to cover the retreat. He swore as he saw the troop of horsemen closing in on them at a fast pace. Reinforcements! His men began disengaging and retreating toward the hills, fighting off the superior English forces. Slowly they fought their way back to the hills, taking a heavy toll of the English horsemen.

"Now!" Davon shouted, and his men abruptly disengaged and raced for the hills. As he thundered over the grass and into the beginning of the rocky gorge, Davon remembered Rufenna, ahead somewhere with Will and Sim. He should not have brought her! He should have left her at Hammond Tower under heavy guard. It was too dangerous to risk her safety in a lightning raid. His inner voice told him he had been reluctant to let her out of his sight. His instinct had warned him that she would stop at nothing to escape from him. Well, it was done and they would soon be safely home with their herd.

The farm was a blaze of light and activity. Men were rushing around dousing the fires and regrouping for the pursuit through the hills toward the rapidly disappearing Scottish raiders.

The burly Englishman lowered Rufenna to the ground and dismounted, holding her arm in a hard grip. She was marched into the farmhouse and dragged into a large kitchen. The room was full of men gathering weapons and discussing the possible route the Scots would have taken through the hills. The big gray-haired man, who was the obvious leader, paid little attention when they entered the room.

"Master Thomas! See what I caught," the Englishman said, hauling her forward. Her leather cap was swept from her head to the floor. All eyes stared in varying degrees of interest and astonishment at the flaming hair that spilled wildly around her face.

"A lass?" Thomas Charlton said, moving to stand before her. "Who are you?"

Rufenna didn't know what to say so she stood silently, meeting his gaze defiantly. His eyes ran slowly over her, taking in the unmistakably feminine form under the shirt and leather breeches. With quiet dignity Rufenna pulled the cloak tightly around her, standing proudly before the angry Englishmen. "You were with Hammond? Well, that's the first bit of luck we've had tonight."

"Hammond must be bored to bring his doxy along on a raid," one man said, provoking laughter among the other men.

"We'll have to deal with her later," said Charlton. "Charlie, gather the men. We've got to move now."

"What about her?" a man asked, jerking his thumb in her direction.

"She'll stay here until we come back. Ian, you and Jock stay with her and watch her carefully, mind. My lord might pay a fancy ransom for her, after we're through with her, of course."

Rufenna shivered at the appraising looks that were directed at her and understood him all too well. This time yesterday she would have been none too sure of his meaning. Now she knew. The Englishmen would take turns with her when they returned and if what they were saying was true, they would watch each other as they mounted her and relieved their pent-up passions. She did not have to listen to their vulgar exchanges to know what they had in mind for her. Cold terror gripped her and she leaned heavily against the wall. The men moved out, with much laughter and joking, until Rufenna was left alone with the two men who were to guard her. They sat down at the rough table and one pulled out a pair of dice.

"Sit down, girl. They won't be back for a bit. You'd best rest. You'll need it," the older man said. He was big and middle-aged and bore a striking resemblance to Thomas Charlton. "Ian, fetch us some ale. I'll watch the lass."

Ian obediently disappeared into the larder and Rufenna, retrieving her hat, moved to the nearest chair and sank down onto it. She had to be gone before the others returned, but how could she do it? These two would never let her out of their sight. She had no weapons except . . . It just might work! When Ian came back with the ale, but none for her, she waited quietly for a few minutes until the two were engrossed with their dice game. She let her body droop in the chair, knowing that Ian was glancing over at her. Holding her breath in fright lest this might not work, Rufenna gave a little gasp once she was sure Ian was staring at her, and slid from the chair into a silent huddle on the stone floor. Scarcely breathing, she waited, lying limply and not moving.

"Jock . . ." Ian dropped the dice and moved around the table, coming to stand by her. "The girl's swooned."

"Damnation! Well, leave her there."

Rufenna's heart nearly stopped at that. It was no part of her plan to be left lying on the cold stone floor.

"But, Jock, Thomas won't like it if she's sick when he comes back! We'd best put her on the bed."

Jock scowled and got up. He came across the kitchen and prodded her hard in the ribs with the toe of his boot. Rufenna nearly gasped at the pain and it took all of her resolution not to roll away from that punishing boot.

"She's out all right. Take her in the bedroom and lock the door. You're to come straight back, mind! You're not to stay there. No touching her until Thomas comes back and decides what to do with her."

"Aye, I know what I'd do with her if I had the say," muttered Ian. He knelt and lifted her limp form and ran a hungry eye over her slim body and sighed. Thomas would no doubt share her after he had had his fill of her but when would that be? He dumped her unceremoniously on a hard straw mattress and shut the door firmly.

Davon rode out of the hills onto the flat Scottish plain. Ahead of him, camped near a straggling stand of trees, his men awaited him. He was sure they had outdistanced the English, and the cattle must be nearly home by now. He cantered into the camp, ignoring everyone, his eyes scanning the clustered men, looking for that fiery red hair. Wat materialized beside him and he drew rein.

"M'lord, Timmy brings news. There's a party of Scotts camped over about two miles. Timmy says they've just returned from a raid. On the Charltons' Gisland farm."

Davon grinned, delighting in the knowledge that this had not been the Charltons' night. He glanced around.

"Where is Mistress Rufenna?"

Wat shifted hesitantly. "Sim says she was taken. By that troop that arrived late. When they attacked, she got away from Sim and an Englishman caught her. He thinks they took her to the farm."

There was a long, terrible silence. "Fetch Sim," Davon said quietly, his voice steely. Wat ran off, eager to be gone, to let someone else share the blame.

Sim, blue eyes uneasy, shuffled awkwardly before his leader and repeated the tale. He was sure the man had ridden with the girl to the farm. He had been too hard pressed to go to her aid.

"M'lord, she just yanked the reins away and fled. I know not where she was going, but . . ."

Davon dismissed him curtly, knowing full well what Rufenna had been doing. She was so hell bent on getting away from him that she had seized her chance and now the Charltons had her. What chance would she have with them?

"Wat?"

"Yes, m'lord?" Wat said, moving forward.

"You said the Scotts are nearby? Pick five men and come with me."

"Aye." Wat hastily called up the men. They trotted from the camp in silence, following the stiff, stony back of their leader. Wat knew the signs. Davon Hammond was livid with fury and somebody would pay for this. He devoutly hoped it was not he!

The Scotts were aware of their approach long before they were within hailing distance and Davon made haste to identify himself. To his relief the tall man who strode from the campfire to meet him was a distant kinsman, James Scott.

"Davon! What do ye out here at this time of night?"

Davon dismounted and handed the reins to Wat.

"Jamie, just the man I need," he said abruptly. "I hear you struck Gisland tonight? We were at Tynehill. Thomas Charlton raided Treelow last night, thinking I was still in France. Jamie, they captured one of my people, a woman. I want her back tonight."

Jamie gaped at him. He knew this cousin well and never had he seen him so icily furious or his frown so black.

"Who is the woman?" he ventured.

Davon shrugged, his eyes glittering. "A kinswoman of mine, who was riding under my protection. The damned whoresons have captured her and have her at the farm. I don't have enough men now to hit them again. Some of my lads went back with the cattle. Will you ride with me?"

Jamie grinned. He was curious about this kinswoman of Davon's who was riding on a raid but decided against probing further.

"I'd be honored. When, Davon—now?"

"Aye, the sooner the better. God knows what they'll have done to her," he growled.

Jamie, hearing the barely repressed rage in Davon's tone, wondered even more about this woman. He felt sorry for the Charlton who touched her, for Davon could be a devil when he was roused. If Jamie was any judge, he was thoroughly roused now.

"Ten minutes. I've fifty men. Will that be enough? If we can wait, I can muster more."

"We can't wait," Davon clipped, turning to his horse. "We'll await you at my camp. I'll leave Tim to guide you there. Make haste, Jamie."

"We will."

CHAPTER SEVEN

Back at the farmhouse the key scraped in the lock, and before Ian's footsteps receded down the flagged hallway, Rufenna was off the bed and trying to adjust her eyes to the darkness of the room. One tall window gave out only a faint light as slivers of moonlight slipped through the cracks in the heavy wooden shutters. Rufenna, making a full circuit of the room, realized her only chance lay with the window, since there was no other door. As quietly as possible she pushed and tugged a heavy, low chest over to the window. Carefully climbing on it, she reached up to the shutters. The iron clasp was large and stiff and did not give way under her tugs. She pushed harder against it, desperation giving her strength, and almost sobbed with relief when it gave under her hand. She eased one side of the shutter open, freezing into petrified silence at the dreadful screech the hinge made. She waited for what seemed an eternity, listening. No sound of footsteps rang on the flagstones; no key turned in the lock. They must not have heard it. Rufenna looked up at the window and wondered how to reach it. The sill was nearly level with her chin and she would have to have something to stand on.

A rickety chair, which she had earlier rejected in favor of the more stable chest, caught her eye. It would have to do and she could only pray that it would not collapse under her. Testing her weight on it, Rufenna sighed in relief when it held. Cautiously she eased the chair onto the chest. Now the sill was nearly at her waist, and she leaned forward and unfastened the window casement latch. The outer shutter opened and a rush of cold air touched her face. She crawled and pulled herself onto the sill, balancing there while she peered into the darkness below the window. It was not an impossible jump, she decided. Only ten or twelve feet.

She hoped the springy grass would break her fall but she had little to lose now. Turning loose her grip with misgivings, Rufenna jumped, sprawling painfully on the grass. For a terrible moment she lay there, winded by the impact. Then she scrambled to her feet and pressed back against the dark side of the building. Her questing gaze caught a movement over by the looming shape of an outbuilding. A horse! It must be Jock's or Ian's. A horse was essential if she was to make her escape before the other men returned and before those two in the farmhouse missed her. She could never travel fast enough on foot. Rufenna, sobbing with strain and fright, flitted as a silent shadow across the grass and reached the barn with a stumbling run.

The horse, saddled and bridled, stood quietly, grazing where he was hobbled by the barn. Her shaking hands made slow work of untying the reins and removing the hobbles; then she was leading him around the barn toward the pasture. She did not dare mount and ride directly for the hills, for that was the way the men would return. Behind the barn, in the deep shadow cast by its bulk, Rufenna mounted and urged the horse into a canter. She made for the line of trees that followed the river, knowing she

would not draw an easy breath until she reached
the cover of those dark trees. She had nearly reached
the river when a shout rang out from the farm. They
had missed her! Ian, no doubt, going to check on
her! She could hear their voices as she galloped wildly
for the trees, hoping they had not yet seen her or
the direction she had taken. If she had not been
spotted, they would assume she would head directly
for the hills and get across the Border as quickly as
possible. Rufenna knew she dared not go that way
so she went headlong for the trees. She had made it!

Bending low in the saddle to avoid the low-hang-
ing branches, she pushed the horse through the trees
as fast as she dared. They would look for her here,
she thought, slowing down so she could think. Her
gaze fell on the river. If she crossed it, they would
certainly waste some time searching this side first.
Making up her mind, Rufenna moved the horse to
the river's edge, looking for a possible place to ford.
It flowed swiftly here and was deep, by the look of
it. Kicking the horse into a canter, she followed the
water's edge, looking for a ford. They rounded a bend
and the bank flattened out where the river narrowed.
It was more shallow here, but shallow or not, she
would have to risk it.

Turning the horse into the water, she took her
feet out of the stirrups, ready to let the horse swim
if it proved deeper than she thought. Water surged
up around her legs, reaching her thighs. Icy cold water that took her breath away! She shivered and held
her breath as the horse floundered suddenly, and
scrambled for secure footing. He made it and moved
on, nearing the far bank. She did not release her
breath until they had climbed out on the other side,
merging into the dark trees. For a long moment she
sat still and shaken, catching her breath and trying
to pull the soggy cloak around her legs. Why had
she not thought to take it off and hold it while she

crossed the river? Too late now. The leather breeches clung to her like an icy shroud, sending chills all through her. Rufenna gritted her teeth against the discomfort and moved on. She had a lot of ground to cover before daylight.

For the second time that night Davon led his Borderers through the hills to Tynehill. As they threaded their way through a narrow pass, the guide he had sent out rode forward to greet him.

"M'lord," he said quietly, since voices carried and echoed through the hills. "There's a sizable force moving through the hills over the ridge."

"Charltons?"

"I warrant so, sir. They're headed for the Border. Looking for us, most like."

Davon considered. Jamie had moved up and listened to the report and waited quietly. Charlton would have taken most of his men in pursuit and both he and Jamie had left their camps lightly guarded. Both had taken every available man with them on the ride, thinking they'd need them at the farm.

"It appears, Jamie, that Charlton is pursuing through the hills. He'll not have many men left at the farm. Take all the men but ten of them back there and strike them before they get free of the hills."

Jamie nodded, grinning broadly at the coming fight. "You'll go on to the farm?"

"Aye. Wat, pick nine men to go with us. Pass the word that the rest are to go back with Master Scott to ambush the Charltons."

Without a murmur of protest the men turned and retraced their route through the hills, moving silently and swiftly to intercept the Englishmen before they could come upon the two unguarded camps. Davon signaled his small band of men to follow him, thinking it was fortunate he had run against Jamie, since if anyone relished a fight with the Charltons, it was a Scott. That feud had raged for years, keeping both sides well occupied.

The farmhouse blazed with light as Davon and his men surrounded it. He could see one man near the barn and another going into the house. Davon frowned. Something was amiss and the only way to discover what it was was to ride into the farmyard. He motioned Wat and two men to accompany him and pointed silently at the two distracted Englishmen who were still oblivious to the presence of the Scottish band. Wat, Sim, and Will, hoping to redeem themselves by finding the lass, moved in and the two Charltons were secured almost before they realized the Hammonds had returned. Davon dismounted, seeing Wat move the two struggling, swearing men into the lighted kitchen, and walked in.

"Where is she?" he demanded coldly, his glance raking the room.

Neither man answered as they stood in sullen silence, pinned against the wall by the big Scottish Borderers. Davon drew his dagger deliberately and approached Jock. The point flashed before the man's eyes and he pricked Jock's throat.

"I asked you where the girl is."

Jock swallowed. "Gone. She escaped."

The dagger dug a little deeper.

"I swear it! She swooned and Ian locked her in the bedroom. She got out the window. She's got my horse. We w-were searching for her."

Davon jerked his head and Wat went down the hall. In a moment he returned. "The window was opened. Na doubt the lass climbed out of it."

"Tie them up," Davon ordered. "First, though. Did you touch her? Harm her in any way?"

Jock, hardened Borderer that he was, shivered at the real menace he read in that grim face. "Nay, I swear we didn't harm her. She swooned, almost as soon as the men left. Ask Ian. We didn't dare touch her. Thomas said . . ."

"Thomas said what?" Davon asked, his voice deceptively silky.

Jock swallowed convulsively. "He said to hold her here until he returned. He was going to ask ransom."

"And that's all?"

The dagger tickled Jock's throat again and he gulped. "I don't know. He didn't say."

This told Davon what he wanted to know, and he mentally applauded Rufenna's quick thinking in escaping before Thomas Charlton returned. Without another word he turned and left the kitchen.

"Wat, have the men start a search. Mistress Lyall escaped and will be heading for the Border."

After an hour's fruitless search Davon gave the command for the men to split into two parties. "Wat, I'll take five men along the river. You take the rest through the hills and be alert. She could easily be lost in there, not knowing the paths. I want her found and now!"

Trying not to think of the endless dangers the girl would be facing on the lone ride across the Border country, Davon began the search. Only his growing anxiety and anger sustained him during the remainder of that long night. It was Sim who found the fresh tracks which showed a single horseman had recently crossed the river, but once on the other side the trail was lost in the thick underbrush in the trees. Davon pressed on, hoping to come by news of her.

By late afternoon of the following day Davon admitted defeat. There was no trace of her. No one had seen her in any of the villages, no traveler admitted to meeting or noticing a lone rider going hard across the Border.

Tired, having gone without rest or food, Davon

called Sim to him. "Sim, I'm taking the men home. Go to Lyall and wait. "When . . ." He would not admit the if. ". . . when she arrives there, you'll find me at Torrey. If she has not reached there in six days, come for me or send word. Her father will have to be told and the Lyalls raised to help find her. Not a word about why you're there, understand? Simply seek shelter from them and stay there until she arrives."

Sim nodded. No castle turned away a traveler asking for food and shelter but he didn't know how he was to remain there for so long without exciting suspicion. He would have the ride to Lyall to consider the problem, he thought, and it had better work!

Davon watched Sim begin the ride for Lyall Castle and turned to his men.

"We go home, lads," he said.

As the cold night air struck into the wet leather breeches, Rufenna felt as though she were encased in ice. She shivered uncontrollably while numbly allowing the slowing horse to follow his head. The night was darker than it had been earlier, with low overcast clouds obscuring the stars and moon. The terrain seemed vaguely familiar and she tried to dismiss the growing certainty that she was going in circles.

If only she could be sure they weren't following her! Every bush and tree represented an unknown terror, for they could be either the English or Hammond men. Was there no one she could turn to? All her life she had been sure of a place to lay her head, warm clothing, and nourishing food, even if it was the plain variety offered by the Abbey. Now in a matter of days she had lost all of these things, as well as her innocence. But no, she wouldn't allow herself to think of that. She had a lifetime to writhe when she thought of Davon Hammond and his high-handed treatment of her. She had been deprived of everything and nothing had been given her to replace it. She was helpless, hungry, wet, miserably cold, and in a totally strange part of the country.

The horse, slowing down gradually as he sensed her abstraction, stopped. She peered ahead in the almost impenetrable darkness, to find another river barring her path. To her inexperienced eyes it looked far wider than the one she had crossed a few miles back. If she had not been so near exhaustion, she would have realized it was the same river, only encountered at a wider place. Rufenna nudged the horse forward, thinking that if she could place another river between herself and her pursuers, so much the better. Tired and confused at this madness that forced him to travel through the dark, cold night in such a senseless fashion, the horse hesitated instinctively.

This only served to irritate Rufenna further. Here, at least, was something she could control! She kicked his ribs savagely and forced him to enter the river. Jibbing, he tried to back away but she made him step into the cold, swirling water. After a few steps the horse's instinct proved far more accurate than hers, because the bottom dropped away, plunging them into the deep water. Rufenna realized her mistake too late and tried to pull her feet from the stirrups. She only succeeded in shoving her right foot completely through the stirrup while freeing the left one. She thrashed around wildly, trying to keep her head above water, but when the horse went under, she was towed along. Coughing and choking, she fought her way to the surface, aware of a sharp pain in her ankle. The hard metal of the stirrup was digging painfully into her flesh and she was still held prisoner by the stirrup. She swallowed mouthfuls of the icy water, feeling her strength draining from her as she unsuccessfully fought the current. Gradually a peaceful euphoria robbed her of the desire to fight and she began sinking deeper into the smothering darkness. Her last thought was of Davon's embrace, the warmth and strength it offered; then she knew no more as she sank into a peaceful void.

Sim urged his tiring horse through the rough terrain, first northward and then slightly west of north, straining to pick up any traces of that elusive trail that occasionally tantalized him with subtle clues. He had lost her trail after they had found it where she crossed the river and had only picked it up again after hours of searching. The terrain did not help the tracking, for the rocky hills and gullies that ranged along the riverbanks did not show marks of the horse's passage. Sim paused for the first time in hours to let his horse drink greedily from the small stream they had just crossed.

Sim enjoyed this type of outdoor work and was one of Davon's best trackers. Had he not felt pressed by time and apprehensive of any mistake that would further incur Davon's wrath, he would have relaxed his pace and enjoyed himself. He studied the rocky ground ahead of him and wondered if the lass would have gone that way. There was, he admitted, no way of predicting which way the girl might have gone, fleeing as she was. He reasoned that Davon was correct in feeling her destination would be Lyall Castle; his problem now lay in trying to intercept her. She would not be taking the most direct route or she would have followed the river, where it ran from Tynedale directly across the Border. The lass was lost, he knew; even now she could be riding deeper into England, instead of nearing the Border.

Sim sighed. If he didn't pick up her trail in another hour, he would be forced to abandon the hunt and head for Lyall. He stirred uneasily in the saddle, turning the horse toward the rocky gorge ahead of him, as he realized that would be the most difficult part of the search. He studied the ground, looking hard at every scuff mark on the bank, every freshly broken branch, as he turned over in his mind how to get into Lyall Castle. It was the unspoken law of the Border that a castle did not turn away travelers. They were provided with food and shelter for the night and expected to resume their travels the next day. Therein lay Sim's problem; how to remain the required number of days at Lyall?

No one traveled through the hills just to see the sights. There were none to see, just endless hills and heavily forested terrain. The closer he came to Lyall, the more Sim sweated over his problem. He was turning improbable plans over in his mind, his attention on how best to remain at Lyall for at least six days, when a rabbit ran directly under the hooves of his horse. Tired and bored by the long ride, the horse was moving nearly in his sleep and reacted violently. Rearing suddenly, the horse neatly unseated his rider. Sim, his attention flashing back to his maddened mount just seconds too late, felt himself falling. He hit the rough ground with a jolt that knocked the breath out of him. Winded, he lay there gasping for breath, but managed to struggle to a sitting position. Lyall lay across the valley from him, crowning the opposing hill. Sim swore violently and at length. At last he got up and called the horse to him. A hot flash of pain tore up his leg and he winced painfully. He had wrenched it in the fall, he thought dazedly. pulling himself back into the saddle. At least the horse had not bolted and left him to make the rest of the journey on foot!

Holding the reins firmly now, he guided his mount across the valley toward the towering castle. Triumph filled Sim. This was the perfect excuse for remaining at Lyall for several days. The leg felt bruised and possibly sprained, but he could make more of it if

necessary. Sim patted the horse, murmuring, "I'll forgive your bad manners this time, my lad," delighted
that he had found the solution to his problem.

A clansman, armed with a pike held at the ready,
challenged the horseman who rode slowly up the
approach to Lyall Castle.

"State your business," he ordered.

"I'm an injured man," Sim called. "My horse threw
me and I have hurt my leg."

"Do you need help?"

"Aye," Sim replied, waiting while the gate was
opened and the portcullis raised. He rode slowly into
the courtyard and two Lyall men ran to help him.
Sim groaned mightily, accepting their help as he
leaned heavily on them. He could have made it indoors on his own but it would be better to appear
completely lame. Settled on a straw pallet on the
cold stone floor of the Great Hall, Sim glanced around
at the other figures sleeping peacefully. Gaining access to Lyall had been easy. Since he was injured,
he had even been housed in the castle with the household servants, instead of in the courtyard in the barracks for the soldiers of Lyall. Warm, fed, and still
feeling the glow of the excellent ale that he had
been given, Sim relaxed. My lord would be pleased
with such cleverness!

CHAPTER EIGHT

Out of the mists that swirled around her, Rufenna
saw Isobel. She and Isobel were at St. Whitby's and
Isobel said she would be glad to do the sewing if
Rufenna would scrub the dairy floor. Rufenna knelt
on the hard stone floor of the dairy, a sudden movement spilling the contents of the bucket over her
skirts. Someone said, "We'll have to get those wet
clothes off her." Then the skirt disappeared and she
was wearing breeches and a man's shirt. One of the
nuns said, "How shameless to wear men's clothing."
Rufenna sank deeper into the darkness as a voice
said, "Shut your mouth, Namara. Either help or get
out." Who was Namara? There was no girl at the
Abbey by that name. Her throat and nose ached.
Evidently she had spilled the water and fallen and
hurt herself. But that would make Davon angry. He
had her in his arms and was holding her. She tried
to struggle and screamed at him to let her go. But
he would not. Someone held her tighter and said,
"Hold still, girl. I'm not going to hurt you." Rufenna
moaned and thrashed. The voice again penetrated the
darkness. "Stay with her, Meg, and see that she doesn't
hurt herself." Then Davon was there with Isobel and

they were telling her to do the sewing. She tried but
the needle was so very heavy and she couldn't lift
it. "I'll beat you if you don't do it," they threatened.
But it made no difference; Rufenna could not.

The mists began to clear gradually and she heard
someone say, "Aye, she's coming around."

She opened her eyes and found she was inside somewhere, in close quarters, and was lying on the ground,
wrapped in furs. She was naked but warm. Her head
and throat throbbed and she felt the first stirrings
of hunger. She tried to sit up but a pair of rough
strong hands pressed her back down into the furs.

"Lie still, child. Is going to be well soon."

Rufenna turned her head with great effort and
saw an old woman sitting on a stool, watching her.

"Thanks be you've come around. For a while we
were afraid you'd die on us."

Rufenna tried to speak and found her voice came
out in a husky croak. "Who are you?"

The woman chuckled. "I'm old Meg. They let me
travel with them because of my cooking. I can make
a tasty dish of anything."

Rufenna thought about this information in silence
while she looked around. She was in some sort of a
tent made from animal skins. The old woman, Meg,
who sat beside her, was enormously fat. Her face
was smooth and without a wrinkle but her hair was
nearly white. Her eyes were large and lustrous and
her skin olive hued. Rufenna was quite intrigued by
the old woman's clothes. She was accustomed to the
plain dresses of the girls at the Abbey and the habits
of the nuns. This woman wore many petticoats that
peeped out from under her skirt, showing their dirty
ruffled edges. Her skirt was made of many shades of
red. Over ponderous breasts a bodice that had once
been white strained and threatened to pull loose
from its fasteners. Her feet were bare. Bracelets of
all colors and shapes festooned her arms. They were

made, Rufenna thought, of silver, ivory, and bone. She smelled like woodsmoke, oil, and old woman.

"Who lets you travel with them?" Rufenna asked.

Meg laughed. "Why the group that's going to put on the entertainment."

Rufenna was thoroughly confused by now. "But who *are* you?" she persisted.

"We're Romanys, child," Meg said.

Romanys! Why, they were Gypsies. Rufenna recalled that when she was a small child, some of them had come to Lyall, asking refuge for the night, and had played and sung for their supper. She had been bundled off upstairs when the entertainment began, for it was decided that Gypsy songs were not suitable for childish ears. However, she had sneaked part of the way down the stairs and heard some of the singing. It was sad and sweet and totally unfamiliar to her.

Then Meg was lifting her head and helping her to drink from a wooden bowl containing some spicy brew. "Drink, child," the Gypsy woman encouraged. " 'Twill help you to sleep and get well sooner. We must be off in the morning. I've had a time keeping the others from going off and leaving you. We're late. So drink."

Rufenna drank the not unpleasant liquid. "How long have I been here?"

"Two days now. You were ill from exposure but you will grow stronger every day. Don't talk na more. Try to sleep. We leave at daybreak."

As the old woman spoke, she spread out some more furs and settled herself for the night. Feeling safer than she had for some time, Rufenna turned on her side and snuggled into the warm fur.

The next morning Meg was gone when Rufenna awakened. A skirt, bodice, and several petticoats were thrown over the bottom of the furs. They must be for her, Rufenna decided. Meg could never have squeezed her bulk into these small clothes. Where were the clothes she had worn? The Hammonds' shirt and breeches? Rufenna got slowly to her feet, delighted that she did not even feel dizzy now and seemed to be all in one piece. She put on the foreign clothes and ventured out of the tent.

A dozen or more dark-skinned people were gathered around the cooking pot and Meg was amicably dishing out some kind of savory stew. Dogs were everywhere, begging, snapping at each other, eagerly grabbing whatever food was thrown to them. A young man detached himself from the group and approached Rufenna where she hesitated in front of the tent.

"I have your boots, stockings, and cloak, mistress," he said. "They're dry but none too clean."

Rufenna took the cloak eagerly and wrapped herself in it. She was shivering with cold but the chill air didn't seem to bother the Gypsies. She smiled gratefully at the boy.

"I'm glad to have them back. Thank you for saving them for me."

He grinned at her. "I'm Geordie, old Meg's grandson."

He bore a striking resemblance to the old woman. He had the same large, lustrous eyes and smooth olive skin. Where Meg had gone to fat, Geordie was muscular. "I pulled you from the water," he added.

"I can never thank you enough," she said shyly.

A young woman appeared suddenly at Geordie's side, putting her hand possessively on his arm. She glared at Rufenna. "You don't need to be flashing smiles at *him*. He belongs to me," she snapped.

Before Rufenna could say a word, Geordie turned to the strange girl and rebuked her. "Now, Namara, no need to make the lady feel unwelcome."

Namara jerked away from him. "Unwelcome, is it? Did I help you get the water out of her? And who went out in the cold and dug up couch roots to bring down the fever and help her to mend? She's even wearing my clothes this minute. Without me, she'd be stark naked! You'd like that, wouldn't you, Geordie! We're two days late as it is because of her, but I vow we can wait while you bed the bitch!"

Before Geordie or Rufenna could respond to this attack, old Meg appeared and yanked Namara to her. "You shut your mouth, Namara. You're talking to a lady and such language is unseemly." She raised a heavy hand to punish the Gypsy girl but Rufenna hastened to intervene.

"It's all right, Meg. Don't bother about me."

Namara flung herself away from the other three and bounced off, her hips swinging. "Just keep your hands off Geordie," she warned.

"Now, Namara," said Geordie, going after her.

Rufenna turned to old Meg. "Can I talk to you?" she asked.

The old woman hesitated. "Well, child, we have to be on our way. It's still a day or two to Rutherford and already we're late."

"I know you're late and it's because of me," Rufenna persisted. "But is there any way you could take me home first?"

"Home? Where is home, child?"

"Lyall Castle. I am Rufenna Lyall."

The old woman sat down heavily. "Maybe you'd better be telling me what the daughter of Lyall is doing on the English side of the Border, dressed in men's clothing and traveling alone."

Rufenna hardly knew what to tell Meg. She didn't want anyone to know about Davon and the fact that he might still be searching for her.

"The English captured me," she began. "I was escaping from them when I slipped off my horse and nearly drowned in the river."

"And drowned ye would have but for Geordie. He found ye dragged by yer horse and rescued ye."

"But, Meg, won't you take me home? My father will pay handsomely for my return."

Meg shook her head. "Aye, that he will but ye will have to go to Rutherford with us first. We have promised to go and put on the entertainment for the gossips' wake. The child is born and they are awaiting us."

"A gossips' wake?"

"Aye," said Meg. "The friends and relatives have been gathering, waiting for the new mother to recover. The child has been baptized but the gossips' wake is later."

Rufenna thought about it. "Oh, you're talking about a cummer fialls."

"Cummer fialls, gossips' wake. It's all the same. One of Lord Rutherford's men came to tell us the child was safely born and to make haste. A right good gossips' wake it promises to be, too. Lady Rutherford was delivered of a bonny son, after having six daughters."

In the face of this enthusiasm Rufenna resigned herself to a few days' delay before she would get home. Rufenna couldn't bring herself to tell Meg that others might be searching for her.

"Meg, my father would pay you a little extra if you would not tell the others who I am."

Meg looked hard at her for a moment. "I'll say nothing, child. But should we encounter strangers, they would know immediately that ye are not a Romany. There are no red-haired Gypsies in this band."

Rufenna took the dirty scarf the old woman removed from her own head and bound up her hair. She gave herself up to this situation and swiftly decided it was better than trying to get home by herself. After a moment the old woman hauled herself laboriously to her feet. She patted Rufenna's arm in passing.

"Don't worry, child. We'll get you home. The reward will stand us in good stead. Now stay out of the way and try not to cause any trouble. Best ye eat so we can be on our way. The others grow impatient."

Rufenna was so hungry she did not need to be told but once. A bowl of stew was thrust into her hand and she gobbled it down so fast she nearly burnt herself. Only after she finished did Namara sidle up to her and sneer, "How did you like your dish?"

Rufenna, thinking the girl was trying to be friendly, said, "It was quite good."

Namara laughed nastily. "I wager that's the first time you've broken your fast with hedgehog."

Hedgehog! Rufenna had never heard of anybody eating such for any meal at all. With an effort she controlled her revulsion and managed to remark casually, "So that's what it was. Very good." She did not notice Namara's unwilling look of respect for her as the girl commented in a more friendly tone, "We caught them yesterday and roasted them in the fire overnight. Then we stripped off the prickles and skin and threw them in the pot."

While this conversation was taking place, the other members of the group were packing up, folding the tents, and loading them and the skins and cooking utensils into small wooden carts. Rufenna looked around for her horse but realized she would not recognize him. She had stolen him from the English in the dark and had never had a good look at him. But what did it matter after all, she thought to herself. The important thing was that she had been rescued from Davon Hammond, from the English, from death itself. These people, if she would only be patient, would eventually get her home to Lyall.

When the preparations had been completed, the little band set forth. Some of the Gypsies rode, but most of the ponies were used to pull the carts. The

progress was slow as they moved north through the
rough foothills that wrapped themselves around the
Cheviot Hills. The paths were almost nonexistent but
the Gypsies seemed to know exactly where they were
going. Rufenna was amazed that these people knew
the area almost as well as Davon Hammond's men.
She was determined that she would not cause them
any more trouble or slow them down. She was weak
from her experiences of the last few days, but her
natural good health came to the rescue and after the
meal she felt herself strong enough to go. Meg rode,
she noticed, in a cart pulled by two ponies. No one
offered to give her a place in the cart and she would
not ask.

Seated on a pile of furs, Meg called good-natured
encouragement to the walkers. Rufenna noticed that
Meg was more than the cook of the band. She maintained order and was respected by the others. She was
a good friend to have. The day was clear but cold
and the heavy cloak felt good to Rufenna. She
wrapped it around herself gratefully. Namara was
nowhere to be seen once they started out. She must
be up front with the first travelers.

Presently Geordie appeared at her side and attempted to help her over the rough spots. She hesitated to accept any favors from him because she
didn't care to cause any more dissension between
Namara and him, but she admitted she could use the
help.

When the sun was overhead, they stopped briefly.
Rufenna wrapped her cloak around her and sat
down, thankful for the respite. She was more tired
than she had ever remembered being. Geordie brought
her some cheese and a mug of ale and she took the
food from him eagerly. He flopped down beside her
and they talked of trivialities, the trip, and the upcoming party at Rutherford. In a very short time the
band was on its way again. They traveled until the

sun was low and then they stopped beside a clear, sparkling burn. Rufenna shed her cloak and splashed her face and hands in cold water. She was hot from the quickened pace forced upon her. The other people made fires and some appeared from the woods with the day's catch, fish and a few rabbits. Old Meg took charge, giving orders right and left and clipping Geordie on the head when he didn't move briskly enough to suit her. Rufenna, after a brief rest, approached Meg.

"Can't I do something to help?" she asked.

Namara, busily skinning a rabbit, snapped, "Help! How could a fine lady such as you help? I warrant you never even laced up your shoes by yourself."

"We'll have our supper ready in a short spell, mistress. But thank you for offering," said Meg, with a frown at Namara.

Rufenna returned meekly to her cloak. She smiled to herself at Namara's reference to her elegant upbringing. Namara would have no way of knowing about the back-breaking work she did at the Abbey in the name of preparation for wifehood. However, if the Gypsy girl chose to believe she was a pampered highborn lady, she had not the slightest notion of disillusioning her.

In a short while some food was brought to her. She gobbled it down, not asking or caring what it was. As the sun disappeared behind the hills, she crawled into Meg's tent, wrapped herself in the furs, and fell asleep to the sound of guitars and fiddles and singing around the fire. She did not stir when Meg joined her sometime later.

CHAPTER NINE

The next few days passed quickly and uneventfully. At last they reached Rutherford. The guards on the battlements were looking for them and Rufenna heard their shouts. Immediately the heavy portcullis was raised and the little band passed through and into the courtyard. All was confusion with soldiers on duty and servants eyeing them curiously, and dogs running back and forth, barking. Then the Rutherford household crowded around them, asking questions, eager in their welcome.

The group parted to allow a tall gray-haired man through, his stern face warming into a smile.

"This is a happy day for Rutherford. My wife has been delivered of a strong son. He has been baptized Richard. We will have the cummer fialls tonight if you can prepare in time."

Old Meg assured Lord Rutherford they could be ready in a few hours.

Rufenna, grateful that her red hair was well hidden under Meg's dirty scarf, stayed out of the mainstream of preparations and watched the activity going on around her. Geordie brushed the dogs and tied red rags around their necks and put them through their paces. Rufenna was amazed at what he could get them to do: bark on command, walk on their hind feet, and jump through flaming hoops. The Gypsies unpacked their skins in the stable but left the cooking utensils in the carts. They would eat what was prepared in the cookhouse and bakehouse while they were at Rutherford. For a minute Rufenna considered asking Lord Rutherford to lend her two men to get her home but she quickly dismissed the idea as soon as it came to her. She remembered as a child that she had heard of her father being at feud with the Rutherfords. She did not know if the breach had been healed, but she chose not to call attention to herself.

When the celebrations began in the late afternoon, Rufenna hung around the edges and watched. She heard some of the ladies talking about the kenno, that large and rich cheese prepared by the women of the family and later shared by all the ladies who had helped at the birth. Every time Lord Rutherford commented on what a bonny boy Richard was, his wife, a tall, distinguished woman with a heartbreakingly beautiful face, would shush him playfully.

"I pray you, John. 'Tis not well that you should praise your son. This unseemly praise may cause him to be forespoken."

Lord Rutherford laughed at this and drew his lady to him. "Aye, you are right, madam. Such an ugly, wizened child should indeed not be praised."

He put his arm around her tiny waist and Rufenna could hardly believe that this woman, who seemed so young, had borne seven children. She only hoped she would be as beautiful and shapely after she produced many heirs for *her* husband.

Lady Rutherford laughed up at her husband and they raised their mugs in a toast to the long-awaited son. Rufenna was puzzled by such behavior. She had never seen a married couple behave toward each other in the manner Lord and Lady Rutherford did. They obviously enjoyed each other's company and there was an underlying current of respect and jesting and something else that Rufenna could not define and did not understand. She had been out of a normal family situation for so many years, and she tried to recall how her father and mother behaved toward each other. Father was always courteous but much involved with masculine affairs and often slept in the garrison's barracks with the men. At such times Rufenna's mother had sought her out to share her bed. She never remembered seeing her parents touch one another.

The feast that Rufenna shared had unfamiliar dishes. She was accustomed to the plain fare at the convent—cheese, bread, and ale, occasionally fish. She slipped up to Meg, who was in the cookhouse sitting on a stool and stuffing food into her mouth as fast as she could. Meg swallowed and wheezed, "Get a bowl, child. We don't stand on ceremony here."

Rufenna shook her head in confusion. "What is all this? I've never seen such in my life."

Meg spoke with a mouthful. "Aye, a bonny feast. That's long kale in that pot and pottage in the other. Over yonder is bannocks of barley meal; sure you know salt herrings and onions. Flummery on that bench. The best are the new oatcakes, the baps in new ale and brandy in stoups. Eat up, child. You'll never find such food among the Romanys."

After the feasting, which went on for many hours, the lords and ladies grew loud and restive with partaking of much food and ale. Then the performers began. Rufenna was more enthralled than anyone. After nearly six years at St. Whitby's she was entirely out of touch with any entertainment at all. The nuns considered any music but the chants to be sinful and often talked of mummers and what a hideous influence they had on those who were drawn to their power. Rufenna didn't quite believe all the nuns said but it was with a delicious sense of wickedness that she unobtrusively slipped into the Great Hall when the performances began.

Geordie took his dogs through their tricks and there was much applause and acclaim after each feat. Then he brought out a small, brown dog and put it on one of the furs. He bowed to the captive audience and said, "Lords and ladies, this sma', wee dog, by the name of Byron he is, is my best-trained beast and can perform many acts of great skill. Aye, give me your attention now and will all be quiet." He approached the brown dog and said, "Now, speak, Byron, to the lords and ladies." The dog did not open his mouth but stared straight ahead. "Speak, Byron," said Geordie again. The dog said nothing. The group snickered. Then Geordie ordered the dog to sit up and it curled itself into a knot. The dog did not move. The group laughed out loud at Geordie's discomfiture. Each order that he gave the dog, Byron did the opposite. At last he ordered the dog to lie down and be silent and it rose up and let forth a great howl. Geordie snatched it up and bowed low to much applause. After that several of the girls sang and then one of the men did a magic act. Then out came the jugglers and astounded the audience and Rufenna with their skill.

Following this act there was a pause while the lords and ladies filled their mugs. Then Namara appeared at the door of the Great Hall. Rufenna had wondered what her skill was as an entertainer; now she would find out. Namara was dressed in a striped skirt, a skirt of all the colors of the rainbow. Her bodice was black and of some soft, clingy fabric that emphasized her proud young breasts. Her skirt came halfway down her leg and showed her feminine shape to advantage. She held a tambourine in her hand

and her feet were bare. She bowed low to the audience, who sat in absolute quiet. She stood for a moment at the edge of the hall; then slowly, sensuously, she walked along the hall to the center. She stood poised, as if ready to fly. A rippling murmur moved through the crowd and then they hushed. From somewhere a guitar began playing, a soft, slow, mysterious melody, and Namara began to dance. She began slowly, moving with feline grace, and playing a steady beat on the tambourine. Her movements were synonymous with the music and expressed a deep, hungry yearning. The music swelled and became faster and faster. Namara's skirt and long black hair swirled about her, creating an image of color and voluptuous movement. On and on she danced. She was acting out a Gypsy girl's seduction of her love. Moving toward the imaginary figure, she touched him and danced around him, then sprinted away, tossing her head disdainfully. When the imaginary figure appeared to leave, she turned and flew to him, wooing him, promising him the realization of his dreams, surrendering at last, ultimately, to his desires. Rufenna felt the blood begin to pound in her head and throat. The movements the girl invented were sheer magic. Rufenna shook herself mentally and looked around the Great Hall. All eyes were riveted to the Gypsy girl and people held their breath lest they miss some moment of it. On and on she danced about the hall, sweeping low, now rising, her skirts straight out from her slim young body. Suddenly her surrender was complete and the dance was over. She bowed low to overwhelming applause. Rufenna glanced up and saw Lord and Lady Rutherford looking at each other. In his eyes she could read mastery and in the lady's triumph. Rufenna looked away quickly, not understanding what she saw. As Namara left the hall, breathless and with a look of gloating on her beautiful face, Geordie appeared from the cook hall and dragged her out in the courtyard and they disappeared into the darkness.

Old Meg, looking on, chuckled. "As long as Namara dances, Scotland and England will be well populated. I wouldn't venture to guess how many bairns will be born nine months from this gossips' wake."

Rufenna stared at the old woman. What did she mean? Surely Geordie and Namara weren't . . . It was as though blinders were ripped from her eyes. Before she could think through old Meg's remark, John Rutherford was calling for order and thanking the troupe for their performance.

"Before we retire for this night, I would ask a question. Who is the young woman with the green skirt who does not perform? Old mother, does she have some act we are being deprived of?"

Before Meg could speak, Rufenna realized that it would call more attention to her if she were called upon to explain her position as a nonperformer than to perform. What could she do? Then she recalled a song that Sophia sang when the nuns were not in hearing. When they first heard it they forbade it as being frivolous and unchristian. But that didn't stop the girls from learning it and singing it whenever they had the opportunity. She turned quickly to Meg, who had opened her mouth to answer Lord Rutherford, and said, "If I could borrow a lute, I will sing a song."

Meg grinned at her. "Good." She reached out and took a lute from one of the Gypsies and handed it to Rufenna.

Rufenna seated herself upon a stool in the center of the hall and smiled shyly at her audience. Strumming a few notes on the lute, she sang the chorus of the old ballad:

Now Cara was a Romany and of this tale you may
    hear,
They cannot stay in one place more than a day and
    a year.
Like a lark inside a gilded cage, she longed to be free,
And so when springtime showed her freshened face,
She traded David for the mountains and a faraway
    place.

The audience responded to the tenderness of the
sad tale about the Gypsy girl who could not stay
with her love but must obey the call of the road.
The sweet, untrained voice of the singer held them
in thrall and her poignant beauty touched everybody.
She flushed exquisitely at the applause and fled from
the hall. Old Meg grabbed her.

"We didn't know that you could sing, child. Mayhap we should kidnap you and make you part of the
show." She smiled as she spoke and Rufenna was
reassured when she realized she was being teased.
Singers could be found anywhere, but a reward for
delivering the lost daughter of a lord was hard to
come by.

After the song the lords and ladies took their leave
and the Gypsies prepared to bed down in the stable.
Namara returned a while later from her rendezvous
with Geordie, a delicate flush showing through her
olive skin. She sniffed disdainfully.

"We are good enough to dance and sing but they
won't have us in their castle when 'tis time to sleep,"
she said.

Old Meg responded, "Hush, slut. Be glad we can
be under roof even if it is only a stable."

It took Rufenna a long time to settle down for
the night. Up until now she had shared the tent with
old Meg. It had not occurred to her that the others
bedded down as couples. She was so intent on getting

home that the mere routine of the Gypsy band eluded
her altogether. The only three whose names she knew
were those of Meg, Geordie, and Namara. She had
heard the others referred to but they seemed to have
outlandish names and she didn't remember who they
were. Tonight she began to notice the relationshisp
of the others and considering it kept her awake. Were
Geordie and Namara betrothed or did he take her
whenever the desire came on him with no thought
of the consequences? They must have some better
relationship than that; else why would Namara be
so possessive of him? Did she really fear Rufenna or
was it her nature to be distrustful of all strangers?
Certainly, she, Rufenna, had done nothing to en-
courage Geordie; they had not touched each other
at all except the times he helped her over the rough-
est parts of the path that first day.

The Gypsies grabbed their covers and their partners and chose a spot for themselves in the stable.
Rufenna was unaccustomed to the crowded quarters,
the smells of the animals so close by, the noise of
the guards. As they were relieved of duty, they sauntered into the courtyard to warm themselves around
the fire burning there. They laughed and joshed each
other. Bawdy jokes were exchanged and Rufenna
heard mention of the Gypsies. She heard the quiet
breathing and occasional snores of her companions
and turned restlessly on the noisy straw. She tried to
force sleep to come but her thoughts returned to the
hope that, with any luck at all, they should be at
Lyall tomorrow night. Perhaps her father was better.
Would she be the one to tell of the sad tidings of
Alexander and his men or had somebody escaped and
gone home to report? Was her father able to continue
the feud Davon Hammond seemed obsessed with?
She couldn't answer any of these questions and they
drove sleep further away.

The courtyard became quiet and the wind rustled

through the stable and blew little bits of chaff about. She could feel it settling on her face. Hours, or so it seemed to her, passed. All the Gypsies appeared to be asleep. At last, warmed and tired by the food and ale, and in spite of the uncomfortable bed, Rufenna began to doze. As she floated off on a soft cloud of slumber, she didn't hear the stealthy footsteps approach her pallet. She was taken completely by surprise when the furs were jerked from her body and a rough hand clapped itself over her mouth. At the same time, a strong body began to force itself upon her. She struggled wildly but the hand kept her from making any but the most muffled, choked sounds. Who was this and what did he want? Instantly she knew the answer to that. He was ready for a woman and she had been chosen.

"Lie still, you little bitch, lie still," he muttered.

She thrashed and turned away from him as he tore at the fastenings of her bodice. He freed her firm young breasts and caressed them with a rough, brutal hand. She moaned and tried to tear herself away and he misinterpreted her moan.

"Thought you'd like that. And we're just getting started." He squeezed and tore at her breasts and pinched her nipples viciously.

She could feel herself losing consciousness from the pain and struggled to keep from fainting. That would be fatal. When he finished with her breasts and began to pull up her petticoats, she heard the fabric tear and thought wildly and irrelevantly of how furious Namara would be. She couldn't believe the strength of her unknown assailant. He was effectively gagging her with one hand and at the same time holding her down and tearing off her clothing with the other. She kicked wildly at him and must have hit a vulnerable spot, because he groaned and moved away from her briefly.

"You'll pay for that, you little . . ." He twined

his hand in her long hair and twisted brutally. "Keep those legs still, my beauty. How else can I mount you?" He removed his hand from her mouth so he could undo his own clothing and Rufenna drew in a deep breath and screamed.

No one came to her aid. She heard the laughter around the campfire as some guards approached and warmed their hands. One said, "The Gypsies are a wild lot. Listen to that one scream with pleasure." The Gypsies themselves stirred but no one moved. She heard shushing noises. A feminine voice giggled and admonished them, "Couple if you will but don't be so loud about it."

"No!" began Rufenna. "You don't—" The hard hand was pressed against her lips again. Through the tumult as this giant struggled with her, she found herself thinking of Davon. What he had done to her was essentially the same. He had used and defiled her. But there *was* a difference. He had wooed her and waited for her passion to match his. He had not simply taken her as this beast was intent on doing. As one animal will take another in heat. The brutal hand at last succeeded in undoing his clothing and pulled her skirts up over her head until she was nearly suffocated. Then the hand pulled her thighs apart with a strength and viciousness that she knew would leave bruises and scratches. She could feel her strength waning. "God help me," she prayed, "for I can no longer fight him."

Suddenly the man above her grunted and collapsed on her. He had not entered her and when she again tried to tear herself from under him, he did not stop her. She rolled away, trying to pull down her skirts and hold together her bodice at the same time. The man did not move.

In the flickering light she beheld old Meg. The Gypsy chuckled. "I got here in time, didn't I, child? After I heard ye holler, I made haste."

Rufenna sobbed and did not speak. She saw that Meg had hit him on the head with a shovel. "Is he dead?" she finally asked.

"Na, child. He'll have a bit of a headache on the morrow, I ken, but I wouldn't kill one of our own tribe. I doubt you'll have more trouble with him tonight," the old woman added, "but come over and sleep near me."

Rufenna quietly moved her furs from under the now groaning man. She was careful not to look at him too closely. She didn't want to know who he was. Now, she was sure, as she settled herself near Meg, she would never shut her eyes, but the next thing she knew, it was morning.

Her bruised and aching breasts and thighs served to remind her the minute she awoke of what had nearly befallen her the night before. She did not inquire who had a headache and no reference was made to the incident except Namara's cutting remark when they were alone.

"You might give yourself airs, but you aren't a woman. You know nothing about pleasuring a man."

Rufenna refused to answer such a statement. The Gypsy girl went on combing her long black hair for a moment and then stopped and looked at Rufenna coldly.

"Making such a fuss about nothing last night. A green girl, that's what you are."

Rufenna stalked away in a rage. Did Namara really think she was a green girl? She could tell Namara a thing or two—about a few nights ago when she lay in Davon Hammond's arms and loved every moment of it—when he . . . But even to herself Rufenna could not put their lovemaking into words. Besides that, she would probably never see Davon Hammond again. That is unless her father chose to continue the feud and then she might see his head upon a

pike. Blood had been shed between the two clans
and the feud had gone far beyond a few barn burnings and stolen cattle. So best she forget him and
think of her upcoming marriage and hope that Neville was . . . But it was no good thinking of that
either. She would find out in good time what her
husband to be was like and she knew she had no
choice in the matter. If she liked him, and someday
loved him, all would be well. She would be one of
the fortunate ones. If not she would spend her life
bearing and raising his children and keeping order
in his household. That was what women were for.
Rufenna shook off the depressing thought and went
to join the others in the cookhouse. The hot por-
ridge and ale heartened her considerably and she
soon became intent upon departure. The day was
overcast and it looked as though it would rain any
moment. She prayed that the rain would hold off
until they reached Lyall. The weather had been cold
but dry since she had joined the Gypsies. Pray God
it would not rain this day. After her breakfast she
loaded up her furs on the cart and waited impatiently for the others to prepare for departure. She
saw nothing of the Rutherfords. Evidently Lord Rutherford had settled up with Meg, because they left
the castle shortly afterward.

Old Meg rode in the lead cart, chortling with pleasure at the money they had earned. "When we get
back to Yetholm, I'll settle up with ye," she told the
others. "Meanwhile are ye content that I should keep
it safe for you?" The others agreed and again Rufenna realized the important place the old woman
held in the Gypsy band. Cook, disciplinarian, now
treasurer.

The day passed. Instead of being glad every time
they stopped to eat or rest, Rufenna found herself
mad with impatience at every delay. She would gladly

have run all the way had her strength allowed it or if she had been familiar with the terrain. In her haste to get home she did not notice that the country through which they were passing was not as rough as that she had encountered closer to the Border.

Late in the afternoon a bone-chilling mist began to fall, soaking Rufenna and the Gypsies as it increased in intensity. She was afraid that they would seek shelter someplace else and was glad that they saw nothing, not even a shack where they could get out of the damp. On and on they walked, into the darkening day. At last the towers of Lyall reared against the unfriendly sky. The guards on the battlements, drawing their cloaks around them to keep out the rain, noticed the bedraggled little band approaching the castle. As the Gypsies came within hailing distance, the guard called, "Go away. There is nothing for you here. This is a house of death."

Rufenna broke away from the others, tearing off the scarf she had used for so many days to hide her identity. "I am Rufenna Lyall," she called to the guard. "Open the gate at once."

The guard called down to someone in the courtyard and after a brief delay the heavy portcullis was raised. Rufenna, feeling strength flowing through her limbs, ran into the courtyard. She spoke to the strange guard. "Where is my father?"

The guard stuttered, "Well, mistress . . ." but before he could speak further, a woman in dark robes, pale and wan, appeared at the door of the Great Hall.

"What's this?' she asked in a dazed manner, and then she recognized her daughter. She reeled slightly and Rufenna ran and took the frail woman in her arms.

"Rufenna," her mother said numbly. "Oh, my child, we feared . . ."

Rufenna held her mother close in a warm embrace. "Mother, how glad I am to see you. Father? Is Father . . . ?"

Tears poured down Wira Lyall's face. She shook her head. "He's no better, I fear. Where have you been all this time?" Then she glanced over Rufenna's head at the Gypsies, who were standing uneasily in the courtyard. "Who are all these people, Rufenna?"

Rufenna clutched at the last question. She hesitated to tell her mother what had befallen her and hoped to forestall further questions.

"They're Gypsies, Mother. I have been traveling with them for days. They saved my life and took care of me. I . . ." She hesitated. "I promised them some money if they would see me safely home."

Lady Lyall passed a weary hand across her face and motioned to the Gypsies. "Come into the hall and warm yourselves. I will have the cook prepare a meal for you. Rufenna," she turned back to her daughter, "you have not been with the Gypsies since . . . They had nothing to do with the attack on Alexander?"

"Oh, no, Mother. It was after that when the Gypsies found me."

"I see," said her mother slowly, and Rufenna sensed that this was not the end of the interrogation.

"Mother, please, can I go to Father?"

Wira nodded and watched the Gypsies flocking into the warmth of the hall. "Old Walter can deal with them," the older woman said. "Come, child."

Rufenna told her mother that she must tell Meg good-bye and sought out the old woman warming herself at the fireplace. "Meg, I must go. My father is ill and I am needed."

The Gypsy turned. "Aye, child. Ye're home now and no longer part of our band."

"Walter will give you some money; I will tell him

to give it to you, Meg. I can never thank you enough for looking after me."

The old woman smiled. "Is nothing. We were glad to do it."

Rufenna looked around but her mother had disappeared up the winding stairs, evidently returning to her husband. "Will you stay the night?" she asked Meg.

Meg said, "We'd be grateful but don't ye be worrying about us. We will bed down in the stable and be on our way tomorrow at daybreak. We have a wedding to entertain at in three days so we have some traveling to do."

Rufenna hesitated only a moment and then embraced the old woman warmly. "Good-bye, Meg. I doubt if I'll see you again."

Meg returned her hug. "Fare ye well, Rufenna."

Rufenna went slowly up the stairs to the third floor where the great bedchamber was located. She felt in no hurry because she hated to find out for sure what she was nearly positive was true. She entered the room that had been her own, but she had been gone so long, she had left little imprint on it. She took off her wet clothing and dried herself as best she could. Just as she was wondering what she could possibly put on, a soft knock sounded on the door. The maidservant entered and bobbed a curtsy.

"Mistress, I am Agnes," the fair-haired young girl said clearly. "Your mother said I would be maid for you from now on. She has sent a dress of her own. Thanks be that you're nearly the same size. We'll have to sew for you when this sad business is over."

"Have you been at Lyall long?" asked Rufenna.

"Aye, since my sister came to be Lady Lyall's maid. I have been trained so that I could care for you when you came home." She stood back and looked at Rufenna. "There, you'll do," she said crisply. As she talked, the trim little maid was busily brushing the tangles from Rufenna's hair and slipping the dress over her head.

Leaving Agnes to deal with the wet Gypsy clothing and towels, Rufenna hurried down the corridor to the great chamber that was her parent's room.

CHAPTER TEN

Rufenna gazed with stricken eyes at the gaunt, wasted figure in the massive bed. She could scarcely believe that this pitiful shadow of a man was her father. He had changed beyond all recognition in the two years since he had visited her at the Abbey. His labored breathing echoed harshly around the room, and she shivered. Her mother lightly touched her arm and Rufenna blindly followed her out the door into the adjoining bedchamber. She went straight to the fire, holding out hands, which were numb with cold and shock, trying to adjust to the situation that she had found here at Lyall. Her father was dying; even her unskilled eyes could see that. Alexander was dead. John, her younger brother, her father's heir, was a minor. She cast a quick glance at her mother.

Wira Lyall's face was a study in grief. She had nursed her husband devotedly for more than a year, trying to hold back the course of the wasting illness by sheer determination. She knew now that she had failed. A quiet, gentle woman, Lady Lyall had wrapped her life around her big, sturdy husband. She had borne him four children, three of whom had grown to adulthood. Even now she grieved over the

wee bairn, a second girl, who had died so swiftly
after birth. But she had watched Alexander grow into
a tall, independent man, had tearfully parted with
her only daughter, who was sent to the Abbey for
schooling and security; she had secretly delighted in
her younger son, so much like her with his gentle
manners, and had been glad she had not yet had
to bid him farewell. Sir Ewen wished the boy to go
to France for schooling soon, possibly to prepare for
the Church.

Now Wira stared at the floor, twisting her thin
hands in her lap, as she braced herself to ask for an
accounting from her daughter. They knew no more
than that Alexander had gone to fetch Rufenna and
had not returned. The meager report they had received had been distressing and for the long days
that Rufenna was missing, the lady of the manor
had held out little hope of her survival. Sir Ewen,
sunk into a stupor that nothing nor no one could
penetrate, had not known of this fresh calamity. Wira
had been forced to bear it alone and this in itself
was difficult for her. Always, since her sixteenth birthday and her marriage to Ewen, Wira had leaned
heavily on the broad shoulders of her husband. Finally she straightened her shoulders and turned to
Rufenna, taking in the vivid beauty of the girl with
wondering eyes. The last few years had made an
enormous difference. The laughing, mischievous child
who had left had not shown the promise of this
beauty. In truth she had blossomed into a lovely
woman. How like Ewen she was!

"I would like to hear of it," Wira said, folding her
hands tighter in her lap. "Tell me now, my daughter,
and let us place it behind us."

"We rode from the Abbey that day and were attacked," Rufenna began, not sure how much she
should burden her mother with.

"We sent a scouting party when you did not return," Wira said. "They found the body of a Lyall man, lying all alone, and no sign of any of the rest of the troop. We feared . . ." she stopped, swallowed the tears gathering in her throat and went on. "Do you know who attacked you?"

"Lord Hammond's men."

Rufenna stared with astonishment at the change that came over her mother at these words. Her already pale face had whitened to a deathly pallor; her eyes widened in horror and, yes, it was understanding, too, that she read in those dark eyes! Her mother knew something of this!

"Mother . . ."

"Nay, child, go on. Tell me."

"Well, Alexander was killed and my horse bolted." Rufenna knew the words sounded stark but she didn't know how to soften them.

Alexander's mother bowed her head for a moment. She had been expecting this. "Lord Hammond killed him?" she asked in a shaken whisper.

"No, not exactly. He was wounded, I think, and fell from his horse. He was trampled. Mama, you know something of this! Why did Lord Hammond attack us? Why did he hate Alexander?"

"You are quite sure it was Lord Hammond?"

"Of course I'm sure! He caught me later that night and took me to Hammond Tower." At the memory of her time there Rufenna blushed and dropped her gaze to the fire, not noticing the look of quick understanding that came into Wira's eyes.

"He released you?"

"Oh, no! I escaped and those Gypsies helped me get home. Mama . . ."

"I cannot talk about it now, Rufenna. Later, we will. I must return to your father." Wira rose, deaf to her daughter's protestations, and swept from the room.

After a moment of indecision Rufenna returned

to her own bedchamber. She felt perilously close to crying. Her mother had been sympathetic and had not, mercifully, demanded an exact accounting of her stay at Hammond Tower. She had no desire to tell anyone of it, much less her already grief-stricken mother. However, she could not escape the feeling that she was being treated like a child, too young to know the true story, being dismissed to her room so the adults could discuss it. Without doubt her mother knew exactly what it was about. She knew why there had been ill feeling between Alexander and Davon Hammond and had not been particularly shocked at Davon's attack upon them. Sorrowed, horrified at Aleaxnder's death, but not surprised! And, too, they seemed to have jumped instantly to the conclusion, when the report of the lone body lying in the valley came back, that all had perished. Had they been expecting just such an attack? Rufenna set her soft mouth, deciding that she would get to the bottom of this matter. Her mother owed it to her to tell her of this feud. After all, hadn't *she* borne the brunt of his rage?

Sir Ewen died quietly at dawn, never recovering consciousness. Rufenna and her mother wept quietly as Father Antonius performed the rites for the dying. John, trying to be manly, fought back tears and stood with his arm around his mother. The priest pulled the cover over the body of Sir Ewen. Rufenna tried to think of words to say to her brother to ease his grief, but she did not know John well enough to do this. At least, she thought, he has been with father all his fourteen years, while I . . . No words seemed to touch Lady Lyall at all. She withdrew to her bedchamber, locked the door, and refused to see anyone but her maid.

Some hours later Rufenna sat in the small withdrawing room, used for generations by the ladies of the family, and gazed with anxiety at Old Walter. Her father's cousin and lifelong friend, Old Walter had been a fixture at Lyall as long as she could remember. Now he patted her hand gently and nodded.

"You must take charge, lass. Decisions must be made for the funeral and there is no one but you to make them. John is indeed your father's heir, but he is over-young to deal with this. As for your mother . . ." He let his sentence trail off, shaking his head sadly. "You must handle it for her."

"But, Walter, I have no idea what to do! Cannot Captain Kincaid do it?"

"Rufenna, lass. He is but the captain of the castle. It is his duty to defend it and carry out your mother's orders but you must give them, child. Your mother cannot. Come, I will advise you. There is much to do. Many people will come to pay their respects to your father. He was much admired. You must be prepared to feed and house them. Father Antonius is waiting to find out what you want done."

Meekly Rufenna went with him to meet with Father Antonius, who was eager to return to the village. "To his doxy, na doubt," whispered Walter, out of the priest's hearing. Antonius had been kept at the castle for several days so he made short work of the funeral arrangements.

"Tomorrow, mistress. Sir Ewen died of an unknown malady and it could be a pestilence—"

"Not so," protested Walter. "He had been ill for many months and no one else has been stricken."

"Nonetheless," insisted the priest, "many a contagion becomes prevalent after the soul has departed. Already the body darkens."

Rufenna backed away, her stomach churning, and hastened to agree with the priest to have the funeral the next day. Old Walter objected to that. Such haste was unseemly and the relatives would not have time to arrive. Rufenna turned a deaf ear to him. After all, he said she would have to take charge.

The priest promised to return after supper for the requiem mass. Rufenna thanked him and descended to the kitchens to order the weeping cooks to begin preparations for food. The maids were sent to open unused rooms and ready them for guests. She set a reluctant John to writing invitations to the funeral and Walter dispatched horsemen to deliver them.

She was exhausted by late afternoon. All the arrangements had been made, all the details handled. The news of Sir Ewen's death had spread over the March. His body had been washed and laid out in the Great Hall so family and friends could pay their respects. She sank into a chair in the withdrawing room and looked up to see John enter and join her at the fire.

"Is there anything else to be done?" he asked. "I pray not. My hand is numb from all those notices you forced on me."

"You were the one to do it, John. You are the heir to Lyall now. 'Twas seemly."

"But tiresome."

"I think everything is taken care of. I might need you to see that the stables are readied to take in the horses. Walter says many people will come," she added, trying awkwardly to include the boy in everything.

"James will see to that." James was the head groom and ruled the stables with an iron hand. "He wouldn't like *me* giving him orders. I hope Cousin Murdoch doesn't come," he added gloomily.

Rufenna was startled by this reminder. She had forgotten Murdoch. She grimaced. "I hope not, too, but I warrant he will. If he hears of it in time."

"He'll hear of it, even though I did not send him a notice. He hears of all that happens here."

"Does he? How?"

"Spies, I warrant," John said, showing more animation than Rufenna had seen since she returned home. "I tried to tell Walter but he shushed me. Rufenna, he does know whatever passes here."

Rufenna frowned over this. "Does he come often?"

"Aye, more often than Father liked. He did not much like Cousin Murdoch and neither do I!" he said boldly, glancing at her out of the corner of his eyes to see how she took this statement.

"I didn't like him when we were young, but I haven't seen him for years," Rufenna admitted, somewhat amused by John's pugnaciousness. Perhaps there was more Lyall in him than she had thought! He was just a lad, but he already had the Lyall height and slenderness. His hair was not as red as hers, being more auburn than red. She had always thought he took more after their mother, but there was definitely a streak of the Lyall independence and stubbornness in John. She was relieved to see it.

"Maybe he won't come," she consoled him. "There is naught for him to do here."

"He'll find something, if nothing else but to 'pay his respects,'" John sneered. "Rufenna, he frightens me. I wish Alexander was here," he added in a rush.

"Did Alexander like him?" she asked in disbelief.

John shook his head violently. "He could not abide him. I think Cousin Murdoch was afraid of Alexander. He frequently came when he knew Alexander was not here. That's what I mean, Rufenna. He always seemed to *know*!"

Rufenna was disquieted by these disclosures but she tried to reassure John. The boy was upset. She hoped it was a young boy's fancy about Murdoch knowing more about Lyall than was reasonable, but she feared it was fact. Rufenna hoped John was wrong and Murdoch would not learn of the death of Sir Ewen until much later.

* * *

John had not been wrong. Murdoch arrived before supper, bringing an unexpectedly large troop of men with him. Even to Rufenna's inexperienced eyes it seemed too many men. She guessed that after hearing of Alexander's death, he felt safer so surrounded. But she had no time to ponder this. She was busy greeting new arrivals and neighbors and thanking them for coming. Finally she was forced to show Murdoch some attention. He stood in the doorway of the Great Hall, waiting.

She recognized him instantly, even though it had been five years since she had seen him. The five years had not changed him or improved him. He lacked the Lyall height and slenderness; he was shorter, thicker of body, but well muscled. His hair was a dull sandy shade, lacking the fire of the Lyall redheads. Old Walter had heard the rumor that he was not a Lyall at all, but the result of a raiding party that sought and gained the favors of the lady of Galzean Castle, his mother.

If Rufenna was not impressed with the changes time had wrought in him, he at least was very impressed with her. He remembered her as a skinny, freckled-face child of twelve, all knees and elbows. His pale blue eyes, nearly colorless in this light, ran over the flaming hair, the beautiful face, the sculptured chin that hinted of a dimple. They lingered on her tall, slim, amply curved body, revealed discreetly by the dark gown she wore. The midnight-blue dress complemented her flawless complexion and vivid hair and the sudden flare in his eyes brought a blush to her creamy cheeks.

"Cousin Rufenna, I scarcely knew you," he murmured, raising her hand to his lips.

Rufenna felt the slightly moist mouth pressed against her hand and recoiled automatically. No, she did not like Murdoch any better than before; neither did she like the look in his eye, an appraising, hungry look that sent a chill down her spine.

"Cousin Murdoch, I did not expect you so soon," she said, aware that John was standing beside her in tight-lipped silence. His dislike showed plainly on his young face and Rufenna nudged him gently. He started and dropped his gaze but not before Murdoch had noticed the little byplay.

"I was grieved to learn of your father's death, Cousin Rufenna, and, of course, that of your brother. It was a scrambled tale I heard, about Alexander. Outlaws, I understand."

Rufenna frowned and shot a glance at her young brother. "Later, if you will, Cousin. I will see that you are shown to your room so that you may refresh yourself before supper. Did Captain Kincaid see to your men?"

"Aye, Cousin, he promised to do so. We will continue this discussion later. I am well nigh parched with thirst, I admit, and some refreshment would be most welcome."

Rufenna signaled and a young page crossed to her side. "See Master Murdoch to his room, Ian. Make sure refreshment is provided for him."

Rufenna watched Murdoch follow the youthful page to the spiral stairs and scowled.

"I told you," John muttered softly. "I knew he would come. How did he know? We didn't send word to him."

She shook her head. "I don't think anyone did, but I will ask him later. If you will stay close to greet anyone else that arrives, I will make sure all is in train for supper. I do not think anyone else will come tonight. Darkness has already fallen."

John reluctantly agreed and Rufenna escaped, still frowning over his open dislike and distrust of their cousin. He had managed to raise doubts in her own mind about Murdoch. How *had* Murdoch known? How had he arrived so quickly? As she went down to the kitchens, Rufenna tried to think it out. Her father had died at dawn. If someone—but who?—had left as soon as the news had been passed to the castle's inhabitants, he could have reached Murdoch's castle, Galzean, by noontime if he rode hard. If Murdoch left Galzean immediately on receiving the news, he would have arrived at suppertime. Rufenna worried over it. It did fit the facts they had, but why would Murdoch have a man posted in the castle? No, surely not! Captain Kincaid would be sure to know of that! Perhaps, thought Rufenna, a word with Captain Kincaid would be advisable!

CHAPTER ELEVEN

Two days later Rufenna said good-bye to still another Border family and fled to the sanctuary of her withdrawing room. She sank into a chair near the fire and closed her eyes wearily. Never had she been so exhausted in her life, not even when the horse bolted and she wandered in the wilderness until found by Davon; not even when she awoke at the Gypsy camp. This was more than physical exhaustion. Her mind was drained and she found it difficult to think back over the last few days with any sense of continuity.

That first evening after her father's death Rufenna had welcomed people she barely remembered: relatives, neighbors, old clansmen who had known and loved her father. She listened to stories about him and tried to dry the tears of those who wept over him. At supper the visitors drew out their own knives and spoons but before they began to eat, they looked around for Lady Lyall. Rufenna had tried to tell people that her mother was prostrate in her room but everyone thought she would appear for supper. Rufenna sat at the head of the table in her father's chair and tried to ignore the scandalized mutterings

that went on around her. The idea of a mere chit
of a girl sitting in the heir's place. Who had ever
heard of such a thing? John, the legal heir, had refused the honor; his mother was his guardian until
he was of age and tonight Rufenna was standing in
for her mother. Therefore she must take the head
of the table. Rufenna did, understanding the boy's
shyness. Even worse than that, Rufenna tried to ignore her father's body laid out at the other end of
the Great Hall. Candles burned at the head and
foot of the bier.

After supper, which seemed to go on forever, Rufenna had hoped to excuse herself and go to her
room. Surely the guests would be tired from their
long, cold rides. But it was not to be. Before the
last place was cleared, while mugs were still being
filled, a small group of musicians arrived and began
tuning their instruments. Rufenna glanced down the
table at Old Walter, a question in her eyes, and he
nodded reassuringly. When she could endure it no
longer, she rose to dismiss the musicians but Walter
stopped her.

" 'Tis the custom, lass. And you must lead the first
reel, your mother not here to do it."

"Lead the reel?" she repeated, scandalized. "You
mean we're going to have a *dance*?"

" 'Tis always done at wakes."

"I won't do it! It's not proper."

" 'Tis entirely proper and would be unseemly not
to do it. Already the guests are shocked by the undue
haste of the funeral. To dispense with the reels would
only give them something else to talk about."

Rufenna digested this in horrified silence. "When
do we have the mass?"

"Immediately, before the dancing begins. Ah, there
is Father Antonius now."

The guests gathered at the far end of the Great
Hall near the body of Lord Lyall. Rufenna, John,

and Old Walter knelt near the bier and the requiem mass began. That seemed to take forever and Rufenna, although accustomed to kneeling for long periods at the Abbey, found her knees throbbing unbearably. Before the service ended, she was beginning to weave back and forth and was afraid she would faint.

The instant the last *amen* was said and the group got to their feet, before Rufenna could have a word with the priest, the musicians began to play and the guests stood respectfully, waiting for Rufenna to begin the dancing. She looked wildly about her, hardly knowing where to begin. From the group Murdoch appeared, bowed slightly, and took her hand.

"Allow me to dance the first reel with you, Cousin."

She gave him a small bewildered smile. The guests quickly chose their partners and the dancing began. Also the drinking. Rufenna had not inquired into the ordering of ale and whiskey from the village and she hoped old Walter or somebody had done so. Never had she seen people so determined to drink themselves senseless. The evening dragged on, with song, dancing, and drinking. Rufenna thought it would never end. She was caught in some nightmare where she would forever be whirling around the hall with near strangers, while the body of her beloved father lay stiff and cold at the other end of the hall. At last she was allowed to escape to her bedchamber, bent on falling asleep immediately. But she found sleep had fled. The instant her head hit the pillow thoughts of Davon, the Gypsies, Murdoch, John and his worries, her mother . . . all jumbled together in her head, allowing her no rest. Long before daylight she was up and dressed.

After their fasts were broken, the mourners gathered in the courtyard with the body and followed the priest to the churchyard in the village. Rufenna and

John walked behind the bier, Old Walter and the other kinsmen a respectful distance behind them, followed by their friends and neighbors and the servants last of all. As they approached the village, the people who lived there came out and joined the funeral procession. The pipes played one mournful funeral dirge after another, and Rufenna, the tears pouring down her face, noticed that Walter was weeping too.

Rufenna stood watching as the grave was dug in the churchyard, aware of the icy wind cutting through her woolen cloak. Then the pallbearers carried the body three times around the grave, in accordance with the ancient custom. This would protect the body in the grave from evil influences. Then the body was placed in the grave, with the feet facing east, and the grave was filled in. Rufenna averted her eyes as the damp, heavy soil was shoveled into the yawning hole. The wake continued back at the castle for the rest of the day and most of the night. By the time they had all left, at midafternoon, Rufenna was exhausted. Only Murdoch had remained.

Rufenna had not seen her mother since the dawn of her father's death. At first she had called questions and requests to her through the door, but the maid said Lady Wira was unwell and could not attend to anything. Rufenna was to do what she thought proper. John went about with a sullen face that grew darker daily. He refused to remain in the company of his cousin and showed his dislike very plainly. Rufenna felt caught between the two of them, Murdoch and John. Murdoch was quiet, polite about John's churlishness, and made Rufenna wonder if perhaps she had let young John's excited imaginings influence her opinion of her cousin. Murdoch was at her side whenever a decision was to be made. He discussed with her what was to be done and then saw that her orders were carried out.

It was a relief to share the new, unexpected burden

with someone. She had not been trained to command a castle, clusters of farms and other holdings, due to lack of interest, and troops of garrisoned soldiers. Rufenna felt only relief at this unexpected source of help.

Now that all the confusion was over, she stared into the fire and hoped she could sleep tonight. As long as her father's body lay in the Great Hall, she could not close her eyes without seeing it. Now he had been safely buried since yesterday and she could go to bed early tonight and sleep. Just then Walter joined her in the small withdrawing room. His wrinkled, weather-beaten old face, resembling a friendly prune, was grave. He asked how she was and then went directly to the reason for his visit.

"Child, I know you mean well, but it is not fitting that your cousin Murdoch should swagger about as if he's now master of Lyall. You do ill to put your trust in a marplot such as he. Young John gave you the warning, I hear. He dislikes him greatly and I think the boy has the right of it. Your brother Alexander stood no nonsense from Murdoch. He sent him about his way red-faced when that windbag came poking his nose into business which didn't concern him. I give ye warning, lass. He has an eye on the estate and you do poorly to trust him."

Rufenna stared at Walter with a kindling eye. "Walter, I know you mean well, but what am I to do? John cannot take charge of his inheritance! I don't know many of the things that are necessary for the Lord of Lyall to know! Someone has to advise me. You're as bad as John, making poor Cousin Murdoch out to be a knave when his only wish is to aid me. Nay, enough, Walter," she said as he moved to interrupt her. "I will care for Lyall as best I can but I must have help and Murdoch offers it. He has not made any move that I have noticed that smacks of undue authority."

Walter stroked his beard and peered at her. "What

need has he of so many men, lass? Were ye aware that he brought o'er a hundred armed men with him? For what? Surely it doesn't take so many to protect one man. Twenty men died with Alexander, girl, and there are near fifty of our men still at Knolle Castle, sent there by your brother before he left to fetch you home. We have scarcely forty men, armed and ready to stand duty, here at Lyall. Your cousin is giving the orders now to Captain Kincaid, and the captain is not happy with them. Master Murdoch's men are guarding Lyall, Rufenna, standing duty on your walls."

Rufenna pushed her heavy hair back from her forehead and sighed. More problems! "Walter," she began. "I know Murdoch's men are helping to guard the castle. He offered them himself when he advised me that most of our own men were still at Knolle. A man has been sent to Knolle to recall them and until they arrive, Murdoch is placing his own men at our disposal. Enough of this, Walter! I am tired and weary of arguments. I must do as I think best."

"You are a stubborn lass, Rufenna; you always were. Nay, I'll have done. But say not to me that I did not seek to warn you. He means mischief, that cousin of yours. He always did and always will. Rest well, child, and think on what I've said."

Rufenna went wearily to her room, wondering if Walter could possibly be right. She knew he disliked Murdoch as much as John did and they both had seen more of her cousin than she had. After all, she had been away from home a long time. Rufenna, instead of lying down on her bed, thrust open the tower door and went hastily up the stairs to the battlements. Perhaps some air would clear her muddled senses. She eased open the heavy wooden door and stepped out onto the battlemented wall, her eyes going immediately to the armed soldier who stood sentry duty not ten feet away.

Ignoring him, she went over to the wall and leaned against the rough stone. From here she had a wide view of the rugged countryside, with its sharp ridges and sheltered valleys. Lyall Castle had been built upon one of those ridges and she could see the village nestled at the foot, secure in the valley below. Spring was in the air now. In spite of the late-afternoon chill she could almost smell it. Faint touches of purple bloom showed in the heather growing up the sides of the hills. The trees, although still gaunt and wintry looking, were beginning to take on that almost imperceptible look of expectancy, of pastel softness. The brisk wind had a cutting edge to it and she moved to the inside of the wall and huddled behind the square tower. The castle lay below her. The tall, four-story keep stood strong and gray, the original fortress built on this ridge by the Lyalls. Wings had been added on either side, then long side walls and a stout front wall, with towers at the corners. Men were moving around down in the square courtyard, framed by the massive stone walls, and she could hear hammering coming from the smithy nestled in the corner.

Thinking of Walter's words, she scanned the defenses and began to frown as she realized that every man that she could see on guard duty belonged to Murdoch. The big, tough-looking troopers wore the usual leather breeches and leather jacks of the Border soldier, but all her men wore the green and white Lyall badge on their shoulder. These men carried no insignia. Where were the Lyall men? Beginning to grow worried now, Rufenna returned her gaze to the courtyard, carefully inspecting every man she could see there. Castle servants, scurrying between the bakery and the hall; more unliveried soldiers clustered in groups, quaffing ale and resting in the shade of the walls; villagers bringing goods for the castle, moving back and forth under the great portcullis that guarded Lyall's gatehouse. No Lyall men were in sight at all! There should be too. Lyall men should be sharing the guard duty on the walls with the men Murdoch had brought. They should also be visible in the courtyard, drinking ale, resting in the shelter of the looming walls. A chill feathered down her spine. If Walter was right about Murdoch's intentions, then the situation was indeed serious. Murdoch, as of this moment, held Lyall Castle and all within it in his grasp. She went inside, wondering what to do next.

Her maid, Agnes, was waiting for her in her room, a strangely agitated Agnes. She took a step forward and three backward, cleared her throat awkwardly, and finally, at Rufenna's exasperated demand to be told instantly what was the matter, blurted out the message.

"The man, Sim, mistress. He said I was to tell you—"

"Who is Sim? One of Master Murdoch's men?" Rufenna questioned sharply.

"Nay, mistress. A traveler." She tried to hide a smile at the thought of Sim. "He came at dusk two days before you returned. He had hurt his leg in a fall and asked shelter. He said to warn you of Master Murdoch, mistress," quavered the maid, now frightened at the rage she saw on the face of her mistress.

Rufenna sank down on the bed and glowered at the terrified Agnes. "Just one moment," she said. "You say this man Sim came several days ago, claiming a hurt leg, and now sends me a warning? Who is he, Agnes? A traveling merchant?"

"Nay," Agnes said hastily, recalling Sim's big, broad-shouldered frame. "He's nae merchant, mistress! I know not who he is but he has remained, caring for his leg. He talks to the soldiers in the courtyard, sitting under the shade by the armory. He said to tell my mistress that Master Murdoch meant mischief. His men have the castle, he said, and mean harm by the boy."

"John?" Rufenna felt a new icy chill sliding down her spine. "He warns me to be careful for John?"

"Aye, for young John."

"Agnes, how could he know this? Fetch me this man instantly! I will question him myself."

Agnes bobbed a curtsy and scampered out, leaving Rufenna more perplexed and worried than ever. Silently she began pacing the floor, waiting to question this chance traveler who sent such a strange message. A muffled knock at the tower door in the corner of her room sent her turning in surprise. Had Agnes brought the man up this way? The heavy latch opened under her hand and a large, burly man ducked into the room, quickly closing the door behind him. Rufenna watched him with narrowed eyes. She did not understand his furtive air, his quick move to conceal his presence here. He met her gaze unflinchingly and she frowned. He was strangely familiar. Something stirred in her memory but eluded her. She had seen him before, but where?

"Mistress, if you would lock your door? I have no wish to be found here by your cousin. 'Twould be dangerous for you."

Rufenna locked the door and confronted him. "Explain yourself, if you please. What is this danger that you prate of? What have you heard that leads you to think my brother John is in danger?"

He moved toward her, stopping only feet away and met her gaze frankly. "You and your brother, Master John, are in grave danger, mistress. This afternoon your cousin issued his captain orders—orders to prepare to escort John to Galzean, which Agnes tells me is your cousin's own castle. He will be held there in 'protective custody,' your cousin said, to safeguard him against your enemies. Do you know of any enemies that would harm the lad?"

Rufenna nearly denied it and then remembered Davon Hammond. Would he carry his feud against a boy? Somehow she could not see him doing so. He makes war on women, however, her mind whispered, so why not a boy?

"Only one," she said slowly. "Lord Hammond. He is engaged in a feud with the Lyalls and killed my brother Alexander."

Something in Sim's face gave her the clue, the recognition that had eluded her before. Into her mind swam the memory of Davon consigning her into a big Borderer's care before riding against the Tynehill farm. This was the man, this Sim!

"Y-you . . ." she sputtered, gaping at him. "You're h-his man, Sim!"

Sim nodded calmly, not showing any unease at her recognition. "He sent me here to make sure you returned safely, mistress. He was nigh distracted when you disappeared. He searched the Border for days until I send word you were safely home. Nay, mistress, whatever m'lord's quarrel with you might be, he would not harm the boy. Think you that Lyall could have held against him if he wished to take it?"

Hot words rose to Rufenna's lips and Sim backed off and quickly said, "That is, with all the confusion and coming and going of the last few days. Lyall has been very vulnerable, mistress."

This amendment did little to soothe her outrage. Stunned by Sim's presence here at Lyall, Rufenna burst out, "He sent you here to spy on me? How dare he go to such lengths! Get you hence, Sim, and tell him that I have no need of his man in my home! Do you suggest he is protecting *me*? After . . ." she choked incoherently on her anger.

"Mistress, I only know my orders. I am to stay here and keep watch for him at Lyall and see that no harm befalls you. You must not put your trust in

Master Murdoch, Mistress Lyall. Yon bully is plotting against you. He means to take Lyall!"

"Does he intend to take *me* into protective custody also? Does he mean to challenge my authority here? John is now lord of Lyall but since he is only fourteen I must see to his interests."

"Master Murdoch will see to them; aye, he will see that it is he who commands here. You are a lass and cannot stand against him."

Rufenna tilted her chin defiantly. "Think you not? He means to remove John, you say? When?"

"In the morning," Sim said confidently. "Have you not noticed that the Lyall men are gone? He has sent them this very day to Knolle. You have scarcely ten able-bodied men at your command, mistress."

Rufenna sank down weakly on the edge of the bed. Something about the big Borderer's straight gaze, his unwavering regard, forced her to believe him. He might be Davon Hammond's man but he swore he was here to protect, not harm, her. If that were indeed the case, then he would be telling the truth. Besides, had she not already seen for herself that there were no Lyall men to be seen on the walls or in the courtyard?

"And Captain Kincaid?"

Sim smiled grimly. "If you sent for your captain, my lady, you would find that he is not here. Perhaps your cousin would say the captain was out with some of the Lyall men; I know not what tale he would tell you, but you would not see Captain Kincaid! He was sent to Knolle, under orders coming from *you*, this very morning. He left protesting, but he had no choice in the matter. Mistress, Knolle Castle is too far away to fetch your men from there, nor is there time for me to ride for help. M'lord has men at Hammond Castle or Treelow that would come to your aid if I can fetch them but I'm not sure the

guards would let me leave the castle. They have
been suspicious of me since they arrived, asking many
questions of what I do here. I doubt not that I'd
be prevented from leaving."

"He has guards at all the towers, I warrant, and
at the gate?"

"Aye. Not a mouse could ride out of Lyall without
his men knowing of it."

"I will think about it and send word to you in
the kitchens as to what I wish to do. Listen well,
Sim; you may hear more of what my cousin is plotting."

Rufenna watched Sim and Agnes leave by the
tower stairs and gazed blankly at the wall. She did
not now doubt the warning. The situation was indeed desperate, Rufenna realized, rising from the
edge of the bed and striding about the quiet room.
By a skillful ruse Murdoch had managed to send away
her captain and nearly all of her men. Her own home
had now become a prison for both her and John,
and Murdoch was in command now. She shivered as
she thought of his plans for John and realized afresh
that she must do something quickly to thwart those
plans. Yet if Sim were right and a mouse could not
leave Lyall unobserved, how could she get John
away? Then a memory of a childhood escapade came
to her mind and a faint smile touched her mouth.
She had one weapon that Murdoch had not considered! She had been born here, reared here. She knew
Lyall as he would never know it, every nook and
cranny of it. There *was* a way out of Lyall that he did
not know of—and she meant to use it. Her thoughts
returned to the big Borderer, Sim. She dared not
take him into her confidence. He was Davon's man,
and would take her and John to his chief. That she
would not tolerate. No, she would go to Knolle. From
there she could consider how best to move against
her cousin Murdoch. With Murdoch's men holding

Lyall, there was nothing she could do here to retake her castle from him. She had to have men to do that and her men were at Knolle with Captain Kincaid. But before she could make any plans for driving Murdoch from her home, she had to get John away. Once Murdoch held John safely at Galzean Castle, there would be little she could do to recover Lyall from him without jeopardizing her brother's life. If she could get John away to a place of safety, then she would be free to move against her cousin. Everything, she knew, now depended on them getting away from Lyall tonight.

CHAPTER TWELVE

Rufenna sent Agnes for Walter just before the supper hour. When he entered her room from the tower door, Rufenna went directly to him, kissed him on the cheek, and smiled. "My friend," she said, "I owe you a great apology. You were right about Murdoch and I was wrong. Come, let me tell you about it."

Taking him by the hand, she led him over to the settle before the fire. Then she recounted to him all that she had learned, skimming over who her informant had been, for she did not yet wish Walter to know about Davon's man being still in the castle. How much the old man knew of the feud, she could not tell, but she would not burden him with the story until later. They had enough facing them now.

Walter agreed with alacrity that Lyall was not a safe place for John. But he increased her foreboding a hundredfold when he began to speak of herself.

"Aye, lass, and you—he's an eye on you too. Think, Rufenna! If something were to happen to Master John, who would be your father's heir? Aye! You, my dear. If the ruffian could wed you, he would be master of Lyall in name as well as fact. Nay," he waved away her argument briskly, "don't prate to me of your betrothal! Do you think Murdoch would honor it if he could have Lyall? As for going to Knolle, that would be the best plan for the moment. Any help you'd get from Sir Robert Kerr of Cessford would bear a heavy price. He gives favors to no one, even his nephew's intended wife. You would only be taking John from one tyrant to another, lass, if you petitioned Sir Robert. He would hold him in such same 'protective custody' while he made free with Lyall. So we go to Knolle. And what about your mother?"

"She must go with us, Walter. You talk to her, make her see she cannot stay here. John and I could not leave her to Murdoch's vengeance. She would be hostage for our actions."

"Aye, that she would. I'll try to talk to her but if she sets her face against going, we must get John away without her. He would gain nothing by harming your mother, child, but much in ridding himself of John and forcing you to wed him. Think on that while I see your mother."

Rufenna went down to supper, her nerves quivering with apprehension. She was glad nothing yet had been said to John, for he would surely have betrayed them with triumphant glances at his despised cousin. As it was, he sat sullenly through the meal, scarcely eating, and speaking to no one. Rufenna tried to appear normal but she was painfully conscious of a sulky John on one side and a very smooth, very attentive cousin on the other. For the first time her previously deaf and preoccupied ears picked up the nuances in his addresses to her: the mocking tone beneath the smooth flattery; the constant brushing of their hands as he passed dishes to her, pressing her to sample each one as if he were indeed the gracious host in his own castle; the sidelong glances, brimming with a mixture of contempt and lechery. She had certainly been deaf and blind to have missed his plans for her!

Abruptly pulling her hand from his light grasp as she steadied the heavy platter he was passing to her, she looked up, and from his lowly position down the table, met Sim's eyes. They were dark with anger at the attentions being forced on her by her cousin. All logic told her not to trust any man serving her enemy, but she still felt vaguely reassured by Sim's mere presence. Here, at the least, was one large, solid, able-bodied man who was capable of defending her if necessary. The longer supper progressed, the more wine Murdoch consumed and the more amorous his attentions became. John, not too young to notice and grasp the nature of the attentions his sister was receiving, grew more like a thundercloud with each passing minute. Down the table, Sim's large, strong hands clenched in frustrated anger as he saw the woman he had mentally tagged as belonging to his chief being harassed by that fusionless little sneak. If he knew his master, Sim thought furiously, Master Murdoch Lyall would pay dearly for every insult he offered her. And he, Sim, would make very sure that nothing was left out in the telling either!

Striving to avoid Sim's outraged gaze, John's scornful eyes, and Murdoch's patting, squeezing hands, Rufenna couldn't get the meal over with quickly enough. As soon as it was possible, she excused herself.

"My dear cousin, there are a few things I need to discuss with you, privately . . ." Murdoch began, the look in his eye betraying just what he would do with privacy, and she shook her head.

"Not tonight, Cousin, please. I am very weary and would ask your leave to excuse me. John, it is time for you to retire as well. Make your excuses to Cousin Murdoch."

John bowed curtly and strode from the hall, leaving behind him an awkward silence.

"You must excuse my brother, Cousin. He is still greatly upset. Until tomorrow," she murmured, suffering him to press damp kisses on her hand and then whisking herself out of reach and up the stairs. Once in her bedchamber she locked both the main door and the tower door, so Murdoch could not decide to pay her an unexpected visit. A timid tapping on the tower door sent her spinning around.

"Who is it?" she asked sharply.

"Agnes, mistress."

Rufenna unlocked the door and Agnes hurried in, out of breath.

"Mistress Rufenna, Sim wishes to speak to you. He says it is urgent that a decision be made before tomorrow."

Rufenna had been expecting this. "Indeed, I agree, Agnes. Tell Sim to come up at midnight, when the servants have retired. We can decide on a plan of action then. My cousin should also be abed by then."

Agnes nodded and turned toward the door.

Rufenna thought to herself that Sim would have no way of knowing that she did not intend to be here at midnight. She planned to be safely on her way to Knolle, a smaller family castle, where she would rally her defenses and decide how best to retake her home.

"And, Agnes, before you go back down, find me Old Walter and ask him to come here. He was going to visit my mother and he will tell me how she is feeling."

Soon Walter was facing her in the bedchamber. "Walter, think back, now. You remember when I was a child, you showed me a secret way to get out of Lyall? You took me and Alexander and led us through. Remember?"

Recollection and admiration lit the old man's eyes and a wide grin curved his mouth. "Indeed, I well remember, lass."

"Walter, does anyone else know of that secret route? Murdoch, for example?"

"Nay, lass, only the Lord and his heir. I took you with me when I showed it to Alexander only because you could ever twist me to your will and did then. Nay, no one knows but your mother, yourself, and me now. It will serve," he muttered to himself. "It should do well."

"It has not been blocked off or closed, Walter? You're sure of that?"

"Aye, I'm sure. Your father would never have done that. You remember why it was built? The first tower built here by the Lyalls was attacked and burned. They had no way to escape and were roasted alive. The descendants of those Lyalls rebuilt the tower and enclosed it, much as it is today. That Lord built in a secret escape route to prevent such a thing ever again befalling the family. Only the master of Lyall would know of it, so that the news could not be broadcast to their enemies. That puppy couldn't know; you can be sure of that."

Rufenna was satisfied by his assurance. "And Mother? Did she agree to come with us?"

Sadly Walter shook his head. "Nay, she did not. She seems not to care o'ermuch what happens to her. Lass, dinna fash yourself about it. You must get yourself and Master John clear. Your cousin will not harm your mother. I will leave guards by her door, just in case. I warrant he will be too occupied in finding you, lass, to give her much thought."

"I have not yet told John, Walter. I sent him to bed, since he seemed determined to stir my cousin to anger tonight. He was very ill-behaved at the table and would have been worse if he had known anything."

"We will not tell the lad until time to go. Rest a bit, child. I go now to take care of your cousin."

Rufenna stared at him. "What do you mean, Walter?"

He chuckled grimly. "He prides himself on his

head for wine but he has met his match in Walter Lyall. I will have him so befuddled with drink in another hour that he will not stir until morning."

"Walter! We can't risk your getting drunk too! Listen to me—I mean it. I count on you to go with us, to guide us to Knolle."

"I will be ready, lass. Fret not about it. No mawworm such as he can match Walter's head for spirits. Even your father, a hard-drinking man that he was, could not pass me. Prepare what you wish to take with us but we must travel light."

"Walter, how do we get horses? We cannot take them from here!"

He admitted that, but assured her it would be taken care of. She watched him leave with a slight smile, hoping he wasn't mistaken about his drinking ability. He turned at the door. "We leave at eleven, lass. Be ready. I will fetch Master John and meet you here."

"Yes, Walter, I'll be ready."

Rufenna spent some time prowling the room. Thinking about the rough journey ahead of them, she realized what a disadvantage her hampering skirts would be. An idea came to her suddenly and she grinned. Her ragged breeches and shirt had been left behind with the Gypsies, but Alexander's room was just below hers! Rufenna slid open the tower door and started down, holding her breath for fear she would meet one of the guards going up to the battlements. She reached the floor below, where the household garrison was quartered, and where her brother had taken over the corner apartment for his own. She tried the door and smiled happily to herself when the latch opened. Rufenna slipped into the dark room and shut the door silently behind her. A candle in a holder should be on the table by the door and her groping hands found it. Easing the door open again, listening intently, she slipped out to the stairs and lit the candle from the tall torch held securely in its iron bracket. Guarding the flickering flame with her hand, she reentered her brother's room. His clothing would be too big for her but surely there had to be something she could use! She opened the chest and began folding back the clothing. Soon she had a neat pile of clothes on the floor and closed the chest. She clutched the garments closely to her and slipped back out the door, being careful to blow out the candle and return it to the table.

In her room she tried on her selection. The heavy worsted shirt was just a bit too long; the sleeves covered her hands. The leather breeches would nearly wrap twice around her dainty waist and were too long. Moving quickly now, Rufenna got out Agnes's sewing basket, thanking God that her mother's clothes had needed to be altered for her when she first arrived. She said a little prayer of thanksgiving that the good nuns insisted that she learn to sew a fine seam. These were no fine seams, she admitted ruefully, but they would shorten the shirt and breeches and make the waist a bit snugger.

By eleven she was clothed in the shirt, breeches, and a leather belt. The belt reminded her painfully of another time, another ride through the darkness, another man! She dismissed these thoughts impatiently and pulled on two pairs of heavy woolen socks and slid her feet into Alexander's boots. They were still a bit loose and somewhat the worse for wear but with socks stuffed in the toes they would have to do. She tucked her hair under a dark leather cap and picked up the leather jacket. As the soft, expected tap came on the tower door, she threw the fur-lined cloak around her as well. It would be a cold ride tonight and she would need it.

Walter was struck dumb when he saw her and

gaped widely. John, wrapped in his own dark cloak, gave her a cheeky grin, greatly pleased with the entire escapade. He relished the thought of thumbing his nose at Cousin Murdoch and had entered enthusiastically into Walter's plans.

"Come, lass, let us be going," whispered the old man, his pungent, wine-laden breath enveloping her. "Murdoch is asleep in his cups and the men are settling down for the night. We must be very quiet."

She nodded and joined him on the stairs. John started to say something and was motioned into silence. Listening hard, they cautiously descended the tower stairs, holding their breath as they passed the main floor housing the Great Hall, where some of Murdoch's men were bedded down for the night.

Rufenna wondered suddenly how many of Murdoch's men were on guard duty on the walls but decided that Walter would know. He would have checked before taking them this way. They reached the lower level of the old keep, slipped past the doorway to the kitchens, and threaded their way through the piles of stores in the storerooms. Walter moved unerringly through the darkness, going directly to the back wall. The rear curtain wall of the castle was twice as thick as the side walls. Walter moved into the corner of the room and felt over the face of the stone wall. He put his weight against it and a section of the wall moved. It swung out on a swiveled rod. Walter grasped the edge and opened the door wider and motioned the girl and boy through. Then he muttered something and told them to wait where they were; he returned to the storeroom and Rufenna saw with relief that he was lighting a tallow candle from the torch that blazed there. He returned quickly and followed them into the narrow tunnel that ran between the outer and inner wall. Rufenna felt fairly certain that all of the castle walls were not hollow, just this one. Walter edged past her in the narrow tunnel, pulling the boy behind him so that Rufenna was bringing up the rear.

The flickering candlelight served as a guide and not much more but Rufenna saw enough to terrify her. Ancient spiderwebs stuck to her face and hair and she tried to wipe them away, only to walk into more. Water dripped constantly down the walls and bats swooped and dived above her head as her passage disturbed them. She stumbled on the rough, uneven floor of the passageway and shivered when she grabbed the wet wall for support. The smell was of cold, musty, unused air, much like what she would expect of a tomb. She determinedly kept her eyes on the candle ahead of her and tried not to think—only move.

She could hear nothing through the walls, only their own breathing and the scuffling of their feet on the uneven floor. From the direction they were heading, she imagined they were moving inside the wall behind the kitchens, which occupied the entire eastern side of this floor. The storerooms filled the rest of the floor.

The tunnel stopped abruptly and Walter began pressing on several stones near the floor. Locating the right one, he pressed hard and a narrow door, not over four feet high, quietly opened. A rush of cold, fresh air stirred around them and Rufenna thankfully followed John out into the chilly night air. Walter closed the door and she turned and looked hard at the massive curtain wall behind her. There was no sign, no hint of a door showing in the wall. How cleverly it had been done. She looked westward down the wall and realized that they were concealed from the view of anyone guarding the outside of the postern gate by the jutting stone of the square tower that interrupted the smooth curtain wall. It would be impossible for anyone on the walls to see them unless they leaned precariously over the buttresses and looked directly downward. They would only be in danger of being seen when they left the shelter of the wall.

Here, along the back wall of the castle, the ridge dropped off sharply, its dangerous edge not fifteen feet from where she stood. It would make it impossible, she realized, for any siege weapons or large numbers of men to mass behind the castle wall, for the ridge was narrow here, dropping more than a hundred feet straight down before it gentled out into a more gradual slope. It would be a difficult place to attack, so the back wall did not need as heavy a guard. That was why the concealed door had been placed there. Walter began moving down the wall to the northeast tower and they followed him, being as quiet as possible. They stopped in the shadow of the massive tower, and Rufenna wondered what they should do now. They were outside the castle but still had to deal with the problem of getting away unseen. Walter turned and drew her near.

"We're going down the ridge at the end, just there. See those bushes? I'll slip down first. Wait a few minutes and then send young John. Then wait a bit before you come. Tell him to move quickly but quietly, lass, for there is a guard on the tower."

She nodded and held John's arm, pulling him back against her and repeating Walter's instructions. John nodded and they both watched the old man scamper across the bare ground to the edge of the ridge. His agility and surefootedness belied his age and also the quantity of spirits he would have had to consume to put Murdoch into a stupor. Rufenna wasn't aware that she was holding her breath until she felt the blood drumming in her ears, and she let it out with a pent-up hiss that made John jump. No shout came from above, no cry of discovery. The ridge dropped off into a series of gullies, broken with thick clumps of gorse bushes. Rufenna, remembering her recent and

painful experience with the prickly gorse, was glad
she was wearing heavy leather breeches and boots.
They would give her more protection than her skirts
had. Nothing moved in the moonlight so she signaled for John to run to the edge. He flitted swiftly
to the edge of the ridge and, moving with the lithe-
ness of youth, vanished from sight. While Rufenna
waited, she tried to avoid thinking of her mother
there at Lyall at Murdoch's mercy. She could only
hope that Walter was right. Lady Lyall was no threat
to her cousin and harming her would only make
matters worse for *him*. If he chose to move into
Lyall, putting his young cousin John under his personal protection, the neighboring families would see
little wrong with that. But if Murdoch harmed Lady
Lyall, who was well liked for her gentle manners,
that would be another matter entirely. Murdoch must
be painfully conscious that Lady Lyall was closely
connected with many of the powerful Border clans,
particularly the Scotts. His own castle, Galzean, lay
well within Scott territory and he would not be
anxious to start a feud with them.

Taking a deep breath, dreading with every moment the cry from above that would mean capture,
she went over the rough, broken ground as quickly
and noiselessly as possible. Her back felt stiff with
strain as she reached the edge and scrambled down
behind the gorse bush. Heart hammering, she waited
until she had caught her breath, and then looked
down.

Walter was taking John down the gully as fast as
the old man could move, not daring to wait for Rufenna. She knew, as did her old kinsman, that it was
imperative that John get away; whether or not she
was caught was not of such urgency. It was John who
stood between Murdoch and the right to Lyall. When
they reached the bottom of the gully and ran for a
copse of trees, Rufenna began the descent. The gully

was rough and treacherous underfoot, with an unwary move causing little stones to roll and clatter to the bottom. If she were heard, she thought, she would run the other way, away from the trees that now concealed Walter and John, leading any pursuit away from them. But she reached the bottom with grazed hands and no shouts of pursuit behind her.

"Good girl," Walter murmured, turning immediately to lead the way through the trees. On they went, fighting through the thick underbrush that entangled their feet. This seemed to be taking a dangerous amount of time, Rufenna thought. It was imperative that they put as much distance between themselves and the castle as was possible before dawn, when the servants would stir and discover them missing. She gave a fleeting thought to Davon's man, Sim, and how angry he would be at being duped in this manner. He would come to her room at midnight as they had agreed and she would be gone! That should put Sim and the Hammonds in their place and make it clear that she did not want their help.

When they reached the edge of the trees, Walter allowed them to rest for a moment. They were standing on a low hill, overlooking the sheltered valley that surrounded Lyall. Beneath them in the valley was one of the Lyall farms, and it was to this farm that Walter was heading. He took them down the slope quickly and Rufenna wondered at the old man's stamina. She was panting openly now and even John was flagging somewhat; but Walter reminded her of a sturdy oak, still standing in the forest as younger trees fell during a storm. A lifetime of campaigning and roughing it on the Borders had inured him to discomfort; his easy, deceptive lope across the ground covered distance at a moderate rate, but he could sustain it for hours. Rufenna and John tried to match their pace to his, and began to get their second wind.

When they reached the edge of the pasture, he motioned them to stay back out of sight. He gave a high-pitched whistle that echoed shrilly across the pasture. Rufenna waited, curious, and saw something move by the stable. It couldn't be! But yes, the tenant, Samuel, had appeared leading four horses. How, she wondered in amazement, had Walter managed that? He had not been allowed to leave the castle! He exchanged a quick word with Samuel and she saw something bright that glittered in the moonlight pass into Samuel's hand. Then Walter was leading three of the horses over to where she and John were waiting.

"How did you arrange that?" she breathed as he helped her to mount.

"Samuel's son is a groom at Lyall," he answered her.

Walter led them northwest at a fast trot and then they kicked their ponies into a canter. Knolle lay northeast from Lyall, set in a curve of the Tweed River. Knolle was smaller than Lyall, but had begun life originally as a peel tower, one of those stout, square stone towers that reared themselves along the hills of the Border. Later Rufenna's grandfather had added a barnekiln, a stout wall, which enclosed the kitchens, stables, sleeping quarters for the garrison and the keep itself. The wooden stables, kitchens, and sleeping quarters could quickly be put to the torch, so they would not provide cover for attacking raiders, as the defenders withdrew into the nearly impregnable keep. At Lyall, built the same way originally, the outer buildings were now of stone, making living more comfortable but making defending more difficult. Rufenna, having spent her childhood within sheltering walls, had never looked at either Lyall or Knolle from a military angle. Now, faced with defending Knolle from Murdoch's men and having to retake Lyall, she was evaluating them in a different way. Her mind, as they made as fast a pace as was

possible through the long series of ridges divided by
valleys, was already turning over possible ways to
retake Lyall from Murdoch.

As they walked the horses slowly down a steep
slope, Rufenna looked ahead, seeing with relief the
open plain ahead of them. The most rugged part of
their journey was now behind them. Alternately trot-
ting and walking the horses, they would use the rest
of the night to cross the moor before reaching Knolle.
She was consoled by the thought that even if the
drunken Murdoch discovered their flight almost immediately and found himself capable of sitting a
horse, he could not make much better time than they
had. The ponies, bred as they were both for endur-
ance and speed, did have a limit and Walter was
pushing theirs as much as he dared. Also, Murdoch
could not know precisely where they were heading
unless he turned clairvoyant and managed to trace
them to Samuel's farm. If the peasant watched which
direction they took and could be bribed or tortured
. . . Without that, Murdoch could guess Knolle but
they could just as easily have gone west, to Sinclair
Castle, to the clan chieftain. Lord Sinclair would give
both shelter and protection, even against Murdoch,
and Murdoch knew that.

Suddenly Walter reined in and dismounted, stretching stiffly. Rufenna slid from her horse and gasped
at the weakness in her legs. She had not ridden so
much in her entire life as she had in these last few
weeks.

"We rest here a little, lass. The lad is weary."

Rufenna looked at John, his eyelids drooping heavily, and nodded. Walter, ever resourceful as most experienced Border men were, opened a saddlebag and
handed out great chunks of bread and cheese. Rufenna
ate hers hungrily, then bullied her brother into making some attempt to eat his. John, exhausted with
excitement and genuine fatigue, was sulky. He was

tired and in no mood to eat, but under Walter's stern gaze he made the attempt.

"Where are we, Walter?" Rufenna asked, looking around in the moonlight. A slight mist was hugging the ground, making the dark hills rise like mysterious peaks through it.

"Near Bedrule. 'Tis over there, to your right. Torrey Castle lies a few miles beyond it, perhaps five, seven miles from here," he said, glancing at her expressionlessly.

Rufenna's heart gave a great leap as she realized she was so close to Davon Hammond's stronghold. If he only knew she were out here! She swallowed nervously.

"What is Torrey?" John grumbled sleepily.

"The Hammonds' castle," Walter said quietly. "Johnnie, are you thirsty? There is a little burn over there. Come, we should water these ponies while we rest."

Rufenna led her horse over to the little stream and splashed some of the cold water on her face. That, and the thought of resting so closely to Davon Hammond's lands, roused her sufficiently to remount and ride on. Trying not to go to sleep in the saddle sometime later, she thought about Lyall and how to retake it. It was a pity, her drowsy mind whispered, that Davon Hammond was an enemy. If he had been an ally, a friend, she could have asked him for aid. If anyone could drive Murdoch from her home, it would be Davon Hammond!

Back at Lyall Castle, all was quiet. Agnes made not a sound and cautioned Sim as she led him up the winding tower stairs to Rufenna's room. It was just on midnight. Sim had lain wakeful on his pallet on the floor of the Great Hall until it was time for his rendezvous with Mistress Rufenna. Being a traveler, he slept inside the keep with the servants in-

stead of in the stone quarters in the courtyard with
the garrison. He was glad of it since it made it easier
for him to get to Rufenna with the assistance of her
maid. Now he followed Agnes up the stairs, moving
quietly on the stone steps. She stopped outside the
door and tapped. While they waited, she whispered
to him: "I did as you bid and checked on Master
Murdoch. He is in his own room, snoring heavily.
Thomas, the steward, said he drank much wine with
Master Walter. Two of his men had to carry him
to his room."

She knocked again and waited. Still no answer.
Casting a troubled glance at Sim, she tried the door,
easing it open quietly. The room lay in darkness
and silence. Agnes glided surefootedly across to the
table and fetched the candle, lighting it from the
torch on the stairs. She returned to the room and
went to the large bed. Sim waited inside the door
as she tugged back the hangings.

"She's not here," Agnes gasped, turning to stare at
him in surprise.

Sim's mouth tightened. "Search the room, quickly."

When it was obvious that Rufenna was not in
either the room or the small antechamber that served
as a dressing room, Sim gave swift orders. He had
an inkling that something was afoot, something he
would not like. "Go to her mother's room and make
quite sure she is not there. Then search the kitchens
and the downstairs hall. I will go to Master John's
room and Master Walter's. Meet me back here. Quickly, lass; time is precious now."

Sim slipped down the dark hallway to John's room.
It was empty. When he reached Walter's, on the
floor below next door to Alexander's room, he knew
before he opened the door what he would find. Darkness, silence, emptiness. They were gone! Cursing
himself for his stupidity, Sim bounded back up the

tower stairs to Rufenna's room to find Agnes waiting for him.

"Well?" he barked, his blue eyes dark with anger.

"S-she's not there, Sim! I saw her ladyship myself," Agnes babbled as she grasped his arm. "Sim, something is badly wrong! Her ladyship's room is guarded by two of the footmen, Peter and Giles. They would only let me in when I swore I was alone and had to see Lady Lyall. I can't understand it."

"I can," he said grimly. "Her ladyship knows all about it and they've provided her with a guard. Devil take the lass! To dupe me so! God's foot, how did she get out of the castle? Or are they out yet? Come, Agnes, do just as I bid you. We have to be sure they are truly gone."

He took her up the rest of the stairs at a run, pausing before the door at the top that opened onto the battlements. "Don't forget now. We're lovers, coming up to be alone. Understand?"

Agnes looked up at the good-looking dark-haired young Borderer and giggled. He put his arm firmly around her and swept her through the door onto the wide stone walk at the top of the wall. The guard was pacing the wall, going toward the opposite tower, and Sim moved swiftly to the outer wall, scanning the terrain with a keen eye. Nothing moved on the ridge or down the slopes. Before the guard reached the end of his walk at the next tower, Sim moved Agnes to the inside wall, where he could see down into the courtyard. They leaned against the stone battlement and Sim pulled her tightly against him. He lowered his head and kissed her soundly, squeezing her hard against him. For a moment his mind, until now intent on his purpose, wavered, and was distracted by the comely armful pressed closely to him, and his hand moved caressingly down her back.

"Here! You, there! What are you doing up here?"

the guard demanded loudly, breaking into a run.

Sim's grip tightened warningly on Agnes and then he straightened up and stepped reluctantly away from her.

Before Sim could speak, Agnes turned to the guard, who was glowering at them suspiciously. "Oh, you scared me," she said accusingly.

The guard looked her over thoroughly, eyes lingering on the soft curves, the sweet pout of the recently kissed lips. He dragged his eyes away from her and glanced at the big, silent Borderer who stood with an arm still around her.

"What ye doing here?"

Agnes tossed her head and met the guard's gaze defiantly. "Thomas, the steward, gave us leave to come up for some air. Do you wish me to fetch my mistress up to give me permission also?"

Sim swallowed hard at this open display of defiance, but saw that Agnes had judged her man correctly.

"Weel, now, no call to get nasty, lass. I got me duty to see to. Orders, ye understand. No one to come up here."

"My mistress gave orders that her own servants cannot come up for some air?" Agnes challenged crisply.

The man hesitated awkwardly. "I got orders," he said again. "But it will be all right if you two are quiet. No roaming about the walls, now. Just get some air."

Agnes sniffed disdainfully and turned her back on the guard. He shuffled awkwardly a moment and then turned around and marched off. Sim let out a great sigh of relief. He met Agnes's mischievous gaze and thought she was very like her mistress, cocky and sure of herself. His arm tightened around her, drawing her close. "We got our orders, lass. No moving around, just get some air," he murmured, kissing her.

Agnes went willingly into his embrace, having been attracted to Sim since the day of his arrival.

After a long few minutes Sim raised his head, breathing hard and forcibly reminding himself why they were there. Agnes's eager response had roused his blood and he wanted nothing more than to sweep her up and carry her to the first quiet corner they could find. However, Davon's dark, forceful face hovered in his mind and he was reluctantly shaken from his amorous state. The chief would skin him alive for dallying here instead of finding Mistress Rufennal

Sim sighed, released Agnes, and turned to look down into the courtyard. His eyes were well accustomed now to the darkness and he searched every corner, every shadow below. No hint of movement, no sound broke the silence, only the cold wind stirring the treetops down the slope. Sim did not know how she had done it, but he was ready to bet his last horse the lass had found a way out of the castle and escaped with her brother. He was also certain that only Lady Lyall could give him the answer and that she would never tell him.

Sim did some hard, quick thinking as he turned slightly to watch the movements of the guard. If the lass were free, where would she go? Knolle? He felt sure that was her destination. Knolle offered men, shelter for young John and herself, and time to plan their next move. Unless something unforeseen occurred, they would reach Knolle by dawn, he reckoned, mentally covering the distance. The passage through the series of hills before they reached the spreading plain would take most of the night, for the way was rough and difficult. Once on the plain they could cover ground more swiftly, if Walter had seen to it that their horses were carefully nursed. From what he had seen of Old Walter, Sim thought sourly, he would bet on that too. What should he do now? Try to get out of the castle and go to the chief? Or stay at Lyall, waiting to see what Master Murdoch would do? There was little protection that he could give Lady Lyall that the two footmen could not. He had seen Peter and Giles, both big, strapping boys. The servants were devoted to their mistress, he knew, and would protect her against Master Murdoch. He'd make sure they got the warning of what was afoot, he thought, and then he'd best ride for Torrey. Lord Hammond would want to know what had happened.

Having made up his mind, Sim began to think around the problem. Agnes was shivering against him, feeling the chill night air through her dress and lacking the warmth of his woolen shirt. In silence he led her to the door and down to Rufenna's room.

"I'll light the fire for ye, lass, and then settle down and be quiet. I have much thinking to do."

Agnes curled up on the bed, a tempting morsel, and pushed the hangings out of the way.

"But the mistress . . . ?" she began.

"Gone. I don't know how she did it but she's gone. Shhh, lass, let me think."

Sim made sure both doors were securely bolted, and built up the fire. When it was crackling merrily, sending out a welcome warmth and light into the room, he paced the stone floor restlessly, trying to decide on the best course of action.

He did not know the way they had used to escape. That one existed, he would take an oath! But Lady Lyall certainly would not give him the secret. He was a total stranger to her and mayhap she knew he was one of Lord Hammond's men. He must find another way. He would be questioned if he attempted to leave in the middle of the night. The main gate was closed and the portcullis down, so that was out of the question. He had noticed the guard at the postern gate, too, so that meant the only way out of Lyall

was over the wall. Dimly he recalled seeing a coil of
heavy rope in the storeroom below, when he had
helped Thomas, the steward, bring up a butt of ale.
If he could go over the wall on the northeast side
by that corner tower, he would come down at the
back of the castle. He had watched the guards closely.
The front and side walls were much more heavily
guarded than the back wall. There were a pair of
men on each section of the front wall and the side
walls, but only two men, one on each side of the
center tower, on the back. He would have only one
guard to silence. The new guards had taken position
at midnight and, by watching carefully the night before, Sim had discovered that Murdoch's captain was
changing the guards every four hours because of the
icy wind that swept the battlements at night. So in
less than three hours new guards would be coming
on duty. It would still be dark enough, give him time
enough to make good his escape before dawn, if he
waited for the guards to change. Sim made up his
mind he would do it that way.

He turned and saw Agnes curled up on the bed,
wide eyes watching his restless movements. Her fair
hair gleamed in the firelight and she looked both
soft and inviting. He went over and sat down on the
bed, one large hand going out to touch her blond
hair.

"Have you decided, Sim? What will you do?" Admiration shone in her blue eyes as she smiled tenderly at him.

He smiled slightly. "When the guards change at
four, I'll go over the wall. There's a rope in the
storeroom. You'll have to fetch it for me and lead
me up to the northeast tower. We'll go up as we did
just now, like two servants getting up early, ye ken?
Seeking a little privacy before everyone else awakens.
The new guards won't have seen us out there tonight
and will suspect nothing, I warrant. 'Twill make it

easier to surprise the guard if I've lulled his suspicions already."

Agnes gazed at him admiringly and his smile deepened.

"Now, lass, we have three hours to wait until it is time. Shall we stay here in the warm?" he asked huskily. As he spoke, he gently pulled back the neck of her dress and pressed a kiss on her bared shoulder. Her arms went up and around him.

"Aye, Sim, we'll stay in the warm," she consented, going into his arms.

At four o'clock Rufenna, John, and Walter were riding the last weary miles to Knolle. Rufenna, chilled to the bone and so tired she could scarcely stay in the saddle, would have ground her teeth in rage had she known her loyal little maid had spent the long, cold night warmly wrapped in the arms of the enemy, in *her* bed!

At four o'clock Lady Lyall gave a little cry and sat up in bed. The movement brought her maid, Mary, sleepily but warily to the side of the bed. "Do you think they're there yet, Mary? Oh, St. Christopher, I pray you to keep them safe!" she murmured, allowing the maid to press her back down and cover her up.

At the same time, the cold, numbed guards clattered gratefully down the tower stairs, leaving the icy walls to their replacements. Sim and Agnes, waiting in the kitchen below, listened to their voices as the men crossed the courtyard and vanished into the sleeping quarters of the garrison. They waited, Sim holding a long coil of rope under his heavy cloak, until silence once again descended on the castle.

The battlements were cold and dark when they eased open the door. Sim peered out, locating the guard. He was coming back this way, having just made

a full circuit of his section of the wall. Sim thrust
Agnes back and closed the door except for a thin
crack. He could watch the guard from here. His lips
brushed her cheek as he whispered, "See that they
take good care of my horse until I can come back
and get him."

Agnes agreed eagerly. That meant she would see
him again. She felt that her life would be bleak if
Sim were gone forever. "Go now, lass, and get to your
couch. I can handle this alone." Sim had decided,
seeing the lone guard on the battlements, that it
might be safer later for Agnes if this guard did not
see her. "You know naught of this tomorrow, remember. We parted after our walk on the wall at midnight and I went below. Quietly, now, but hurry."

She kissed him swiftly but passionately and hurried down the stairs. Sim eased his dagger from his
belt and waited. The guard came toward him, stopping almost at the door, and then turned. As he completed his turn, Sim thrust open the door and struck,
slamming the hilt of the heavy dagger against the
man's head. Knocked out cleanly, without a sound,
the man crumpled onto the stone walk. Sim moved
to the edge of the tower and secured the rope around
the sturdy stone buttress. He threw the coil over the
side and was over and moving down it before Agnes
reached the kitchens. Sim went down, his hands feeling for the heavy knots he had made in the rope,
guiding himself with his feet against the wall.

Dropping onto the ground, he hugged the wall and
moved to the corner. Now that the tower was unguarded, he didn't hesitate as he dashed to the edge
of the ridge and started down the gully. It could be
hours before the man recovered consciousness or was
found and he didn't intend to waste them. Treading
unknowingly the same paths that Rufenna, John, and
Walter had traversed earlier in the night, Sim made

for the farm he had noticed from the castle walls. He would buy or steal a horse there, for he had to carry his news to Torrey and Davon Hammond as quickly as possible.

CHAPTER THIRTEEN

After Rufenna was revived with hot food, drink, and dry, warm clothing, she welcomed Captain Kincaid into the room. The tall captain of Lyall betrayed his anger and humiliation with steely blue eyes and a tight face.

"Mistress, forgive me, for I have ill-served you and Master John. I was suspicious of the orders your cousin gave, but allowed him to persuade me they came from you."

She looked at the angry soldier curiously. "What did he tell you, Captain? He said naught to me of your going."

His face darkened. "He said he had knowledge of a raid on Knolle and you wished it reinforced at all speed. We rode hard and have been sitting here await-ing the sight of raiders for two full days! It was a ruse, mistress, to get us away from Lyall. Master Wal-ter has told me all and if you wish to discharge me from your service, it is naught more than I deserve!"

"No, Captain, I would not do that. I have need of your skill and courage, I promise you. You have been in my family's service for many years, even be-fore I was born. My cousin duped us all, so do not be disgusted with yourself; I was as finely tricked. But we got Master John away and must hold him safe from my cousin."

"Aye," he growled, still burning with anger at how he had been used. "And what of Lyall?"

"We take it back," she said calmly. "Mother would not come with us and remains at Lyall. We must take the castle from my cousin. First, Captain, there is the matter of Knolle. I warrant my cousin will send men here in search of us when he discovers that we are gone. Can we defend Knolle?"

From his expression it was obvious the captain hoped Murdoch Lyall would try to take Knolle. "Aye, we can hold it. Taking Lyall is another matter, however. I have defended it too many years not to know its strength, mistress."

"How would you take it, Captain?"

He frowned thoughtfully. "We have no cannon, mistress, and Lyall is impregnable to a raid. We could starve them out but that would take much time, ye understand."

"And if we could get men inside without their knowledge? Men who could take the walls and open the portcullis?"

He laughed mirthlessly. "We would hold the castle in less than an hour, lass, but it's not possible. There is no way in except over the wall!"

Rufenna smiled warmly at him. "But there is, Captain Kincaid! How do you think we got out?"

Sim stared blankly at Luke Daniels, Captain of Torrey Castle. "He's not here? But, man, where is he? 'Tis urgent."

Captain Daniels shrugged. "He was sent for by the Queen Mother, Mary of Guise, several days ago, Sim. He's in Edinburgh."

"When does he return?"

"He did not say. Sim, where have you been? I've

orders about you. M'lord said any message from you
was to be given top priority." The captain was eyeing Sim with curiosity. Luke had heard of the ambush of the Lyalls, of the red-haired lass, and her
capture by the English. "Thank God you found the
lass. He had all the available men out searching the
Borders for her until he had your message she was
safely home. He cursed fearfully when the summons
came from the Queen and even considered not going!
Think of that! Here, wet your thirst and tell me
about it."

Sim sank down on the bench in the guardroom and
thankfully took the tankard of ale offered to him.
He and Luke were cousins, related to the Hammonds
and devoted to their chief. "Luke, I wish he had not
gone. Things are amiss and I know not what to do."

"He had to go! What's the matter? Mayhap we can
deal with it?"

As he drank the ale, Sim poured out the tale of
Rufenna's arrival back at Lyall with the Gypsies,
about her father's death and Murdoch's arrival and,
taking a second tankard of ale, related the events of
the last few days. "The bloody whoreson will be hot
after her by dawn, I warrant, and I know not how
matters stand at Knolle. If the bastard gets his hands
on her and Master John, the chief will be fit to murder me," he ended, looking dismally at his cousin.

Luke leaned back and thought about it. "You say
Murdoch Lyall will pursue them? This morning?"

"Aye, he will. He must get his hands on the boy,
y'see. He sent the Lyall men to Knolle, but I'm not
sure how many there are or if they could hold against
him. He has over a hundred men, Luke. Have you
seen Knolle? Is it strong?"

Luke nodded. "I've seen it and it's strong enough.
Thirty men could hold it, if need be, and you say
they've more than that. Aye, lad, let me think. I've
got it," he said, sitting up, his dark eyes gleaming.

"They must cross Hammond land, must they not, to reach Knolle? We will not allow them free passage," he said simply. "M'lord does not like armed soldiers crossing his lands," he added with a pious look that was quite wasted on his cousin. "If he must go back and circle around to avoid crossing Hammond land, well, it will give us plenty of time to warn the garrison at Knolle. He may even think better of it, Sim, and return to Lyall. What do you think the lass will do?"

"If I know her, and I'm beginning to do that, she'll not sit still while he lords it at Lyall Castle. Luke, this is the very thing. The fact that he is prevented from crossing Hammond land in pursuit of her will tell him that m'lord is taking an interest in this affair and I cannot see Master Murdoch Lyall willingly crossing m'lord! He'll retreat to Lyall and concentrate on holding it, awaiting another chance to get the boy. They'll be safe at Knolle, if they'll but stay there!" he added doubtfully. "I'd best get to m'lord and tell him of this." Sim rubbed a weary hand over his brow and stood up. "An hour's rest, Luke, then I'm to Edinburgh. You'd best post guards to warn you of his coming. I know not when the alarm was given but he must know by now."

Luke agreed and went off whistling to send out scouts. He ordered a troop readied to ride, awaiting his command, and went up on the massive walls of Torrey. It would be good sport thwarting a yellow bastard such as Murdoch Lyall, who made war on women and young boys, he thought, looking forward to it.

Sim had changed, eaten, and ridden for Edinburgh, bemoaning his favorite horse still stabled at Lyall, when the scout rode in announcing that a large troop of men were coming from the southwest. Luke Daniels smiled, pulled on his steel helmet, and signaled his men to mount. They cantered easily out of Torrey and cut across the valley to where they would intercept the hard-riding troop. Luke stationed his men in a fringe of trees and took twenty men forward with him. They formed a single line across the path through the valley and waited.

Murdoch Lyall, leading his troop, had not anticipated any such problem. He reined in and frowned at the stationary line of soldiers. When he recognized the black and silver badge they wore, proclaiming them to be part of the Hammond entourage, he cursed long and hard. He *was* on Hammond land. He walked his horse forward, knowing his men to be following slowly behind him.

"State your business!" Luke ordered before Murdoch could speak.

"We seek passage across your land," Murdoch snapped.

"For what purpose?"

Murdoch ground his teeth and tried to be civil. "Personal business."

Luke shook his head. "I have orders not to allow armed troops to cross m'lord's land, sir, so you must return the way ye came."

"What?" bellowed Murdoch, his hand flying to his sword.

Luke saw the suggestive move and raised his right hand in a brief signal. Silently a line of horsemen rode out of the trees and halted at a distance. Another line of men followed, then another. Murdoch, gaping at the rows of armed soldiers, could not know how many were hidden behind them in the trees.

"Return the way ye came, sir," said Luke coolly. "You'll not cross Hammond land today."

"God damn your eyes, I have urgent business . . ."

"Not so urgent, sir, that you cannot find a different route. We mislike strangers on our land and my men are getting restless."

Murdoch met that steely gaze, looked once more

at the silent horsemen, and admitted defeat. "Your master will hear from me, Captain!"

"I'm sure of it," Luke answered, trying to smother a grin. " 'Tis uneasy country, sir, in these hills. My men will see you to our boundary."

Cursing furiously, Murdoch realized there would be no way he could turn back and then sneak around this small army of men. They would be escorted, politely but firmly, to the edges of Hammond land and watched until they were out of sight. Scouts would be deployed so the captain would know if they again tried to cross! Murdoch knew the rules by heart. He had used them often enough himself. There was more here than met the eye, he realized, turning about and leading his men down the valley. Why did the Hammond captain block his pursuit? They did not ordinarily challenge men crossing their land, although they were well within their rights to do so. Once assured it was a peaceful party, with no designs on the property in sight, they were allowed to pass. Why had he been stopped? Murdoch, escorted well outside the Hammond territory, took his men back to Lyall, determined to discover what was behind this strange behavior on the part of the Hammonds. He knew of the ill feeling between Alexander and Davon Hammond; knew of Alexander's death at Davon's hands. If the Hammonds were genuinely at feud with the Lyalls, why were the Hammond men aiding the lass? Why would they interfere in this struggle for power between himself and the girl? Yet it was apparent to him that they *had* interfered! For all he knew, the girl could have been given shelter at Torrey . . . or Lord Hammond had allowed her to pass on to Knolle, had perhaps warned the garrison at Knolle of his coming . . . or even, he thought, scowling, even reinforced it with some of the Hammond men! *Why?* Riding furiously toward Lyall, Murdoch swore to get to the bottom of this. Damn Davon Hammond! Another one he had a score to settle with!

At Knolle Castle a rested, well-fed, and determined young lady faced Captain Kincaid. "How many men have we here, Captain?"

Kincaid, accustomed to taking orders from Sir Ewen or Alexander Lyall, tried to mask his confusion and chagrin at such a discussion with young Rufenna. However, he still stung with humiliation at the way he had come so near to betraying her when he followed Murdoch's orders and allowed himself and his men to be sent away from Lyall. It was his fault she was in the position of having to take back her own castle. He swallowed his protests and answered respectfully, "Nearly a hundred, mistress. Master Alexander had sent fifty of the men here before he rode to St. Whitby's to fetch you, and I brought forty with me. The garrison here could spare another ten, I warrant, so we have nearly the number of men your cousin has at Lyall."

"And John?" She turned to her old kinsman, who stood by, proud of the way she was taking the responsibility. "Walter, what should we do with John? Leave him here under guard?"

Walter scratched his graying hair thoughtfully. " 'Twould be safe enough, unless . . ." He did not finish the sentence but Rufenna knew what he intended to say and said it for him.

"Unless we are defeated by my cousin and then John will be vulnerable to him here. Let me think, Walter, for there has to be another way to safeguard John, no matter the outcome."

"You could send the lad to Lord Sinclair," Captain Kincaid suggested, referring to the clan chieftain.

She shook her head. "Not yet; m'lord is old, Captain, and I mislike embroiling him in this fight against my cousin. Who could hold John safe for us?"

A slow smile spread across Walter's face. "The Queen! Rufenna, send him to Edinburgh to the Queen Mother. Even your cousin would not dare harm the lad if he was under the care of the Queen! Your father was a favorite of hers, you know. He was a strong supporter of the King and detested the thought of a betrothal between little Queen Mary and Henry of England's spawn." He cleared his throat and spat contemptuously. "Mary of Guise won't have forgotten that. Aye, that's it. We'll send the boy to Edinburgh."

Rufenna nodded, thinking around it, feeling great relief. Of everyone in Scotland, the Queen could offer John the strongest protection.

"I thought the Queen was still at Linlithgow," Captain Kincaid murmured.

"Even so," Walter argued, "John would be safe at Holyrood. The Cardinal is there and he will have a care for the boy."

Rufenna absorbed this information with a brief silence and then tossed back her head. "Captain, pick several trusted men to take charge of John and I'll give them their instructions myself. As for us, we ride to Lyall this afternoon."

The captain nodded at her first order and frowned at the second. "In the morning, mistress, if you please. We need time to ready the men. We can send Master John to Edinburgh then also. I will see to it." He looked at Rufenna to see if this arrangement met with her approval.

"We ride for Lyall at dawn," she agreed.

It was a brave sight the next morning as the hundred armed and rested men rode out of Knolle and headed west. Rufenna, flanked on one side by Walter and on the other side by the captain, watched with a slight lump in her throat. These were her men, riding to follow her orders and retake her home. Could she lead them? Would they accept her? For a moment her inexperience nearly overwhelmed her; then she straightened her shoulders. She was a Lyall, after all, and she would lead her men today.

"Mistress, are you ready?" the captain asked, eyeing the slight figure doubtfully.

"I am ready."

Walter made a motion to move to the front, slightly ahead of her, but Rufenna wheeled her Border pony and walked it to the front of the line. She saw twenty men ride out, heading north, taking a reluctant John to Edinburgh. Last night she had turned a deaf ear to his protests at being left out of the fight. She finally won him over by appealing to his importance. After all, he was the head of the Lyalls now but he would need to keep himself safe until his age allowed him to take over in fact. He brightened considerably as she impressed upon him how valuable he was. She made him understand that this was not a game, but a dangerous mission she was undertaking, and that only he stood between Murdoch and Lyall. Today he rode north, somewhat mollified but still sulking, and she felt a great weight of anxiety lift from her shoulders. John would be safe with the Queen and now she was free to turn her full attention to driving her cousin from her home.

When the towers of Lyall came into sight, they reined in and scattered the men in the thick trees. Captain Kincaid and a single trooper joined the waiting Rufenna and Walter and they turned their horses and rode toward the village that sheltered at the base of the ridge.

"Mistress Rufenna," Captain Kincaid began, already having second thoughts about this scheme, "I do think it would be best if you would let me send one of the men into the castle in your place. I don't like this plan, mistress, 'Tis too risky for you."

Walter nodded his agreement. "Something could go wrong, lass."

Rufenna reined in her horse and turned to the two anxious men. "Nothing is likely to go wrong, Walter," she said quietly, trying to soothe his qualms. "You know we must get someone into the castle; there is no other way. Someone must be smuggled into the castle to open the door for the rest of the men."

"Aye, I know that, lass," Walter argued. "But it does not have to be you."

"Yes, it does," she insisted. "It was my plan, Walter, so I should be the one to do it."

"I can't like it," the captain muttered. "Surely we can think of some other way!"

Rufenna shook her head and smiled warmly at him. "Captain, the door does not open from the outside; in fact, it cannot even be seen from the outside! Someone has to get into the castle to open it from the inside! Come, Captain, would you have allowed Lyall to have a door that could be opened from the outside? Would you want to defend one that had such a door? Of course you would not! And Murdoch does not know of the door's existence! If we can get someone inside to open the door, we can get our men back into the castle before he even knows we're here!"

"I know that," the captain admitted, "but it's too risky for you, lass."

"Risky or not, it has to be me, Captain. Only Walter and I know about the door and how to open it and I would never agree to let Walter go."

The two men, recognizing defeat, fell silent and led the way into the village and straight to the shop of the wine chandler. They dismounted in the yard and Walter went inside to talk to the merchant. Rufenna walked about the yard, trying to work some of the stiffness out of her limbs, and turned expectantly as Walter hurried out of the shop, followed by the beaming wine chandler.

"Mistress, my poor shop is at your command," the merchant murmured, standing aside so that Rufenna could enter

"You have been told to deliver wine to the castle?" Walter asked, looking around the dim interior. Butts of wine, casks of whiskey, of ale and cider, were stacked high along the walls.

"That is so, Master Walter. The order came this morning."

Rufenna smiled at the captain. Their thinking had been correct, then. Murdoch, expecting a siege to drive him from the castle, was ordering provisions. Walter, conferring with the astonished merchant in one corner, was insistent and the man finally agreed.

"It is done, lass. He will take you in."

"I will go with her," the captain said suddenly, having fresh apprehensions about this harebrained scheme.

The merchant ran his eye doubtfully over the tall, broad-shouldered figure of the captain and shook his head. "Mistress Lyall, yes, but, sir, you would not fit."

Captain Kincaid walked over to the large wooden butt that the merchant indicated, and frowned. It would be quite difficult to fold his length into the butt and his shoulders would never go. He went to the door and motioned to the soldier he had left outside with the horses. "Fetch me Jed and be quick about it," he barked.

Jed arrived shortly and the plan was unfolded to him. After learning what he was to do, he began to grin. He looked at the wooden butt, the slender young girl who was being lifted into one of the butts, and nodded briskly. "Aye, I'll be pleased to go with her. Is this one for me?"

"Get in it and remember, not a sound," the captain said sternly, eyeing the young Borderer. Jed was nearly the same age and size as Rufenna and would fit nicely into the wooden butt. "You're not to make a sound no matter what happens, lad. When the storeroom is quiet after supper, you're to get out and release Mistress Lyall. Then you do exactly what she tells you. Understand?"

"Aye," said Jed cheerfully, delighted with this novel change in routine. He climbed into the butt without another word. The tops were put onto the butts and only lightly hammered down so Jed could push his off from the inside. With many misgivings the captain watched the wine chandler load great butts and kegs of wine onto his cart, telling his helpers to handle those two butts gently. He himself would accompany the cart and see to the placing of the kegs and butts in the storeroom.

Curled up in the butt, Rufenna could hear what was going on but could see nothing. The wine chandler had made small airholes for them in the butt but only tiny points of light came through. They were not large enough to see out. She braced herself against the side of the butt as it was lifted and put on the cart and then silently endured the bouncing, jolting ride up to the castle in the rough cart. She felt shaken to the core by the time they rolled into the castle courtyard and began unloading. Rufenna and the trooper, Jed, were safely unloaded in the storeroom. The hours passed slowly. Rufenna grew more and more cramped and suffered from hunger and thirst. She wondered if she would be able to stand once she was released from the butt. What would happen if she were discovered?

At last the storeroom lay in silence. Jed had napped, awakened, and napped again. He had heard Thomas, the steward, come down after dinner to fetch several bottles of French wine for Murdoch, and since then the room had been quiet. Nothing stirred as he gently pressed his shoulder to the lid of the butt. More pressure, and it started to give. In another minute it was off and he cautiously looked over the rim. Darkness lay upon the room, broken only by the flickering light of a torch in the hallway outside. Jed eased himself out of the butt and moved silently to the doorway. He could hear a faint chatter of voices coming from the kitchen and stole nearer. Supper was over and the servants had nearly finished clearing away the debris. From their talk he gathered it must be almost ten o'clock. He slipped back into the storeroom and went to the butt holding Rufenna. She gasped as the lid was quietly removed and let him lift her out. Her legs betrayed her as she had feared and Jed eased her down on a wooden crate while she got her breath and massaged her stiff limbs.

"What do we do now, mistress?"

Rufenna looked around and then at Jed. "We open the door when the castle is quiet and bring some men inside. Before dawn, they are to silence the guards and take command of the main gate, so they can open it for the rest of the men. It is not time yet, is it?"

Jed shook his head. "The servant girls are still stirring, mistress. 'Twill be several hours before they settle down for the night. Do they sleep in the kitchen?"

"Some do. The cook and the girls that work in the kitchen, I think. Jed, I'm so hungry and thirsty. Do you think we could find something to eat?"

He grinned. "Drink is easy, mistress; we have ale and wine for the taking. Food . . . I don't know. Let me look." Jed began prowling around the high-piled crates and barrels. He came back over to her. "Nay, mistress; barrels of corn, rye, oats. Spices, foodstuffs, but nothing we could eat. Is there anyone in the kitchen you can trust, mistress?"

"Thomas, the steward—my maid, Agnes . . ." she

began doubtfully. "But, Jed, we cannot take the risk of attracting attention. There has to be something to eat in here."

Rufenna came unsteadily to her feet and joined Jed in his search of the storeroom. Her eye fell on some small barrels stacked in one corner and she worked her way to them. "Help me, Jed. Ah, I thought so!" she said in relief, watching him pry the lid from one with his dagger. Her hand dipped into the barrel and came out clutching a handful of dried fruit.

Jed didn't bother to wait for an invitation. Sitting on the sealed barrels, they munched companionably on the dried fruit and took the edge off their hunger. Rufenna tried not to think of the haunch of venison or beef that had been cooked on the spit tonight. Or Cook's rich gravy, or the oatcakes . . . Cook made the best oatcakes in the world, Rufenna thought. Jed, finding himself even thirstier after eating the dried fruit, uncorked a small keg of ale. They hunted around the room until they unearthed a crate of horn cups her mother had stored there. Blowing the dust out of two, Jed poured the golden ale into them and they drank deeply. Rufenna felt the small glow of the ale spread through her stomach and sighed. She knew she would not relax until this dangerous misson was over and she was safe, but, unbidden, sleep overwhelmed her. Her eyelids were too heavy to remain open another minute. With a word of caution to Jed she retreated to the stacks of hay in the corner and was soon asleep.

The Great Hall had been dark and quiet for more than an hour when Jed awakened Rufenna. She rubbed her eyes sleepily, stretched, and then, remembering where she was and what her responsibilities were, came fully awake with a start. Having him light the tallow candle from the hallway torch, Rufenna went to the corner and opened the door. Silently she led Jed down the tunnel between the castle walls and within minutes she had opened the concealed door.

Captain Kincaid had sent a man up the gully, ordering him to lie hidden and watch for the opening of the door. Jed motioned her back and slipped out the door, moving quietly to the corner tower. A faint rustle in the gorse, then he was looking into the sharp gaze of the scout. Jed nodded and the man disappeared. Jed pressed back against the wall, knowing he was hidden from the view of the guard in the tower, and waited. The captain was sending up fifteen men, Rufenna had said, and Jed relaxed when he saw the last five slip like dark shadows to the wall. Waiting in the tunnel, Rufenna strained her ears to hear any sounds of movement and heard nothing. She gasped in surprise as Jed led the men into the tunnel and motioned her to lead the way back. Once in the storeroom the men settled down in dark corners, hidden behind tall piles of stores. Between the clutter and the darkness they would be safe should anyone come into the room. Rufenna curled up on her pile of hay again and went over the plan. It had to work! There were twelve guards on the walls: two on the back, four on each side, and two on the front. Inside the gatehouse Walter had seen guards on each side when he had checked before their midnight flight to Knolle Castle. The two men assigned to silence the guards on the back wall would move to the side walls to help there and so on to the front. With luck all the guards would have been taken care of by dawn, when the loyal Lyall men would open the gate for Captain Kincaid and the remainder of the men. Rufenna frowned. She had not considered the fact that the portcullis made so much noise when it was raised and would surely awaken the garrison in the courtyard. Well, by then it would be too late, she hoped, determined that by that time she would be upstairs making sure her mother had not been harmed by Murdoch.

Jed lightly shook her shoulder. "Mistress," he whispered, " 'tis nearly dawn. The men are ready to move. Will you stay here until the captain and his men are inside?"

Rufenna nodded without speaking. She had no intention of staying here but felt it was not the time to argue it with Jed.

"You'll be safe enough, I warrant," he muttered, wondering if he should stay with her.

"Go with them, Jed, and do not worry about me."

She watched the men quietly leave the storeroom, their woolen stockings making no sound on the stone floor and their boots tied neatly to their belts. Each carried a dagger and a short sword. Rufenna was glad she did not have to go with them. She shuddered at the thought of being witness to what would happen next. Her men would creep up on the unsuspecting guards and slit their throats. It had to be done, she knew, but she was glad she would have no part in it.

The first rays of the sun were beaming over the horizon when Rufenna heard the faint rumbling of the portcullis. Though there had been no other sound to give away the fact that the castle had been invaded during the night, she knew her plan had worked—at least so far. She flew across the storeroom, running for the kitchen and the tower stairs to her mother. In the courtyard she could hear the sudden shouts of men, half awake, partly dressed, tumbling from the sleeping quarters to respond to the horsemen who were even now pouring in the main gate. The kitchen was the scene of chaos, as servants leapt up, crying out with fear, running madly in panic. Thomas, the steward, ran into the kitchen and saw her.

"Mistress!"

"Thomas, quiet them and keep them here. It is

our own men retaking the castle and they have no need to fear. My mother?" she demanded, moving toward the tower stairs.

"M'lady is well, Mistress Rufenna. Peter and Giles are even now on guard outside her chamber. Mistress—"

"Not now, Thomas. Do as I bid you and quiet them."

Rufenna went up the stone stairs as quickly as she could. She was panting slightly, propelling herself up the tightly spiraling stairs by sheer determination. Then she collided with someone; strong arms went around her and held her firmly. She gasped and tried to pull back. Murdoch! He held her arms in a hard grip, staring furiously down at her.

"I might have known," he muttered, yanking her against his left side, freeing his sword arm from her body. "Later you will tell me how you did it, but now, my dear cousin, you will be my safe passage out of Lyall! Come!"

Rufenna struggled wildly against him and he slammed her roughly against the stone wall of the stairs. "It will do you no good," she panted, her senses reeling from the blow.

"We will see about that."

Holding her in an iron grip, his naked sword in the other hand, Murdoch started down the stairs. As they went, Rufenna stumbling and nearly falling at the pace he set, they could hear the sounds of combat in the courtyard. Murdoch reached the kitchen landing and jerked her to a stop. Sliding his sword into its sheath, he pulled out his dagger and crushed her against his side. The point hovered near her throat.

"No tricks, girl, or I'll kill you. Now, walk out into the hall."

They emerged on to a noisy scene. Shouts of pain were mingled with screams of triumph as the two bands of soldiers fought it out. Several lay quiet and Rufenna knew they would never rise again. The strong smell of blood mingled with sweat and fear. Her senses reeled at the reek of it. The few guards who had reached the Great Hall were rounded up by Captain Kincaid. Murdoch's gaze went to the tall captain and his grip on Rufenna tightened.

"Captain!"

Captain Kincaid turned, sword at the ready, his eyes widening as he beheld Rufenna grasped tightly in front of Murdoch, with that deadly dagger just touching her throat.

In an instant Murdoch summed up the situation. Captain Kincaid had retaken the castle and by threatening Rufenna he, Murdoch, could force Kincaid and his men to throw down their arms. But what then? If he harmed her, those sturdy Borderers would die to the last man to avenge her death . . . and in the struggle perhaps even he . . .

No, the best course of action would be to remove her, to leave doubts in the mind of the good captain. With Rufenna in his grasp he could find out what he wanted to know: namely, how the Lyall men got back inside to retake the castle and what had been done with young John. That there would be ample opportunity, once safely at home, to enjoy and otherwise subdue this impertinent girl, his cousin, was also to his liking. Best to let Kincaid have Lyall. He had still won the day.

"Call off your men," Murdoch shouted. "Release my men and have our horses brought into the courtyard. If you do not, your mistress dies," he added, letting the point of the dagger dig into the tender flesh of Rufenna's neck. She swallowed convulsively and dared not make a sound. She realized she was in the clutches of a desperate man who would stop at nothing to gain his own ends.

Captain Kincaid eyed the droplets of blood that

welled from a surface cut on that white throat and lowered his sword. The men in the Great Hall stood frozen, watching this tableau, and the captain was the first to move. He walked to the main door and shouted orders to his men. One wary step after another brought Murdoch to the door, making sure the captain moved ahead of him. Rufenna glimpsed Walter's outraged face and then Murdoch had moved down the ramp into the courtyard. He held her fast until his men had been allowed to mount and ride out, dragging her with him to the waiting horse.

Captain Kincaid watched helplessly. If he tried to rush Murdoch, the man was close enough to Rufenna to kill her before the captain could even reach him. Grinding his teeth in fury and frustration, the captain watched as Murdoch tossed Rufenna up into the saddle and hastily mounted behind her, the dagger still threatening that slim throat.

"Do not pursue us, Captain, or she will pay for it. Have your men stand away from the gate."

Nearly bursting with impotent rage, Captain Kincaid had no choice but to watch Murdoch ride out of the gate, taking Mistress Rufenna with him.

CHAPTER FOURTEEN

Sim pressed his mount as hard as he dared but he well knew he could not ask the horse to go much farther. Reining in on a slight rise, he looked about him. Through the trees he glimpsed high, white turrets and he smiled with relief. At last here was something familiar.

"Come, lad, not much farther now," he told the horse, setting him at a walk toward the tree-sheltered lane. Seton Castle lay behind those trees and Sim was assured assistance there. He eyed the dense trees lining the lane that led to the castle, and grinned. You could conceal an entire army in those trees, he thought, knowing that Lord Seton paid little attention to that aspect of his famous park. Far enough from the Border to render him safe from raiding parties, Lord Seton had turned his castle into a garden. He reasoned, Sim understood from Lord Hammond, that since any castle in Scotland, or anywhere else in the world, was vulnerable to the siege guns of an army, he might as well enjoy some luxury and so the affable lord spent his hours fashioning gardens. Sim shook his head in confusion. In his own rough Border country beauty took a low second to the se-

curity that was mandatory to survival. Never would
he have cluttered up the approach to *his* stronghold
with dense trees! He rode unchallenged to the gate,
thinking poorly of Lord Seton's defenses, and in a
short time found himself in the courtyard. As he
dismounted at the stone steps leading up to the main
door, a tall man came out.

"I wish to see the captain," Sim said quickly,
mounting the stairs at the same time.

"I am Captain Preston," the man replied as he
looked Sim over carefully.

"I am Lord Hammond's man, Sim. I ride to Edinburgh with an urgent message for m'lord and am in
need of a fresh mount. Will his lordship gie me the
loan of a horse?"

Captain Preston frowned. "Trouble with the English? We've been hearing rumors . . ."

Sim snorted. "There's always trouble with the English on the Border, Captain, but nothing new that
I know aught of. Nay, this is urgent family business
and I must reach m'lord this day."

The captain asked no more questions and sent a
servant to the stable. He knew that his master, Lord
Seton, was a friend to Davon Hammond. Both Cath-
olics, they had fought to see the treaties arranged with
England for the marriage of the infant Queen Mary
and the son of Henry of England rejected in Parliament. Now, rumors of Henry's rage over the rejection of the treaties, and the suggestion of a possible
Scottish alliance with France, had sparked new tales
of English retaliation. The captain questioned Sim
closely on the state of affairs on the Border, while
they waited for the horse to be saddled and brought
to the courtyard.

"Aye," Sim conceded grimly. "Old Henry'll not
like it and there has been fresh activity on the Border. He won't take it lying down, not Henry! He'll
not rest until he has Scotland in those fat, grasping

hands of his, m'lord says. Ah, here's the horse. I thank
you for it and will tell m'lord. Would you wish me
to leave it at Lord Seton's stables in Edinburgh?"

The captain nodded. "When your own is rested,
I'll send it on to Edinburgh. M'lord is at his house
there? Good. Fare you well."

They parted with a friendly wave and Sim pressed
on to Edinburgh.

Davon Hammond had his audience with Cardinal
Beaton. He gave his report on his trip to France and
his talks with the French minsters about the possibility of a marriage for the young Queen with the
Dauphin of France. The Queen Mother was still in
Linlithgow, fretting at being separated from her little
girl, who was now lodged in Stirling Castle for safekeeping. The Cardinal, spearheading the attack on
the English treaties, had personally urged the Queen
Mother to send Davon to France. The old Cardinal,
with a fanatical hatred of the Protestant English,
would go to any lengths to prevent any sort of alliance with Henry VIII of England. He knew, as the
Queen Mother did, that once Henry had little Mary
in his clutches, he would virtually control Scotland.
This proposed marriage between the young Queen
and Henry's son, Edward, had nearly sent the Cardinal into an apoplexy. He had fought it with every
weapon at his command and had rallied the Catholic
nobles to bring to bear their pressure on Parliament.
At Christmas the treaties had been rejected and the
Cardinal, knowing well Henry would in no way take
that insult lightly, waited impatiently for the English
King's next move. Davon assured him that the French
did not view favorably an allegiance between Scotland and England and were interested in negotiating
a marriage for the young Queen with a French prince.
Following his instructions, Davon had suggested the
Dauphin, heir to the French throne, but the minis-

ters had not promised anything. However, they were interested. His report made, Davon thankfully left the overbearing Cardinal's chambers, to find a page awaiting him in the hall.

"M'lord, a messenger has come for you. He waits in the courtyard."

Davon went out to the courtyard of Holyrood Palace to find one of his men leaning negligently against the stone wall. The man straightened as his chief advanced and hurried to meet him.

"M'lord, Sim has come. He says it is urgent."

Davon's black brows snapped together. "He's at Hammond House? Well, hasten, man, don't stand there waiting. Let's to Hammond House without delay."

Sim gulped down the tankard of ale and rose as Davon strode into the room. A quick glance told Davon that his man had ridden hard so he motioned Sim to sit back down.

"M'lord, I bring urgent news from Lyall."

Doggedly Sim recounted the tale, beginning with the death of Sir Ewen and progressing through Murdoch's arrival, his attentions to Rufenna, and the midnight escape of Rufenna, Walter, and the young heir to Lyall, John.

"Once I was sure they were gone to Knolle, m'lord, I got out of the castle, o'er the wall, and went to Torrey." He paused in the story, remembering the sweet hours he had spent with Agnes before he went down the rope.

Davon growled, "For the love of Christ, get on with it, man."

"Captain Daniels made sure that Master Murdoch's path was blocked, so the man and his troop could not pursue them easily to Knolle but I know not what is happening now, m'lord. I warrant the lass is plotting how to retake Lyall and Captain Kincaid will help her. I bethought it best to bring the news to you."

Davon's face had darkened with the telling of the story until now it was grim with anger. The lass would be foolish enough to lead her men against Lyall, he thought furiously. "God's blood!" he swore. "I never knew a woman with such a penchant for trouble. You did well, Sim. When do you think they will move against Lyall? Immediately, I warrant. What chance have they of taking it?"

"Judging by the temper Mistress Rufenna was in over Master Murdoch's plans, I doubt that she would eat or sleep until Lyall is back in her hands. It is the boy she is most concerned with, m'lord. If Master Murdoch can remove the boy, he will force the lass to wed with him, y'see, and then Lyall will be his."

Sim pretended not to notice the towering rage on his lord's face when the word *marriage* was mentioned and continued hastily with his theories.

"Master Walter, an old kinsman of Sir Ewen, had long mistrusted the cousin and tried to warn the lass. I would have brought them to Torrey Castle, m'lord, but she duped me well. I still don't know how they got out. They did not go over the wall as I did. There was no rope left hanging, you understand. I looked to make sure. If there is a secret way out of the castle, which I ken there must be, then they can use it to take Lyall. Captain Kincaid is no fool, m'lord, and he has nearly a hundred men at Knolle."

"Do not praise Kincaid to me, Sim," growled Davon. "He is not so smart or he would not blindly have followed Murdoch Lyall's orders and been so eager to leave Lyall without consulting with Mistress Rufenna, Walter, or *somebody* in authority. Too late to think of that now." Davon looked out the window at the late-afternoon sunlight. "Tell the men we ride for Lyall within the hour."

"Aye, m'lord," Sim murmured, getting to his feet.

He left the room satisfied. His chief would settle that slimy Murdoch Lyall!

The journey from Lyall to Galzean, Murdoch's castle, was a nightmare Rufenna would always remember. Even when she reached her middle years, the horror of that desperate ride would invade her dreams without warning and she would awaken, screaming with terror and with Murdoch's name on her lips. But her husband would draw her gently down beside him and reassure her with promises that all was well; Murdoch could never touch her again, and, soothed by his voice and concern, her sobs would cease and she would at last turn and sleep peacefully.

Fearing pursuit on that fateful day, Murdoch took the men on a rough, circular route, knowing that if Captain Kincaid came after them, going to the castle by the direct route, he would find it empty except for the small garrison Murdoch had left there. Baffled at the disappearance of their prey, the Lyall men would then begin to search the area, knowing Murdoch could hole up in any one of four towers held by the Lyall family. None of the towers would be staffed by more than a dozen men, Murdoch reasoned, and his identity would open the gates to him. Once inside, his men could hold the tower for months against a raiding party. This was an old and often used Border trick.

Rufenna, thinking this through herself, wondered if Murdoch intended to do just that and pondered on it in despair during the long weary day as they twisted and turned. They worked their way to Galzean Castle by a torturous and little used path, arriving just at dark.

"Has anyone been here asking for me?" Murdoch demanded of the guard at the gate.

"Aye, Master Lyall, a troop of men from Lyall Castle were inquiring if you had arrived. We thought you were there but told them nothing but that we did not expect you."

Murdoch's thin lips curled in a satisfied smile. His ruse had succeeded. He had intended for the Lyall men to reach Galzean first. That was why he had taken the roundabout way home. Now Captain Kincaid would be riding hard through the Scottish Border, carefully checking each of the towers that could harbor them.

"The Abbot has come daily, sir, asking to see you."

"Is he here now?" Murdoch demanded sharply.

"Yes, sir, he is still within."

"Tie him up, take him to the dungeon and I will deal with this pesky Sir Abbot."

Murdoch led the horse across the rough cobbled courtyard and dismounted, dragging Rufenna roughly from the saddle. Her knees nearly buckled with weariness and he pulled her up the stairs to the Great Hall. She stood in a daze of fatigue while Murdoch talked to his steward and Galzean's captain. So great was her exhaustion that it did not occur to her to look around or perhaps request food and drink. Then she was pulled roughly through the hall and taken down the flight of stone steps leading to the storerooms.

Galzean was basically a square keep of the older Border type. It had later had four stout square towers built, one on each corner, and was encircled by a rough stone wall. The air was dank and musty as she stumbled down the dark stairs and she shivered against the chill. Lights were flaring below as they rounded the last turn of the stairs and she blinked as they dazzled her eyes. She had never been to Galzean before and had not known that the lower level of the keep was fitted out as a dungeon. Her grandfather had long ago ripped out the rough cells in the cellar at Lyall and converted them into dry, clean storerooms. Surely Murdoch did not intend to put her down here! Her appalled gaze went from the rows of barred cells that lined one wall of the massive room to the shrinking figure of the Abbot, bound and trussed like a fowl on the floor in front of the great fireplace. Used as a second bakehouse in time of siege, the room was fitted with an odd mixture of damp cells, an enormous fireplace that would roast an entire deer, and worktables and shelves of cooking pots. Murdoch advanced on the Abbot, pulling Rufenna along with him. His grasp was so strong that she was nearly faint from the pain and did his bidding silently. He signaled two men to hold her and turned his attention to the miserable Abbot, now looking up at him with apprehensive eyes.

"Sir, I protest . . ." began the Abbot, breaking off with a gasp of agony as Murdoch prodded him with his boot.

"Nay, it is I who protest, Sir Abbot. I mislike having you invade Galzean in my absence, thinking to cozen my steward with tales of theft."

The Abbot drew a painful but outraged breath. "Sir, the gold chalices you took from the Monastery were not yours. You must return them!"

Murdoch sneered. "How concerned with gold and riches have become those who pledged their lives to the service of the Mother Church. I don't recall reading of a gold cup at the Last Supper!"

"Your knowledge of Holy Scripture will not save you on the last day when you will be condemned as a thief."

"You will be sorry for those accusations presently, Sir Abbot," said Murdoch, prodding him again with his boot. Then he turned to the two men holding Rufenna. "Enough of this. Has he signed the deeds?"

"No, Master Lyall, he refused."

"Then we must persuade him to change his mind! Abbot, I tire of this little game. I want that land and you will sign that deed, do you hear me? If you do not agree, we will be constrained to force you to reconsider." Murdoch's tone was soft but menacing.

The Abbot, showing a strange dignity in spite of his bindings, shook his head. "It is Church land and I cannot give it to you. I will protest this, sir, to the Bishop. He will never countenance such treatment. . . ."

Murdoch sat down on a wine keg and looked at the man waiting quietly by the stairs. "Fetch two more men, quickly. We must give Sir Abbot reason to change his mind."

Under Rufenna's horrified gaze the three men tore off the Abbot's robe and linen undergarments, lifted him and bound him fast to the large metal spit, and swung it into the fireplace, over the smoldering coals.

"When you change your mind, Sir Abbot, speak out," Murdoch murmured, directing the men to build up the fire.

Rufenna struggled wildly; she could not stand there and watch a man of God, or any man, for that matter, being burned alive. Her struggles were futile, however, and she only hurt herself. She closed her eyes, fighting down the nausea that rose in her throat as the flames licked the Abbot's bare skin. His screams and prayers for mercy pierced the silence in the dungeon, making Rufenna shake violently. She would not look; she would not show her sickness before Murdoch. The wavering light of the torches pressed against her closed lids. She sagged and only the firm hands holding her prevented her from falling onto the cold, stone floor. Just before she lost consciousness, she heard Murdoch order the men to take her upstairs and lock her in a chamber. He ordered a guard to remain outside the door.

Rufenna awoke to swimming darkness. She tried to move, and felt her hands bound tightly. Faint light came from the single candle standing on the table by the door. The room was empty. She pulled at her wrists, her heart pounding with fear, and discovered they were tightly bound with cord. The end of the cord had been secured to the tall bedpost. She rolled over on her stomach and tried to rise to her knees just as the door crashed open. She fell over onto her back and stared at her cousin with frightened eyes. He slammed the door, locked it, and advanced to the bed.

"Well, well, what have we here? You didn't care for the entertainment I provided you? Pity. You should have stayed. The Abbot changed his mind, after all, and was happy to sign the deeds. No, he's not dead, just blackened a bit. Nothing like a taste of fire to make a man change his mind. Now, my dear cousin, to more pressing matters," he said silkily, reaching over and catching her chin in his hand. "Where is your brother?"

Rufenna didn't answer and his grip on her chin tightened. "You will tell, Rufenna. Like the Abbot, you need persuasion. Did you take John to Knolle and leave him there?"

Stubbornly she remained silent, determined not to tell him anything.

"Answer me," he growled.

She pulled her chin out of his grip and raised her head defiantly. "He is where you will never find him, Murdoch."

"You will tell me where that is before the night is out, girl. You will beg me for permission to tell me anything and everything I want to know."

"I will never betray my brother to you," she said firmly, putting more strength into her answer than she felt she really had.

It convinced Murdoch, however, and with a curse he lunged at her. His brutal hand caught her linen shirt and ripped it furiously from her. Helpless to cover her naked breasts, Rufenna kicked out at him and he caught her legs. Her leather belt was un-buckled, the breeches ruthlessly dragged off, until she lay twisting on the bed, her white body gleaming in the soft candlelight.

Murdoch licked his lips. Seldom had he seen such beauty. But sudden rage at her defiance blocked out his lust. The little bitch would tell. Oh, yes, she would tell. Rufenna saw him raise the belt and instinc-tively rolled over onto her stomach, away from the blow. The leather snapped across her shoulders, leav-ing a searing welt, and she gasped. The pain envel-oped her. Again and again the belt fell, crossing and crisscrossing her back, her buttocks, her legs. After that first involuntary cry she held her lip tightly in her teeth, determined not to beg him for mercy or to play into his hands. She endured the lashing of that malevolent belt, nearly losing consciousness from the burning pain. When he could wring no cry from her, he flung the belt from him in a fury, grabbed her shoulders in iron hands, and turned her onto her back.

"Where is John?" he ground out between clenched teeth.

"I will not tell you," she gasped, tasting the blood welling from her cut and swollen mouth.

He shook her until she feared her neck would break. Then he struck her brutally across her face and she closed her eyes. He let her drop back to the bed and then his hands were moving on her body, leaving pain and bruises behind them, forcing her legs apart as he flung himself on her, so enflamed with rage that he was nearly maddened with it. When he forced himself into her, she felt as if she were being impaled upon a dagger. The pain that the beating caused was mild compared with this agony. She felt that her entire being was being torn in two. Mur-doch was skilled at this kind of sadism and inflicted all the agony he could. Rufenna blanked her mind, willing her senses to dull, to release her from this torment. She could feel herself slipping into darkness and welcomed it. Under his merciless hands she went limp and he realized she was no longer aware of him or what he was doing to her. Murdoch flung himself from the bed, pulling his clothing around him, trying to calm his frenzied mind. The timid rap at the door brought him around, his hands shaking, his heart beating hard.

"Master Murdoch?"

He recognized his steward's voice and, without a backward glance, walked out of the room, locking the door behind him.

The steward looked at him curiously, seeing the streaks of blood on his clothing, his distorted and mottled face, but he knew better than to show any interest.

"Well, what is it?"

"This message has come, sir." The steward handed him the sealed note and Murdoch opened it unsteadily. He frowned as he puzzled over the nearly illegible handwriting and curtly dismissed the steward.

"I ride to Hermitage to meet other gentlemen," the note read, "who have urgent news from H. Do not"—Murdoch puzzled over the word and decided it was *allow*—"allow aught to delay you. Come at once. G."

Murdoch scowled blackly. Trust the Earl of Glencairn to give such a note to a messenger! Damn, he thought, not now! But Glencairn said it was urgent. Murdoch crushed the note in his hand, determined to burn it at the first opportunity, and strode down the hall.

He pulled on fresh clothing, collected his cloak, and returned to Rufenna. She had not moved since he left her. He noted that her hands were still bound to the bed. Warning the guard to allow no one to enter the room, he locked the door, secured the key in his pocket, and stormed down the stairs.

"Captain," he barked to the startled soldier. "Fetch me a horse and ten men to ride with me. Guard the castle well in my absence."

"Aye, Master Lyall," the captain said, wondering where his master was going this time of night.

After giving his steward some hasty instructions about his two reluctant houseguests, Murdoch led his small troop of men out the gate, heading southwest to Hermitage Castle. When this emergency was over, he would conclude his dealings with his dear cousin in a way she would mislike even more than she had the previous persuasions. He smiled to himself as he rode through the darkness.

It was not long after the sun had risen when Davon and his men approached Lyall Castle. He had ridden his little troop hard through the night, but made the journey from Edinburgh easier by using the main roads as much as possible. Their horses covered the long, flat miles and sped on through the dark until they reached the rolling hills marking the beginning of Border country. Davon was not sure of his reception at Lyall. Surely the captain knew of the feud that existed between the two families, even if he did not know the reason for it. If only he had not been called to Edinburgh at such a time, but he was the Queen's emissary and he well knew the dangers of falling out of favor with her. Not that he would. Once he pledged his honor and his word, he would keep it to the death. But the timing had been so bad. He wondered who held Lyall. Rufenna, that spunky little convent lass who had swept into his life, had left an indelible imprint on it and just as swiftly swept out of it. He would barely admit to himself that she was seldom out of his thoughts. Or did Murdoch hold the castle? That loathsome bit of humanity. Davon had never met him, but stories of his brutality and treachery swept down the Border from time to time.

As they approached the castle, he walked his horse up the slope, riding directly to the main gate. He saw no one familiar but there was no evidence of battle, at least none from outside the wall.

"Who goes?" came the cry from the guard on the wall.

"Lord Hammond to see Mistress Lyall."

There was a stir on the walls and Davon sat back and waited. He was not particularly surprised to see Captain Kincaid look over the wall, staring at the man waiting impatiently on horseback with his ten men clustered around him. So the lass had managed to take the castle back after all, Davon thought.

"Open the gate," Captain Kincaid called, disappearing into the tower. Davon smiled grimly. Feud or no feud, the captain knew well that ten men could pose no danger to the castle. He was quite willing for them to come inside, but Davon knew that if there was any trouble, getting out would be an entirely different matter. As Davon led his men inside, the captain was waiting for them in the courtyard.

Sim moved up beside his chief and murmured, "The old man hurrying out of the castle is Master Walter Lyall."

Davon nodded and dismounted. He eyed the tall captain wearily. "Mistress Lyall?" he questioned.

Old Walter reached the group and met the captain's eye in a quick exchange of glances. Davon frowned. All was not well here. "She *is* here?" he asked. "I see that you have retaken the castle, Captain, so I assume that Mistress Lyall returned with you? I intend to see her," he added, setting his jaw grimly. He wondered briefly what his reception would be, meeting the lady on her home territory.

The captain met that steely gaze and decided that

frankness was the best course. "Mistress Lyall is not here. During the fight yesterday morn, her cousin took her prisoner and used her as hostage to get him and his men away."

A sharp silence fell. Davon's hands clenched and his face clearly reflected exactly his opinion of a captain who allowed his mistress to fall into the hands of the enemy. A slight flush rose in the captain's cheeks, but he stood his ground. He knew that if he had offered resistance to Murdoch, another Lyall wake would be taking place today.

"You have not found her?" Davon demanded.

"No, not yet . . . not that we didn't—"

"And young John?" Davon interrupted. "Did he capture the boy too?"

"No, the boy is safe."

"You're sure of that?" Davon asked with searing sarcasm. "You haven't allowed the boy to slip through your fingers as well?"

The flush deepened on the captain's face. "M'lord," he said, attempting to move the conversation into safer territory, "this is not your concern! I am charged with the safety of Lyall—"

"And a damned poor job you've done of it! Listen well, Captain Kincaid. I am making Rufenna's safety my concern! Where have you searched for her?"

The captain, goaded by that taunting remark, started to answer angrily and then restrained himself. There was some justice to it, after all. He swallowed his anger with poor grace. Not a man present, including old Walter, had missed this furious nobleman's casual use of Mistress Lyall's Christian name. Kincaid decided to answer as reasonably as he could.

"Galzean first, but they had not been seen there. Then we went to each of the Lyall towers but no word of them. There are a dozen places he could take her."

"When did he take her from here?" Davon asked,

his mouth becoming tighter and more grim by the minute.

"During the attack at dawn. Yesterday," the captain added. "We searched all the day and most of the night. We are planning to widen the search today."

"You went straight to Galzean, I understand? And he had not been there?"

"No sign of him. His men seemed surprised that he was not still at Lyall. M'lord, 'tis a big area . . ."

"Perhaps, but we'll find her," Davon ground out, restraining his rage with the greatest of difficulty. These fools had let Murdoch pull the oldest Border trick in the world on them and still did not realize it. Murdoch had deliberately taken the roundabout route home and let his pursuers reach Galzean before he did. Then they would spend days searching all other possible places while he coolly settled at home. He turned to his horse, motioning for his men to turn about. Old Walter watched that enraged nobleman ride out of Lyall, thoughtfully revising his opinion of the gentleman.

"Master Walter, do you think . . ." the captain began.

Walter Lyall chuckled grimly, deep in his beard.

"I think, sir, that I would not stand in Master Murdoch's shoes this day for all the gold in London!"

Davon rode furiously to Galzean, making plans as he went. When the old keep at last stood before him, he sent one man to the gatehouse. Soon the man was back where his chief was resting and watering the weary and thirsty horses by the sheltered stream.

"M'lord, he is gone, they say. The guard at the gate said Master Lyall rode out last night with ten men. The young lady must still be in there," he added, watching the hard muscle flicker at the corner of his chief's grim mouth.

Davon turned to the waiting men. "Wat, stay here with three of the men. If we do not come out in less than an hour, ride for Torrey and fetch the rest of the men. There must be well over a hundred men in the castle so I think we'll try to bluff our way in," he decided, looking through the trees at the keep.

Minutes later Davon rode proudly up to the gate, holding his head high and looking every inch the nobleman. "You, there," he shouted imperiously to the guard. "Open this gate! I have urgent business with your master."

The startled guard gazed down at the haughty nobleman accompanied by so few men, and wondered what to do. He was considering sending for the captain when the nobleman began to shout again.

"Damn my eyes! D'you keep me waiting here, you rogue? Open that gate!"

The guard scrambled to the gate and swung it open and was nearly trampled by the nobleman's impetuous entrance. Davon dismounted in the courtyard, throwing his reins to one of his own troopers and his alert gaze went quickly around the walls. There were a few men visible on the walls so the bulk of Murdoch Lyall's men must be in the barracks. "You," he said shortly to the gate guard. "Where is your master?"

"He's not here," the guard stammered.

"I'll see your captain, then," Davon said, waiting impatiently in the center of the courtyard. The man scurried off without a protest and vanished into the stone barracks. Too many unexpected visitors had ridden in recently to confer with his master for him to be much surprised at this one's arrival. He returned quickly with the captain of Galzean.

Davon ran an appraising eye over the sleepy man, who was hastily pulling his jacket on against the cool early-morning air. "Are you the captain?"

"Aye, sir, I am," the captain admitted, wondering just who this nobleman was and what to say to him. He was just formulating an explanation of his master's absence when the nobleman nodded.

"You'll do perfectly," Davon said, reaching out and catching the startled captain firmly by the arm and spinning him about. The captain opened his mouth to protest, saw the wicked length of steel hovering near his unprotected throat, and swallowed his hasty words.

"Sim, have a man keep the gate open. We won't be here long."

Sim signaled to one of the waiting troopers, who promptly seized the gate guard and, dagger at the ready, kept him pinned against the stone wall.

Moving his prisoner before him, Davon went toward the main steps. "You will order any soldier we meet to stand aside, is that clear?" he demanded, forcing his prisoner into the Great Hall of Galzean. The man nodded. The steward, crossing the Great Hall, found himself confronted by a big, angry stranger who held the castle's captain in a tight grip. "Mistress Lyall? Where is she?"

The steward slid a glance at the angry-looking troopers who were crowded behind the nobleman, and swallowed. "Upstairs. The master—"

"I will deal with him later. Take me to Mistress Lyall at once! Sim, bring this man with us," he said, thrusting the captain at Sim. The silent procession went up the stairs and stopped before the door to Rufenna's chamber. A guard, lounging against the door, straightened as the little group came down the stone hallway, his gaze widening as he saw his captain held by a big Borderer.

"Open this door instantly."

The guard's gaze shifted from Davon's furious face to the pale, sweating face of the captain, and he hesitated. "Sir, I cannot. Master Murdoch took the key with him when he left. Captain," he began, turning to appeal to his superior, "we must not let—" His hand rested on the hilt of his sword.

The guard did not finish the sentence as Davon felled him with a single blow. Then Davon jerked down a battle ax attached to the wall and began to chop furiously at the heavy door. Would to God, he thought, that Master Murdoch Lyall was under this ax! In a short time the sturdy door gave in to his force and he pushed it aside.

He stood in the doorway for an instant and his hard eyes scanned the room. A stifled curse left his tight mouth and he turned to the steward, who promptly fled down the hall. This was not his doing, the terrified steward thought, but he would be blamed for it if he stayed.

In two strides Davon was by the bed, staring down at Rufenna. She lay on her stomach, her face buried in the tumbled covers. His shocked gaze traveled down from her tightly bound wrists, still secured to the bedpost, down her bruised back and legs, to the telltale streaks of blood on the inside of her thighs. His dagger was quick in cutting her bonds and he eased her over, believing her dead. His heart leapt with hope when he saw a faint movement of her torn, bloody lips. His hand was trembling with rage and tenderness as it went to her throat, feeling for a pulse. It was there, feeble but beating under his fingers. Bitter, dark eyes scanned her bruised face and body and rested for a long moment on the angry marks on her white breasts. Without a word he pulled the blanket from the bed and lifted her onto it. A moan escaped her and her eyelids fluttered. Davon knelt by her, brushing back the tumbled hair, as she gazed up at him with blank eyes.

"Rufenna?"

After a long agonizing moment the blankness lifted and recognition dawned. A quivering sigh went through her. "D-Davon?"

"Rest, child. I'll take you away from here."

"T-the Abbot, Davon. H-he . . ."

Davon frowned in perplexity. "Abbot?" he echoed in confusion.

"In the dungeons. Oh, Davon," she sobbed, letting the tears flow for the first time.

"All right, Rufenna. We'll see about the Abbot. I'm going to lift you up and it will hurt. Just hang on, child, and you'll soon be home."

He wrapped her tightly in the blanket and carried her from the room, a grim-faced Sim behind him. His men waited, silent, tight-lipped, downstairs in the Great Hall. They glanced from her bruised, bleeding face to their chief's, and shivered.

"Sim, she says there is an Abbot in the dungeon. See to it."

One of Davon's troopers stepped forward and relieved Sim of his prisoner and, as Sim went quickly down the stairs to the dungeon, the little group went out of the Great Hall into the bright morning sunlight flooding the courtyard.

Davon carried his light burden to where a trooper waited with his horse, steeling his heart against Rufenna's sobs of pain. A large group of Murdoch's men had gathered in the courtyard, and they stirred uneasily as they saw the tall nobleman carrying his burden across the courtyard. Davon flicked a glance at the silent captain, still held firmly in the grip of a trooper, the dagger at his throat glinting in the sunlight. "Order your men back into the barracks until we leave," Davon said curtly.

For a tense moment the captain met that cold, dangerous gaze and fresh beads of sweat formed on his brow. If he let this man leave with the girl, Master Murdoch would have his hide. If he did *not* allow this haughty nobleman to have his way . . . He sweated harder, seeing certain death waiting ahead in that implacable gaze. "Return to the barracks and remain there," he called to the Lyall men. "Do it at once," he cried, feeling the sharp point of the dagger dig lightly into the soft skin of his throat. The men shuffled awkwardly, then began to move across the cobbled courtyard toward the barracks. Davon mounted, letting one of his men hand the quivering bundle up to him. He looked down at the trooper still holding the captain hostage. "Bring him with us. We'll release him outside the gates when all of our men are out."

"M'Lord, we found the Abbot," Sim said, coming to a breathless stop by Davon's mount. "He's been burned, or something, but can stand. He won't leave without a chalice he talks about, which he says Master Lyall stole from the Monastery."

Davon flicked a glance at him. "Find it, Sim, if you have to tear this place down to do so, and then return the Abbot to the Monastery. We'll go on to Torrey."

"Aye, m'lord," said Sim, looking as though he would enjoy tearing down Galzean.

"No, give the orders to the men, Sim, but you come with me."

"M'lord!" The quavering voice came across the courtyard and Davon turned impatiently.

"M'lord," the Abbot gasped, leaning heavily on one of Davon's men. "I give you my blessing for what you do this day. If there is anything Cairnbrae can do for you, come to us."

Davon nodded. "My men will see you to—Cairnbrae, is it?—and take care you do not come near Galzean or Master Murdoch Lyall again. I may not be at hand to rescue you."

"My Bishop will deal with this, m'lord . . ." the Abbot assured him.

"No, Sir Abbot," Davon said softly. looking down at his burden. "I will deal with Master Murdoch myself—in my own time."

The little Abbot glanced from Rufenna to the dark face of Davon Hammond and watched him wheel his horse and ride slowly away from Galzean.

CHAPTER FIFTEEN

As the cold, early spring sun rose higher in the sky, the silent troop rode through widening vales toward Torrey. The rounded hills were opening out, spreading into the burgeoning green valleys of Teviotdale. Carrying his light burden firmly, Davon passed near Stobs and Ormiston but headed in a direct line for the rising towers of Torrey. Twice they stopped in a sheltered vale, watering the horses from the icy, sparkling stream that bubbled merrily down the valley. Rufenna roused slightly when she was laid on the new grass by the stream and accepted the cup of water held to her lips by Davon. The cold water stung the cut flesh of her mouth and she winced, taking care not to meet his dark gaze. One swift glance at that set face had been enough and she felt wary of prodding his tightly controlled temper by rousing it further. The men waited in a silent little group, containing their curiosity about this lass and intending to pry the information out of Sim the instant they reached home. Many of them recognized that fiery hair and knew her to be the lass taken to Hammond Tower and then lost on the raid over the Border. What had occurred during their time in Edinburgh that had led to this? Sim had spent some time at Lyall and would know. Their speculative glances rested on the big Borderer watering his horse in stubborn silence.

"Aye," said Wat in a whisper to the others. "Several goblets of wine and Sim's tongue will be loosened and we'll know everything."

Rufenna was settled across the saddlebow and they pressed on. The motion of the horse was agony but she bit her lip and kept silent. She was acutely conscious of the strong arms holding her so closely, of the steady beat of his heart against her cheek. She moved uneasily, trying to assume a more comfortable position. Davon looked down at her, feeling her movement, and let her ease herself into a more comfortable position. He murmured encouragingly, "Not long now," looking down at her white face. He had little need to repress *his* curiosity; the nature of her injuries had told him all he needed to know about what had happened to her. He would still have the full story from her, just to be sure he had not missed anything important, but he could make all too shrewd a guess.

Before they reached Stobs, he drew rein and turned to Wat. "Wat, send a man on to Lyall. He is to tell the captain only that Mistress Lyall is safe and in my care. He is then to come on to Torrey."

Wat nodded and rode back down the line to summon one of the men and give Davon's orders. Wat watched the man leave and turn south, headed for Lyall, and Wat wondered. He had been with his lord for many years. They had grown up together at Torrey, had learned the use of the sword and lance together, had learned to ride. He had attended his lord first at Court, when King James V had been alive, and to France where Davon had gone on business for the Queen Mother. He had seen his master have many women over the years, but he could never remember his lord so disturbed over one. As Wat rode back up the line and fell into place beside Davon, his glance slid to the mass of red hair that tumbled around the rough woolen blanket. The faintest touch of misgiving prodded him; this lass was going to be trouble!

By the time the towers of Torrey rose above the woods, the entire troop was regarding the girl with new respect. From the little they had gleaned from the servants at Galzean, they too had made a fair guess of what the lass had endured there. They also knew about her leading the Lyall men and retaking her castle and had watched her quietly on this long ride to Torrey. Not a whimper, not a cry, had escaped those bruised and cut lips. She had endured the agony of the ride with stolid acceptance and had wrung the grudging respect from every man of them. This, they decided, was some lass.

The portcullis stood wide and Luke Daniels waited in the courtyard. Davon rode up to the stone steps and, waiting for Sim to approach, handed down his burden carefully. Luke's startled gaze flew from the slender, blanket-wrapped figure to his master's grim face. He looked questioningly at Sim, but Sim shook his head slightly, turning to hand back his light burden to his master.

"Luke, close the gate and see that the men are rested. They've had a long, hard ride. Sim," Davon added, "before you take off your boots and reach for the ale, find Andrew and have him fetch Old Nell."

Davon started up the stone steps to the main door, ignoring Luke's attempts to detain him.

"M'lord . . ." Luke said, moving several steps behind Davon. "I must tell you . . ." Luke broke off, shrugging, as his master strode purposefully through the doorway, not waiting to hear the news. He would find out soon enough, Luke decided, returning to the courtyard to see about the tired men waiting in groups.

The steward, Andrew, hastened across the Great Hall, gazing at his lord in some considerable surprise. "M'lord . . ."

"Send Old Nell up immediately, Andrew, and bring up hot water and towels."

"A-aye, m'lord," the steward stammered, turning back and hurrying for the kitchen.

Davon went up the winding staircase rapidly and pushed open the massive door with his foot. Sim was close on his heels and moved to the bed and drew back the heavy velvet hangings without waiting for the order.

"Thanks, lad. Now, get to your rest."

"Aye, m'lord," Sim said, withdrawing and nearly colliding with a slim figure standing in the doorway. He hesitated, eyeing the girl curiously.

"Davon?"

Davon straightened abruptly from laying down his burden and spun around, staring in astonishment at the girl standing in the doorway. She moved into the room, hurrying to his side and gazing down at the blanket-clad figure on the bed.

"What in hell are you doing here?" he demanded angrily, looking down at his sister.

Two pairs of dark eyes met for a brief instant and then she said, "That can wait. Who is that? What has happened to her?"

"Elizabeth, I asked what you are doing at Torrey? I . . ." Davon broke off, seeing Old Nell hovering uncertainty in the doorway. "Nell, I have a patient for you. See to her," he ordered, taking his sister's arm in a firm grasp.

Elizabeth Hammond smiled stubbornly at Davon and removed her blue velvet sleeve from his grasp. "Later, dear brother. I will help Nell first and then

we can talk. This girl needs attention now. Nell, ask
Andrew for hot water and towels."

"I have done that already, damn it," Davon said
impatiently, gazing angrily from his sister to Nell.
The old woman had nursed and cared for two generations of Hammonds and she moved to the bedside. "Elizabeth . . ."

"Presently, Davon, please," Elizabeth said, placing
a placating hand on his arm. Her composed face betrayed no sign of the unease her brother's anger
roused. Time enough to enrage him later, she thought
to herself. "Please let me attend to the girl first."

With a curse Davon turned from the bed and
stamped from the room, sending his sister a frustrated and darkling glance. She was supposed to be
in Linlithgow with the Queen Mother! What the
devil had brought her to Torrey? Not *more* disgrace!
As he stamped down the hall, Davon decided that he
would soon find out.

Sim, a silent witness to the confrontation, moved
to the door and started to follow his master. His
movement caught Elizabeth's eye and she turned.

"Sim, please carry the girl to my chamber. She
cannot remain here. What is Davon thinking of?"
she murmured, moving aside so Sim could approach
the bed.

The big Borderer, who knew fairly well what was
in his master's mind, hesitated. M'lord had given the
order to have the lass placed in his own chamber.
Sim hesitated to go directly against his lord. "If my
lord wants her here . . ." he ventured, uneasy but
not about to enlighten Lady Elizabeth about Rufenna.

The small, dark-haired Hammond girl stamped her
foot. "Name of God, Sim! It is not seemly to leave
her here." A low moan from the bed attracted her
attention and she lowered her voice. "She needs close

nursing and I can see to her better in my chamber,"
she continued firmly.

Sim gave in and lifted the semiconscious girl from
the bed. He followed Elizabeth down the hall and
carried Rufenna into Elizabeth's chamber. His master wouldn't like it, he knew; he would be angered
afresh by his sister's meddling. As he retreated, before
the determined mistress of Torrey could ask awkward
questions about the girl, Sim wondered about this
intriguing situation. He knew full well why m'lord
had brought her to Torrey instead of taking her back
to Lyall. He knew what his lordship intended; Lady
Elizabeth did not. The question that accompanied
Sim back down to the soldiers' quarters and his ale and
rest, was just how m'lord intended to accomplish his
plans with his sister in residence! Sim reached the
quarters in the courtyard, removed his boots and
drew a mug of ale, and sat down gratefully. He hoped
that Lord Hammond would not blame him for these
complications.

The same thought had occurred to Davon and only
fed his growing anger. He had taken refuge in the
small room at the end of the long hall, a room usually
reserved for guests. The page had removed his boots,
brought food and wine and hot water. Davon ate,
washed the dust of travel from his face and hands,
and nursed his wrath until it simmered satisfactorily.
Once Rufenna had recovered from her injuries, he
had intended to keep her here as his mistress but
that would be impossible if Elizabeth remained at
Torrey. Elizabeth would have to go tomorrow, he
decided. He would bundle her off to Linlithgow
where she belonged. He thrust away his half-eaten
supper in frustration. Damn the girl, he thought furiously. She could not have chosen a more awkward
moment to come home. The page hovered in the
corner, watching him with apprehensive eyes. Davon
turned and looked at him.

"Fetch me writing materials, Peter, and send word to Captain Daniels that I will need a messenger shortly."

In her own chamber Elizabeth helped Nell wash the dust and dried blood from the girl's body. The eyes of the young and the old woman met in shocked disbelief at the wide red welts that crisscrossed her white back, welts that were swollen and ugly and beginning to turn black. The girl had been beaten; there was no doubt of that. The marks were unmistakable, Elizabeth realized, swallowing painfully. The girl, her eyes tightly closed, endured their ministrations silently.

They washed her gently and put on a balm made from Aaron's rod for her bruises. Old Nell mixed a dried powdery substance made from the flowers of cowslip that aided in reducing fever. She mixed it with a little warm water and spooned it into Rufenna's mouth. Then she cut the root of Fuller's herb and held it to the worst bruises, murmuring to Elizabeth that it would help to fade the discoloration and aid in healing. As did most women of the time, Elizabeth had some knowledge of herb craft and she was familiar with Old Nell's treatment.

Elizabeth was burning with curiosity about this girl. Where had Davon found her? Who had mistreated her in such a way? As they rolled Rufenna over on her back and began bathing and medicating the bruises on the front of her body, Elizabeth and Nell again exchanged startled glances. They, like Davon, realized from the nature of her injuries that the lass had received more than a beating. Old Nell muttered under her breath and stirred another spoonful or two of an evil-looking liquid into the mug and forced it between Rufenna's lips.

"What is that?" asked Elizabeth.

"Not fit for virgin ears to know," retorted the old woman.

"Nell," answered Elizabeth, "I will be caring for this girl and I need to know what you are giving her."

The old woman hesitated but weakened at Elizabeth's insistence. "If the girl is impregnated by the man who beat and . . . er . . . hurt her, then this will take care of it."

"You mean you gave her an abortifacient?"

"Aye."

"What was it?"

"I will not tell, mistress. A good lass like yourself has no need of it. The herb will bring on her fluxes; that is all you need to know."

And with that, Elizabeth had to be satisfied.

Just then the girl stirred and a soft moan escaped her. She opened her eyes and stared in confusion at the two figures bending over her.

"What is your name?" Elizabeth asked softly.

"Rufenna."

"Rufenna? Rufenna who? Can you tell us who you are?"

"Rufenna L-Lyall," the girl murmured, writhing painfully from the gentle hands smoothing salve across her bruised breast.

Elizabeth was so shocked that she nearly dropped the pot of salve. Lyall? Oh no, she thought. *Lyall!* With horrified eyes Elizabeth watched Nell ease the girl into a clean linen nightshift and settle her more comfortably against the pillows. A sleeping draught was coaxed down her, for rest would be the best medicine of all. Elizabeth turned blindly for the door, her mind reeling with shock, leaving Nell to take up a vigil by the girl's bedside. A Lyall? Could Davon have done this? she wondered in horror. She knew he had a terrifying temper when it was fully roused, but would he have beat the poor girl like that? As Elizabeth made for the door, she wondered how on earth to approach Davon. But she was determined to find out what was going on.

A messenger handed the sealed letters to Captain Kincaid at Lyall and rode out the gate. He had been ordered to deliver the letters and not to linger so that he would avoid awkward questions. Captain Kincaid looked at the letters, noticing that one was addressed to him and one to Lady Lyall. He broke the seal of his and spread open the page. The strong black writing leapt from the page, telling him, if he had needed telling, who the author of this missive was. He began to read.

"Well?" demanded Walter, waiting impatiently as the captain read over the letter a second time.

Captain Kincaid looked at Walter. "'Tis from Lord Hammond. He says . . . Here, read it yourself."

Walter handed it back. "I cannot read, Captain; you know that! Come, what does he say about the lass?"

"He begins: 'Captain Kincaid, I found Mistress Lyall at Galzean. She is safe at Torrey but unable to travel at the present. She has been badly beaten by her cousin. I have not told Lady Lyall of her daughter's condition. You must decide how much you wish her to know. Murdoch Lyall was gone from Galzean but I give you this warning. He may attempt to retake Lyall, so be on your guard. I will have Mistress Lyall escorted to Lyall Castle when she is well enough to travel.'" Captain Kincaid looked over the letter at Walter. "It is signed 'Hammond.' Master Walter . . ."

"Damn," expostulated Walter. "We should have died, every man of us, before we let that bastard have her. 'Tis ashamed I am to claim kin to such a one as Murdoch Lyall!"

The captain was also furious and ashamed at what

had befallen his mistress but he kept silent lest he further enrage Walter. After a moment the old man brought his temper under control.

"Curious," Walter said. "He could just as easily have brought her to Lyall. I wonder what Lord Hammond has in mind?"

"Master Walter, what do we tell Lady Lyall? Her condition is yet frail, so says her maid. I hate to burden her with more distressing news. And what do we do about Mistress Rufenna? Do we fetch her from Torrey?"

Walter, deep in thought, roused himself and looked at the worried captain. "Captain," he said slowly, "has it occurred to ye that m'lord is pursuing this feud in a strange manner? You saw his face, sir, when he discovered that Master Murdoch had the lass; you saw his rage. Why is he so anxious to have the lass at Torrey?"

The captain thought about it. It was, now that Walter had mentioned it, strange indeed. When a blood feud sprang up between two Border families, entire clans were killed. The feud was not just directed against the individual who began it; it involved both families. So the Hammonds had been injured by the Lyalls and would, by right, turn their sword against any Lyall. Yet Lord Hammond had not. He had searched the Border for the lass when the English had taken her; he had put a man into Lyall to see to her safety, a man who had warned both Walter and Mistress Rufenna of Master Murdoch's intentions. The Hammond men, for no apparent reason, had prevented Master Murdoch's pursuit of Mistress Rufenna, Walter, and young John. Captain Kincaid did indeed remember Lord Hammond's anger when he learned the lass had been abducted by her cousin. He had ridden off with a small troop of men and had taken her back, traveling to Torrey with her instead of returning her to her home. Yes, it was a strange way to conduct a feud! "Master Walter, do you think . . ."

A slight smile touched the old man's lips. "I think there is more here than meets the eye, my friend. Lord Hammond's interest in the lass is not what one would expect in a feud." He scratched his head thoughtfully. "I also think that, feud or no feud, the lass is safer at Torrey with Lord Hammond than she would be here! I think even m'lord is not sure of his intentions toward her! The lass has a way with her, ye understand, and I think m'lord is finding that out. Aye, 'tis interesting, and I think we'd best not interfere. If he does not return her when she is recovered, then we'll decide what to do. We can be sure he has told Lady Lyall nothing. We will not tell her either. She can be happy in the knowledge that Mistress Rufenna was rescued by m'lord and is being kept safe at Torrey—until we finish dealing with Master Murdoch. The warning is well given. We need to be alert to Master Murdoch's next move against us. I agree with m'lord; we are not yet done with that scoundrel!"

"So we do not send men to Torrey to fetch Mistress Rufenna?" questioned the captain.

Old Walter grinned. "From what I know of the lass, I'd say m'lord is in more danger than she is. Nay, we do not interfere. 'Twill be interesting to see m'lord get himself out of this coil!"

Back at Torrey Castle the master of the house prowled his room like a caged panther. He turned as the door was opened unceremoniously and Elizabeth stood there, calmly meeting his smoldering gaze. He was surprised to see the determined set of her mouth and the question in her eyes. He could not know that only by great concentration was she keeping her limbs from trembling. She had seen Davon in a temper before but this was more than even *she* had believed possible.

"Davon, what happened to that girl?"

Davon forced himself to calm down a bit and shut the door. He indicated a chair but she chose to ignore it and turned to face him in the middle of the room.

"Davon, did you know that she is a Lyall? Who did that to her?"

Davon saw the horrified question in her face and his black scowl lifted. "Are you suggesting I am the villain?"

"I-I don't know!" she stammered. "Davon," she urged, her voice pleading, "tell me what she is doing here and who beat her like that."

"You really think I am responsible?"

"No—no. I don't know what to believe. But, Davon, she *is* a Lyall!"

"Aye, little sister, that is true," Davon confirmed. "She was with her brother, Alexander Lyall." He ground out the name from between clenched teeth. Then he turned and changed the subject. "This is none of your affair, Elizabeth, but I did not beat the girl. She was taken by her cousin, who has designs on Lyall, and mistreated, as you saw. I fetched her away from him and brought her here. Elizabeth, I will not discuss it further. It is none of your concern. What I wish to hear from you now is why *you* are here! You are supposed to be in Linlithgow with the Queen Mother."

Elizabeth shrank under his piercing gaze and went quietly to the chair he had indicated and sat down, bracing herself for his anger. "I came home to see you, Davon, with the Queen Mother's permission. I have a matter to discuss with you."

"What matter is this? I am waiting for a full explanation, Elizabeth."

She twisted her hands nervously in her lap and took a deep breath. In less than a minute I will know, she thought. "I wish to marry Patrick Douglass, son of Sir William of Drumlanrig."

A taut silence followed her words, stretching out until she stirred uneasily.

"No," Davon said firmly. "You will not wed a Douglass."

"Davon . . ."

"It is out of the question, Elizabeth. I have been arranging a marriage for you with Lord Herries, for his second son. Colin Maxwell is a fine lad . . ."

"Davon, I love Patrick and he loves me. His father will agree to the match if you will. I know Colin Maxwell; I have no desire to wed with him, Davon. I agreed to wed Michael Scott because Father desired it. When Michael was killed and then Father died, I thought . . . I hoped . . . Davon, let me have my choice this time! I was willing to do my duty before; let me select my own husband this time."

Davon looked at her for a long moment, and then he hardened his heart against her appeal. Much as he loved Elizabeth and was concerned for her happiness, this was too much.

"Elizabeth, if I could agree, I would. But, my dear, a Douglass! It is out of the question."

"Why? Oh, I know about their troubles, Davon! They were long at war with the King and were forced into exile in England. But things have changed now, Davon! The King is dead; the baby Queen is held safely at Stirling and the Queen Mother and the Regent, Arran, both agreed to allow Lord Angus to come home. The Douglasses are no longer exiles! Sir James is highly respected by the Queen Mother, Davon, and Patrick is accepted at Court."

Davon put another log on the fire and poked it absentmindedly. He knew that Elizabeth's arguments were sound, but they barely scratched the surface of the matter. His first impulse was to tell her that his decision was final and he would discuss it no longer. But she was so lovely sitting there, with her dark hair rumpled and her eyes flashing; she looked so much like his mother that he sat down again and softened his voice.

"Elizabeth, it is not that simple," he began. "When the English King, Henry, released the Scottish lords taken at the battle of Solway Moss and allowed them to return home, Angus, the Red Douglass, was given permission to come with them. You are forgetting, however, that Angus and most of the other Douglasses are in sympathy with England. Angus himself is brother-in-law to the English King! They worked for this marriage proposed between King Henry's son, Edward, and the baby Queen Mary. When it was defeated and the treaty rejected, they continued to work for an alliance with England. My dear, Scotland would not survive if we allied with Henry. Like his forebears, he covets Scotland and will take it any way he can. Failing to get possession of our young Queen—and you must know he tried to get custody of her, by fair means or foul—he will try to take Scotland another way. No, the Hammonds have always stood fast against England. We have served our Stuart kings for centuries and will continue to do so. We will have no part in giving Scotland to Henry of England!"

There! he thought to himself, that will make it clear.

"But Patrick is not . . ."

"He is a Douglass, Elizabeth, and the Earl of Angus is head of their family. Where Angus goes, so go all Douglasses. As long as Angus works for England, we will not ally ourselves with them. I have worked hard in France for an alliance there; they have long been our allies against England and will continue to be so. There is no question of allying with a Douglass, Elizabeth. I'm sorry that you have so chosen, but I will not allow it. If you do not wish to wed Colin Maxwell, then we will seek another young man for you, but you will *not* wed with Patrick Douglass! That is my last word on it."

Elizabeth sat quietly, repressing her tears. It was no more than she had expected. Patrick had warned her it would be thus but, still, one could hope! Somehow, some way, Davon must be made to understand that Patrick did not involve himself with English politics. Davon must be made to change his mind about him.

"You will return to Linlithgow and stay there, Elizabeth. It is dangerous here on the Border with Henry in such a temper over the rejected treaty. He will retaliate, of that you may be sure! We must be prepared. At Linlithgow you are safe, and will remain so. Stay with the Queen and put aside any thoughts of marrying Patrick Douglass. I will order a troop to escort you back tomorrow."

Elizabeth rose and faced him. "No, not yet, Davon, please. There is the girl to be cared for. I have had her removed to my chamber, where I can more easily see to her. She will recover soon, Old Nell says, and then I will go, but I wish to stay for a time."

After considering it, Davon nodded. He could do nothing about Rufenna until she was well again, so he would allow Elizabeth to remain and care for her and then she would return to Linlithgow. He watched Elizabeth leave and close the door. She knew about Alexander Lyall's dastardly conduct and what it implied to find a Lyall here! But it was nothing he was willing to discuss with his sister, particularly his plans for Rufenna. He sighed. Women could certainly complicate matters! He would have to make it clear to Elizabeth that she was not to concern herself or meddle in the matter.

A rapping at the door pulled him out of his musings. He opened it and took a letter from the page.

Oh-ho, a reply already from Lyall, he thought. He threw himself into the chair recently vacated and loosened the seal with his dagger. Moments later he flung the missive into the fire with an oath.

How clever was the answer from Captain Kincaid. It was couched in careful terms, thanking him, in Lady Lyall's name, for the rescue and care of her daughter. It advised him that the captain accepted his hospitality for his mistress and would stand ready to send an escort to bring her home when m'lord judged her able to travel. Until that time the family of Lyall were content to leave her safely in his hands, secure in his care. Davon snorted in amusement, thinking of that phrase. That wily old devil, Walter! His hand showed mightily in this missive, Davon knew. Under the unwritten code of the Border, Davon was now responsible for the safety and well-being of the daughter of Lyall! He would be held accountable for any harm that befell her and now stood to her as a guardian! Clever, he thought, to make it official as they had done. It would successfully tie his hands, branding him as an honorless man if he harmed her. Well, time enough to think around this when Rufenna was well, her bruises healed and her white skin smooth and tempting. He smiled in memory and flung open the door and went down the stairs, shouting for the steward and food and drink.

CHAPTER SIXTEEN

Rufenna lifted her head from the pillow and rolled over. Sunlight lay in a warm bar of gold across the floor, lighting up the room with an amber light. She stretched cautiously, wincing with the pain of movement. Her gaze moved around the room, coming to rest on the girl sitting quietly in the tall chair by the bed. Her lap was filled with colorful strands of silk thread, and seeing the green eyes resting on her, Elizabeth laid aside the linen coif she had been embroidering. Emerald green eyes met dark brown eyes and they surveyed each other thoroughly. Seeing a slight smile touching the older girl's lips, Rufenna relaxed and allowed her own to curve in an answering one.

"How do you feel?"

The girl's voice was cultured and sweet. Rufenna eased herself up on the pillows and instantly Elizabeth was by her side.

"Do not try to move too much right now. Are you still very sore?"

Rufenna settled down carefully and found a more comfortable position. "I think I'm better. How long have I been here?"

"Since the day before yesterday. Don't you remember anything?"

"A little, but things are muddled in my mind. Did Davon bring me here from Galzean?"

"Yes, you're at Torrey Castle now, and safe."

"Who are you?" Rufenna asked, although by now she was sure of the answer.

"Elizabeth Hammond, Davon's sister. You are Rufenna Lyall?"

Rufenna nodded. "You're Isobel's sister? She talked about you. I thought you were a lady-in-waiting to the Queen Mother."

"I am."

Rufenna looked the girl over thoughtfully. She was only two or three years older than Rufenna and looked much like Isobel. The same curly black hair, dark eyes, and sweetly curved mouth. In fact, all the Hammonds that she had met had the same handsome family resemblance.

"Tell me about Isobel," Rufenna said suddenly. "I was at the Abbey with her, you know. I was so sorry when she left. Is she wedded to Ian Hunter? How does she go on now?"

There was a strange silence. Rufenna looked at the stricken girl, taking in the sudden pallor, the hard clasping of the slim hands. She raised herself up in the bed.

"Please, is something amiss?" she persisted. "Is Isobel not well?"

Elizabeth was at a loss as to what to say. It was obvious that this girl did not know about Isobel; and yet, if she did not know, why was she here? She was a Lyall, after all! Elizabeth frowned. There was a mystery here and she was going to get to the bottom of it.

"Isobel is dead, Mistress Lyall. I will tell you of it later but first—"

"Dead? Isobel? What happened to her? She was well when she left the Abbey . . ."

White-faced, Rufenna stared at Elizabeth. She could scarcely believe that gay, laughing Isobel was dead!

"I will tell you of it presently, but first you must tell me why you are here."

Now it was Rufenna's turn to be bewildered. She gazed in confusion at the older girl, wondering what to say, how much to tell her. Yet she was Davon's sister! Was she an enemy too? Perhaps . . . yes, the truth might serve her best, Rufenna decided, might make it possible for her to find out from this girl just what it was all about.

"You know your brother brought me here. He rescued me from my cousin. Lady Elizabeth, there is much here that is puzzling. Do you know why your brother brought me to Torrey instead of taking me back to Lyall?"

Elizabeth shook her head. "No, I have no idea and please, call me Elizabeth. May I call you Rufenna? Good."

"I will tell you all I know and perhaps, between us, we can discover the truth of this," Rufenna said firmly, sitting up and pulling the bedcovers warmly around her. "My brother, Alexander, came to the Abbey to escort me home. On our way, we were attacked by your brother and his men. Alexander was killed and they later captured me. Your brother talked of revenge, of 'an eye for an eye.' I did not know what he meant, nor why there was ill feeling between Alexander and Lord Hammond. Do you know?"

Slowly Elizabeth nodded. Her face was deathly pale but tightly controlled. "Rufenna, six months ago Davon was sent to France on a mission for the Queen. The Queen Mother, I mean," she added, making sure that Rufenna didn't think she meant the tiny babe was giving orders yet. "Three days after he sailed, Isobel left the Abbey with your brother, Alexander. He had met her there when he went to visit you and she fell wildly in love with him. So, she ran away with him. He took her to Knolle and kept her there. As his mistress," Elizabeth said clearly, making sure that Rufenna understood. "Everyone knew. At Court all the talk was of Isobel and your brother. I-I thought he would marry her. She was mad with love for him, else she would never have gone with him. S-she stayed with Alexander those six months at Knolle, while Davon was gone. I wrote to her, imploring her to return to Torrey. She refused. The Queen would not allow me to go to Knolle to reason with her, saying it was Davon's responsibility and he would deal with it when he returned. Then I heard that there was talk of a marriage between your brother and the daughter of Lord Kennedy. It would be a much more advantageous match, of course, for your brother. Mary Kennedy was well dowered and is Lord Kennedy's only child. I couldn't believe it, Rufenna, that your brother would use Isobel in such a way. She believed he would marry her, of course. She told me so in a letter. Then I got another letter from her, the last one she wrote me. She had learned of the talk about Alexander Lyall's alliance with the Kennedys and she had confronted him with it. He had admitted it. Mary Kennedy is her father's heir, he said, and it would be a much richer marriage than if he wedded Isobel. Isobel would have been well dowered but she was not father's heir. It is all Davon's. And he would wed eventually. There was talk, then, about Davon and Janet Gordon. She is at Court, one of the ladies-in-waiting to the Queen, and Davon has been interested in her for a long time."

"She is his mistress?" Rufenna demanded.

Elizabeth flushed slightly. "Yes, at least the gossips say she is. I believe it, for she flaunts her name with his. I don't like her at all," Elizabeth said, wondering why she felt she had to explain Davon to this girl. "A scheming hussy, if ever there was one, I think, but Davon—"

"Davon beds with her," Rufenna interrupted bluntly, wondering why such information hurt.

"I suppose so. Everyone says so and she does not deny it. She thinks to trap him into marriage but I don't think she will succeed. Others have tried but never managed to get him to the priest. So, the next thing we heard was that Isobel was dead, by her own hand."

Rufenna stared, appalled, at Elizabeth. "You don't mean . . ."

"I do. In her letter she said she was with child and that Alexander would not marry her. She could not bear the disgrace. She was ruined and knew it." Elizabeth broke down and sobbed. It was a long moment before she regained her composure, dried her eyes, and continued. "I wrote to Davon but he was already on his way home. A few days later, he reached Edinburgh to see the Queen. I saw him and had to tell him. Rufenna, I have never seen him so— so angry. He did not wait for an audience with the Queen but rode for Lyall in a white-hot rage. Luke Daniels told me that when Davon reached the village near to Lyall, he learned your brother was on his way to St. Whitby's, so Davon followed. He was so furious! I think he was half crazed with anger and grief. He was determined to kill Alexander for what he had done to Isobel. Luke said that Davon caught Alexander and his men on the way back and Alexander was killed. I didn't know about you. You said he captured you? I don't understand this, Rufenna. Please tell me about it."

Rufenna hardly heard the last things Elizabeth said. She was deeply immersed in sorrow for Isobel and could think of nothing but her lonely deed that led to a burial, unblessed by Mother Church, a burial apart, not even in hallowed ground. Rufenna, steeped in the rules of the Church, believed that even now Isobel was in purgatory and would be there for a long time. Her hopes for heaven were remote. I will pray for her, Rufenna thought. Then she was brought back to the present and the horrifying facts that had led Isobel to suicide. She stared blindly at the coverlet, scarcely knowing what to think. Alexander and Isobel! It explained so much! Isobel's dreamy state, her mysterious departure that the nuns would not talk of. And Willy! He knew but could not tell her! Her mother, of course, also knew, and that was why she had not been overly surprised at Davon's attack on them. An eye for an eye, he had said, she remembered. Now she understood precisely what he meant. Her brother had flaunted his sister before the world and ruined her. Davon was going to extract his revenge on the Lyalls by doing the same. He would keep her here at Torrey, keep her as his mistress, until he tired of her. Or until—who was it?—Lady Janet Gordon talked him into marriage. Then she, Rufenna, would be ruined. Her betrothal would be at an end, her chances of marriage over. She shuddered.

"Rufenna," Elizabeth prompted.

"They caught me that night," Rufenna said dully, frightened again by the seemingly hopeless position in which she found herself. "They took me to Hammond Tower and he . . ." She broke off, her glance meeting that questioning dark gaze. A warm flush spread over her cheeks and her gaze fell. Elizabeth's eyes widened in understanding and she gasped.

"Rufenna, he—didn't hurt you, did he?"

Rufenna blushed more deeply. "N-not exactly, but he . . . I didn't understand *why*," she added, shying away from telling Elizabeth the details. Their quick meeting of eyes had told her that Elizabeth understood what had happened at Hammond Tower and was stunned by the fact. "I had done nothing to the Hammonds," Rufenna continued, "and couldn't imagine why . . . I knew it must be Alexander but I never, never thought of Isobel! Oh, Holy Virgin, what am I going to do? You know what he intends, don't you? He told me! An eye for an eye, he said, making it clear he intended to bring me here and keep me openly. He still intends to do that!"

"If so, why didn't he bring you here before now?" Elizabeth suddenly demanded.

"I escaped. I got home to Lyall and then my father died. My cousin Murdoch arrived . . ." Rufenna told the horrified Elizabeth about Murdoch and what had happened to her at Galzean.

"But, Rufenna, he rescued you! Davon, I mean. He brought you here and—"

"And means to keep me here! Elizabeth, I will not stay here and let the world think I am his mistress! I had nothing to do with Alexander and Isobel and he will not make *me* pay for it! If he wants a mistress, he can go fetch Lady Janet! What am I going to do?"

Elizabeth, repelled yet fascinated by this recital of her brother's sins, sat back and considered it. She could not help but be struck by his determination to bring Rufenna back to Torrey. He must still intend to carry out his plan, she admitted, and then suddenly she grinned.

"Rufenna, think! God's teeth! No wonder he was so angry when he arrived and found me here! How can he flaunt you to the world as his mistress while I'm here? I'm an adequate chaperone, you know. You have only to say that you were here with me! Besides, he can do nothing at all until you are better. Even Davon wouldn't force you to . . . well, he wouldn't! Not while you're so ill."

Rufenna sat up abruptly and stared at Elizabeth. "You're right! As long as I'm ill . . ."

They looked at each other and Rufenna smiled. "Elizabeth, are you willing to help me? I know he's your brother, but . . ."

"Yes, he's my brother," Elizabeth said firmly, "but I don't approve of what he's doing. He should not make you pay for what Alexander did. I mean, you already have. Oh! Rufenna, he won't hurt you, I'm sure he won't. If you could have seen his face when he carried you in here! Holy Mary, he was fit to murder someone, your cousin most likely."

"Only because I was taken to Galzean and beaten," Rufenna reasoned, refusing to believe what Elizabeth was implying. "He does not care about me, Elizabeth. Only, he thinks I am his for a time now, until *he* tires of me. I expect he was angry because he thought if anyone was to give me a beating, he was entitled to do it."

Elizabeth protested that. "No, I'm sure you're wrong about that. Rufenna, he's not like that! He wouldn't, *couldn't* beat a woman as you were beaten. Not Davon! He might, well, he might . . ." She stumbled to a stop, trying to think of a tactful way to discuss it.

Rufenna saved her the trouble. "He might rape me but he wouldn't beat me?"

"R-rape? Rufenna, he didn't! I mean, oh, dear, I don't know what I mean."

Rufenna looked at Elizabeth's flushed cheeks and suppressed a smile. She knew perfectly well what Elizabeth didn't say. Naturally she did not want to believe her brother was capable of raping a woman.

"He did," Rufenna said clearly. "It was against my will!"

"But you said he didn't hurt you!"

Rufenna flushed painfully, seeing the trap too late. "Well, he didn't, Elizabeth, but he did force himself on me! It wasn't like Murdoch, yet . . . I mean, this is not . . . not . . . We won't talk of it! He *did* and he intends to continue doing so if you don't help me get away from him!"

Elizabeth, although older, was much more innocent. Her mind teemed with confused thoughts as she wondered how Rufenna could have been *raped* by Davon and yet lie there and maintain that he had not hurt her. She had always heard that being raped was, well, different from that. She was burning to ask Rufenna if it had really been so bad, if she had *really* hated it. Davon was so, well, damnably attractive; even his own sister knew that! Elizabeth's impressions of being raped tallied a lot more with the treatment Rufenna had received from Murdoch than the girl's admissions concerning her time with Davon at Hammond. Elizabeth did want to hear more about that night at Hammond but refrained from asking. She was sure Rufenna wouldn't tell her any more, and so she was left with a number of unanswered questions. She could not dispute Rufenna's insistence that Davon intended to keep her here and continue to, well, force himself upon her. He had practically confirmed that to her himself. It was the *way* it was being handled that puzzled her. He wasn't expecting to find Elizabeth at Torrey, that was true; still, he could never have had the intention of bedding Rufenna while she was ill. He would know that he would have to wait.

"Rufenna, as long as you're ill, he'll let me stay. He agreed to that. He said I could stay and nurse you until you were better. Then I must return to Linlithgow."

"So I have to stay ill, don't I, until we think of something," Rufenna mused. "You're sure he said that? Then I just won't get better."

Elizabeth grinned. "That will work, I think, for a time at least. That's what we need, Rufenna—time. We've got to have a plan to get you away. Luke Daniels will never allow you to ride out, even with

me. He'll have his orders by now. We'll have to think
of something."

When Elizabeth went down to supper, Rufenna ate
the light meal brought up by a serving girl and settled back against the pillows. She had to think of
a way, she thought sleepily, easing her bruised back
carefully against the bed. She was not badly injured,
but did he know that? How much of her injuries
had he seen? she wondered. The beating had left
black, swollen welts across her back and buttocks but
they were already eased by the salve. The swelling
had gone down and the bruises were not nearly as
painful as they had been. Her other bruises would
fade in a few more days and then what? Elizabeth
would be sent away. . . . She stirred in the bed,
realizing that they did not have much time. He would
not be too patient, she felt, knowing his temper. He
would not be fooled for long.

Rufenna, feeling herself safe for the moment, dozed,
waking slightly at the sound of the closing of the
door. Had Elizabeth returned from supper already?
A hand touched her forehead and she opened her
eyes. Davon stood by the bed, thoughtfully surveying
her.

"No fever now," he murmured, his quick gaze
scanning her face. Healthy color bloomed in her
cheeks and her lips were no longer so swollen and
bruised. Instinctively Rufenna pulled up the bedcovers to her chin but he ignored that.

"Let me see your back," he said quietly, taking
away the covers with a firm hand.

She shook her head nervously and pressed deeper
into the feather mattress. His dark eyes met her green
ones and she read determination there.

"Roll over and let me see your back, Rufenna. Do
not put me to the trouble of making you do so," he
added coolly.

Rufenna knew he would. With a set mouth she

rolled over and stiffened as she felt his hands drawing the nightshift up to expose her back.

"Davon, what are you doing?" Elizabeth demanded, coming into the room.

"Looking at her back," he said calmly. "I wish to see for myself how she is healing."

Elizabeth stared at him in frustration. "She is still quite ill, Davon, and it is not proper . . ."

He turned and met her indignant gaze with an amused glint in his eye. Knowing his sister, he was quite sure that she had had the entire story from Rufenna by now. "Proper, dear sister? I have seen her naked back before," he said deliberately, dragging the linen nightshirt up to Rufenna's shoulder blades.

Elizabeth gasped at this frank statement and fumed. "Davon," she protested, "please leave her alone. I am caring for her!"

Davon ignored his flushed and protesting sister and proceeded to inspect every inch of Rufenna's rigid back and softly curving hips. "It is better," he murmured. He laid a gentle finger on one of the dark streaks and pressed gently. "Does it still hurt?"

She winced and nodded, her face buried in the pillows. The touch of that warm, firm hand on her back was stirring emotions she was determined to suppress. She felt his hand lift and then slide gently down the curve of her spine. She trembled under his touch and knew full well he was aware of it. Then the covers were drawn up over her naked back and he turned to Elizabeth.

"Undoubtedly, she is better. The bruises are fading nicely now and she has no fever. I will send Sim to move her to her own chamber. She no longer needs your nursing, Elizabeth, and you need your rest."

"But, Davon . . ."

He strode to the door, disregarding her protests,

and Elizabeth stared after him. So much for fooling Davon!

"Elizabeth, what am I to do?" Rufenna gasped, seeing the door close firmly behind the tall, dark lord. She sat up, straightening her nightshift, and looked at her ally "He means it. He could see I am better."

"I don't know," admitted Elizabeth thoughtfully, sitting down by the bed and chewing her lip thoughtfully. "Once he has moved you into your own chamber . . ."

"He will send you back to Linlithgow soon. Mayhap tomorrow!"

Elizabeth shook her head. "Not tomorrow, Rufenna. He would have told me so that I could prepare for the journey. Not before the day after that. We don't have much time," she worried.

"No," sighed Rufenna. "We don't. We must think of a way."

Later that night, lying in the large bed in the guest chamber given to her, Rufenna stared with unseeing eyes into the dark. He had wasted no time in having her moved. Sim had arrived shortly after Davon's departure and had silently carried her to the new room. She felt quite sure it was near Davon's bedchamber. It was at the other end of the hall from Elizabeth, far enough away from her that she would be powerless to interfere if Davon . . .

Rufenna rolled over carefully onto her stomach and thought hard. Somehow she had to get away! The sound of a door opening brought her head around, and she sat up, peering into the darkness. The door to the room was still shut! Another slight sound sent her head swiveling around, searching for its source. A door had opened in the wall, and she could see the flicker of a candle. Davon walked in and put the candle down on the table beside the bed.

"W-where did you come from?" she stammered.

He gestured at the open door in the wall. "My

bedchamber is through there. This was my mother's room," he added, sitting down on the side of the bed.

Which, she thought, explains the door in the wall! It joined the two master bedchambers. Rufenna flicked a glance at him, sitting so closely beside her on the bed. He wore a woolen dressing gown and her heart began to hammer.

"I came to see if you need anything," he said quietly. "Did Elizabeth put fresh salve on your back?"

Before she thought, Rufenna shook her head and then realized what she had done. "Oh, yes, I mean . . ."

His glance lit on the china pot of salve on a table by the door and he got up and went to get it. "Turn over."

"Really, m'lord, I don't need—"

"Turn over," he repeated quietly. "I am only going to put this on your bruises."

She sighed and rolled over, stiffening as he pulled up the nightshift for the second time that night. She winced elaborately, affecting more discomfort than she really felt, as he smoothed on the salve. If he thought she was still too ill . . .

"There, that should help it. You are healing nicely." He wiped his hands on a linen towel and tossed it over the side of a chair. Rufenna hastily pulled down her nightshift and turned back over, avoiding his gaze. "Are you in much pain, Rufenna?"

"Yes," she said quickly. "I am. It still hurts quite a lot."

He looked down at her and reached out a hand to touch her lips. "I thought I once warned you not to lie to me, Rufenna! It is sore, yes; but you are not in great pain. What's the matter?" he murmured, leaning down and letting his lips touch the corner of her mouth. "Are you afraid to get well?"

She was but did not think it prudent to say so.

She remained silent, turning her face away from his lips. "I want to go home, m'lord."

"In time," he said softly, his mouth caressing her ear. "When I say you may."

"I want to go now. My mother needs me."

"I am sorry to hear that. It is out of the question. Elizabeth leaves the day after tomorrow and then there will be just you and me."

She swallowed hard at the implications of this information and knew perfectly well what pleasure he was taking in baiting her. Rufenna gritted her teeth and tried to ignore that warm mouth teasing her ear.

His hand caught her chin and turned her face around. She opened her lips to protest, but he covered them, silencing her. She pressed back against the bed, trying to get away from his hard, warm body. His hand left her chin and slid down her shoulder to her breast. His caressing fingers pressed on a bruise and she winced. He lifted his head and looked hard at her.

"No," he agreed, sitting up. "You are still sore, aren't you? I can wait a few days and Elizabeth will shortly be gone. Then we'll resume this . . . conversation."

Rufenna shook her head. "I will not be used by you, m'lord. I learned of Isobel and Alexander and protest that it has nothing to do with me. I will not pay for my brother's crimes," she added, throwing caution to the winds. Better to have this out once and for all. "It is unjust of you to think I should. Besides, you have had your revenge of me. What more do you want?"

He looked down at her, his black eyes glittering. "I want you, my little red-haired witch! I want you here, for my convenience, until I tire of you. Then, and only then, will you go home."

"No! I won't do it! Anything you get from me

will be by force! What kind of pleasure will that be for you?"

He leaned forward, capturing her face again, imprisoning her head between his hands. His mouth was hard and forceful, demanding a response from her, and stubbornly she withheld it. One hand was loosened from her hair and slid down her body, caressing her stomach. She tightened her muscles against him, willing her treacherous body not to respond to him. It wasn't fair! she cried silently. He covered her face and throat with kisses, his hands coaxing, caressing, tantalizing her. She forced her limbs to remain stiff and cold, to reject the flood of warmth surging through her. She tried to concentrate on the slight soreness of her bruises, exaggerating this discomfort in her mind to oppose the growing heat spreading through her loins. His hands grew more urgent, demanding, and she trembled violently under them. He could feel her inner struggle growing, her fight against giving in to the hot pleasure of surrendering to him.

"By force, is it?" he murmured, his lips nibbling at her ear. "If that is so, you must like force," he added.

"No, stop," she cried, thrusting him away and rolling onto her stomach. Tears poured down her cheeks, tears of strain and fright, and she struggled against his hands as he tried to turn her over again. "Leave me alone, please! I can't . . . I won't be used like this. . . . Davon, please. I am n-not well! Leave me!"

He stared at the tears coursing down her cheeks and felt his resolve weaken. He could not bring himself to force an admission of desire from her. Her body had told him what he wanted to know; in her stubborn determination she would not admit it with her mind, yet. He touched her wet cheek, thinking she must be weaker than he had thought to give in to tears. Well, he would be patient for another few days. She would be stronger then, less emotional. His finger stroked her damp cheek and he rose, pulling the dressing gown more closely around him.

"If you need anything during the night, Rufenna, just call out. I'll be in the next room and will leave the door open. Sleep well, my dear."

Rufenna turned her face into the pillow, torn between anger at him and at herself. She must force herself to be stronger, more determined. She had to resist his attraction, she told herself. It would be so wonderfully easy to relax, to melt into his arms, to let him warm her and love her. She swallowed the lump in her throat and reminded herself of his other woman, Lady Janet Gordon. He didn't need her, Rufenna, except as an instrument of revenge. He didn't care about her. He was only concerned with carrying out his plan, no matter what *she* suffered. No, she must get away. If she stayed here, with him . . . Rufenna felt a cold chill touch her as she realized how vulnerable she was to him. How easy it would be to accept what he offered, for as long as it lasted. It wasn't fair, her heart cried, for he was the enemy! It wasn't fair he could arouse such violent emotions in her, could reduce her to quivering with longing with a touch, a caress. Disaster could be the only result of that course of action, she knew. She reminded herself of what had happened to Isobel, who had cast aside discretion to follow her lover. Isobel, ruined, carrying an illegitimate child, finally rejected for a richer heiress. No, Rufenna decided, it will not happen to me! I will escape him if I have to tie the bedclothes together and climb over the wall. Death would be preferable to the fate that awaited her if she stayed with him, she told herself firmly. She quelled the rebellious corner of her mind that questioned that wild statement. She would trick him; she would defeat him. She was a Lyall! She would not let him humble her. She crept out of bed and felt her way to where she thought the door in the wall was located, closed it quietly, and placed a chair against the stop, knowing full well it was a futile effort. However, the action made her feel a little more secure, and on that note she crawled under the covers, settled herself comfortably, and slept, to dream of dark eyes and a tender, coaxing mouth.

CHAPTER SEVENTEEN

Temporary reprieve came with the morning. After breakfast Elizabeth rushed into the room bearing news.

"Davon has left, Rufenna! He had to ride to Hammond for a few days and won't be back until the day after tomorrow at the earliest. It might even be longer!"

"You don't have to leave now?" Rufenna asked, sitting up in the bed and staring excitedly at Elizabeth. "It will give us more time."

Elizabeth sank down on the bed. "Well, no. He said that I was to leave tomorrow, early in the morning. I heard him tell Luke to see that the escort was prepared. But he won't be here today or tonight, so mayhap we can think of something. You must be gone from here before I leave."

Rufenna sat back against the pillows and tried to think. "You know Torrey Castle, Elizabeth, I don't. Is there any way out? I don't want to climb over the wall unless there is no other way."

"C-climb over the wall! Rufenna, you couldn't! It's hundreds of feet down. Torrey stands on a ridge and the cliff drops straight down. It's only flat at the base of the wall at the front, where the guards would see you."

"Oh, God! Is there no other way out?"

"Not that I know of and I know every inch of Torrey. Oh, if only you could leave with me!"

A sudden gleam lit Rufenna's green eyes. "Do you have your maid with you?"

Elizabeth, puzzled, nodded. "Marie will leave with me in the morning."

"No!" Rufenna said suddenly, bouncing on the bed. "*I* will leave with you and she will take my place in this bed."

Elizabeth's dark eyes widened and then she started laughing. "He'd murder us, or want to! To come back and find Marie!" She began to giggle, seeing her plain maid ensconced in their mother's bed when he returned.

"Elizabeth, will you do it?"

"Yes, of course I will. How shall we work it, Rufenna? Andrew would soon know, or the maid who brings your food."

Rufenna thought about it, preparing a plan. "No, you said you would leave early in the morning. You and your maid, Marie, will prepare to go. Andrew will send up my breakfast, which I will eat here. Then I'll tell the maid who brings the tray and takes it back to the kitchens that I am feeling unwell and am going to sleep. You will come in to bid me farewell, bringing Marie. Let's see, she'll have to change places with me. Elizabeth, it has to work; I know it will. We'll have to contrive it so that you are mounted and ready to ride when your maid rushes out to mount her horse. If I were to stay in the courtyard for very long, someone would be bound to notice that I look nothing like Marie. You'll have to keep the captain's attention on you, Elizabeth, so that he doesn't look closely at me. We'll have to be very careful on the trip. It is fortunate that the men do not know Marie or me. The men escorting us must not know who I am or they would bring us back. Oh, I'm sure it will work. They won't miss me for hours, too late to come after us. How early could we leave? If it is very early, still dark, I mean, it would be easier."

"Leave Luke to me," Elizabeth said firmly. "Davon left orders we were to leave Torrey tomorrow but he did not say what time. I'll tell Luke I wish to make an early start so that we can reach Edinburgh by midday the day after. They could still come after us," she added doubtfully. "Well, we'll have to persuade the men to go another way to Edinburgh, different from the usual road. I'll think on it and decide what would suit us best. Yes, it will work. Could you be poorly today too? So they won't be suspicious?"

Rufenna could. Throughout the long day she lay in bed, chafing at her inactivity, ready to rise and get away from Torrey. She would never escape from here while Davon's observant eye was on her, so it had to be now.

While Rufenna lay in bed, alternating between confidence and terror and wishing the day over, Elizabeth was having her own troubles. She returned to her room after her talk with Rufenna and summoned Marie. As she laid out the plans for the morrow, she watched with apprehension as Marie's expression changed from puzzlement to amazement, and then to shocked disbelief and obstinacy.

"Nay, I won't do it, mistress. 'Tis wrong to fool m'lord."

Elizabeth had no intention of explaining to Marie why this deception was necessary. In her simple peasant fashion she would probably think that Mistress Rufenna was making a great deal of fuss about nothing. Any girl in Scotland should consider herself fortunate to have taken the eye of the handsome Lord Hammond.

"Marie, you will do as I say or I will discharge you."

"Nay, mistress!" cried Marie. "You wouldn't be so cruel."

"I will and you can return to that hovel you came from." Elizabeth felt guilty at the savage way she was attacking the maid, but she knew full well how much Marie enjoyed the small luxuries of being a lady's maid and how she would hate to give them up.

"I'll go to m'lord, I will!"

"He is not here, Marie. That's why the deception will work if only you will help. There now, don't cry. Davon will not be angry with you, I promise, and I will send for you as soon as I get to Edinburgh."

"Well, mistress, I will do your bidding, but I think little of being a party to such."

Marie left and Elizabeth sat down, breathing a sigh of relief.

The long day and even longer night passed, and after a quick breakfast Rufenna sent away the unsuspecting maid, asking not to be disturbed until late afternoon. Elizabeth came to say good-bye and Rufenna bounced out of bed, not even conscious of her still slightly sore bruises. She felt brimming with life and excitement. The still-protesting Marie was quickly undressed, ruthlessly thrust into Rufenna's nightshift, and put into her bed. Rufenna glanced at the dress Elizabeth was carrying.

" 'Twas my mother's, Rufenna. It should fit you. She was a tall woman, too."

Rufenna donned the dark dress and then the heavy enveloping cloak. They hid her vibrant hair under a starched coif and pulled the hood of the cloak up over that. For the rest they would have to count on the darkness of the overcast day to aid them. Elizabeth handed Rufenna the jewel case that Marie would normally carry and went out to start the prepara-

tions for departure. Rufenna waited in the room with
the muttering Marie and then lurked in the hall,
listening to the growing bustle down in the courtyard. When she heard Elizabeth's clear and louder
than usual voice inquiring where Marie could possibly
be, she quietly went down the steps and out to the
waiting horse. Luke Daniels, kept occupied by a conversation with Elizabeth, barely gave the cloaked
figure a glance. Rufenna accepted the help of the
trooper to mount, keeping her face turned away in
the still gloomy courtyard. Dawn was just breaking
as they rode out and headed north, to Edinburgh.
Their way should take them down the well-worn paths
by Melrose Abbey and Galashiels, past Crichton
Castle.

"We normally stop for the night near Lauder,"
Elizabeth said to Rufenna as they made their way
down the rocky path. "We will have to change the
route somehow, or Davon could find us. I will tell
the men that we wish to rest at Stow instead, with
Lord Steels. I know his daughter well, Rufenna, and
the men should agree. By swinging toward Stow instead of going toward Lauder, any troop coming after
us will be on a different road. It's the best I could
think of."

Rufenna agreed easily to it, determined to put the
most distance possible between Torrey and herself.
She said prayerful thanks that Sim had not been
given the task of escorting Elizabeth to Edinburgh.
He knew her too well and would be bound to scent
a trick. These men had only seen her once that she
knew of, on the night of the raid into England. They
would not be as likely to look for a trick, nor as
quick to recognize her. And, for all they knew, she
was still abed, moaning from the beating. She must
keep her hair covered at all times, for it was that
which would give her away.

As the day passed, they crossed out of the Border,

leaving Teviotdale behind and riding into the Southern Uplands. With each mile Rufenna relaxed a bit more, amusing herself on the journey by imagining Davon's rage when he discovered their substitution. She hoped that Elizabeth was correct in thinking that Davon would not vent his anger on poor Marie. After all, the lass was only following her mistress's orders. Elizabeth had no doubts of it at all. He would be furiously angry, of course, but at them, not at Marie.

The men were persuaded to break the journey at Stow, finding argument with Elizabeth a profitless business. She had pointed out, gently but firmly, that their task was to see them safely to Edinburgh and they could please take them there by the route that the Lady Elizabeth Hammond desired! Rufenna was kept well out of sight at Stow, once Lord Steel's daughter had been let into the secret, and the unsuspecting troop of men rode out the next morning still with no idea that they escorted their master's intended mistress farther and farther away from his bed.

By the time the outskirts of Edinburgh were reached, Rufenna and Elizabeth had worked out a plan. Somewhere in that vast spreading pile of gray stone that was Holyrood Palace was the Queen Mother, briefly in town on State business, and also John, Rufenna's brother. Once inside, they could take refuge in Elizabeth's room until Davon's men had returned to Torrey. Then Rufenna could make her curtsy to her Queen. Mary of Guise would welcome her, she knew, as Sir Ewen's daughter. She could explain that she had come to bear her brother company for a short visit, before returning home to Lyall.

They entered the city unchallenged and Rufenna was hastily smuggled up to Elizabeth's room, away from the prying eyes that might notice her and cause word to sift back to Davon's men.

She waited, her heart beating rapidly, for John to enter the room.

"Rufenna, h-how did you get here?" he exclaimed as he ran across the room to hug her.

"I decided to come and see how you are doing," she answered, "and Lady Elizabeth invited me to come with her."

"Many thanks to you, Lady Elizabeth," said John, acknowledging her. Then he turned back to Rufenna. "Did Captain Kincaid succeed in taking the castle? What became of Cousin Murdoch?"

"Our plan did well, John, and Murdoch was made to understand that he was not welcome at Lyall," said Rufenna, with something less than the truth.

"What did you do to yourself?" John asked. "Your lip is swollen."

"Oh, nothing much. A silly fall."

"There is much to see, Rufenna. Come, let me show you."

Elizabeth interrupted. "If you will excuse me, I must go and leave a message for someone. And, Rufenna, I would advise you to rest. After all, you have had a fall and a very long ride."

Rufenna smiled her thanks to Elizabeth. She knew that the someone referred to was Patrick Douglass. On the long, hard ride and overnight stay Rufenna had learned of Elizabeth's great love for Patrick and Davon's stubborn refusal to allow them to marry. Rufenna was very grateful that Elizabeth mentioned the fact that she should rest. It was essential that she keep out of sight until the Hammond troop went home.

After Elizabeth left, John began to talk about how much he enjoyed city life. "But I still prefer the horses, Rufenna. The stablemaster here is not so cross and abrupt as James at home and he said I know as much about horses as anyone he has ever met!"

"When I have rested a bit I will be delighted for you to take me everywhere and show me everything," Rufenna said, hugging him briefly.

For the two days that the Hammond troopers rested their horses and partook lustily of the varied pleasures of the capital city of Scotland, Rufenna stayed out of sight with John. In the short time that John had been in Edinburgh, he had matured at an amazing rate. Rufenna was relieved to discover that her decision to send John to Edinburgh had benefited him immensely. He was changing rapidly from the baby of the family, much coddled by his devoted mother, into a spirited young man—a Lyall!

At last Elizabeth came in to tell Rufenna that Davon's men had departed and she was now free to move around the palace, to meet the Queen, to mingle with the other ladies-in-waiting.

Rufenna had been whisked upstairs in such a rush that she had no opportunity to look at the palace. Now, clad in a borrowed dress of Elizabeth's, she nearly stumbled and fell down the wide staircase, as she tried to see everything at once. Unaccustomed to such luxury and opulence, she clutched the banister in astonishment, thinking that even banisters were a rare thing. They did not have them at the Abbey, Lyall Castle, or Torrey!

The Great Hall, to which they were descending, had such a variety of wall hangings that the cold heavy stones of the walls were nearly hidden. The hangings were of velvet, of colors Rufenna had seen only in sunsets and rainbows, never in woven cloth. The fringe that hung from these tapestries was nearly a foot long. Where tapestries and hangings were absent, scenes were painted upon the walls, scenes much larger than life, hunt scenes interspersed with battle scenes. Battle axes and claymores were hung upon the walls, as well as bows and arrows. Sconces filled with glowing candles and ornate chandeliers brightened the room. At one end was a fireplace large enough to roast a whole ox. The ceilings were divided into squares and ornately carved. All the doors Rufenna had seen thus far were carved elaborately and so heavy she could barely push them open.

Before she could begin to absorb all this splendor and beauty, Elizabeth touched her arm and made a slight motion. Rufenna followed her gaze to the raised dais that held the carved and red velvet throne, upon which sat the Queen Mother of all Scotland.

Mary of Guise was a tall woman, but was delicate and graceful. Wideset dark eyes, a straight Grecian nose, and a softly curved mouth, set in a round face with a decidedly sculptured chin—all these features made it a pleasing face. She was dressed in black velvet with the fashionably lifted sleeves at the shoulders, a style that made her look more broad-shouldered than she was. The sleeves were decorated with embroidery and jewels and were very full above the elbow and tapered down to sheer ruffled cuffs. She wore rings on two fingers of each hand. The neck of the dress was square and set near the shoulders, and the white sheer material of the cuffs formed the insert across her breast. Her cap, of black velvet also and quite plain, was smaller than that of anyone else in the room and had a short headdress. As they crossed the room to the throne, Elizabeth whispered to Rufenna that the new headdress must be the newest fashion to come over from France because Mary of Guise led the capital in the latest innovation.

"And many of the girls here will stay up half the night changing their headdresses so they will look more like the one Her Majesty is wearing," concluded Elizabeth.

After the introduction, at which the Queen cordially but briefly took Rufenna's hand, she began to speak. "So you are Sir Ewen's daughter. You favor him, as does young John. What a loyal subject he was to us. We have grieved his untimely death, although it is God's will," she said in her delightful French accent, crossing herself as she spoke.

Rufenna, after a glance at Elizabeth, hastily crossed herself and thanked Queen Mary for her cordial reception of John and herself.

"Now, my child," said the Queen, "Elizabeth must introduce you to my ladies."

The two girls curtsied again and moved toward the ladies, who were eyeing Rufenna with avid curiosity. Elizabeth introduced her as her dear friend, Rufenna Lyall, and the ladies were pleased to accept her, with one exception—Lady Janet Gordon. Rufenna instantly remembered her as the woman Elizabeth had mentioned as being in love with Davon.

The tall, richly curved girl had black hair and eyes to match. Her high cheekbones and generously curved mouth combined to make her a striking-looking woman. Her red dress was daringly cut to show a white, firm bosom. She was as fashionably dressed as the Queen and flaunted more jewels. She took an instant dislike to the newcomer. The flutterings of the girls would be as nothing once the young men spotted this redhead, thought Janet Gordon with hate and envy. She swept up to Rufenna and glanced at her coolly and with studied indifference.

"I wonder at Elizabeth Hammond's acceptance of the family that murdered her sister . . ." said Janet, her dark eyes filled with dislike.

"For God's sake, Janet, where will your tongue lead you?" snapped an older girl.

Before Rufenna could speak, Elizabeth was at her side.

"Keep quiet, Janet, lest you say something that cannot be excused," Elizabeth said quietly.

Janet flashed her dark eyes fearlessly. "She is the sister of that blackguard, Alexander Lyall, who sullied—"

"Nay, no more. We all know the story and say it once I will and there's an end to it. She is my friend, and Davon's also," Elizabeth added pointedly.

As Janet flounced off in a temper, she was heard to remark that when next she saw Davon Hammond she would question his idea of friends. She said his taste had altered deplorably since she last saw him.

Rufenna knew immediately the cause of her antagonism. Janet Gordon cared not a whit about who befriended whom as long as her place with Davon was secure. Instinctively she realized that Rufenna threatened her. She and Elizabeth exchanged glances and when Lady Janet was safely out of earshot, Elizabeth whispered, giggling, "She would have a screaming fit of rage if she knew Davon had carried you off, Rufenna. He's never carried *her* off!"

"Nor had any need to, I warrant," sniffed Rufenna. "She is probably quite available to m'lord."

"Shhh," cautioned Elizabeth. Just then the outer doors were flung open and a dozen or more young nobles came into the Great Hall. The first thing they did was to pay their respects to their Queen, then they warmed themselves at the roaring fire. After that they strolled casually over to chat with the ladies and paired off for dancing or cards or whatever the entertainment of the evening proved to be.

Rufenna glanced from the young men to Elizabeth and, at the transformation of her face, knew that Patrick Douglass was among the arrivals. Elizabeth's face, heart-shaped and beautiful, now glowed with a passion that Rufenna could only guess at. The look on her face told the world that she loved and was loved in return. Before Rufenna could move, a young man separated himself from the others at the fire and came toward them.

"Ah, so this is Rufenna, whose praises you have been singing, Elizabeth. You have not exaggerated, my love. She is beautiful," Patrick said, looking at Elizabeth.

Elizabeth laughed comfortably, as befits a woman who knows that Helen of Troy could appear among them and Patrick Douglass would have eyes for no one but herself. She placed a small hand on his sleeve and he covered it possessively with his own hand, smiling down at her, a smile of such warmth that Rufenna turned away and glanced down, embarrassed at being a witness to such intimacy.

Rufenna looked at this red-haired giant and spoke cordially to him and then decided to acknowledge the three young gentlemen who were now with them, clamoring for an introduction. It was obvious that Patrick and Elizabeth had eyes for no one but each other and wished to be alone, as alone as two people could be in a hall full of others. As she allowed the three lords to introduce themselves, she heard Patrick murmur, "Don't be cast down, love. We will find a way to make your brother change his mind!"

When next she looked for them, Rufenna found that Patrick and Elizabeth had disappeared from the Great Hall.

On the third day the Queen and her retinue returned to Linlithgow Castle. Rufenna said a sad farewell to Elizabeth and was an unwilling witness to the poignant and tender farewell between Elizabeth and Patrick. She wondered if it would help if she talked to Davon about Patrick but she hastily dismissed the thought as quickly as it came. With luck she would never see Davon Hammond again to discuss anything with him. Then she wondered at the odd, blank feeling that caught her heart at the thought of Davon going out of her life forever. Immediately she gave herself a mental shake and, waving a last good-bye, went in search of John.

The middle-aged tutor, into whose care John had been placed by the Queen Mother, admitted that his charge could almost certainly be found in the stables. While they waited for John to answer the summons sent by the tutor, Rufenna listened to a very satisfactory report on her young brother. She was pleased that he was doing well with his studies and appeared to be settling down to life at Court so well. John, learning that his sister was to move into the rooms which had been given to him, was delighted and cajoled permission from his tutor to suspend his studies for the next few days so that he could show Rufenna about the town.

Although he had grown in experience and maturity overnight, there was no one his own age around and he was pleased to expound his knowledge to Rufenna. She had already decided that she must have some clothes. She had arrived at Torrey wearing a blanket and since then had borrowed from Elizabeth. Elizabeth had kindly lent her a few gowns but Rufenna looked with distaste upon the hand-me-downs. Elizabeth was not as tall as she and the dresses, although fashionable and not worn, were somewhat skimpy. If she was going to stay in Edinburgh for a week or more, she would have to have clothes to wear. Besides, there was little wearable in her own room at Lyall either.

John proudly escorted her, and after the proper introductions to the merchants, she found them more than willing to extend credit to Mistress Lyall. They had been pleased to serve Alexander and Sir Ewen in the past and she was welcomed. John, as soon as the introductions and business were finished, grew increasingly bored and restive as Rufenna tried to make a decision of what to order. The array of fabric, ribbons, and lace almost overwhelmed her. Because of her need for haste, the dresses had to be kept simple. The dressmaker promised some for day after tomorrow, at least the green silk and pale blue brocade. She would have to wait for the others. The ones that could not be ready before her departure from Edinburgh were to be sent on to Lyall when they were completed. Rufenna picked out green satin slippers to match the dress and insisted upon carrying them with her. She had longed for fancy footwear for so many years that she intended to wear them tonight, although it would have to be with Elizabeth's green velvet dress. They were too beautiful to wait for a ball to wear them.

After the shopping she put herself in John's hands and they spent hours walking through Edinburgh. Rufenna had lived at the castle until she went to the Abbey and she was completely unfamiliar with city life. The crowds, the bustle, the young men on horseback, the litters carrying great ladies, the beggars—all tended to overawe her at first. She noticed that John appeared to be entirely at home and she modeled her behavior on his.

"You know, Edinburgh was named by the Gauls; it means *slope* or *hill*," explained John as they panted to the top of a steep hill.

"Now, how would I know that?" retorted Rufenna breathlessly. "But it's well named."

"What *did* they teach you at the Abbey?" asked John.

"Nothing that was so frivolous," giggled Rufenna, thinking of the utter dullness of sewing and churning and the eternal prayers. Then she remembered Isobel and sobered up a bit and said a little prayer for her that her sojourn in purgatory would be short.

"This is the Canongate, where the hostels and some town houses are. It is so named because the road was used by the monks. Gate means *way*," John added.

The road that impressed Rufenna the most was Cowgate, an inelegant name for the road that held the residences of the very wealthy: the town houses of the Douglasses, the Hamiltons, the Stuarts, whose lords wished to be comfortable when they came to Edinburgh to deal in business or pleasure. Rufenna looked at the deep glen of Cowgate and then looked up on the north side, through sunny gardens planted with trees. Some of the houses were of stone with steep roofs; most of them were timber fronted with galleries and gables breaking out into many shapes and angles. The houses of the servants and less rich were put together with whatever material was available and roofed with a thick thatching of grass. When she looked south, she saw more gardens, together with orchards, pastures, and wastelands running behind them. There were also religious houses on Cowgate, each with its own church, cemetery, and collection of outbuildings.

John and Rufenna walked past Blackfriars and he told her he had heard they were the richest religious order in all of Scotland, with lands extending all the way up the hill and beyond. At the foot of Blackfriars he pointed out the palace of Archibald Beaton and then said, "See across the street, Rufenna. That's the town house of Gavin Douglass, the third son of the Earl of Angus. Don't you think his is the finest, except for Cardinal Beaton's?"

Rufenna had to agree but she felt so weary she suggested they turn back. On the return to Holyrood she asked John to identify the church that was adjoining Blackfriars.

"Aye, sister. That's the Collegiate Church of Our Lady of the Fields, but it's been shortened to Kirko'-Field."

John asked if she wanted to see anything else and she said that tomorrow they could finish with High

Street. He agreed, adding that Tweeddale House, with
its garden and grove of lime trees, was also worth
seeing.

"Did you know, Rufenna, that the furniture for
these big houses is imported from faraway places—
Spain, Italy, France?"

"I wonder that we don't buy some from England."

"A Scot has no desire to enlarge the already swelling coffers of Henry Tudor."

"And how did you get that bit of information?"
she teased.

"One learns quickly in the city, sister."

When they were a short distance from the palace,
a woman, skirts flying, headdress in disarray, ran by
them, screaming.

"The English are massing at the Border and there
are English soldiers in the harbor!" she shrieked.

Rufenna cast a frightened glance at John, who suggested she return to their rooms and rest. He would
see what he could learn. He would go to the stable,
often a hotbed of gossip.

"Don't worry, Rufenna. Rumors like this fly around
Edinburgh every day. The English are angry about
Scotland rejecting the treaty but that doesn't mean
they're going to attack us. Don't fash yourself. Go
and rest."

Moments later Rufenna sat before the fire, admiring the green satin slippers. She had wanted silks
and satins and now she could indulge this taste for
luxury. She gave a fleeting thought to the coarse
woolens she had worn for so many years in the Abbey and smiled at her reflection. She could hardly
wait to wear that green silk gown. Two days seemed
an interminable time to have to wait for it. She wondered if the dressmaker could be hurried. Then she
soothed herself with the thought that she had waited
eighteen years for it. Surely she could survive for two
more days.

Her pleasure was shattered by the tempestuous entrance of John, bursting with news.

"Rufenna, it is true! The English are sending an army. The word is all over the palace."

Rufenna turned wildly to John and stared at him. "John, we've heard that before and you promised me minutes ago that it was just a rumor."

John sat down breathlessly. "Aye, I know, but this is different. A courier just came in for the Cardinal and he told us the news in the stable. The little Queen has been moved by the Regent from Stirling to Dunkeld for safety and the Cardinal himself is riding to Stirling at this hour. The Regent has ordered a force to be gathered, led by Lord Bothwell, Rufenna. He's also ordered that the lords held in Blackness Tower be released."

Along with everyone else in the palace, Rufenna knew that a number of the lords who had been captured at the defeat of the battle of Solway Moss were imprisoned in England, then released, and were thereafter arrested for treason. They had been charged with conspiring with Henry of England to open Scotland to English domination. It was known that these lords had supported the treaty; how much more they had done for England was not certain. But the Scottish government meant to find out.

Lord Maxwell, lodged in Blackness, had been caught carrying a letter addressed to the Earls of Cassillis and Glencairn, from Henry of England, outlining what he required from them in the way of support. Lord Fleming was imprisoned there, as was George Douglass and his brother, the Earl of Angus. All had been arrested by the Regent for conspiring with the English. These Protestant lords had supported the treaty and a union with Protestant England rather than Catholic France. Angus had been quite vehement about his innocence on a charge of treason. He pointed out to the Regent Arran that

he had openly worked for the treaty, as had other
lords. Why was his family singled out to be arrested?
He had not been caught carrying or receiving trea-
sonable letters! Now, it appeared, Arran had released
them, on their promise to assist him against the invading English.

Rufenna listened to John's news with growing uncertainty. It did sound more serious than before.
Perhaps she should leave the palace, she thought,
taking her problems out into the gardens to think
about it. Spring was everywhere, on this, the second
day of May. The shrubs in the garden, unfamiliar to
Rufenna, who only knew medicinal bushes and herbs,
were bursting with buds and new leaves. The flowers
in the formal gardens were just beginning to show
hints of color. Rufenna wandered the paths, considering what was best to do and wishing she had a
wiser person to consult. If the English came, and she
rode with John for home and the Border, they could
run right into an invading army. Surely the army
would not reach Edinburgh! Or if an army actually
crossed the Border, they would have news of it soon
enough to get away. She could take John north, to
Stirling or toward the Highlands; or west, circling
down the west coast to the Border, well out of the
path of an approaching army. The English in the
past usually crossed at Berwick, because that town
frequently was held by the English. After Berwick
the army would march up to Edinburgh along the
east coast. She would have to wait, she decided, to
see what the morrow brought. News could reach
Edinburgh tomorrow and it would help her decide
the best course of action.

The next day was strangely quiet. Rufenna and
John went to mass. Rufenna found that she had
quickly grown out of the habit of frequent prayers
and her knees were quite stiff when the final amen
was said. John seemed at loose ends too and she did

not know quite what to do with him. She hesitated to confide in him what the possibilities of flight would be, should the necessity arise. The hours dragged and Rufenna breathed a sigh of relief when the day crawled along to the end and she could dismiss John and go to bed to spend a strange and restless night.

The night brought several alarms and frights. Rumors flew wildly around the palace. Twice Rufenna was aroused from her half-sleep to find John at the door.

"They say the English have arrived, Rufenna. Quick, get up!"

Rufenna lit a candle and stumbled to the window and pulled the heavy hangings aside. The street was dark and quiet. She turned and attempted to reassure John.

"Go to bed; there is nothing out there. And even if they do come, we will have a better chance of escape if we have had a good night's sleep."

John left but he was back within the hour, saying that the English army was even now in Edinburgh, sacking the town. Rufenna again pointed out the quiet streets and the darkness and this time threatened him if he disturbed her again. He withdrew reluctantly and muttering.

A servant girl burst into the room a little later to tell Rufenna that the English army had been sighted coming up the west coast, not the east. When Rufenna demanded a confirmation of this, the little maid departed, saying that she had heard it from a stablehand. After that Rufenna gave up trying to sleep and lay in the big bed, wondering if morning would ever come. The only real news she had heard in two days was that Lord Bothwell, at the head of four thousand men, was on guard at the capital city.

Daylight brought the terrifying truth.

Rufenna, in her chamber dressing for breakfast, was startled by the sounds of shouting in the hallway. She flew to the door and threw it open, calling to a scurrying page.

"Wait! What is it?"

"The English are here! They landed at Leith Harbor and are already in the town."

"No, don't go yet, tell me!" she demanded, catching the frightened page by the arm. "What of Lord Bothwell's army?"

"They retreated! The English have twenty thousand men and they couldn't stop them. The city is lost!"

Rufenna stared at the page in horror. Another courier coming down the hallway from delivering a message to Lord Arran confirmed the story. Henry had fooled them well. He had embarked an army of ten thousand, commanded by his brother-in-law, the Earl of Hertford. They had landed at Leith, Edinburgh's port city, during the night, had burnt the shipping in the harbor and sacked Leith. Now they were encircling the city, entering by the north gate. The Scots army was gone, falling back toward Stirling, to hold it if possible. Rufenna, coming out of her horrified state, flew back into her chamber and dragged off her gown. She must find John and they had to escape from the city. With forced coolness she made herself go to his bedchamber and rummage through his chest of clothing. She found breeches, shirt, and cap that would enable her to move more freely. She would be less vulnerable dressed as a boy, with the streets full of soldiers. She shivered, thinking what soldiers do to captive women. As she forced stiff, nervous fingers to button the shirt and tie the laces of the breeches, she could hear firing begin. The shouting and confusion increased, as did the clash of swords. It sounded like the end of the world. The English were here!

Rufenna had nearly finished dressing when the door burst open and John ran in.

"Rufenna, we've got to get away from here. The English soldiers have taken the palace. Come quickly! We can go down the back stairs to the stables. They're fighting now in the Great Hall and will be upstairs in a few moments."

Rufenna belted her breeches and reached for the leather jacket, just as the heavy door crashed back against the wall. Three English soldiers stood there, their bloody swords giving evidence of their recent fighting.

"Well, look what we 'ave 'ere," one muttered, coming forward into the room.

John stepped in front of Rufenna, barring the man's way.

"'Tis a lad and a lass. Or is she a lad too?" The soldier who quite obviously had been drinking heavily of the palace's stock of wine, staggered toward them.

"Do not touch her," shouted John, standing his ground.

The second soldier looked at John and interfered. "Who are ye, little bantam?"

"Sir John Lyall and you will not harm my sister," John said firmly, his young voice quivering only on the last word. Rufenna felt a surge of pride in the boy, standing so straight and tall before the three armed soldiers.

"Lyall, eh? Of Lyall Castle?"

John nodded curtly. "My father was Sir Ewen Lyall," he added, keeping a wary eye on the drunken soldier, who waited impatiently for his sergeant to finish the questioning.

"Take him," the sergeant said to the two men. "M'lord Hertford will be glad to have such a hostage."

"'Is bloody lordship don't want no bloody boy," the other soldier insisted.

"Lord Eure will," the sergeant reminded him.

Rufenna's heart sank at this reference to the too-well-known Warden of the English East March. Lord Eure would indeed relish having as a hostage the heir to Lyall. Such a swine was he that his reputation had seeped through the sheltered walls of the Abbey. Rufenna feared him as she would have feared Satan himself.

The second soldier apparently thought that Eure would be pleased to have John. "We'll take him with us," he added, moving in on the boy.

Rufenna tried to push John aside and was roughly grabbed by the drunken soldier, who held her while the sergeant and the other soldier were seizing the struggling boy. John, tall for his age and quite strong, was giving them a hard fight of it when the sergeant eased his dagger from his belt and brought the heavy hilt of it down on the boy's head. John sagged without a word and they dragged him to the door.

"Come on," the sergeant murmured, casting a glance back at the man who still held Rufenna.

"In a minute," the man murmured, holding her clamped tightly against him. "We were a long time on the sea and the cabin boys are a poor substitute for what I got against me now."

"Well, don't be too long," the sergeant said.

"Man, the way I feel, 'twill not take long at all. I'll meet you downstairs."

The sergeant gave a crude laugh and went out, leaving his companion to hoist the unconscious boy over his shoulder and follow.

Dimly Rufenna could hear the growing sounds of fighting as the soldiers penetrated deeper into the palace. She began to struggle anew against the man and he laughed, swinging her around to face him.

"Now, lassie, don't give me no trouble and I'll not 'urt ye," he muttered in her ear, his reeking breath washing across her face. He staggered slightly and she tried to kick him, aiming her booted foot at his shin.

She got one hand free and reached up and clawed him wildly in the face, kicking out at him again.

"Spirited little bitch, ain't ye," mumbled her captor.

. Her struggles threw him off balance and he wobbled, tried desperately to regain his footing, and went down with her under him.

"Aye, nice; this is the way it should be," he said, breathing hard in her face.

The impact knocked the breath out of her and she lay helpless on the floor, pinned down by his weight, gasping for breath. He recovered first and started clawing at her shirt, ripping the heavy material away from her shoulders and breasts. She fought him with all her strength until he caught both of her hands and held them firmly in one of his large ones. He was lying heavily on her and rolled slightly to one side so that he could reach the laces on her breeches. She twisted and squirmed, making the task as difficult for him as she could, her body straining away from his large, rough hand. Her eye caught the gleam of metal and she concentrated on it, identifying the location of the dagger thrust in his belt. If she could just get that dagger!

He tore the laces loose, pulling wildly at the heavy leather of the breeches while he forced her knees apart. She heard him muttering that if she had on petticoats like a proper woman he wouldn't have all this trouble. Then he drew in his breath and said at least there was proper woman under them breeches. While he muttered, he was bending over her, kneeling above her, his free hand gropingly untying his own laces. His hot, sour breath was as nothing to the reek of sweat and dirt from his body. She felt nauseated; her head was swimming. She was tiring quickly, knowing she could not continue the struggle much longer. Sweat ran down her face and trickled across her bared breasts. The sight of those white, firm breasts, rising and falling rapidly with her harsh breathing, seemed to spur him on, and he ripped at his laces, freeing them finally. Rufenna tensed against him, determined to deny him entrance to her body. This was not going to be as it was with Murdoch, she vowed to herself. That time she was tied up, had been beaten, and was weak and completely helpless.

Her eyes had not left that tantalizing dagger in his belt as she struggled against him. Suddenly, his wits addled by his drunken state and the lust that was driving him on, he released her hands, needing his other hand to force her thighs apart so he could take her. It was all the time that Rufenna needed. Instantly her hand flashed down, sliding the dagger from his belt. He was so intent upon satisfying his lust that she caught him by surprise. By the time he realized she had the dagger, it was too late. From her cramped position beneath him, she could not get a full thrust at his heart but she drove the dagger up at his massive chest. It penetrated the heavy leather jacket and slid through the flesh before hitting a rib. Gasping in agony and rage, he hurled himself into her and for a moment the pain was so intense she could not think. She willed herself not to lose consciousness.

Then, as from another life, she heard a cool, calm voice commenting to her about daggers. It was the morning after Davon had caught her, after she tried unsuccessfully to stab him and had succeeded only in scratching him. She was frightened when she saw the bandage and he had said: "Daggers are meant for throats, mistress. Remember that."

She jerked back her arm, realizing she could not be sure of a clean thrust and looked upward at him, as he tried to focus his bleary eyes on her hand. Quick as she could, Rufenna gripped the dagger more firmly and, as he leaned down to take it, drove it upward, slashing at his throat. The wicked ten inches of steel sliced cleanly through the tender skin of his throat, laying open the flesh in a gaping wound. Her wild cut had severed the jugular vein and he stared at her for a few seconds in total surprise. Then he rolled over, clawing wildly at his throat. Rufenna fought her way from under that gasping, struggling body, as the blood spurted from his throat like a crimson fountain. She could feel the warm stickiness splashing on her, spraying her face and naked breasts, and she freed herself of his imprisoning weight with a desperate jerk. Sobbing, sickened by the blood and the terrible gasping of his increasing struggles to draw breath, she got to her knees and turned her face away from the painful sight.

She staggered to her feet and lurched heavily against the bed, trying to regain her composure. Pulling the coverlet from the bed, she tried to wipe the sticky blood from her face and body and refasten her shirt and breeches with trembling hands. She tried not to look at the blood that spotted her shirt and pants and groped for the leather jacket she had dropped when the three English soldiers had first appeared. She was moving in a daze as she stuffed her hair under the cap and made herself pick up the dripping dagger. A sound in the doorway sent her spinning around, eyes wide and frightened.

A tall man stood there, a nobleman by his velvet doublet and hose. A naked sword, smeared with blood, was gripped firmly in his hand. He was a middle-aged man, heavy through the chest, and looked familiar.

He looked from the English soldier, still immersed in hideous death throes on the stained floor, to the slender figure by the bed, still clutching the bloody dagger. His gaze went over her again but he did not remark on the slightness of the lad. Deep blue eyes, surrounded by wrinkles in a weather-beaten face, met her eyes and she lowered her dagger. The shadow of a smile passed over his face and he lowered his sword.

"Lad, we'd best get away from here. The soldiers hold the palace. Come, we had better try the back stairs."

Without a word Rufenna moved to join him, not daring to look at the sprawled figure on the floor. The raspy breathing still filled the room and she felt she could not get away from it quickly enough.

"I must find my brother," she murmured, joining the man in the doorway. "The soldiers took him."

"His name?"

"John, John Lyall."

"Sir Ewen's boy? Your father? Well, there is naught we can do for your brother now, lad. We must make some attempt to save ourselves. Come, we have no time to lose."

With a persuasive hand on her elbow he urged her down the hall, steering her around the crumpled figures of palace guards who had been killed by the English soldiers. They flew down the back stairs, flattening themselves against the wall as voices reached them from the lower floor. Then he led her into the deserted kitchens and out the back door. The cool morning breeze hit her face as she stepped into the back courtyard. Here was more evidence of the fight, with bodies of servants littering the rough cobblestones.

Her burly companion muttered, "Looks like this whoreson Hertford makes war on anybody who stands in his way, even the unarmed."

They stayed close to the wall, moving toward the back gate. Later Rufenna scarcely remembered that wild dash out of the city. As they emerged from the gate into the dirt lane at the back of the palace, they saw the damage already wrought on the city. Hand-to-hand battles raged in the streets; buildings were going up in flames as the English burned the city;

cries and shouts rang through the streets as the citizens of Edinburgh tried vainly to defend their city against overwhelming odds. Once he pulled her into a dark doorway and pressed her hard against the door, covering her with his own body, as a troop of soldiers came running down the narrow street. Then he was threading his way through the back alleys of the city, weaving in and out, running her up and down wynds she had not known existed. Finally he pushed her into a doorway and told her to wait.

"I know where there might be some horses and we'll need two to get away from the city. Stay here and don't show yourself."

She watched the big man race down the street, moving like a man half his age. Recognition dawned on her. She *had* met him before! Three days ago, no, four, at the palace. Lord Ashkirk! A Borderer! She had met him before that too. All the Ashkirks had come to her father's funeral but in the confusion she had found no time to talk to them. Kirkhill Castle lay near Knolle, she thought, light-headed with relief. Her father had known this man well!

The clatter of hooves on the rough cobbles caught her attention and Rufenna peered out of the doorway. He was coming quickly down the street, riding one horse and leading another. She was out of the doorway and mounting almost before he had halted. He turned, still holding her reins, and headed back down the narrow wynd.

By late afternoon they were out of the city, having outrun one patrol of soldiers and barely escaping being caught by a pair on horseback. Rufenna settled herself in the saddle and looked back once, as they rode south. The city was in flames. The black smoke rolled up in billowing clouds, covering the city with an inky cloud. Then she turned and followed her rescuer blindly. On they thundered, riding their horses hard, racing through Loanhead, past Roslin

Castle, riding for Peebles. They avoided the main
roads, keeping to rough paths and going across country. As the moon came up, he called a halt, stopping
first at a small farm they had nearly ridden past. Rufenna drooped in the saddle, so tired she was sure
she could not dismount. He walked up the lane and
hammered on the farmer's door. Shortly he was back,
holding a bundle in one hand, and remounted. He
cast a quick glance at her and reached over to take
her reins.

"There's a burn over there in the trees where we
can rest and water the horses. Not long now and you
can rest, my brave lad."

Rufenna, moments later, lay sprawled on the cool,
damp grass by the clear little creek, watching him
watering the horses and then hobbling them while
they grazed. Then she sat up and regarded the bundle he was opening with interest. He broke the freshly
baked loaf of coarse dark bread in two, handed her
a sizable wedge of cheese, and pulled the corks from
two bottles of home-brewed ale.

" 'Tis the best the farmer could offer."

Rufenna remembered suddenly that she had neither
eaten nor drunk since the day before. The cheese,
bread, and ale was more tempting and satisfied her
better than all the epicurean dishes at the Rutherford cummer fialls.

"Drink up, lass, er, lad. You'll need your strength
to make it to the Border."

His slip, calling her lass instead of lad, brought
her sitting up straight, her wide eyes meeting his. He
regarded her in amusement.

"What's your name, lad?" he said deliberately.

"Uh . . ." She thought fast. "Rufus."

A quick grin touched his mouth. "I didn't realize
Ewen had a son named Rufus," he mused, breaking
the cheese into bite-sized pieces. "He did have a

daughter, I recall, Rufenna or some such name. I met her at the funeral. A beautiful lass. Rufus—" he chuckled, his dark blue eyes twinkling at her, "a good name for a lad. A brave lad, at that. Eat up, boy. We can't tarry here long. You're for Lyall? I go to Kirkhill."

Rufenna, answering that smile, relaxed. He knew exactly who she was and was amused by it. She certainly had nothing to fear from him. "Knolle, I think. It's on your way, isn't it?"

"Aye. You'd be secure at Knolle? I could take you to Kirkhill and send you on to Lyall with an escort. You're not to try to reach Lyall by yourself, lad. The hills are full of English soldiers now. D'ye wish to fall afoul of more?"

She shuddered and shook her head, her mouth full of bread and cheese. "I'll go to Knolle. There's a garrison there that will see me to Lyall." After thinking about it at length, she decided on the ride that it was in her best interests to confide in Lord Ashkirk. So, carefully leaving out the sordid details, she explained to him her troubles with her cousin Murdoch. It was essential that they find out who held Knolle Castle before she showed herself. Lord Ashkirk insisted that he be the one to find out who held Knolle and she stay out of sight until this was accomplished. He would ask entrance at the gate. He would inquire for the master and discover if Murdoch were there. If so, he would ask food and water, which would be given. Then, saying nothing, he would depart, come back to her waiting place, and take her to Kirkhill with him.

"So be it," he said, eating as quickly as he could. Rufenna chewed methodically, but she was too tired to know what she was eating. Soon, too soon for her weary body, they were back in the saddle, entering the spreading plains near Melrose. The stone castle of Knolle rose before them and Lord Ashkirk left her in a concealing copse of trees while he rode to the castle gate.

Rufenna dismounted as her gallant rescuer rode toward Knolle. She said a little prayer to St. Christopher for her safe deliverance thus far. But she would not feel entirely secure until Lord Ashkirk had carefully investigated Knolle Castle. In her ten days absence from home a great deal could have happened.

Rufenna watched until she saw the gates open to admit him and then settled down on the damp grass to wait. The sun had not long risen and washed the native stone in a rosy glow. Her eyelids drooped and she forced them open. She could not go to sleep now! She vowed to herself that as soon as she got back to Lyall, if ever, she would have a tub bath or maybe more than one and then give orders not to be disturbed for two days. She ached with anticipation at the thought of her huge, soft bed, with the comfortable coverlets and big pillows. It seemed like forever since she had slept in it.

Long before she expected him, she heard the clatter of hooves and peeped from her hiding place among the trees. Ashkirk was riding up the slope to the copse of trees, accompanied by Jock, the soldier in charge of the garrison at Knolle.

Jock surveyed her impassively but his keen eyes missed nothing: the weary droop of her mouth and lids, the travel-stained, blood-spattered breeches and shirt front. His mouth tightened. Lord Ashkirk, who was preparing to ride on to Kirkhill, had told him the tale, omitting nothing. The lass was worn out, needing sleep and food.

"M'lord, how can I thank you for your kindness," Rufenna murmured, looking up with eyes dazed with fatigue at the waiting nobleman.

"Aye, lass, none of that," he said, relinquishing the pretense of Rufenna being a boy. "It was a pleasure to help Ewen's daughter. He will be sorely missed. Give your mother my regards and you're always welcome at Kirkhill if your cousin gets troublesome again. I'll give you aid and gladly."

"Thank you, Lord Ashkirk. I will remember you in my prayers every night," she said, watching him mount.

They rode back down the hill and she waved to him as he turned for Kirkhill.

"Ye canna stay at Knolle, mistress," Jock said bluntly, as they rode toward the open gates. "The damned English are raiding every night and we expect to see an army cross any day. M'lord told me of the fight in Edinburgh. 'Tis a sad thing and I misdoubt that they'll go home this way. Nay, you're for Lyall in the morning, mistress, for I'll not have the responsibility of keeping you here."

Rufenna nodded wearily. In spite of her exhaustion she knew that Jock knew what was best, and had it been possible, he would have let her stay at Knolle until she was thoroughly rested and recovered. If ever that could be, she thought, forcing her thoughts away from the soldier in Edinburgh and what he had done to her.

"I'll gladly go home," she murmured, riding into the courtyard and hearing the heavy gates close behind them. "Any sign of Master Murdoch?"

"Nay, not a peep. His lordship sent a man, asking for ye. We told him ye had not been here nor were expected," Jock said, sliding a sideways glance at her, wondering about this. It had excited his curiosity then and he still wanted to know what it was about.

"His lordship?" wondered Rufenna. "Whom do you mean, Jock?"

"Why, Lord Hammond, mistress. 'Twas a week hence, I think. Came asking if ye were here. We told him ye were at Lyall, as far as we knew. Is something amiss? Why would m'lord seek you here?"

Rufenna could scarcely tell Jock that Davon Hammond was searching for her to drag her into his bed, so she chose her words carefully. "M'lord rescued me from Galzean, when Cousin Murdoch carried me there. While m'lord was away from Torrey Castle, I left, meaning to go home. The message I left for him must have been misunderstood and he believed me to have come here instead of home to Lyall."

Jock stared hard at her, not accepting this as full truth in the least. He could not say so, however, so he nodded. "'Tis fortunate that you have the support of Lord Hammond, mistress. He's a good man and neighbor to ye, and your father thought well of him."

Rufenna kept silent and simply nodded. She wondered if Jock would believe her if she did tell him the truth.

She dismissed him and, not waiting to eat or wash, tore off her bloodstained clothing and fell into bed, thinking and worrying about John. The English had him . . . or rather, Lord Eure had him, which was infinitely worse. Her father had been at odds with Lord Eure for years, long before that Englishman had been made Warden, or Sheriff, of the English East March. He would relish having Sir Ewen's son as his hostage! She would have to get home to Lyall and consult with Walter and Captain Kincaid. For one sleepy moment she thought wistfully of what Jock had said about Davon Hammond. *He* would know what to do! If only things were different between them!

CHAPTER EIGHTEEN

Rufenna bent over her household accounts, laboriously adding up a long column of figures. She detested this type of work and wished her mother felt well enough to do it. The nuns had spent years teaching their charges to do their sums because it would be one of her responsibilities, as mistress of a household, to supervise and approve the household accounts. Thomas, the steward, had respectfully presented them to her this morning and mentioned that Lady Lyall was not yet well enough to do them. They must be examined before the monies could be paid on account.

She had been back at Lyall for three days now, and had promptly consulted with Walter and Captain Kincaid about how to recover John. They had both advised her that until the English army returned to England, and they were notified by Ralph Eure (Old Walter's lip curled contemptuously when he said the name) that he held John as a hostage, there was little that could be done. The latest news to reach the Border carried word that the English army, reinforced by Lord Eure with four thousand mounted English Borderers, had just left Edinburgh in ruins and was burning and sacking its way back down the east coast toward the Border. The Earl of Hertford was grimly carrying out his orders to wreak as much devastation as was possible in Scotland. He had left Edinburgh, leaving a raped and ravished city behind him, and had turned aside long enough to burn and pillage Lord Seton's unfortified castle. Lord Seton, as one of the prominent Catholic lords who had fought against the treaty, was high on Hertford's list for reprisal. But Hertford did not draw his bloody sword against only the influential and those known to be enemies of England. With grim delight he burned the crofters' hovels and killed anyone who got in his way.

News of the sacking of Seton Castle reached them this morning, by a party of Borderers who had escaped from Edinburgh and been caught in the ring of soldiers Hertford had thrown around the city. They had managed to hide and make their way out during the night and had stopped at Lyall long enough to beg food and drink for themselves and their horses.

Captain Kincaid promptly ordered tighter security at Knolle and at Lyall and increased the sentries at both castles. Daily scouting troops were sent out, cautioned to be on the alert for any large body of troops moving across Lyall land.

"Mistress Rufenna," Thomas said quietly, entering the small withdrawing room off the Great Hall where Rufenna was struggling with the accounts. "The captain sends word that a small mounted troop of men is heading for Lyall and should be here within the hour. The scouting troop believes they are Sir Robert Kerr's men."

"Thank you, Thomas. See if you can find Master Walter and ask him to join me here."

What could Sir Robert Kerr be sending to Lyall for? she wondered, aware of a growing uneasiness as she thought about it.

"Walter, have you heard?"

Walter came into the room and moved to the narrow window that overlooked the courtyard. "Aye, I've heard," he growled. "I wonder if Kerr is with them."

"Sir Robert? Why would he come here?"

Walter turned and looked at her. "Lass, you're betrothed to his nephew and ward, and your wedding is supposed to be set for the summer. There must be many arrangements to make."

Rufenna sank slowly back down into her chair and stared at Walter in astonishment. She had completely forgotten the existence of Neville Kerr!

"But, Walter, with things as they are here, I could not marry this summer! Surely Sir Robert . . ."

"Make not your excuses to me, lass," Walter said with a grin as he turned to the window to look out. "There they are," he reported, watching the heavily armed troop ride through the gate. "He *is* with them. Ye can tell Sir Robert how ye feel, mistress, and much good it'll do ye. Powerful set on having his way, is Sir Robert!"

Rufenna's soft mouth tightened slightly. "So, Walter, am I! You'll stay with me? I'll not see him alone."

"Aye, I'll stay if he'll let me."

"I am in charge here, Walter, and if I wish you to stay, you will stay," said Rufenna firmly, determined not to be bullied by Sir Robert Kerr. He might be a powerful man in the Borders, particularly as he was the Warden, or Sheriff, of the Scottish Middle March, dispensed the justice, and was in charge of governing this March, but she had had her fill of domineering males telling her what to do!

"Sir Robert Kerr, Mistress Rufenna," Thomas broke in on her fuming as he stood aside to let Sir Robert enter.

Rufenna, having never actually met Sir Robert before, used the time while the formalities were going on to study him. As he expressed his sympathy for her loss of both brother and father, she examined his face. It was long, narrow, and cold. Light blue eyes appeared almost colorless in his pale face, a slightly pointed chin, thin, hard cheeks, a tight, humorless mouth. Rufenna, by the time he reached the real reason for his visit, had decided that she not only did not like Sir Robert, she was afraid of him. There was something cold, implacable, about that face. He appeared hardly human, bloodless, not moved by human emotions.

"I am sorry that Neville is not with me, my dear, but I am only passing by on my way back from Riccarton. He wished to accompany me so he could see you but I needed him at Cessford. Such troubled times," he sighed, turning so that he was excluding Walter from the conversation. After the first introduction he had ignored the old man, had ignored him very pointedly, Rufenna thought indignantly.

"Perhaps he could call some other day," Rufenna murmured politely, wary of discussing Neville, or indeed anything, with this man.

"Ah, yes. There is much to arrange before the summer, of course. What plans have you decided upon for the wedding? Have you drawn up a list of guests yet? I have several in particular that I would wish to be included."

Rufenna clasped her hands in her lap and met that cool gaze. "I have as yet made no plans, Sir Robert. You must know how we are situated at Lyall."

"I am aware of your problems, my dear, and we can take care of them. I intend to take young John back with me today. He needs a man's guidance and would be better off under my care at Cessford until you and Neville are wed. I believe it would be best for Neville to remain with you here after the wedding, instead of bringing you to Cessford. Your mother will need your help and support for a time yet and Neville would be here to see to the affairs of the estate. I assure you that I have trained him well and he will do justice for Lyall. He will instruct your brother of what is expected of a Lyall of Lyall, of course. . . ."

"Sir Robert, that is quite impossible," Rufenna interrupted gently. "I have recently come from Edinburgh, where my brother was sent for safety. The troublesome times," she added, so he would not inquire as to the reason John had been removed from Lyall. "He was under the care of the Queen Mother. During my visit there, the Queen and Lord Arran both agreed that I was the natural choice of a guardian for John and they confirmed it."

The Queen had done so and Lord Arran had agreed, but Rufenna had not brought any official papers from Edinburgh and hoped he would not ask to see them. "My mother, as you pointed out, is not well, so I have been charged with John's safety."

Her guest frowned, bringing a colder light to those pale eyes. "I should have been consulted in the matter! Besides being the Warden of this March, I stand to you as guardian now that your father is gone."

"My mother is still my guardian, Sir Robert, and I am now in charge of John," Rufenna contradicted, beginning to enjoy crossing swords with this arrogant man. "I regret there was no opportunity to consult you but the visit was not planned in advance."

"After your marriage to Neville . . ."

"It is out of the question, sir, for me to marry your nephew this summer. Not only am I in charge here at Lyall, there are other matters which demand deferment of our wedding. We were in Edinburgh when the English army arrived, sir, and John was taken prisoner. I escaped only with the help of Lord Ashkirk, who kindly brought me back to Lyall."

Stunned, Sir Robert gaped at her. "John . . . a prisoner of the English?"

"I am afraid so. He was taken by Lord Eure's men, for ransom, they said."

"Why was I not informed of this?" he thundered, livid with rage. His tight mouth was a line of anger as he glared at her.

"There has scarcely been time," said Rufenna, thinking to herself that nobody thought of informing Sir Robert of anything. "I just arrived back here myself. There is little we can do, either, until we receive word from Lord Eure that he does indeed have John."

"I will attend to this, my dear. You leave it with me. I will have a messenger leave at once for Lord Eure. . . ."

"I understand Lord Eure is still with Hertford's army around Edinburgh. Until they return to England, there is nothing we can do."

He didn't like it and didn't want to admit it was so, but finally nodded. "You send word to me the moment you receive a message from Lord Eure. I will address him on this matter myself. As the Warden of this March, my word will carry considerable weight with him and we should have the lad back quickly."

Old Walter chuckled grimly and Rufenna interpreted him correctly. If Lord Eure hated anyone more than Ewen Lyall, it was Sir Robert Kerr!

"I thank you for your concern, sir, but my cousin is aiding me on this matter," she said, gesturing toward Walter, who still stood silently by the window, filled with amusement and respect at the way the lass was defying the old devil. He was hard pressed to keep a straight, serious face.

"As for your wedding being delayed, mistress, I see no reason—"

"My mother is unwell, Sir Robert. I could not consider having a wedding while she is so ill. It must wait, at least until we are out of mourning," she added, knowing she would hit him in a tender spot with this reasoning. "You would not wish me to be disrespectful to the memories of my father and brother by wedding your nephew so soon? It would be improper," she said quietly, folding her hands demurely in her lap. "My mother would never hear of it."

"Perhaps if I spoke to your mother about the urgency of the situation? Neville is badly needed here, my dear, to lift this burden from your slender shoulders."

"She is not well enough to see anyone, I'm afraid, and we are going on very well here at Lyall. If I need assistance," she added, prompted by some devil inside her that wanted to pierce this man's cold shell, "I have only to send to Torrey Castle and Lord Hammond will aid me. He has been most helpful," she said, ignoring Walter's choked cough at this blatant lie.

"Hammond? Lord Hammond has been aiding you? My dear, if you need any assistance, you must come to me! I insist! You should not have to rely on such a one as Davon Hammond!"

Rufenna bit her lip and looked down hastily to stop the smile hovering on her mouth. Walter had mentioned that Sir Robert hated the Hammonds and was fiercely jealous of Davon Hammond's influence in the March and with the Queen. Rufenna suddenly remembered Davon's contempt of Sir Robert when she had told him she was betrothed to Neville Kerr and Sir Robert would avenge her honor. Then she turned her mind quickly away from Davon and the events in Hammond Tower that night.

"He has not embroiled you in this latest trouble, has he?" Sir Robert demanded suspiciously.

"What trouble do you refer to, Sir Robert?"

"This problem with Jamie Scott," Kerr said impatiently. "Hammond sent to me for men! I received the request yesterday. The English apparently captured Jamie Scott during a raid over the Border, and Davon Hammond, who is a kinsman of this Scott, had the temerity to ask *me* for men to attempt to get him back! I did just wonder, when you mentioned Hammond's name, if he had applied to you also. He'll need more men than Torrey can supply to raid the English camp!"

Rufenna exchanged a quick, startled glance with Walter and turned to Sir Robert. Later she could not say what had prompted her, but she picked up the gauntlet he had thrown down. "Yes, we just heard. I promised Lord Hammond as many Lyall men as he needed. You forget, sir, that my mother is also a Scott," she added, "a kinswoman of Jamie Scott. Naturally, she wishes us to do what we can to aid him."

Rufenna blandly met Walter's astonished gaze and braced herself for Sir Robert's anger.

"You promised him Lyall men? Mistress, regardless of your mother's concern, you have no business—"

"Sir, you forget that I am in charge at Lyall now and will remain so until my brother is of age. Lyall has received aid from the Scotts many times over the years and I think you know that my father would have ridden with his men to assist Jamie if he were here. Alexander, too. Surely, as the daughter of Lyall, I can do no less," she responded, throwing caution to the winds.

"You do not intend to lead your men personally?" Sir Robert stared at her in frank horror. "Your captain is fully competent to do that for you. A woman—"

"Naturally, Captain Kincaid will do so," she murmured, not agreeing to or denying his demand. "I am sorry to have displeased you on this matter but our assistance has been promised."

By the time Sir Robert left, Walter was well nigh speechless at Rufenna's defiance of one of the most powerful men in the March. Sir Robert was livid with a cold, dangerous fury that this chit of a girl was refusing to do *anything* he suggested, and Rufenna herself was exhilarated at her successful stand against a man she knew she should fear. He was scarcely out of the door before Walter turned to her.

"Lass, are you out of your mind? We have promised Lord Hammond no such aid! We did not even know of Jamie Scott's capture!"

"I have promised it now, and if Sir Robert, as you say, knows everything that goes on, we must make good our promise. Walter, go and ask Captain Kincaid to ready a messenger for Torrey while I write to Lord Hammond."

"Lass, you're not really going to write Hammond and offer our men, are you?" Walter said despairingly.

"Certainly I am," Rufenna said, sitting down at her desk and drawing forward a clean sheet of parchment. "Would my father have done less, Walter?"

"No," he admitted reluctantly. "Old Kerr hates the Scotts. They've been at feud since, let me see, 1526, I think it was. Naturally Kerr won't give aid to rescuing a Scott, even if he is the Warden of the March."

"It is part of his duty to give aid to his people," Rufenna said fiercely. "Just because it is a Scott—"

"That's the way it is, lass, and don't forget it. I can scarce believe *you* mean to offer Lord Hammond your assistance when he has not even asked for it!"

"I am not aiding Davon Hammond!" she said hotly. "I am aiding Jamie Scott, my mother's kinsman. It is a different thing entirely!"

Walter considered bringing up the fact that the Lyalls and the Hammonds were carrying on a feud but he had long since decided that Davon Hammond was feuding in a most unusual fashion. Admitting defeat, Walter headed for the door. "I'll see about the messenger and tell Captain Kincaid about this latest start of yours. Not that he'll be surprised!"

Rufenna smiled at him and turned back to the desk, concentrating on just what she should say in her letter to Davon. Finally she wrote: *"Lord Hammond, Sir Robert Kerr just visited us at Lyall and told us of the capture of Jamie Scott. If you have need of the Lyall men to effect his rescue, send word to Lyall. Rufenna Lyall for Lady Wira Lyall."*

She looked at the short note with satisfaction, knowing that Davon was perceptive enough to read between the lines and know that this was her doing, even if it was done in her mother's name. Then her pulses began to race at the thought of seeing him again. She paced the room, wondering impatiently how long it would take the messenger to go to Torrey and return with an answer.

The letter that was sent back by the messenger matched her own in brevity and coolness. Evidently Davon Hammond was desperate in his need for men. The note was addressed to Lady Lyall and simply asked that any Lyall men who could be spared be led to Hammond Tower on the morrow. The large raiding party was assembling there, under the command of Lord Hammond. The messenger also brought back the details, gleaned while he was given a rest and ale in Torrey's kitchens. Rufenna pulled the information from the reluctant man, who dared not say that such details should be left to the captain of the guard and she should tend to her embroidery. Rufenna knew exactly what he was thinking as she questioned him. Jamie Scott, leading a small raiding party into England above Kielder, had been taken by a large band of Charltons. The few of his men who managed to escape and get back rode for Sir

Walter Scott of Buccleuch, the head of the family,
only to find Buccleuch was believed to be in Edinburgh when the English army surrounded it. Whether
or not *he* was also a captive of the English was unknown. Tim Scott of Tushielaw had willingly agreed
to send the few men he had available, the bulk of his
men having accompanied Buccleuch, and old Wat of
Harden was also supplying troopers. Jamie Scott's
wife, also related to the Hammonds, had sent word
to Davon, who had taken charge of the raiding party.
Word had been sent throughout the Scottish border
of the raid, asking for men. So far, only the Kerrs
had refused to send men to aid the Scotts. Rufenna
permitted the messenger to leave and sent for Captain Kincaid.

"Captain, how many men can we send to Hammond Tower without leaving Lyall vulnerable?"

He considered, having thought about it after Walter told him of the plan. "I could easily take fifty,
Mistress Rufenna. We have reinforced Knolle with
as many as we could spare, so I could not send more
than that unless I strip the castle of her defenses."

"Fifty will do. Have them ready at first light tomorrow and we'll ride for Hammond."

He stared at her. "We? You do not intend for *me*
to take them?"

She smiled at him, knowing she would have to
coax him. "I'm afraid I don't, Captain. I will take
them myself. Who is your most trusted lieutenant?"

"David Shelby," he said absently, still considering
her previous statement. "Mistress, I must protest . . ."

"I know you must, Captain, but I want you to stay
here and guard Lyall. My cousin Murdoch must know
of this raiding party; we have word that it will be
of considerable size and he does seem to know much
of what occurs here. Knowing also that my mother
was a Scott, he would feel sure that we would send
aid to Jamie Scott! It may be the very opportunity he

is waiting for and we cannot take that chance. I can see the men to Hammond, where they would be commanded by Lord Hammond anyway, but you are badly needed here."

"Mistress, this entire plan is unwise. To take any men away from Lyall at such a time! There is not only the threat from your cousin, mistress; there are also the English raiding parties to consider."

"Believe me, Captain, I do not intend to leave Lyall vulnerable. You yourself just assured me that we could spare fifty men for a space of a few days. My cousin would have great difficulty in taking Lyall by force in that time, you must admit that! Besides," she added, firing her parting shot, "think how displeased Sir Robert Kerr will be!"

Rufenna had her way and rode out of the gate of Lyall at first light. She had not the slightest idea how she would be received at Hammond by Davon and was afraid to guess. He would not refuse the Lyall men, she knew; he had accepted their assistance and would not order her to return with them to Lyall. She had also made sure that David Shelby, Captain Kincaid's most trusted officer and her old friend, understood that where he went, she went. She would not take the risk of falling into the hands of Davon Hammond again! He would not be granted the opportunity to have her carried off to Torrey and could scarcely seize her in front of her men! Pleased with herself, Rufenna led the men down the path, riding east to Hammond Tower.

CHAPTER NINETEEN

After some time they passed the last of the guards posted by Davon around Hammond Tower. Rufenna led the Lyall men up the rough track to the gates of the tower. The area seemed to teem with men and horses, camping in clusters in the green valley around the base of the rise. They watered their horses at the little stream that meandered through the valley and pressed on up the track to the tower gate.

"How many men would you say he has?" Rufenna asked David Shelby, who was riding silently beside her. David had known the daughter of Lyall since she was a young girl. He was not much older than she, and was a kinsman of Lady Lyall. Lady Wira, upon learning he had been orphaned when he was eight, had taken him into the household. He had played with the young Rufenna when they were children, and had ridden the last few years with Alexander, before being made Captain Kincaid's lieutenant. He had been much less surprised by this mad plan of Rufenna's than the captain, as he had known the girl much better. However, he rode the miles between the two castles in uneasy silence. Now he looked around with an experienced eye and made a rough guess.

"I'd say a hundred in the valley and probably at least fifty in the tower itself. We will see. Mistress Rufenna, will you not reconsider and let me have you escorted back to Lyall?"

"Certainly not," she said smartly. "David, these are my men now and I will go with them. You will actually lead them," she admitted with her natural frankness, "but they will be represented by a Lyall."

He grinned at her, admiring, in spite of his unease, her courage and determination to do the right thing by her men. "All right, lass, as you please. I doubt not that Lord Hammond will dislike it. He cannot approve of women on raids."

Rufenna longed to tell David that it was Davon who had taken her on her very first raid but she prudently held her tongue. It would call for far more explanations than she was willing to give to David and so was best left unsaid. They reached the gates and were admitted to Hammond Tower and drew rein in the crowded courtyard. Rufenna had just slipped down from her horse when that familiar dark-haired figure appeared in the doorway to the Great Hall. Her heart started hammering and her mouth went dry. Perhaps she would have done better to stay at home, as far away from this man as was possible. But no, she reminded herself proudly. Her place was here with her men. She lifted her head and preserved her composure and quietly handed her reins to a waiting trooper. David, after one uneasy glance at her, went forward to greet Lord Hammond.

"M'lord, David Shelby," he said, shaking hands with Davon. "I bring the Lyall men. Fifty strong," he added, aware that Davon was looking over his head at that tall figure with the blazing red hair.

"And your mistress as well?" Davon questioned, his eyes narrowed in the sunlight.

"Sir, she brought herself," David admitted.

A slight smile touched Davon's mouth. "I'm sure she did, knowing Mistress Rufenna! Master Shelby, see my man Wat and he will arrange for your quartering. I will see to your mistress."

David frowned. He had his orders from that same lass that he was to stick by her side like a burr. Now what to do? "Sir . . ."

"I'd appreciate it if you would join us in the hall when you have seen your men settled," Davon said smoothly, taking the wind out of the younger man's sails.

There was little David could do but agree. He turned away, aware that Davon had passed him and was advancing on that fiery-haired figure who waited patiently in the middle of the courtyard, still surrounded by her men.

"Mistress Rufenna," Davon murmured, casting a swift glance over her. His eyes missed nothing, the hair swept up under her hat with small tendrils curling around her ears, the firm jutting breasts pushing against the man's shirt she wore, the slim thighs and calves outlined in the leather breeches. There was something else about her. She had matured in these few short weeks. No longer was she weak and bruised, shrinking away from him. For a long second she looked him full in the face and then cast down her eyes.

"Or is your name perhaps Marie?" he murmured softly, referring to her escaping with Elizabeth and leaving Marie at Torrey.

Rufenna could think of nothing to say.

"No matter," he continued. "Elizabeth will hear of it when next we meet."

"No doubt," she said, hoping he would change the subject.

"I did not expect to have you arrive with your men."

Rufenna had been quite sure of that. She said nothing.

"Let me show you to your quarters," he added, taking her elbow in a firm grasp. "Master Shelby is seeing to your men and will join us shortly."

Rufenna resisted the pressure of that hard, slender hand. "I prefer to remain with my men, m'lord, if you please," she said with what decorum she could muster.

"No doubt," he agreed quietly, but with a thread of steel in his voice. "It would not be seemly for you to do so. You will join us in the hall."

Rufenna was aware that her men were listening curiously to this exchange and she swallowed angrily. Now was not the time to display her temper, however, so she allowed him to escort her up the ramp and into the dim coolness of the Great Hall. It was crowded with men and she recognized Sim immediately. He came forward, giving her a warm grin, and reluctantly she returned it. She was developing a fondness for the good-looking Borderer, she thought!

"Sim, how are you?"

"Fine, mistress. I did not expect to see you here," he added.

"You should have," Davon said dryly, frowning at the warmth in her voice as she greeted his man and wondering what it meant.

"Aye, no doubt I should," Sim agreed, grinning at her again.

"Will you see Mistress Lyall to her chamber, Sim? I'm sure we can find her one."

"She can have mine," Sim said promptly, leading Rufenna up the twisting stairway in the far corner of the hall.

Rufenna tried to protest but Sim silenced her. "Nay, mistress, 'tis no trouble. We are near full to the rafters today but we ride at dark. You must have a chamber to freshen up in and mine is handy."

Handy to what? Rufenna wondered, going up the stairs with him. Handy to Davon's? She did not recognize the chamber. It was not Davon's, which she had cause to remember well, nor the first room she had used at Hammond. It would do, however, for the few hours she would use it. Sim collected his gear and came back with a fresh towel and basin of warm water for her. He waited tactfully in the hall while she washed her face and hands, removed her hat, and smoothed down her unruly hair. Then she followed him back down to the Great Hall. It was still full of men, lounging in corners, sitting at the long wooden tables playing a game of dice, drinking ale, and eating great chunks of bread and cheese. Her empty stomach suddenly reminded her that she had not eaten since before they left Lyall that morning and it was past midday now. Sim's eyes had followed her wistful glance at the food, spread out on one of the tables.

"Are ye not hungry, Mistress Rufenna? Come, let me find you a place to sit."

"I'll wait for David, if you don't mind, Sim. He hasn't eaten either."

"Na doubt David Shelby is eating with the men, lass, in the courtyard, and won't be back for a time. Come, I'll sit with you and you can tell me how things are at Lyall."

He led her over to a table holding Hammond men, men who had recognized the red-haired girl instantly from their ride from Murdoch's castle, where she had been held captive by her cousin. Admiring glances were exchanged among them as they realized she had brought her men here to join the raid. As Rufenna arrived at the table, there were smiles and shuffling around as they delightedly made room for her. She returned the smiles shyly and allowed Sim to place her in the quickly emptied section of the bench. He fetched two large wooden platters, heaped with bread, meat, and cheese, and a tankard of cool ale. Rufenna ate hungrily, aware that the men were still quietly observing her as they ate their own meal. When Sim had satisfied the worst of his hunger, he turned to her.

"How is your mother, lass? Still the same?"

Rufenna pushed away the nearly empty platter and took a last drink of the ale. "Aye, Sim, about the same. She grieves much for my father and will not come from her chamber."

He nodded. "I expected it to be so. And your cousin, Master Murdoch? Has he tried to retake Lyall?"

"No, we've seen nothing of him, thanks be to God. Lyall is strong, Sim, and he knows it."

Sim agreed, for he had made an intimate inspection of Lyall's defenses. "He had the chance when he was inside with his men but taking it from without is quite another thing."

The men, listening to this interchange, rumbled angrily about Murdoch, their keen sense of Border fairness pricked by that rogue's treatment of the lass.

"If he bothers you again, lass, come for us. We'll settle yon poltroon!" a trooper muttered.

Rufenna flashed him a glowing and grateful smile. "'Tis kind of you but I think he will not trouble us further now. He has not enough men to take Lyall."

Sim, watching her discussing it with the trooper, was burning to ask about Agnes. He hesitated to do so. He had not been able to forget that comely lass and her warm embraces and wished very much to have news of her.

"And everyone else at Lyall? Master Walter? Is he well?" Sim persisted, hoping that Rufenna would mention Agnes.

"Walter goes on fine, as usual. He is taking care of the household while I am gone. Sim, has there been any news of Lady Elizabeth? Were they safe in Linlithgow?"

Sim nodded. "Aye, m'lord sent men to see about her and found the English did not go near Linlithgow. The last word we had was that the army was preparing to leave Edinburgh. Have ye garrisoned Knolle well, mistress? 'Tis in their path back to the Border."

"Captain Kincaid says so. I brought fifty men from Lyall and he has sent all we could spare to Knolle."

"You came with the men alone, lass? 'Tis not wise for you to ride alone through the Borders."

Rufenna grinned. "Did you expect me to bring my maid and steward and cook?"

This was the opening Sim was waiting for. "Your maid, yes. 'Twould have given you female company here. Is Agnes well?"

Rufenna smiled to herself at Sim's efforts to mask his eager interest. "Indeed yes, but she would never willingly have come with me. Agnes is a poor traveler, Sim, and can barely sit a horse. Come, don't scold me! David Shelby has already done enough of that! They are my men and I ride with them."

Sim, amused by the thought of the luscious Agnes repeatedly falling off her horse, smiled and admitted defeat. "You'll stay here during the raid?"

"Certainly not," she retorted, just as another voice interrupted.

"She will," Davon said, from just behind her. Rufenna stood up and glared at him but he ignored her. He was looking at Sim. "She will wait here in the safety of Hammond."

"I will not, m'lord," she said firmly, angered that she was being treated like a child. "My men go with me. If you wish them to ride with you, then I also ride."

There was a taut silence, while every man at the

table waited to hear how m'lord would settle this one. Davon's dark eyes raked up and down the boyish clothing, which did little to hide the womanly curves, and he smiled a little.

"Bloodthirsty, Rufenna? Want revenge on the English? I would have thought you had had enough dealings with them already."

She paled and took a step backward. For one hideous moment she thought that he knew what had befallen her in Edinburgh. Then she realized he had no way of knowing. He must be referring to her capture on the raid and escape.

"No, m'lord, I'm not bloodthirsty, but I will go with my men."

Davon had noticed the pallor that swept over her face at his words, and wondered. There was something here that he did not know, he thought, and he would have to get to the bottom of it. Perhaps, knowing the lass, it would be just as well to keep her under his eye.

"Very well, mistress, but you will ride with me. We will take no chances on your safety this time."

He turned on his heel and walked off, going in search of David Shelby, who might be able to tell him what had caused that stricken, white look to appear on her face. Rufenna gazed at his retreating back and wondered if she had won a victory or not. He needed her men and could not allow her to take them back to Lyall. So he had given in, or had he? Then Rufenna wondered what the nuns would say if they could see her now. They would deplore her unwomanly raiment; she would be sent fasting from the table for her lack of retiring behavior. They would say sharp words to her about challenging a man after they had impressed upon her the superiority of the masculine sex.

The rest of the afternoon she spent at the table with the troopers, relaxing until it was time to ride.

They were teaching her to play dice, to their great amusement, and minded their tongues and manners under Sim's protective eye. Sim, watching that vivacious face as she threw the dice and laughed happily when she won the silver pennies she had staked, did not wonder at his master's interest in the lass.

Sim had ridden with m'lord to Hammond when Rufenna had made her escape from Torrey with Elizabeth. On their return he had been a witness to that nobleman's thunderous rage when they found her gone. A troop of soldiers had been sent out after them when Luke realized that the lass had tricked him, but they had not found them. Davon sent a second troop to search for them but the girl and Elizabeth had well nigh vanished off the face of the earth. Then the rumors of an English invasion had occupied everyone's time and energy. Sim was very curious about what had befallen Rufenna in Edinburgh.

"Lass, were you still in Edinburgh when the English came?" he asked in a casual tone during a lull in the conversation. He noticed her sudden stillness and the draining of color from her rosy cheeks as she admitted she had been. He was not fooled by her offhand manner and let his glance flicker over that slender white hand, painfully gripping the dice.

"How did you escape from the city?" he pressed, determined to get what information he could from her.

"W-why, Lord Ashkirk helped me," Rufenna stammered, refusing to meet those keen blue eyes. "He was at the palace when the English stormed it and got me away." Swiftly she changed the subject. "Sim, tell me about the raid tonight. Where are they holding Jamie Scott?"

Sim smiled knowingly to himself. If the lass was bent on changing the subject, so be it. He gave her the briefest of details, leaving the final orders on the raid to be explained by m'lord. As soon as she was again immersed in the game, he quietly excused himself and sought out Davon to report what he had learned. Davon, entertaining suspicions that he still had not heard the whole story, had already gleaned the same information from David Shelby. He knew that the information had been reluctantly given by Rufenna's lieutenant, but he had deliberately left David no choice. To refuse to answer would have been considered rude, but David had admitted as little as possible.

David had not told Davon about her bloodstained clothing and bruised face, which shocked him considerably when she had arrived from Knolle. Although she had begged other clothes from the captain of Knolle, the troopers who accompanied her had given David the tale of her condition when she arrived at Knolle with Lord Ashkirk. David had his own suspicions but was not willing to discuss Rufenna with Davon. She would be furious if he did. So he said only what common politeness demanded and left that angry lord to seethe with questions that only Rufenna could answer.

They rode out after dark. Rufenna, riding beside Davon, was aware of David and Sim on her other side. Davon had had his way and had made sure David Shelby and Sim understood that Rufenna was to stay close by Davon's side during the raid. Jamie Scott had been taken near Kielder and held there by the Charltons. The intelligence that Davon had managed to get said that the Charltons, unwillingly, were turning their prisoner over to Lord Eure. The orders were that the prisoner was to be taken to Alnwick, and be held there pending Lord Eure's return with his army from Edinburgh. The troop sent to escort Jamie to Alnwick would make the transfer tonight. Davon planned the raid to do the most possible damage to the English. He had decided that they would strike both at the Charltons at Kielder, and the second arm of their force would intercept the English soldiers escorting Jamie at the ford of the Rede River, just below Otterburn. He would lead the force riding for Otterburn, and Wat would take the other half of the men to hit the Charltons. Rufenna and the Lyall men would ride with Davon.

They crossed the Border, riding south, fording the west end of the Rede River shortly after entering England. Here the two forces split, half silently turning west to ride for Kielder as Davon led his men south, to make the ford near Otterburn. The men rode silently, grimly intent on carrying out their purpose this night, and all were aware that they had a woman in their midst. Sim, remembering another night, another raid, stayed close behind Rufenna, determined that she would not get herself into any more trouble that his master would blame him for!

Finally the hills thinned out, and they entered the spreading plain of Redesdale. Otterburn lay ahead, across the river, and they scouted the ford carefully. No troop had yet crossed the river here, the only easy ford along this entire stretch, and they relaxed a bit. Davon took them into cover in a copse of trees fringing the river, where they could await the approach of the unsuspecting English troops and ambush them as they were scattered across the ford. He discussed the plan with David Shelby and the Scotts, led by Tim Scott of Tushielaw. They decided to plant half the force on this side of the ford and half on the other side. They must be sure of getting to Jamie quickly, freeing him and rushing him to safety in the trees. The men posted scouts in a circle around the ford and sat down to wait.

Rufenna, sitting on the heavy cloak spread for her by David, leaned against the trunk of the massive tree and closed her eyes. They had ridden hard and fast, using the darkness to cover them but also having to reach the ford before the English troop. She imagined that the return trip would be even faster, pursued as they would be by the English!

"Tired, lass?" Davon's quiet voice came out of the darkness and she was aware of him moving to sit down beside her.

"A little," she admitted, knowing it would be useless to lie to him. "It's been a fast ride."

"Aye, and the night's not over yet. You'll stay in the trees, Rufenna, and don't try to argue with me. The fight is no place for you. Sim will stay with you."

Rufenna protested. "Sim will be disappointed if you leave him here with me! One of my own men will stay with me, m'lord. I will remain here, I promise." She knew she would only make their job more difficult if she insisted on trying to join in the melee.

He agreed to that and swiftly turned the subject. "I understand that you were in Edinburgh when the English sacked the city?"

Rufenna stiffened and wondered how he knew. Sim, no doubt. "Aye, I was."

"And . . . ?"

She knew perfectly well what he was probing for, and would not tell him. "I escaped," she said lightly. "Lord Ashkirk helped me and escorted me to Knolle. It was a terrible sight," she added, trying to divert him, "to see the city burning."

"I'm sure it was. Were you hurt, Rufenna? Did they . . . ?"

"M'lord?"

Davon broke off, to Rufenna's great relief, and looked up to see a trooper standing before him.

"The English are coming, m'lord. Jem just rode in."

Instantly Davon was on his feet, sending Jem to order the men to mount. As the trooper departed, Davon looked down at Rufenna.

"We will continue our discussion of your stay in the capital at a later time," he promised her.

Not if I can help it, Rufenna vowed silently.

A trooper, already mounted, went across the ford to warn David of the coming of the enemy, and Rufenna quietly went to her own horse. Sim appeared from the darkness and helped her to mount, and she looked down at him.

"Fetch one of my men, Sim, to remain with me. M'lord needs you with him."

Sim grinned and willingly went off to do her bidding and soon one of the Lyall men moved to sit his horse by her side. From his sullen face Rufenna realized that he was disappointed to be left out of the fight but he did not protest his orders. M'lord had given them personally, telling him in terse detail what he would do to him if Rufenna were harmed.

The English, their force about the same number as the waiting Scots, rode toward the ford. Through a break in the heavy foliage, Rufenna could see them riding quietly and steadily in their orderly ranks. Where was Jamie? she wondered, her eyes scanning the troops. Then she caught a glimpse of fiery hair that nearly matched her own in color and smiled. He was there! Placed in the center of the troop, he was well guarded.

The first soldier splashed across the ford and Davon held his order to ride until the English were strung out in a double file across the shallow river. Then, kicking his own horse into action, he led the sudden charge from the trees. Within seconds all was confusion and noise. The Scotsmen assigned to get to Jamie and get him away went directly to him, cleaving their way through the confused ranks of English horsemen. They formed a guard around Jamie, forcing the indignant Scotsman to leave the scene of the battle and ride for the safety of the trees. Jamie, still protesting at being taken out of the action, was cut

free of his bonds and left seething in the hiding place
in the forest with Rufenna and their increased guard
of six men.

Jamie, suddenly breaking off his steady cursing,
realized that the slender horseman at his side was
a girl! He turned and stared curiously at her and
she smiled.

"Master Scott, we're glad to see you. I am Rufenna
Lyall."

He gaped at her, amazed to see her here. "I'm
glad to see you," he murmured. "I was not willing
to stay much longer with the English. Mistress Lyall,
may I ask what *you* are doing here?"

"I brought the Lyall men," she whispered, keeping
her voice low, as he had done.

"And Davon allowed that . . . for you to come
along, I mean?" He was obviously astounded by this.

"He had little choice in the matter. I go with my
men," Rufenna assured him coolly.

Jamie, knowing Davon Hammond very well, stared
at her. It was not like Davon to be coerced by a
woman, however charming, into doing something he
did not wish to. If he had not wanted her along, he
would have done something about it. Jamie was sure
of that. Now, seeing that vivid face and red hair,
rumors that had reached his ears about a red-haired
lass were recalled. This must be the girl that Davon
had searched for over the Borders! His curiosity
piqued now, Jamie was determined to learn more of
this situation. He had just opened his mouth to ask,
when Rufenna, still keeping an eye on the battle
raging across the ford, let out a cry. Surely that tall,
black-haired man who had just gone down was Davon? Before the startled Jamie and the guards could
stop her, Rufenna had spurred her horse forward,
riding rapidly out of the trees. She heard the shouts
from behind her but ignored them. Sim suddenly ap-

peared at her side, his sword dripping with blood and his face furious.

"Mistress!" he shouted, as an English horseman pressed against her other side, reaching for her.

Warned, Rufenna turned and brought her riding crop down across the man's face with her full strength and kicked her horse forward. She went toward where she had seen Davon fall, followed by the protesting Sim.

"Sim, m'lord has fallen. I saw him. Over here," she shouted, pointing with her whip to a spot ahead of them.

Sim fell silent and moved with her, his alert gaze scanning the fight, ready to defend her if necessary. Then she was stopping, sliding off her horse and kneeling by a still figure on the ground. Sim dismounted and moved her aside, motioning for her to remount. Rufenna ignored him, her wide gaze on the spreading circle of fresh blood on Davon's leg. She heard him moan, and realized that he had been stunned by the fall. The blood welled rapidly from the jagged wound and held her horrified gaze. Then she recovered her wits. She was oblivious to the fact that two of the Hammond men had realized what had happened and were now standing guard on horseback over the fallen man and the two people beside him. One mounted guard moved off to rejoin the battle that had surged away to the other side of the river as the English began a confused retreat. Rufenna looked wildly around for something to use to bandage the leg, to stop that dreadful rush of blood, and found nothing. Without a moment's hesitation, she slipped off her cloak and jacket, took off her heavy outer shirt, and knelt by Davon's injured leg. The cool May night air struck her through the flimsy linen of her remaining shirt and she stopped long enough to slip her jacket back on. With trembling hands she bound up the leg, winding the bandage tightly to stop the bleeding. She became aware of a fixed gaze and turned her head to see Davon's dark eyes on her.

"Get her away from here," he muttered to Sim.

Rufenna ignored his order and finished tying the bandage. Then she stood up. "Sim, can you get him on my horse? I don't see his. He is hardly conscious, I think, and I'll have to ride with him."

With admiration for her cool-headed reaction, Sim agreed and signaled the Hammond man guarding them to help him. In minutes they had Davon on Rufenna's horse and she mounted behind him. Sim took the reins as she wrapped both arms around the large man in the saddle before her, steadying him against the movement of the horse. Slowly they left the field and reached the safety of the trees.

Sim hesitated now that his master was no longer able to issue orders and looked helplessly at Rufenna.

"Sim, go back and get the men away. Give me these six men and Master Scott and we'll head back for Hammond now. We cannot keep the pace you'll have to set when you withdraw. We need a head start," she added firmly, drawing herself up as tall as she could and looking fiercely at Sim, determined that he would obey her.

"Aye, that would be best. I'll give you as much time as I dare, lass, and then pull the men out."

Torn between the necessity of taking command now that Davon was injured, and the wish to see his master safely home himself, Sim rode out of the trees, trusting to the lass to do the job for him.

For Rufenna it was a nightmare ride back to Hammond Tower. They could not move swiftly, for Davon would fall off the horse if they did. He was partially conscious, trying to retain his seat in the saddle, leaning heavily on that slim figure behind him. Up gorges, down slopes they went, threading their way quietly through the rough terrain that marked the Border. Rufenna was ready to ask one of the troopers to take Davon for a while when the battlemented tower of Hammond appeared. Just as they rode up the rocky path to the gates, the rest of the men, led by David and Sim, appeared, riding fast. Sim caught up with the little group as they reached the courtyard. Rufenna could have cried with relief. Her arms ached dreadfully, as she struggled with his weight, and her legs felt numbed from gripping the horse so tightly with her knees. When they halted in the courtyard and she surrendered her burden to willing hands, she could hardly stand. Davon was lowered carefully to the ground and she knelt by him, checking the tightness of the bandage. Suddenly the black eyes opened and he stared at her, his gaze clearing and sharpening.

"What happened?" he muttered, reaching for her arm.

Rufenna took his hand firmly in hers and attempted to soothe him. "You were wounded. We're at Hammond now and they're going to take you up to your room. Everything's fine, Davon. We got Jamie and all the men are back now. Don't fash yourself," she added, aware of the tight, painful grip of his hand.

"I must talk to you," he muttered, refusing to release her hand. "You must stay until I can talk to you!"

Gently Rufenna disengaged her hand and nodded. "I'll wait, m'lord. Take him up now," she added to the waiting men. They lifted Davon carefully and moved into the Great Hall with him. Rufenna followed slowly, thinking about what to do. Her men would be ready to return to Lyall in the morning. Captain Kincaid might need them and she could not keep them waiting at Hammond. Yet there was no one here to nurse Davon and that was a terrible wound in his leg. Could she leave him to the well-meaning but untender mercy of his men? The thought of Elizabeth and how she would feel if Rufenna left her brother bleeding and ill, without proper nursing, stiffened her spine. Rufenna went up the stairs, knowing what she must do.

CHAPTER TWENTY

Rufenna followed the men into the large bedchamber, the bedchamber that she had so much cause to remember, and instructed them to lay Davon on the bed. Having eased their limp burden down, they turned and waited respectfully for their orders. Rufenna thought frantically. She had never seen such a wound, much less nursed one, but she *had* helped Sister Angelica at the Abbey the day Willie cut his arm so badly. Taking a deep breath to calm herself, Rufenna tried to think back, to remember exactly what Sister Angelica had done. She had bathed the wound and then bandaged it tightly, wrapping the strips of linen sheeting over a folded pad, to stop the bleeding. Then she dosed him with a mixture of herbs to reduce the fever. Well, she could bandage the wound and try to stop the bleeding. But she did not know for sure what herbs to brew for Davon if he started a fever, which she feared was inevitable from so terrible a wound. The nuns had tried to teach her about herbs; why hadn't she paid more attention? she moaned to herself.

"Sim," she said, turning naturally to the one man here whom she knew best and who could be counted on to help her. "Bring up water and some clean linen sheets. Have the men slit the sheets into long strips and get those breeches off him," she added, sending a swift glance to the unconscious figure on the bed. Sim snapped out a few quick orders and, motioning to two of the men, approached the bed. He looked back over his shoulder at the girl standing helplessly in the middle of the room and gave her a reassuring smile.

"Mistress, if you would wish it, you could freshen yourself from the ride while we get him ready for you. You could use the chamber you had this morning."

Rufenna hurried down the hall, not waiting to watch them slit the breeches and remove them. She could trust Sim and those large, capable hands of his to handle his patient gently. She would be better able to manage after she had washed her own face and hands.

When she returned to the main bedchamber, Davon had been stripped, his muddy face and arms cleaned, and Sim waited quietly by the bed. The other two men were gone. With her heart beating rapidly and the palms of her hands sweating with nervousness, Rufenna went to the bed. Davon, mercifully unconscious, lay quiet and still, his face pale, his body, except for the injured leg, covered by a clean linen sheet. Rufenna looked at the spreading scarlet stain on the rough bandage she had put on and she swallowed hard. Not meeting Sim's anxious gaze, she began unwrapping the bloody bandage, exposing the wound, and heard his gasp as he saw the jagged, torn flesh. An English soldier had driven his lance, with that terrible steel point, into the thigh, penetrating the right side and ripping through the flesh. The sharp steel point had laid bare a jagged furrow along the leg, running for about ten inches up the thigh. Blood was still flowing in a crimson stream from the wound.

Rufenna knew the first thing to do was to stop the bleeding. She folded a thick pad of clean linen and they strapped it tightly over the wound. It reddened almost immediately. After three such attempts, Rufenna was nearly in tears of frustration and felt utterly helpless.

"He's bleeding to death, Sim, and I don't know how to help him!" she whispered.

"We must sear the wound, mistress," Sim said.

"How do you do it?"

"Well . . . er . . . er . . ."

"Tell me," she demanded.

"We will heat a sword untitl it is red-hot and then burn the wound. That will stop the bleeding."

Rufenna reeled from the bed, her head swimming, bitter bile rising in her throat. She fought it down and sat down weakly on the side of the bed. "Is there no other way, Sim?"

"None that I know of," he admitted.

She stood up, clinging to one of the bedposts. "Very well, Sim," she said resolutely. "I will sear the wound."

Sim smiled a little. "Not you, mistress. I know how 'tis done and I will do it."

"Very well, but let us hurry before he loses more blood."

Sim left the room and returned with four of the brawniest, strongest Borderers Rufenna had ever seen. Then he put his sword in the fire. And they waited. At last the moment arrived and Sim turned to Rufenna, standing white-faced and determined by the bed.

"W-what do I do?" she quavered.

"Mistress," Sim said gently, "you wait outside the door."

"But . . ."

"Please, mistress. 'Tis a most unpleasant thing we do here and I fear if you stay we will have two invalids on our hands."

"But I want to . . ." she argued weakly.

"No," said Sim and with firm hands he put her outside the door. As he was preparing to shut it in her face, he said: "I will call you when we need you."

In only a few seconds Rufenna heard a scream of agony and knew it came from Davon's throat. It was followed by a low cry and then more screams. She sat down on the floor and held her hands over her ears, but she knew that sound of agony would follow her to the grave. Then there was an ominous silence. She waited fifteen impatient minutes and finally beat upon the door.

"I'm coming in," she threatened.

The four Borderers who had helped to hold Davon down filed past her as she opened the door. Their faces were chalky white. The terrible stench of burning flesh almost overwhelmed Rufenna as she edged, tentatively, into the room.

The wound was seared and blackened and only a trickle of blood escaped it now.

"I have some horse salve that we use—will that do?" Sim asked.

"Is there nothing else?"

Sim shrugged. "Nothing that I know of."

She smoothed the sticky, smelly horse ointment over the wound and bandaged it firmly. When they finished, Rufenna straightened and pulled the sheet over the leg.

"Where is the nearest village, Sim?"

"There's a hamlet about two miles from here. What would you be needing?"

"Is there an herb woman there? Someone skilled in nursing? When his fever rises he must be dosed, and I don't know what to give him."

Sim frowned. "I wish we had Old Nell from Torrey here. She'd know."

"Could you bring her here?"

"Aye, but it would take time. She is old and could not travel quickly."

"Then in the morning we'll go into the village and see if we can find someone. Sim, what about Jamie Scott? He must be wanting to go home. Could you send some men with him in the morning?"

"He's down in the hall, lass, if you'd like to speak to him. He can go with Tim Scott's men. What about you?"

"I will stay until he's . . . better. I'll send my men home tomorrow, Sim, and ask to borrow some of your men to see me home when m'lord is recovered."

"Gladly, lass. Shall I tell Master Shelby for you?"

"Please—and, Sim, have you heard about any casualties?"

"All of no account, mistress. We hit the English by surprise and by the time they drew their swords, it was too late to do much to us. We lost four or five horses but the men patched themselves up when we got back."

"Praise to God for that. Ask David to take the men home and tell Walter I will come as soon as I can."

Stretching her tired back, Rufenna moved to the deep armchair before the fire and sat down. "I'll stay with him for a time."

Sim nodded and went quietly out the door, closing it softly behind him. Rufenna leaned back against the soft cushions in the chair and fought her weariness. She was unutterably tired! She had had a long day and a longer night, with far too much time in the saddle. She longed for a bath and a soft bed but someone had to stay and watch Davon. Gradually her lids drooped and she slid deeper into the cushions. She was just dozing off when the door opened to admit Sim. He stood aside and motioned for the man behind him to enter and place the steaming bowl of hot water near the hearth. The man left and Sim came forward, resting the heavy tray on the table by Rufenna's chair.

"I've brought you hot water, a towel, and some food, lass. You'll need to eat if you're going to sit up with him for a time."

Rufenna sat up and sniffed appreciatively at the savory smell coming from the big bowl of stew. It seemed a long time since she had eaten with Sim in the hall below, before their ride to the Border. She realized that she was ravenously hungry.

Thanking Sim, she took the towel and thoroughly washed her face and hands again, this time with hot water. She then turned greedily to the tray, eating stew and the large chunk of fresh bread and cheese. The ale sent a warm glow through her stomach and relaxed her. After she put the tray outside on the floor, she checked Davon's bandages and was relieved to notice that, as yet, there was no hint of the telltale scarlet seeping through. Evidently the searing had done its work effectively.

She settled herself with a rough wool blanket in the big chair. Twice during the night she awoke, when Sim came in quietly to replenish the fire. Together they checked the quiet figure on the bed. Davon was sleeping heavily, his face still pale but cool, and the bandages seemed to be controlling the bleeding. Exchanging relieved glances, Rufenna and Sim settled down to their vigil, Sim taking over the other big chair and Rufenna returning to her own.

The next morning, Rufenna left Sim watching the patient and went down to the hall. By dawn Davon had started running a fever and had grown increasingly restless. Rufenna was determined to find help in nursing him if she had to inquire in every house in every village in the area!

Jamie Scott was waiting on the front steps, surrounded by a troop of Scott men. He asked about Davon, frowned, and wondered aloud if he should leave her to manage alone.

"There's naught you can do, Master Scott, and your wife will be waiting word of you. We will take good care of Lord Hammond, I assure you."

Jamie surveyed her tired face with an inquiring, curious gaze. He had not wasted his time during the evening, and had discovered that this lass was indeed the one whom he had tried to help rescue from the English. He had *not* been able to find out why she had been riding with Davon at that time or what a Lyall was doing riding around the countryside with the Hammonds. Especially a woman! Davon's men had told him of her capture by her cousin and their rescue. The more Jamie learned, the more curious he became, but found that the men, while eager to speak highly of the lass's courage and spirit, would not tell him how she came to be with Davon on the raid. David Shelby, also at the table, was listening avidly, storing up the information to take back to the captain and Master Walter. He too found the situation strange, even though he knew how she came to be with Davon on the raid. Like Walter and Captain Kincaid, David knew of the attack on Alexander, the abduction of Rufenna, and her return with the band of Gypsies. He also thought it a strange way for m'lord to extract revenge on the Lyalls. He thought it even more peculiar that Rufenna, the supposed victim of his revenge, was determined to take her men to help him on this raid and then to stay and nurse m'lord while sending her men back to Lyall! Having no idea of the seething curiosity of the two men, Rufenna watched them both gather up their men and ride out, one to Lyall, the other to Buccleuch.

As soon as they were gone, she asked for an escort to the nearest village and rode out of the gates of Hammond Tower herself. Allowing Will, who was in charge of her escort troop, to guide her to the nearest village, Rufenna explained to him what she needed. When they rode into the tiny cluster of houses, just stirring in the morning chill, Will questioned the first man he saw and came back to where she waited with a smile on his face.

"Widow Harkness, the man says, mistress. She's the local herb woman and said to be very skilled."

"Did he say where we could find her?"

"Aye. This way, mistress. It's the last cottage down the lane."

Rufenna dismounted before the tiny thatched cottage and waited while Will hammered on the door. Slowly the door opened a crack and a woman's face appeared. She was old, tiny, and appeared to be a walking collection of rags. Her thin, stooped figure was so swathed and wrapped in ragged shawls and scarves that one could scarcely believe that a person was inside them. The cowl that covered her hair and part of her face was worn but clean. Rufenna explained to her their errand and found that Widow Harkness was willing to accompany her to Hammond. The old woman's dark eyes snapped with excitement at the thought of tending to m'lord, and she hastened back indoors to collect what herbs she would need. Will and Rufenna exchanged triumphant glances and waited impatiently for her to return. Soon they were cantering back up the track, the widow mounted before one of the troopers and hanging on in terror.

When they reached Hammond Tower, Rufenna rushed to Davon's room.

"Sim, how is he?" she asked from the doorway.

"Not good, lass. His fever has risen and he's getting restless. Did you find someone?"

Rufenna stood aside and let the old woman enter, and she and Sim watched anxiously as Widow Harkness examined the patient. Before the hour was up, a soothing draught of lockleburr was mixed and the old woman watched while Sim and Rufenna forced it down Davon's resisting throat. Then she mixed a salve of serpent's tongue and two other herbs which Rufenna did not recognize. Rufenna's timid questions were met by incomprehensible mutterings. She then demanded Rufenna's help in taking off the bandage and smoothed the herbal mixture over the wound and replaced the bandage with clean pads. After that she retreated to the chair by the fire and waited. As the day wore on, Davon grew more and more restless. His fever was mounting steadily and Rufenna was wringing her hands with worry. The old woman, in her dry, thin voice, reluctantly assured them that it was only to be expected, that the fever would have to run its course but she could ease it with some more of her remedies. Again they forced a bitter draught down the reluctant Davon's throat. He was delirious now, fighting them and refusing to swallow it. As fast as Rufenna would spoon some of the medicine into his mouth, he would spit it out.

Then, in despair, she remembered something she had seen her brother do when dosing a favorite dog. Rufenna told Sim to spoon another lot of the mixture in. Instantly she forced up Davon's chin, pressing his mouth closed with a quick hand, and then pinched his nostrils shut. Involuntarily he swallowed and then she released him so that he could breathe. Sim grinned and nodded and they repeated the maneuver, managing to get most of the draught into him by this method. After a while he relaxed, sliding into a deep sleep. Rufenna collapsed into the chair.

He was going to be a terrible patient. It was bad
enough now, while he was delirious, but it would
be even more difficult when he recovered his senses.
She felt sure he would refuse to drink anything so
evil-tasting and then what would they do?

Slowly the night passed, Rufenna dividing the
watch with Sim. When it was time for her to take
over the vigil, he fetched her from her chamber and
reported that Davon had been quiet, still under the
effects of the medicine. Rufenna curled up in the
big chair and dozed off, awakening instantly to find
the patient thrashing about in the bed. She was
quickly at his side, pressing his broad shoulders back
against the pillows and trying to keep him from using
the injured leg. It would not do for him to thrash
around like that, as it could cause the wound to
break open and begin bleeding. With a lunge that
caught her by surprise Davon sat up, knocking her
from the side of the bed to the floor. He was muttering wildly and she scrambled to her feet, grabbing
his flailing arms.

"I must talk to her! Make her come back!" he
mumbled, trying to throw back the cover and get up.

Rufenna exerted her full strength in forcing him
back on the bed, realizing she could not hold him.
Either she had to take the risk of leaving him or she
had to break through the haze of fever and talk him
into quieting down. The first idea she rejected immediately. During the time it would take her to summon
help, he could get off the bed and then the damage
would be done. Rufenna decided to talk to him, and
if that didn't work, then she would be forced into
finding Sim.

"Davon, I'm here," she repeated over and over, "it's
Rufenna." She was struggling to make him lie back
down. "Davon, stop it! It's Rufenna."

For a long instant the cloud of semiconsciousness

veiling his dark eyes lifted and she saw him compre-
hend her words.

He sank back against the pillow, grasping her arm
in an iron grip. "Rufenna?"

"It's Rufenna. I'm here. Lie down, Davon."

He let her settle him but did not release her arm.
"I must talk to you," he muttered.

"You will," she said clearly, easing herself over
him and lying down on his other side, away from the
injured leg. "I'm here and you can talk to me whenever you wish."

He lay quietly for a long moment and she thought
he had slipped back into that semiconscious state.
She felt his forehead, smoothing the tumbled hair
back out of his eyes, and worried about the heat under her hand. His fever was still high.

Suddenly his eyes opened again. "You won't leave?"

"I won't leave," she promised. He sighed and closed
his eyes and Rufenna felt his body relax. He still
held her arm tightly so she made herself as comfortable as she could, her body turned awkwardly
because of his tight grip. After a long wait she moved
slightly, watching to see if he would rouse if she
slipped out of his loosened hold. Instantly his hand
tightened, as if he held onto her as a lifeline in his
dark delirium. Persuading him to shift his grip to
her free hand, she managed to get under the covers
and pull them up over her shoulders. With a relieved
sigh she snuggled down against his side, listening to
his heavy, raspy breathing as he moved restlessly in
the bed. Then he began to quiet down a little, turning slightly so he lay close against her, his hand releasing hers and going across her waist, drawing her
against him. Hardly daring to breathe, she waited,
studying his strong, pale face in the flickering firelight. Even when he was unconscious, unaware of her
as a woman, her body quickened at the feel of his

strength against her. Rufenna sternly subdued such reactions and made her body relax against him, letting him bury his hot face against her cool throat.

When Sim came quietly in to relieve her, he stared in astonishment at the entwined figures in the bed. Rufenna was sleeping peacefully in Davon's warm hold and Sim gazed thoughtfully from her calm face to his lord's pale one. A light touch assured him that his master still had the fever but surely it was not so high as it had been. Sim built up the fire and left as quietly as he had come, grinning slightly to himself. Trust m'lord to make the most of even this situation. Sim went back to his cold bed, wondering if he dared tell m'lord about this when he recovered. The lass would be angry if he did, but m'lord would be very interested to learn that the lass had held him all night against her breast like a babe. Slipping into his damp, clammy bed, Sim was sure the fever would be broken by morning. M'lord must have come out of his delirium for a time, at least, to have inveigled the lass into his bed! If that was so, and it must be so, then the fever must be breaking. Satisfied, Sim turned over and went back to sleep, to dream of another lass, Agnes, and of her warm soft body against his.

CHAPTER TWENTY-ONE

Sim was mistaken. The fever did not break by morning, or even by the morning after that. He and Rufenna, assisted by the old woman, Widow Harkness, fought the fever and dosed Davon repeatedly with the mixture of herbs and bark. At last the fever began to subside on the third night. Rufenna had found that her presence in the bed beside him during those long, feverish nights seemed to soothe him. It was as if he knew she was there, watching over him, fighting with him for his life. The wound, swollen and inflamed for those days, began to look better, and Rufenna and Sim took their first relieved breaks from the sick room since Davon was wounded. Rufenna felt sure she could not have managed if Sim had not been there. All Davon's men were loyal and would have done their best if asked, but Sim seemed almost to anticipate her needs before she voiced them. He was there when Davon needed to be moved or cared for. He was always ready to fetch Widow Harkness whenever Rufenna felt her assistance was needed. He was willing just to be there to lend her his moral support. Sim quickly moved into the position of

brother, the older, wiser, understanding brother that
Alexander had never been for Rufenna.

It was the first time in her life she had ever had
the responsibility of nursing a gravely sick person.
Rufenna was painfully aware of her inadequacy.
They were doing all they knew to do for him and
could only wait and watch. And pray. Rufenna's prayers during these troubled days had never been so
fervent. Once she thought how pleased the nuns
would be to know that she had learned one lesson
well. She was so tired from her long hours of careful nursing that it was easy not to think about what
could happen; she didn't *want* to think about it. She
told herself wearily her anxiety and prayers were
caused by the responsibility involved in nursing any
sick human being; the fact that it was Davon made
no difference. During those nights when she lay by his
side, reassuring him with her presence, she carefully
blanked her mind, courting sleep, ignoring the physical responses his very proximity roused. Reluctantly
she admitted to herself that it was a physical attraction and she was ashamed of it. It was a base thing,
something to be fought against, to be ignored or
suppressed. How could there be deeper feelings when
this man was her enemy! He had kidnapped her, ravished her, held her against her will. He was not to
be trusted and any emotions she felt toward him
must come from the devil and hell itself!

Sim, watching this intriguing situation, was torn
between amusement and sympathy. He knew, none
better, what fate his master had planned for her.
However, Davon had not behaved as he should have
either. Lost in the tangle of illogic that seemed to
govern this situation, Sim dismissed it. He could not
understand the lass's mind nor fathom how she could
continue to consider the man lying there so ill and
quiet her enemy, and still spend her days and nights
nursing him. But she went far beyond the normal

nursing duties. She shared her warmth and reassuring presence during the nights in his bed, and agonized over his continuing fever. Sim decided that if that was typical of a woman's reasoning, he would never understand them. To Sim's more simple philosophy, bred on the rough, turbulent Border, an enemy was an enemy and you gave him no quarter, no succor, no sympathy. Being enemies by day and lovers by night was beyond his understanding and he shrugged and fervently hoped that Agnes did not turn out to be as baffling!

By the third night Rufenna was certain that Davon's temperature was beginning to come down. His forehead felt cooler, he was less restless, less inclined to mutter and talk so wildly during the night. Yet he showed no signs of regaining his wits and it worried her. She lay by his side, aware of his strong arm wrapped tightly around her, and tried to puzzle it out. He seemed to require her presence as much as, if not more than, he had done during the worst of his delirium. He held her more closely, slept more soundly now, his lean body warm against hers. Often, in his sleep, he would stroke her back or thigh, yet he never woke, never seemed to recognize anyone. By the fourth night she was wondering if she should confide these troubling thoughts to Sim. There must be some reason why he had not regained full consciousness.

Rufenna put the question to Widow Harkness the next day. The old woman was repacking her precious herbs to return to the village. The widow felt she had done as much for her patient as she could; only time and rest would complete the cure. She shot a wary glance at Rufenna, muttered something indistinguishable under her breath, and shrugged.

"But he should have come to his senses by now, should he not?" Rufenna persisted, determined to get an answer.

"Mayhap, but it affects different, mistress."

"It affects different people different ways? The fever? Well, then, when do you think he will know us?"

The widow shrugged and hunched her shoulders, glancing at the quiet figure on the bed. His breathing was easy, steady. His forehead was cool now and she was perfectly sure he was no longer feverish. "Mayhap he hit his head when he fell," she offered, it being the only suggestion she would make.

Rufenna frowned. It was possible, she supposed, but only increased her worry. They had not noticed any head injury but he could have struck a rock in the dark and they wouldn't have noticed it. They had thought him merely stunned by the impact of the fall but what if he *had* struck a rock? Sim was also noncommittal about it. He listened to her worried summation of what the widow had suggested and he, too, shrugged. He appeared not to be so concerned as before and this, instead of reassuring Rufenna, only served to irritate her. Time would tell, he suggested casually, urging Rufenna to go out into the courtyard for some air. More and more, Sim was taking over the day watch, freeing Rufenna to rest, to get some fresh air, to be ready for the night shift. She still spent it sleeping beside Davon in the big bed, close by if he should waken and be conscious, or if his fever should rise again. At the end of a week she was wondering if she needed to continue her night vigilance and told Sim so.

"He is obviously so much better, Sim, I don't think I need to stay with him tonight. His wound is healing now and the fever seems to be gone. I can't help but think that if he would just recover his senses, he would be nearly well."

They were in the hall, just outside the open door. Rufenna could see the quiet figure, lying on his side facing the wall, and sleeping deeply.

Sim frowned. "I know, mistress, but not yet. I

mean, you need to be with him at night until he does come to his senses. If he awoke during the night and could not recall what had happened and tried to get up . . ." He let the sentence trail off suggestively.

"I hadn't thought of that," she admitted, knowing that Davon's leg was not yet healed enough to be walked on. "You're right, Sim. I'll wait until he seems to know us. Perhaps tonight."

"Aye, lass, perhaps he'll recover his wits tonight," Sim agreed.

As had become the habit now, Rufenna ate supper with the Hammond men in the Great Hall while Sim took up Davon's tray and spoon-fed his invalid's diet of broth to him. Sim had insisted upon it and Rufenna agreed, for she enjoyed sharing the meal with the men and hearing about the day's hunting. It made a welcome change in a day's routine, which was growing increasingly boring, she thought, letting the men further her education in dicing. They beamed proudly on her when she won and consoled her when she did not, treating her with a curious mixture of respect and camaraderie. She was, in their eyes, m'lord's property and not a man in the hall would have dared to offer her the least insult. They teased her, drew lots to see who would cast dice with her, competed to tell her the most outrageous stories of hunting and fighting prowess, and yet gave her the respect m'lord's lady would expect. By the end of that long week there was not a man there who would not have died protecting her and it gave her a warm feeling, a feeling of belonging, which she had never really known. They liked her for herself, accepted her, and she grew increasingly fond of them.

By the time Sim appeared that evening, letting her know that Davon was fed and settled down for the night, she was tired but happy. She went quietly into his bedchamber, slipped off her borrowed dressing gown, and crept into bed. Davon didn't stir and she drifted quickly off to sleep. Hours later she awoke, stretching drowsily, feeling someone moving beside her. Her lids flew open just as a pair of warm lips touched her throat, moving caressingly down to her shoulder and the tantalizing warm hollow between her breasts. Rufenna stiffened in shock. Davon?

"Ummm, nice," he murmured, his face against her throat.

"Davon!" she gasped, trying to sit up. Strong hands caught her and pressed her back down, hands showing no sign of weakness from fever and his wound!

"Y-you, Davon . . ."

His mouth silenced hers and she knew without doubt that he had certainly recovered his wits. His hands, urgent and yet coaxing, caressed her and her body flamed into warmth. Rufenna gently pushed him away, freeing her mouth, and, by the light of the fire, gazed astounded up at the dark face above her.

"You're awake!"

His lips quirked into a smile. "Obviously," he said, brushing her tumbled hair from her brow. "Far more awake than you realize."

"But you . . . Davon, how long have you been conscious?" Suspicion was entering her mind, for here, plainly, was no wasted invalid, no man who had lived on thin broth for a week! The sheet and coverlet slid down to his waist and she could see clearly the broad, muscular shoulders and hard chest. He had not lost an ounce, she realized, wondering just what was going on here. "When did you . . ."

His dark eyes narrowed in amusement and he shook his head. "Why, I just woke up and here you were. What a wonderful surprise!"

She didn't believe him for a minute. Rufenna's wits were working quickly now and she began to grasp the fact that he had not just recovered consciousness; he had not been living on gruel and broth!

"Sim!" she sputtered. "He's been lying to me and I swear I'll—"

"Don't blame Sim," Davon said quietly. "He's only following orders."

Rufenna gritted her teeth in rage. "How dare you, Davon? How long have you been awake?"

"Long enough," he admitted, stroking her cheek.

She pushed his hand away, too incensed to have her anger softened by a caress. "And all those nights . . ." she accused.

He grinned unrepentantly. "Wasted, of course, but I was too ill and weak to do much about it. Until now," he said softly, lowering his head.

Rufenna jerked her face away, not mollified at all by this statement. "You've deceived me!"

"It was necessary, Rufenna. You'd have gone back to the other room if you'd known I was conscious. I enjoyed it, really, but it was a bit frustrating. Having you in my bed and not being able to do anything about it," he explained, capturing her head in his hands and holding it still.

"I'll never forgive you!" she burst out. "Either of you!"

"Ummm," he answered, finding her mouth.

In spite of her anger Rufenna could not deny the surge of warmth that flowed through her. She wanted to strike out at him, or run away, and could do neither. He was in no shape for a struggle and if she tried to escape him, he could injure that leg, open the wound again, trying to stop her. So she fumed and tried to hold her body stiff and unrelenting. But Davon read her emotions clearly and took base advantage of the situation. He knew she would not dare fight him and he was determined to melt that icy resistance. His fingers began to trace lacy patterns across her breasts while his mouth teased and tormented her ear, her cheek, feathering kisses over her face. With infinite gentleness he wooed her, teasing, stroking, his hands warm and knowing just where to touch or stroke to add to the burning ache growing in her.

Rufenna stood it as long as she could, fighting herself since she dared not fight him, her resolve and anger melting away under the throbbing need of her body. With a sobbing gasp she flung her arms around his neck, pulling him closer to her, molding her body against the taut length of his. She was trembling now, no longer caring what he was doing. She was only aware of the fires flickering down her limbs, coursing through her stomach, sending her nearly wild with desire. Words of love trembled on her lips and she caught them back, momentarily shocked into stillness by their very existence. She could not love this man! It was madness, impossible! Then even these thoughts were driven out of her mind as he roused her to a fever pitch of ecstasy and she was lost in flowing waves of passion.

Spent, past caring about his deception, she lay in his arms, her cheek resting against his broad chest. She could hear the steady beat of his heart under her ear. After a long, quiet moment a thought came into her drowsy mind and she asked him:

"What did you have for supper?"

He chuckled. "Same as you: mutton, potatoes, cheese, and bread. Sim has been looking after me well."

She raised her head and scowled at him. "I'll get even with both of you, Davon Hammond! Just wait."

His flashing smile warmed her. 'I'll enjoy it, I'm sure. Besides, lass, just think how quickly I'll get well with this kind of medicine!" He traced a lazy finger down her breast. " 'Tis better than that old crone's brew you forced down me."

"But you . . . Davon, when *did* you recover consciousness?"

He grinned and pulled her back into his arms. "Go to sleep."

Tomorrow, she thought sleepily. I'll tell him what I think of him tomorrow!

CHAPTER TWENTY-TWO

Rufenna's mind was made up the next morning, when, on leaving the bedchamber shortly after dawn, she met Sim's knowing grin.

She had to leave. The memory of last night's passion and tenderness would follow her to her grave but there was no sense to it. Davon Hammond had used her and she could not allow herself to forget that for a minute. She was needed at home and if she didn't leave while Davon was at least partially helpless, he would never allow her to go. She closed her mind to the thought that she was becoming so passionately attached to him that she would soon find it impossible to leave him. She kept her thoughts firmly on his deception.

No longer would she allow Davon either to trick her or force her into such a situation again. Anyone as well on the road to recovery as his performance last night proved did not need her constant nursing. He could just get along with Sim, she decided, and determined to leave for Lyall immediately. Opening her door, she saw a young clansman going down the hall and asked him to fetch Sim to her. Her feelings toward him this morning were far from sisterly and

Sim realized it the minute he took a good look at her. He entered her room quietly, forewarned by the militant gleam in her green eyes.

"Would you order your captain to ready a troop to escort me to Lyall?"

Sim frowned. "This morning, lass?"

"Now," said Rufenna firmly.

"Did m'lord agree to your leaving, lass?" he asked frankly, surveying her flushed cheeks and the determined jut of her chin.

"I do not need m'lord's permission to leave, Sim. I'll be ready in an hour."

"Lass, he will not permit you to leave until he talks to you. Will you come now and discuss this with him?"

"No! I have nothing to say to him, Sim. He is recovering quite well and no longer needs my nursing and you know it. I don't want to see him, Sim, and I intend to leave. Will you grant me an escort or not?"

Sim scratched his head anxiously. "I cannot order it without m'lord's approval, mistress. I'll just have a word with him about it."

Sim started to leave and Rufenna called him back. "I mean it, Sim. I intend to leave Hammond today with that escort or without it."

Sim was soon back. "Lass, he says you cannot go until he speaks to you. He's expecting you now."

Rufenna, her face washed and her hair tidied, was just sitting down to the breakfast tray the page had brought up. "No," she said baldly. "I do not want to talk to him about anything."

Sim, not knowing what to do, reported this to Davon and was disquieted by the immediate spark of temper in his master's eyes.

"Then I'll have to go to her," Davon murmured, throwing off the bedcovers and reaching for the dressing gown lying across the foot of the bed. He carefully maneuvered his leg from the bed to the floor and looked up to see Sim gaping in astonishment at him. "Don't stand there, man, help me! Fetch me my walking stick." When Sim didn't move, only looked pleadingly at him, Davon frowned. "Now, Sim," he said softly, "and I warn you not to tarry."

Reluctantly Sim fetched the heavy gnarled stick, lovingly carved from stout oak and given to Davon's grandfather by an elderly clansman. Davon leaned his weight on it and held out his free arm to Sim, demanding his assistance. Mentally cursing women and their stubbornness, Sim helped Davon down the hall to the door of Rufenna's room.

Rufenna had no warning of the sudden descent of her host and nearly dropped the mug of ale when the door crashed back and Davon came in. Her gaze flew to his grim, taut face, to the bandaged leg and back, and she slowly rose to her feet. Still silent, Davon limped to the bed and sank gratefully upon it. His dark gaze flashed to Sim, standing helplessly in the doorway. "Shut the door, lad, and wait outside."

Sim gratefully did so, glad to escape the sulphurous atmosphere brewing in the room.

"You should not have come," Rufenna burst out, turning to face him.

"You refused to come to me," he reminded her, letting his gaze rest thoughtfully on her pale, determined face. It shifted to the cloak folded over the back of the chair, and hardened. "You were planning to leave this morning, without that talk you promised me?"

She flushed slightly. "There is nothing to say."

"I think there is. Sit down, Rufenna. I don't like having to cramp my neck looking up at you." He waited until she was sitting down. "So you're going to abandon me to Sim's mercies?"

"You're doing very well," Rufenna said tartly, remembering last night. "You don't need my nursing any longer and I must return to Lyall."

He did not attempt to deny that she might be needed at home. "You believe your cousin will try to retake the castle in your absence? He will not succeed. Captain Kincaid is perfectly capable of holding Lyall indefinitely."

She wouldn't meet his gaze and merely nodded. "Nevertheless, I am needed there."

Davon leaned back against the piled-up pillows and studied her narrowly. "I'd like to hear what happened in Edinburgh, Rufenna. I have had a very confusing report."

She longed to say it was none of his business but did not quite dare. However, she had no intention of telling him the truth.

"I was in Edinburgh when the English army attacked it. Lord Ashkirk very kindly assisted me to escape. There's nothing to tell."

"Is there not? You were at the palace, visiting your brother, John, I understand. The soldiers took the palace, I've heard, and burnt it. You were hurt?"

"No," she said, wishing he wouldn't probe so.

"That's not what I heard, Rufenna." It was a shot in the dark, knowing the ways of enemy soldiers, and it worked. The color drained from her face and she refused to meet that dark, penetrating gaze. "Tell me," he said again, softly.

"Three soldiers burst into our room and two of them t-took John. The third one a-attacked me and I . . . killed him," she said, her voice faltering at the end.

Davon, hearing exactly what he feared he would hear, was now as pale as she was. His mouth was a grim line and his eyes dark and angry. He realized it would do no good to press her for details so he shifted his attack.

"Did they say where they were taking young John?"

he demanded, not indicating by a flicker of an eye-lash that until now he had known nothing of the boy's capture.

"T-to Lord Eure, they said. We are expecting a ransom demand when he returns with the army to England."

"It will be a high one," Davon said, thinking hard. "Eure hated your father."

"I know that. However, we shall raise it, however much it is."

"What did Sir Robert Kerr say about it?"

Rufenna remembered belatedly that she herself had told Davon in the note that Sir Robert was at Lyall. "He said he would negotiate the ransom with Lord Eure but," she added, raising her chin defiantly, "I declined the offer. We will manage it ourselves."

She did not see the glow of admiration in Davon's eyes. Here was a spunky lass. "I will manage it," he contradicted. "That bastard Eure will bleed you dry, Rufenna. Leave it to me. What else did Sir Robert say?"

Rufenna stared angrily at him, her growing fury overcoming her discretion. "He is arranging my marriage to Neville this summer so if I need any assistance, m'lord, in getting my brother back, my *husband* will help me."

A flame leapt into life in his dark eyes and he stared at her with a narrowed gaze. She knew that for some reason she had flicked him on the raw and infuriated him.

"You will not marry that weak-chinned puppy, mistress, so do not think you will."

"You have nothing to say about it," she pointed out, deliberately adding fuel to his anger. "It was legally arranged between Sir Robert and my father and it has nothing to do with you, m'lord. It is none of your affair."

"I am making it my affair!" he said darkly, when

there was a discreet tap on the door and after a moment Sim's head came around the edge.

"A message for you, mistress, from Lyall."

Rufenna moved toward the door but Sim opened it to allow the travel-stained man to enter. The messenger glanced curiously at the man sitting pale and silent on the bed and then turned to his mistress.

"Mistress Rufenna," he said, "I come from Master Walter with an urgent message. He asks that you return immediately. The English army has crossed the Border, back into England, and attacked Knolle on their way. It held against them," he added hastily, seeing her angry color fade abruptly. "The captain says all is well there but great damage was done to the east coast."

Davon sat up and caught the man's attention. "What type of damage?"

"I understand, m'lord, that they besieged Tantallon but could not take it without siege guns, so they marched down the coast, sacking Fast Castle and Home, and damaging both Melrose and Jedburgh abbeys. 'Tis fearful damage they did, I hear, m'lord. All the crops were destroyed that were in their path and every tower and castle within easy reach. There was some damage at Knolle but most of the army was attacking Home Castle and so they did not take Knolle."

Davon laughed grimly. "Sir Robert Logan will be in a fine stew about Fast Castle, though why the Logans should be so partial to it when they have a town house such as Restalrig is beyond my understanding. But then, the Logans have always been hard to fathom."

"Aye," said the messenger, impatient to hear what Rufenna would say.

"They did not take Tantallon either?" Davon asked, astonished that the English army would dare touch the mighty Douglass stronghold. Were not the Douglasses sympathetic to the English cause? What had possessed the English to attack Tantallon?

"No, m'lord, Tantallon held. 'Tis impossible to take by siege, without cannon. Mistress Rufenna"—his voice grew urgent—"Master Walter begs that you come home. Master Neville is at Lyall, awaiting your return, and Captain Kincaid hopes to hear from Lord Eure anytime now that the English are gone home."

Rufenna stared at the man. "Neville Kerr is at Lyall? What brings him there at this time?"

"Master Walter said that Sir Robert had sent him. He is under Sir Robert's orders to see to Lyall, and Master Walter is mightily put out, mistress, o'er his giving the orders there."

Her eyes narrowed with anger, Rufenna demanded, "*Neville Kerr* is giving the orders at Lyall? He has no right!"

"So Master Walter says, but Sir Robert—"

"The devil take Sir Robert! He has no legal right to give orders in *my* home! My mother is mistress there, not Sir Robert!"

She turned to Davon, a silent spectator to this exchange.

"I must leave for Lyall immediately! This is not to be borne! Will you order a troop to escort us?"

Davon nodded reluctantly. He had little choice and knew it. The lass was so angry she would go without an escort if he refused it.

"He is welcome to visit Lyall but he will not rule there," she muttered, catching up her cloak and nodding to the messenger. "I will come immediately."

"Sim, order a troop to escort them and see that this man is given some refreshment and a brief rest before they leave. Just a moment, mistress, I have not finished our discussion."

Sim signaled to the man to follow him and closed the door.

"What do you have to say now?" Rufenna demanded. "I have told you what you wish to know, have I not?"

He looked steadily at her. "You choose to regard me as your enemy, Rufenna, but listen well to my advice. Do not allow this marriage to take place at this time. Sir Robert's intentions are all too clear and you will need to go carefully to avoid the trap he has set for you."

"Trap?"

"Aye, that's what it is. If you marry young Kerr, Sir Robert will be lord at Lyall. Have you considered that? He is not a man to be trusted and if you allow him to become involved in ransoming your brother, you will find that you have exchanged one kind of prison for another for John. Kerr will detain the boy under so-called protective custody and, having your brother fast at Cessford, he will be in a position to rule Lyall. Surely Master Walter does not approve of this marriage now?"

"No," she admitted, knowing he was saying only what she had already said. "He sees the danger as you do. Do not fash yourself over it, m'lord. I will not allow my brother to fall into Sir Robert's hands. I am mistress at Lyall now and will guard it well."

"You will give me your promise that you will not marry young Kerr at this time? Your solemn word, Rufenna? I have only your safety, and the safety of your brother, in mind."

She hesitated.

"If you will not promise," he added quietly, "I cannot allow you to leave Hammond. If you are so foolish—"

She exploded with anger. "Foolish! You talk of my safety but I am not safe at Hammond! Not from you and your twisted idea of revenge! You are my enemy also, have you forgotten? You began a feud with my family, killed my brother . . ."

"No, I did not kill your brother. I do not deny that I am responsible for his death, just as he was responsible for Isobel's death, but I did not kill him. That, however, is not the point, mistress. However justified I was in your brother's death, and I will never admit it was not justified, I did rob you and your brother of your sole protector. The only adult male member of your family capable of offering you assistance and protection is dead. The responsibility is now mine."

"You shan't be responsible for me," she cried, her voice trembling with anger. "I am responsible for myself. Besides, I have Walter and Captain Kincaid . . ."

"And your good friend and cousin, Murdoch," he reminded her dryly. "Rufenna, we are talking about an old man and a soldier, who, though a good captain of the garrison, is not the same as a brother or guardian, and an inexperienced girl! No, lass, you should not scorn my protection. I have no designs on Lyall *or* your brother. Being under my protection will keep Sir Robert from taking Lyall and securing your brother. He may be the Warden of the March, but my influence counts at Court and he knows it! Sir Robert Kerr will not pit himself against *me*, lass, and you remember that! Also, do not be deceived that because the English army has recrossed the Border into England that they will stay there. The summer will be hard on the Border counties as the English will be riding nightly on raids, authorized by none other than the King of England. Henry is furious; make no mistake of that. He will make us suffer for what he considers an insult. Knolle has felt it, possibly Lyall will be next. Sim will accompany you and remain at Lyall. I will authorize him to call on my garrison at Torrey for defense of Lyall, if it is needed. When the ransom demand comes, he will bring me word and I will get young John back for you."

"I don't need Sim," she protested. She was still smarting from Sim's part in the deception. All those days he was watching her and wondering when his master would be ready to "wake up"! She ground her teeth in irritation at the thought of Sim.

"He will accompany you or you do not leave. Do I have your promise?"

Rufenna knew that he meant it. Reluctantly she gave it, wondering if she would regret giving in to him on this point. She would never have admitted it to Davon, but she would be relieved to know that Sim, with the Hammond men available to him, would be at hand at Lyall. She would have to forgive his part in the deception . . . for now. Besides, she had only promised not to wed Neville this summer, which she had not intended to do anyway.

"I will go home to Torrey Castle as soon as I can travel," Davon said, "and I'll advise Sim of our return. Until he hears differently from me, he can find me here, if the demand should come quickly. Don't worry overmuch about the lad, Rufenna. Eure won't harm him. He's a valuable prisoner and worth a goodly ransom. So he'll see to the boy's safety because of that." He did not add that a dead prisoner was worth nothing to Eure.

She had worried about it and hoped Davon was right. Prisoners held for ransom were usually treated very well, she knew. She could only hope he had been delivered swiftly to Lord Eure's custody when Edinburgh fell.

Davon, knowing full well that she would not tell him anything of the ransom demand if she could help it, was not fooled for a minute. He would rely on Sim to keep him advised and make the lass accept help. She would only bungle it, and give Eure the opportunity to keep raising his ransom demands.

"I thank you for the nursing, Rufenna," he added, his mocking gaze sliding down her shapely figure in the boyish clothes. He didn't like the despondent droop of her mouth or the worry in her eyes but he could remedy that. "I am sure I would not have recovered so quickly without it." He was instantly rewarded by a flush of anger on her cheeks.

For an instant she was half tempted to throw her nearly empty mug of ale at his insolent head, for she had not needed that reminder. Flouncing from the room in a rage, Rufenna knew that she would not forget last night. Now he was just making fun of her! She would not be able to repress the memory and it would come all too often to haunt her. She could only writhe at the memory of Davon Hammond and hope that she never had to see him or those mocking dark eyes of his again. She could manage Lyall and Lord Eure very well without his help, she thought furiously, storming down the stairs to the Great Hall. Never would she ask *him* for help!

help, she would only break it and give him the
opportunity, to keep them for your own demands.

"I thank you for the warning, Marquis," he added,
... meeting ... sliding ... had slightly ... in
the ... dishes ... didn't ... her ... expression
... of her mouth ... the worry in her eyes ... just
... could remind ... am sure ... would not have
returned to ... without ... He ... it was a pity
... interested by ... of them ... her cheeks.

For a ... the ... half ... to draw her
... lips ... of ... his ... head, but
she had not ... that reminder ... embarrassment
... was, in ... Suddenly ... the world
... longer ... night. Now he was just making fun
of her. She would not be able to ignore the memory
and it would return all too often to haunt her. She
could only ... of the memory of ... if
... and hope that the ... to see him or
... thinking that ... of his ... She could
manage ... and ... your ... well without his
help, she ... nervously ... about the same
... she would rather would she ask him for help?

CHAPTER TWENTY-THREE

Rufenna stood at the narrow window in the small withdrawing room, which she had taken over for her own use in seeing to the chores of running the estate. She felt that if she heard the phrase *my uncle Robert says* or *Sir Robert says* one more time today, she would scream. It seemed to preface every remark Neville Kerr made and unfortunately, holding his uncle in aversion as she did, it exasperated her thoroughly. Just once she wished he would say, "I think it should be done this way" or "Do it this way." Make a decision on his own, without justification, qualification, or equivocation! Now she turned slightly and studied the fair, handsome face of Neville, her betrothed, as he talked to Walter on the far side of the room. He was certainly handsome to look at; she could not deny that. Above medium height, slender but wiry, he was nicely built and his smooth fair hair and blue eyes should make him an unusually attractive man. Perhaps it was the indecisiveness of his expression or the unassuming manner that marred the picture. He was not forceful or domineering, as Davon was. He thought things through with careful, *obvious* deliberation before voicing his opinion. Or rather, Sir Rob-

ert's opinion! Even now she could hear him advising
Walter on the sowing of the crops in the west pas-
tureland and the phrase *Sir Robert believes* reached
her where she stood. Rufenna sighed.

The past week had been an irritating one. She had
returned to find Neville in command at Lyall, issuing
orders in his quiet, calm way, upsetting everyone with
his insistence that things be done the way Sir Robert
preferred. Rufenna had spent her first days acting
as peacemaker. She had soothed Walter's ruffled feath-
ers, assured the steward, Thomas, that she certainly
was in command of the household and he would take
his orders from her, and pacified the household servants. To make it even more difficult, she had spent
an entire morning convincing Captain Kincaid that
he was to use his own discretion in the placement of
guards and pay no attention at all to Neville's arbi-
trary orders.

She had been forced to tackle Neville himself, trying to make clear, in a tactful way, that he had no
authority at Lyall, no matter what Sir Robert had
told him, and could not issue orders as its Lord. As
the week passed, Rufenna realized more and more
that although Neville was a nice lad and she liked
him, being married to him would drive her mad.
He had lived under Sir Robert's thumb all his life
and genuinely believed that Sir Robert was the top
authority on everything. Rufenna, disliking his uncle
and determined not to put herself under his control,
would not marry Neville if it meant spending the
rest of her life doing as Sir Robert said. The situation was difficult; they were legally betrothed; there
was a binding contract that both Sir Robert and her
father had signed. She had gradually noticed that
Neville, attentive and polite as he was, did not appear greatly enthusiastic about their marriage either.
Not once had he attempted to do more than take
her hand politely, at their first greeting, or to hand

her up into her saddle when they went riding. If he had any interest in her as a woman, she had seen no sign of it. Instead he treated her with polite respect, a slight condescension for her status as a woman, and offered only the bare minimum—what was actually demanded by convention—of gallantry. When he offered her a compliment on her gown at supper, he could not have spoken more correctly if she had been her own grandmother, three times his age. It relieved Rufenna, who would have violently rebuffed any sly attempts at intimacy, and at the same time annoyed her that he treated her with such impersonal politeness. It was, she realized, a far cry from Davon's high-handed treatment of her but at least he had treated her as a woman!

Sim, meeting Neville and summing him up swiftly with those shrewd blue eyes, relaxed. This weak young man, who didn't even seem to notice Rufenna's inviting curves, presented a poor rival for m'lord, Sim thought. He was careful to avoid the young man, knowing perfectly well that Mistress Rufenna had not told Master Kerr that he, Sim, was not a Lyall man, but belonged to Davon Hammond. Keeping appraised of the goings and comings of the household by the faithful Agnes, Sim settled down to enjoy the relative peace of Lyall, a welcome respite after the hectic pace m'lord had set during the last months. His moments alone with Agnes more than compensated for the inactive life he was living, he thought.

But as the weeks passed, the fragile peace of Lyall gradually disintegrated. The English, following orders from their angry king, were intent upon making life miserable for the Scottish border. Nightly raiders came over the Border, striking farms, fields of grazing cattle and sheep, burning, looting, leaving death and devastation in their wake.

Every night Rufenna stood with Agnes on the battlemented walls and watched the signal fires spring to life across the hills, blazing a warning of the approach of the raiders. The nobles and lesser gentry of the Border were safely locked into their stout castles and peel towers but the peasant folk and merchants suffered badly. Fields of wheat and barley were razed by fire. Lighted torches were pitched into the rude hovels most of the peasants called home, leaving them without food or shelter. Herds of cattle were driven away, while the distraught farmer prayed for the assistance of his overlord. Captain Kincaid had the Lyall patrols ranging from one section of the Lyall lands to another, trying to keep them mobile enough to dash to the stricken area. The hot, dry, dreadful summer wore on, taking its toll of nerves and property.

Rufenna leaned against the battlemented walls, staring intently into the night. While she watched, the fires began glowing in the east, and she sighed. It was a peculiar thing, she thought. No matter where Captain Kincaid sent the patrols, the raiders would strike elsewhere, hitting a lightly guarded farm or tower, skillfully avoiding the patrols on their way in and back out. Lyall's losses had been great. After what the lands had suffered this summer, she had no idea how she would raise the ransom money.

There was still no word from Lord Eure about John. The English army, bearing their prisoners from Edinburgh, had been back across the Border for more than two months! Walter, counseling patience, reminded her that these things always took time. After the Battle of Solway Moss the Scottish lords taken prisoner by the English had waited a year before being ransomed.

Rufenna knew the waiting was wearing on her mother, who still kept to her chamber, but asked every day if news had come yet of John. And Rufenna did not know what to say to reassure her. Well, she could only continue to do as she had been doing. Wringing every available penny from the sale of cattle, crops, and sheep; holding down the household expenses until Thomas, the steward, complained; tightening security on the farms and pastures to reduce the losses of stock and crops. It was all she could do until they heard the amount of the ransom. Wrapping her light cloak around her against the cool breeze sweeping the walls, Rufenna went back inside to bed, hoping tomorrow would be better.

It was not. It began with the news of a terrible raid near Knolle, where three farms had been burned during the night. Before she could absorb what a loss the burnings had been, she was confronted with a tearful Agnes.

Rufenna stared at the distressed face of her maid, now blotched with tears, and slowly repeated the news she had been given. "You are with child? Agnes, are you sure?"

Agnes, ashamed of her condition and distressed at having to confide in her young, unmarried, and supposedly innocent mistress, hesitated. Then, "Aye, mistress, I'm sure." Agnes sniffed loudly, rubbing her wet cheeks with trembling hands.

"Who is the father?" Rufenna demanded gently, determined to stay calm and not frighten or upset Agnes any more than was possible.

Agnes began sobbing again.

"Agnes, you must tell me, you know that. How can I help you if you don't? Now, who is it? One of our lads? What is his name?"

Agnes sobbed harder but shook her head. "I . . . 'Tis Sim, mistress," she whispered, hanging her head.

"Sim! *Sim!* That young devil! I'll . . ." She broke off, biting off the angry words that hovered on her tongue, and made an effort to control her temper. "Is he going to marry you, Agnes?"

"I-I don't know," Agnes confessed. "I don't t-think . . ."

"Have you asked him?"

"No."

Rufenna stared at the girl in exasperation. "Does he know you're pregnant? Have you even told him that?"

Agnes dolefully shook her head. "I didn't know what to do."

"Very well. I'll handle this. If he is willing to marry you, will you agree?"

Agnes's face cleared like magic and she beamed. "Oh, yes!"

Rufenna stormed out of the chamber, searching for Sim. Agnes was in love with the man; that was certain. Irrationally, Rufenna felt this was Davon's fault. If he had not sent Sim here . . . Why, she must have gotten herself pregnant while Sim was here that first time!

When she located the prospective father, he stared at her in astonishment. "Agnes is pregnant, mistress? Did she tell you so?"

"How else would I have found out such a thing?" Rufenna snapped. She watched the flush come into the tall Borderer's cheeks. "She says you are the father. Do you deny that?"

"Oh, no," he said hastily. "I'll not deny it, if Agnes says it's so. Mistress . . ." He looked at her helplessly, curiously vulnerable in his distress.

"Sim, had you ever thought of Agnes as a wife for you? She's a nice girl."

His flush deepened. "I had, mistress, from the beginning. I am very willing to marry the lass, but what m'lord will say . . . !"

Rufenna stiffened. "You leave m'lord to me, Sim! I'll get you permission to wed Agnes. I promise you that."

With a militant light in her eye Rufenna retired to her small withdrawing room and composed a letter to Davon Hammond, now back at Torrey. She briefly told him that Agnes was pregnant, that Sim was the father of the child, and that Sim had agreed to marry the lass, with Davon's permission. Rufenna made it clear she expected Davon to give that permission! Smiling slightly to herself, she dispatched the letter by a messenger and returned to her chamber to acquaint Agnes with the latest developments.

Shortly before the supper hour a servant came seeking her. "Mistress Rufenna, m'Lord Hammond is here, asking for you."

"Here? Now? Where is he?"

"Master Walter put him in the withdrawing room to await you, mistress."

"I'll be down to him in a minute," Rufenna murmured, moving to the small square of glass on the wall to straighten her hair. What could Davon be doing here? Why had he come?

She riffled through her dresses and found them all unsatisfactory. Finally she reluctantly chose a green silk one that had been her mother's and had been taken in to fit her. As she washed her face and hands and slipped into the dress, she thought irritably that she never stayed in one place long enough to accumulate a wardrobe. Everything she owned was a hand-me-down from her mother. The lovely dresses she had ordered in Edinburgh had not, of course, come. No doubt the poor merchant had been burnt out by the English army.

She entered the withdrawing room a few minutes later to find Davon sprawled in her chair, long legs stretched out on an embroidered footstool, strong hands grasping a tankard of ale.

"M'lord, I was not expecting you," she said coolly, moving into the room and closing the door behind her.

Davon wore leather hunting breeches and jacket. Evidently when her letter came to him about Sim, he had not bothered to change his attire. He looked her up and down for a long minute, his eyes glinting with amusement. "You should have, Rufenna." He took a long swallow of the ale and added, "No lass, no matter how comely, writes me letters telling me what I must do or must not do! Now, perhaps you will explain yourself."

Rufenna sank down on the nearest chair and stared at him. Holy Mother, she thought, he is the most perverse man on earth! "M'lord," she said, "it was all quite clear in my letter. My maid Agnes is with child and Sim admits to being the father. He is willing to marry her, so . . ."

"Is he? Willing, or have you coerced him?" Davon asked quietly.

"No! He said he wanted to marry her!"

"Rufenna, have this clear! Sim is not just one of my men; he is also my cousin! I will not be a party to forcing him into a marriage with this lass, whether she is bearing him a child or not! Agnes," he added, giving her a mocking smile, "is your problem. Sim is mine."

"Oh," Rufenna cried, jumping angrily to her feet. "It's just like you to say something like that! You don't even care . . ."

He rose too. "I care about Sim's happiness and I don't know this Agnes at all. If Sim genuinely chooses her for his bride, *and* if I deem her suitable, I'll give my permission and not before. You shan't bully Sim into something he will regret."

"What about Agnes's happiness? If you had not forced Sim into our home this would never have happened."

"I misdoubt that Sim forced himself on your Agnes, Rufenna. Did you think to ask that?"

Rufenna stared angrily at him, suppressing the urge to throw something at that arrogant head. Before she could speak, the door opened and Neville walked in, stopping short at the sight of the tall stranger across the room.

Rufenna reluctantly turned and met Neville's questioning gaze. "Neville, are you acquainted with Lord Hammond? M'lord, this is my betrothed, Master Kerr."

"M'lord," Neville said, nodding stiffly, his face expressive of his shock and disapproval.

Davon surveyed Neville lazily, giving a slight, mocking bow before acknowledging the introduction. "Master Kerr," he murmured, insinuating his long frame back into the chair.

Neville stared at him briefly and then quickly turned to Rufenna. "My love, I did not mean to interrupt your talk with Lord Hammond. I will come back later, when your business with m'lord is completed. M'lord," he said, again nodding in Davon's direction, in a clear farewell.

Davon grinned. " 'Tis not good-bye, sir, for my business with Mistress Rufenna is not yet completed. I will see you, no doubt, at the table tonight. She has kindly offered me her hospitality."

Neville flushed angrily and cast a glance at Rufenna. Then he turned on his heel and left. Silence fell behind him, broken by Davon's amused voice. "He's a pretty boy, lass, but not suitable for you."

She passed over that challenging remark, unwilling to enter into any discussion with Davon about Neville.

"I note he calls you his love. You have evidently not taken my advice about allowing the Kerrs to become involved in the Lyall affairs."

She ignored that too. "I do not recall inviting you to come here or to stay the night," she said coldly.

"No," he admitted, still lounging at his ease in her chair. "But I was sure you would not turn me out into the dark, lass, and I have yet to talk to

Sim. I am sure you wish this matter settled without delay."

Grinding her teeth in frustration, Rufenna glared at him. "Yes, I do. A simple permission, by letter, would have been sufficient, m'lord, and this visit was unnecessary."

"And unwelcome, you mean. How inhospitable you are! Didn't they teach you more gracious manners in that abbey of yours, child? You should not try to drive your visitors away! As to a letter, why, if I find the girl suitable, and Sim does indeed wish to marry her, I would not dream of insulting my young cousin by being absent from the ceremony! A handfasting is what you planned, is it not?"

It was and she had to admit it. Handfasting was a quite common practice in Scotland, where a priest was not always readily available. The couple exchanged their vows before witnesses, and it was legally binding for a year. If, after a year, the couple wished to part, and no children had been born of the union, they were allowed to dissolve the relationship. If they wished to remain married, they could do so or avail themselves of the services of the first priest that came by. A handfasting was as binding and as legal as one performed by a priest. With the Border so turbulent Rufenna had never considered a chapel wedding at one of the abbeys. The trip would be too dangerous and would take them away from Lyall at a time when they could not be spared. The village priest was away, on one of his mysterious errands, probably to visit one of his mistresses. Rufenna held him in contempt, remembering how he had rushed through the services at her father's death. He had convinced her that Sir Ewen had died of a pestilence and should be buried without delay. She had not been home long enough nor had her wits together enough to challenge such a statement. If her father had a disease that others could catch, would

they not have come down with it in the long months
her father lay ill? So, with no priest available, a hand-
fast ceremony it would be—if Davon gave his permission!

When she joined the men for supper, Sim gave her
a sheepish grin and nodded. So Davon had talked to
him! Her gaze went to their guest, sitting quite at
his ease at this table full of Lyall men. They smiled
or nodded quietly to him, showing Rufenna clearly
that they liked Davon. They ignored Neville, never
bothering to acknowledge his presence. She sat down
beside her guest, where a place had been left for her,
and glanced uneasily across the table where her betrothed sat in sulky silence. Avoiding Davon's amused
glance, Rufenna tried to concentrate on eating her
supper and listening to the flow of quiet talk around
the table as Davon and Captain Kincaid discussed
the English raids.

"You are very quiet tonight," a soft voice said in
her ear. Rufenna refused to turn and look at Davon.
She recognized the light thread of amusement underlying his soft tones. "I talked to Sim," he continued.
"He is quite anxious to marry the girl and I have
seen and approved of her."

"And is she honored by your gracious approval?"
Rufenna asked bitingly.

He chuckled. "She is. Quite overcome, in fact. I
thought for a moment she would kiss me."

"And is Sim planning to ask my permission for
him to marry Agnes?" Rufenna demanded, forcing
herself to ignore his remark. She choked back the
feeling she had when he mentioned kissing someone
else and how repugnant the thought was to her.

"No, I'm afraid not. At my suggestion, he waited
upon your mother and received permission from her.
She is, I understand, the actual mistress of Lyall.
Isn't she, Rufenna? When you write me those prim
little letters you always sign her name to them!"

He had her there and he knew it. "Yes, she is," Rufenna said shortly, turning back to her food. "I'm glad she approved."

"She quite likes Sim," Davon added.

"So do I, most of the time."

His eyes glinted. "I am aware of that. The ceremony will take place at supper tomorrow night."

"Tomorrow night!" Rufenna was dismayed by his words, realizing he intended to remain at Lyall for the ceremony. "Why not tonight?"

Davon shrugged. "Your mother wished time to make arrangements and chose tomorrow night. If it does not please you, I suggest you discuss it with Lady Lyall."

Rufenna bit hard into the crusty bread to stop the retort that rose to her lips. She would not quarrel with him here, in front of Neville and her men. She would ignore him. She was torn between anger at Davon's pleasure in thwarting her and joy that her mother was at last showing interest in the happenings in the castle. Perhaps this handfasting was just what was needed to pull her out of her apathy.

"Your beloved is not happy about this ceremony, or so Walter tells me. He does not like the idea of even your maid becoming allied with the Hammonds," remarked Davon.

"Sir Robert Kerr doesn't like you," Rufenna reminded him.

He grinned. "I know that, lass, and what Sir Robert doesn't like, young Kerr doesn't like. Do you know, I've yet to hear him express his own opinion on anything. I expect if I asked him if it would rain before morning, he would send a messenger to Cessford to consult Uncle Robert before he dared make pronouncement on it."

"I will not discuss my betrothed with you, Davon."

"Why not? I find him quite amusing. Did you know that he fell violently in love with Patricia Rutherford but Sir Robert wouldn't hear of the match? It seems he represented old Robert at a cummer fialls not too long ago and met the young lady. But Kerr is determined to marry the boy to the Lyall lands, of course, and young Neville agreed."

Rufenna swung around and looked at him. Was it possible that Neville was at that same cummer fialls she had attended with the Gypsies? She tried to remember if anyone had pointed out Patricia Rutherford to her. But no, the Gypsies were there to entertain, not to meet the gentry.

"You're making that up, Davon Hammond!"

"I am not, lass! The girl's father told me. He had no objection to Neville Kerr but Sir Robert wouldn't allow it. He had decided on you and he was determined to have Lyall. Sir Robert would have no chance of getting anything at Rutherford when Sir John has six daughters and now they have a wee bonny son."

So it was the same Sir John Rutherford! With determination, Rufenna changed the subject.

"My brother owns Lyall now."

"Does he? How interesting. Could he stand against Sir Robert? I doubt it. No, I warned you once before, you know. You'll get a husband who is in love with another girl and an uncle-in-law who will control you, John, and Lyall. Not a pretty fate, is it? You can do so much better than that, Rufenna! Why don't you send him packing?"

She lowered her voice so no one could hear but Davon. "Why do you care? You have done everything in your power to destroy Lyall. You killed my brother; you abducted me and would still have me, I vow, if I hadn't escaped from you." Rufenna pushed back her chair and rose. "Pray allow me to manage my own affairs, m'lord."

He eased back his own chair and stood looking down at her. "I would, Rufenna, if I thought you could do so. Wear your prettiest gown tomorrow for the festivities. I intend to dance with you."

Deciding that it would be impossible to have the last word with this odious man, Rufenna left the Great Hall and sought the sanctuary of her bedchamber. She latched the door after Agnes had departed. For a long time she lay awake in the dark, half expecting Davon to knock on her door. The pleasure she would receive at refusing him would be lovely. But the hours passed, the castle quieted, and no knock came.

CHAPTER TWENTY-FOUR

Once Davon decided the handfasting met with his approval, he took charge of the arrangements. Rufenna came down to a late breakfast, after a restless night, to find that he had called upon her mother again and they had made plans that he was already carrying out. Lady Lyall, pale but calm, was seated at the head of the table and all during the meal she and Davon consulted. Occasionally Rufenna saw a wan smile light up her mother's sad eyes. Rufenna was overjoyed to find her mother downstairs, taking an interest in something besides her own grief, but her alliance with Davon so infuriated Rufenna that she could scarcely eat breakfast. She had already tried to discuss this strange alliance with her mother and had been quietly silenced. She did not understand how her mother could accept Davon, who had killed her son, in her home as a guest, much less allow him to arrange this ceremony. But her mother had denied Rufenna's reasoning of the situation and reminded her that, by the law of the Border, Davon had done no more than was his right. Rufenna knew that her mother grieved more over her son's dishonorable actions toward the Hammonds than she did over his

violent death. Lady Wira had even expressed gratitude that Davon Hammond had contented himself
with avenging his honor on Alexander and had not
carried the blood feud, as he was within his right
to do, against every Lyall in the Border. Rufenna,
watching her mother placidly agreeing to every suggestion Davon made, was not so easily mollified. She
knew that the custom of the Border was that once
honor had been satisfied, the two families resumed
cordial relations—since obviously if they did not, no
two families on the Border would be speaking to
each other—but she was in no mood now to accept
that time-honored tradition. The fact that he was
not pursuing the feud against two women and a boy
spoke well for his integrity throughout the Border,
but Rufenna ignored all that and sat and fumed.
She much preferred that he keep out of the way
and allow her, the daughter of Lyall, to handle the
arrangements, with her mother guiding her, of course.
Arguing the point with him resulted in nothing.

"Rufenna, do not be so inhospitable, my dear. We
should be grateful for Lord Hammond's help," her
mother reproved.

Davon, standing behind her mother's chair, grinned
his most maddening grin at her and she retired to
her room in a rage, defeated. The last straw was
when he took her elbow and murmured, "I am only
acting for Lady Lyall and this will spare you, already
busy with the normal household chores to see to.
You don't need any further work or worry."

After that she slammed into her bedchamber and
flung the door shut with an oath. "Jesus, Joseph, and
Mary, what a monster he is!"

The fact that he was sparing her the extra expenses also did not escape her and she was torn between anger and relief. He had already, with Lady
Lyall's permission, sent some of the Lyall men hunting. He had then sent one of his men off to bring

back the itinerant musicians he had heard were in the next village. He himself rode down to Lyall village to select the wines, after a lengthy consultation with Thomas.

The kitchens were bustling with helpers, pressed into service by the kitchen staff, and Rufenna, sulkily leaving her room, found there was, in fact, little for her to do. Between Davon and her mother, with Thomas's and Walter's help, the preparations were well under way. By midday the hunters had returned with a deer and several rabbits and confusion reigned. Rufenna avoided a grouchy Neville and went back to her room to help Agnes get ready for the occasion. Again she was maddened by the lack of any really pretty clothing or fabric.

She examined and rejected Agnes's few gowns as unsuitable for the ceremony, and finally, with her mother's permission, riffled through that lady's wardrobe and came upon a pale blue gown that was not new but would do very well. She drove the sewing maid into a frenzy of alterations on the dress that had to be let out and the hem shortened. Davon, she was determined, would find no fault with the bride's appearance! Between Rufenna and Lady Lyall's maid, Agnes was made ready. Her long hair was washed in scented water, dried before a fire, and arranged by Mary, Lady Lyall's maid, into a smooth coronet upon her head. Agnes was so excited that she babbled incoherently and giggled through most of these procedures. But during the preparations when Agnes and Rufenna were alone, the little maid found time to say: "Sim tells me that m'Lord Hammond is having extensive refurbishing done at Torrey Castle. He has ordered furniture from France and new hangings for the beds."

Rufenna said nothing to this disquieting bit of news. But she knew what it foretold. If Davon were refurbishing the castle, it must be for a purpose. She

had not noticed that it was shabby when she was
there with Elizabeth. He must be doing it for one
reason: he was planning to bring home a bride. Lady
Janet Gordon?

"Come, Agnes, enough chattering. Let me help you
on with the gown or you will be late to your own
wedding, girl!"

"Yes, mistress," and Agnes fell to giggling nervously.

With Agnes ready at last, Rufenna turned to her
own dressing. To her dismay she found that the best
gown she had was the green one she had worn the
evening before. Nothing else in her limited wardrobe
was nearly as new or becoming. She wondered miserably if she would always have to wear rags. She remembered with great regret another gown, of shimmery
French silk, in the exact shade of green of new spring
leaves. It also had had the flowing lace and the enormous sleeves that were so popular now. She wondered
what had become of that dress and the green silk
slippers she had left at Holyrood Palace. They were
no doubt burned with the rest of the city. She reluctantly put on the old green silk dress, frowning at
its inadequacies and wondering what scathing thing
she could say to Davon Hammond when he commented that he had seen it before. "It will be just
like him to mention it!" she muttered to herself. She
had Mary dress her hair in a becoming fashion, swept
off her lovely white neck but with loose curls here
and there. Over her hair she wore a small cap she
had made, much like the new cap worn by Mary of
Guise, and thus attired, swept down the stairs and
into the Great Hall.

The ceremony was brief. Agnes, pale, and Sim, red
with embarrassment, joined hands and promised to
be true to each other. Davon told the witnesses to
acknowledge the same as sworn witnesses. Then there
was much hugging and kissing. Rufenna found herself being kissed not only by a smiling Sim, but by

Old Walter, Davon, and a diffident, and almost casual, Neville Kerr. She wondered if Sir Robert had suggested that it might be a good idea.

Afterward the hall was cleared for the entertainment. The musicians that Davon's man had found sang several songs and some rollicking and slightly bawdy ballads. Rufenna found herself blushing at the frankness of some of them. A little later the dancing began.

Rufenna stood near the fireplace some time later, her cheeks already flushed with dancing and the heat of the crackling fire. Even in late summer a fire was necessary to warm the chilly stone of the walls and floors. Neville, who had been her recent partner in the dance, had gone to one of the long tables to get her a goblet of wine. It would quench the thirst caused by the quick-stepping reel. Aware of sudden movement beside her, Rufenna turned her head to find Davon's lazy gaze resting on her. Now, she thought, he is going to say the maid is better dressed than the daughter of the house. Or he is going to accuse me of being absentminded and wearing the same gown two days in a row. She braced herself for his taunting.

"Are you enjoying the dancing, Rufenna? You haven't yet danced with me."

She was so surprised at the civil, polite remark that her own mood altered. She pushed back her hair and nodded. "Very much. Should you dance? Is your leg healed enough for that?"

He smiled. "I am well enough to dance with you, Rufenna." His glance shifted to her mother, dressed in mourning, but sitting quietly and contentedly at the head of the table, watching the dancing. "Your mother seems to be enjoying herself. Is today, at breakfast, the first time she has been down since your father died?"

"Yes, it is. And you are responsible for it. How did you persuade her to attend, m'lord?"

"M'lord? Such formality between us, Rufenna. Can you not call me by my name?"

She ignored this and repeated her question. "How did you persuade her?"

He shrugged. "She felt it was only fitting that she attend the ceremony, and I agreed with that. She's worried to death about your brother, of course, and that drags her spirit down. Have you heard anything from Eure?"

"Nothing at all. Walter keeps saying that these things take time but he has been gone for nearly four months and I am afraid something has happened to him. Perhaps he never got out of Edinburgh."

"Be patient. They *do* take time. The English army has been back across the Border for several months now, so you should hear something soon. A messenger from Hammond Tower arrived today with some rather curious news. It seems our Queen Mother and Lord Arran, the Regent, have appointed Lord Angus the Lieutenant of Scotland for South of the Forth. They must be desperate for aid in beating off the English attacks if they make a Douglass the Lieutenant of Scotland," he added dryly. "That was several weeks ago, I understand, and it seems that m'Lord Angus immediately let his force be felt. The English had taken Coldingham Priory and put in a strong garrison. Lord Arran wanted it taken back so he appealed to Angus for help. I'm sure you are aware that William Douglass, brother to Angus, is Prior there? That may have helped Angus decide to lend his assistance—I don't know. Still, they besieged it but couldn't take it. From the account Luke Daniels sent to me, they were succeeding when a strong English force appeared to reinforce the garrison. The Earl of Glencairn, who had agreed to help Arran take the Priory back because he had just recently been arrested and released for possible treason, promptly fled and Arran was close behind him."

"The Regent fled?" Rufenna demanded in astonishment.

Davon grinned sardonically. "I can see you don't know much about our beloved Regent! Arran is not a competent soldier, Rufenna. Nor is he very competent as a Regent!"

"Then why is he the Regent?"

"It is an hereditary office, my dear, and he had a right to it. Didn't they teach you anything in that abbey?"

"Not politics," she admitted. "I don't know very much about it."

"Obviously! I suppose," he added, trying to be just, "that it ordinarily wouldn't matter that you don't. Most women do not need to have much of a grasp of politics, I admit. But if you intend to command Lyall until your brother is of age, my dear, you had better acquire at least a smattering of knowledge, if nothing more than learning who your friends are and who your enemies are. Well, to make matters simple, Scotland is in a very sorry case if our defense must rest with Lord Arran! Whatever else may be said about Archibald Douglass, Earl of Angus, it will never be said that he is not a competent soldier. Legend has it that all of the Douglasses are born with a sword in their right hands! He managed to save the little army of Arran's at Coldingham, I hear. Arran abandoned the siege guns and fled, but Angus led a force back in and recovered the guns and then covered the army's retreat very competently. What strange bedfellows war makes," he murmured, his glance resting on the play of firelight over her burnished head. "Arran and Angus, actually on the same side for once. I wonder how long it will last?"

Rufenna blushed at his reference to bed and forced herself to concentrate on Scotland's political situation. He had been right, she admitted, to point out the necessity of her understanding some of what was going on in Scotland. The safety of Lyall could depend on it. "Why shouldn't they be on the same side?" she asked. "They are both Scots, after all."

"My poor child, do you think that matters to either of them? The Douglasses have always looked after the Douglasses first and Scotland second and Arran is too ambitious for my taste. He is busy proposing his son as the natural candidate for the hand of our baby Queen. Not that I think anyone is likely to agree with him! But he and Douglass . . . well, there's long been a hatred between the Hamiltons and the Douglasses. They have been the most powerful families in Scotland for many centuries and so it seems strange to see them working together on anything. The Queen Mother, of course, would rather treat with Angus than with Arran; she loathes Arran and doesn't trust him. She doesn't trust Angus, either, but I agree with her. I would rather deal with Angus than Arran, who is a slippery devil. Look at how he's dealing with Glencairn! The man was actually caught carrying letters from Henry of England, admitted his complicity, and was arrested for treason. He was promptly released by Arran when Hertford's army appeared at Leith. He wasn't the only one, either. Lord Maxwell, Lord Grey, Lord Fleming, George Douglass, Angus himself—all were imprisoned at Blackness on a charge of treason. Arran released them all, on the understanding that they would help defend Scotland against the English. You see how Glencairn defends Scotland? He flees with his men at the first sign of resistance."

He stopped to take a long drink of wine and Rufenna remembered hearing about the prisoners being released by Arran when she was in Edinburgh, before the arrival of Hertford's army. She hadn't understood, then, why it was a significant act on the Re-

gent's part. But if Angus was half the warrior that
Davon's words implied, she was glad Arran had released him! His presence in the Border now with
an army could be of help to the landholders here.

"And Lennox! Our noble Earl of Lennox," Davon
continued, bitterly. "A Stuart, cousin of the baby
Queen, and he has just been made a lieutenant for
the North of England and the South of Scotland by
Henry of England! He has raided, with English
troops, along the west coast, taken several important
fortresses, and makes his intentions very clear. He
is pressing for his own claim to the throne, of course,
and a warrant for *his* arrest has not even been issued!
One wonders what Arran is up to, Rufenna. The
man has peculiar notions on what constitutes loyalty
to Scotland. I tell you this, lass, so you will get it
into your head that because a man is Scottish does
not mean that he can be trusted! Many of the Border
lords are working for that damned alliance with
England and are actually in Henry's pay. I believed
Douglass to be one of them but we shall see. If he
has recollected his duty to Scotland and carries out
his authority properly, we may gain some relief from
these raids that are ruining the entire Border. You
have been particularly hard hit, haven't you?"

"It is almost," she sighed, watching Neville crossing the room toward them, "unbelievable, Davon. As
if they know! Where our patrols will be, which farms
are guarded—Captain Kincaid is very troubled about
it."

His gaze had narrowed suddenly. "Is that so? I'll
speak to the captain about it, with your permission?"

She stared sharply at him. He didn't usually ask
her permission for anything he chose to do!

"If you wish," she murmured, aware that Neville
was nearing them and frowning heavily.

Davon bowed mockingly to the young man and
sauntered off, making no mention of the dance he

had suggested earlier. Rufenna was briefly torn between disappointment and relief that he seemed to have forgotten. Then she turned her attention to Neville, who handed her a brimming cup of wine and scowled.

"What did *he* want?" he demanded, taking up a position at her side.

"Just discussing the raids," Rufenna said, trying not to compare the two men. Then something sprang into her head, something Davon had said about Neville being in love with another girl. She decided to see what he would say if she mentioned the girl's name.

"What is Patricia Rutherford like, Neville?" she asked suddenly. "Davon tells me she is a bonny lass."

Neville jumped guiltily and she saw a light come into his eyes that she had never seen before. It vanished as quickly as it had come and the frown deepened on his face. "What has he been telling you?"

"About Patricia Rutherford," she said patiently. "The rumor is that you would like to wed the lass but your uncle refuses to consider it. He is determined to wed you to me. Is this true, Neville?"

A hot flush had flooded his cheeks and he stared helplessly at her. "Rufenna . . ."

"Oh, Neville, this is not the time for lies! I know about Patricia Rutherford and your uncle's orders. You don't seem to realize that I am betrothed to you by my father's wishes, not through any desire of my own!"

"Are you implying . . . Rufenna, are you saying you do not wish to wed with me?"

She was so exasperated she could have stamped her foot. "Neville, I have no wish to wed anyone! I think you should tell your uncle that you intend to wed the Rutherford lass and be done with it. We would not hold you to the contract."

"I c-couldn't! Rufenna, Uncle Robert says—"

"I don't care to hear what *Uncle Robert says!*" she snapped, her angry voice lost, fortunately, in the music. "I only care about what *we* say and want to do. I will not marry you, Neville. I will postpone the wedding indefinitely until even your uncle understands that! If necessary, I will have the Queen Mother cancel the contract with a royal decree! If Patricia Rutherford looks anything like her mother," Rufenna went on, lowering her voice and remembering the beautiful lady at the cummer fialls, "she must be lovely. So I advise you, stand up to your uncle just once in your life and marry the girl! I will not wed you."

Stunned, gaping at her, unable to take in the enormity of what she was saying, he passed over the remark she had made about knowing Patricia's mother. "Uncle Robert . . ." he bleated uneasily.

"Can go jump off the battlements," Rufenna said coldly. "I care not a whit what Sir Robert says, does, or thinks. I will do what I wish to do and my mother will never force me into a marriage that is repugnant to me. So you can tell your uncle what I have said and that I will enlist the support of the Queen if he forces me to it. As far as I am concerned, our betrothal is at an end. You may tell him so!"

"Rufenna, are you sure?" he asked, finding it impossible to smother the hope that leaped into his thoughts, the hope that perhaps it would be possible to have Patricia after all. Then another thought crept into his mind. "Or is it Hammond you intend to have?"

Her head snapped up, fire in the green eyes. "I would not have Davon Hammond under any circumstances! I have no wish to wed yet and would not consider marrying you anyway. I could never endure your uncle's domination, Neville, and I pity the girl who does marry you! She will have her entire life decided by Sir Robert Kerr, regardless of what she wants or feels. He has no consideration for the feelings of others, that man, and you are so blind you cannot see it. You do exactly what he tells you and never once have you questioned whether or not Sir Robert is always right! You'll never be allowed to have any life of your own, Neville, and neither will your wife. So if you are too afraid of him to tell him the truth, then I will write and do so myself! He will never control Lyall, our lands, or me!"

Rufenna swept away, leaving Neville pale and stunned against the wall, and ran straight into Davon. He was smiling devilishly, obviously having a good idea of what had been said across the room, and he lightly caught her arm and detained her impetuous progress.

"What have you said to the boy to reduce him to that red-faced silence, Rufenna? That is no way to treat your beloved. Dare I think that you told him what you thought of him?"

Rufenna suddenly recalled what Agnes had said about the castle at Torrey being refurbished and new furniture and hangings ordered. She jerked back her arm. "It is none of your affair, m'lord, and I'll thank you to keep out of my business," she said haughtily, moving past him. She had noticed that her mother had retired, leaving Walter alone at the table.

"I have told you before, lass, that I'm making it my business. Is your betrothal at an end?"

She looked at him for a long, cool minute in utter disbelief. "If you will excuse me, m'lord . . ."

"I won't," he said bluntly, holding her wrist in a firm grasp. "Not until you answer my question."

"Davon! You have no right to ask such a question or to force me to stand here like this. I wish to retire, sir, and I will not discuss my personal affairs with you."

"Then I will ask your beloved," Davon said smoothly, releasing her wrist.

"You wouldn't! Davon . . ."

He bowed. "Do not let me detain you against your will. Good night, mistress."

"Davon! Yes, I told him to tell Sir Robert our betrothal is at an end. There, are you satisfied?"

He smiled. "Far more than you know. I'll see you to your chamber."

"There is no need of that, m'lord. I'll see myself to my chamber."

"Don't you trust me on those dark stairs?" he murmured, openly laughing at her. Then he bent a long, cool stare on her. "See here, mistress. I would never do anything to defile the honor of the daughter of Lyall while she is safe in the confines of her own home and I am her guest. You must think me entirely without honor."

She checked the angry and obvious words that rose to her lips, and flushed. "Walter will accompany me upstairs, if it is necessary for someone to do so."

"As you wish," he said indifferently, making her even more angry. He made a quick signal to Walter and waited until the elderly clansman reached them. Then he solemnly consigned Rufenna into her cousin's care. "Good night, lass, dream of me," he added, with a flashing grin, not caring that Walter was listening to this exchange with a knowing smile.

Rufenna turned on her heel and swept angrily across the room, leaving Walter to hasten after her. The nerve of the man! she thought, fuming, as she went rapidly up the winding staircase. He thought she would jump at the opportunity to mount the dark stairs with him, did he? Davon Hammond was just too sure of himself!

But later, lying in her big bed, Rufenna tried to force her clamoring body to calm itself so that she could go to sleep. A wild restlessness had seized her, a restlessness and yearning that she remembered from her Abbey days. Now, however, this yearning was not inexplicable and she groaned, refusing to accept what she knew as the truth. She wanted Davon Hammond!

To her relief but secret regret, Davon left the next day, waiting only to speed Neville on his way to Cessford before announcing his own departure. He had spent the morning closeted with Captain Kincaid and David Shelby, while Rufenna endured an awkward farewell with Neville. Watching the Hammond men canter out the gate, seeing Davon's dark hair glinting in the midday sun, Rufenna turned back into Lyall, telling herself that she was glad he was gone, as they could now have a bit of peace. But inside she didn't believe a word of it.

CHAPTER TWENTY-FIVE

The political situation in Scotland was worsening by the month as summer faded into autumn. The Border lay in a smoking ruin, creating terrible hardships on gentry and peasant alike. Lord Home, Rufenna heard, had been so completely impoverished by the English raids that he had asked for and received royal assistance in maintaining Home Castle. He had been reduced to the position of having scarcely a penny to repair the damages the English had wrought and keep Home Castle a stout defense point against the English army. Rufenna began to feel that she knew how he felt. Money was now so tight at Lyall that she could barely raise the wages for the garrison. Homeless families, their crude huts smoldering amidst burning fields and pastures, were crowding into the villages and castles for food and shelter. The vassals could rebuild their little houses in a day or so, but when night after night they were burned, they lost the hope and will to try. The beacons still blazed across the hills at night, sending the weary, discouraged soldiers out into the dark to protect the pitiful remains of what had once been prosperous farms and herds.

If Henry Tudor thought that his terrible punishment, what history would call "the rough wooing," was succeeding, he had misjudged his foe. Families such as the Crosers, Nixons, and Grahams, who had earlier been joining the English raiders for their share of the plunder, were defecting from their treacherous alliance. The savage raids, laying waste the entire Border country, had left such slim pickings for raiders that the Scots suddenly realized that there was little left to steal. Across the Border in England, fat, rich farms, sheltering the stolen herds, waited. Slowly the Scots rallied, joining together to conduct a few raids of their own. Rufenna, standing on the battlement walls that late afternoon, wondered dismally if they shouldn't join their neighbors in trying to recover what was their own. Her family had always held against raiding. For many Borderers it was their livelihood, but for the Lyalls it was only permissible to pursue a raiding party to get back the stolen goods.

Her mother, although still keeping much to her room, was gradually regaining an interest in what was happening, but she left the management of the castle in Rufenna's hands. Rufenna knew that if her mother were consulted, and she would have to be, that she would never agree to an actual raid on English farms and would be very upset if Rufenna authorized any such thing. Yet what would they do when the ransom demand came? They had no money left to pay it. Rufenna was barely managing to keep Lyall running, to feed all the castle's dependents and the homeless, desperate people from the Lyall farms. She shivered in the chill wind sweeping the walls and tugged her woolen cloak more closely around her. There was no fall harvest to gather in, nor had there been much of a summer one. The few animals they had left were driven into the gates at night, to be guarded inside the walls of Lyall. What were they going to do this winter to feed these people? Her responsibilities were bearing so heavily on her that she longed wistfully for help or advice. Walter repeatedly told her not to worry. They would manage with what they had stored so carefully in the basements of Lyall during the spring and summer. But Rufenna could not help but fret.

"They said I'd find you here," Davon said, having stood for a long moment by the tower door, watching her. She spun around, staring at him, startled by his sudden appearance. His thoughtful gaze took in the thin figure barely outlined by the woolen gown, a figure pounds thinner than it had been at Sim's wedding. Her face was also thinner, and dark shadows left smutty marks under her eyes.

"Why are you here?" she demanded, her voice sharp with strain.

"Several reasons, Mistress Lyall. The first is, I've brought you a present."

"Oh," she said, not very interested.

"A deer. We had good hunting nearby and I remembered how much the Lyall folk enjoyed the deer we had at the handfasting. With Walter's permission, I instructed the cooks to begin roasting it at once."

"Thank you," she said dully. "And the other reasons you are here?"

"I have news that concerns you, Rufenna. Could we go inside? You're chilled to the bone out here."

Silently she led the way into the tower and took him downstairs to her withdrawing room. While he undid the clasp of his heavy, dark riding cloak, Rufenna studied him. He looked tired, cold, and stern. She knew, instinctively, the news was not good.

Without a word she rang for Thomas, instructing him to bring food and ale. Then she knelt by the fire, lighting it carefully, hoping he wouldn't notice the pitiful pile of wood centered in the wide fireplace and realize how they were already, with autumn not gone, rationing fuel for the fires in anticipation of a cold winter. Davon's gaze flicked to the meager fire but he didn't comment directly. Instead he waited until Thomas had placed the tray with bread and cheese and heated ale on the table and departed.

"Luke managed to capture a load of peat from an English raiding party which was unwise enough to cross Hammond land. 'Tis more than we can use at Hammond, Rufenna, wagons of it. If I send some over, could you use it? Perhaps you know of some village folk who will be needing extra fuel this winter. Our villagers are well supplied now and I would not want it to go to waste," he added, hoping he wasn't touching that tender pride of hers. She flushed slightly, in relief at the offer and glad he wasn't offering Lyall charity.

"We would be happy to take it, m'lord. Many of our villagers are in terrible straits and in no condition to face the winter. Our own supply is sufficient, if we conserve it," she said quickly.

He smiled gently at her. "Ours is too, now. Before we were not in such good case but we are fully stocked after securing this bounty. 'Tis amazing that we have managed to retrieve even this much from them."

She nodded, knowing he had not come here just to bring her a deer and offer some fuel. She waited for what she knew was bad news but suddenly she was not anxious to hear it.

"Is your mother well, Rufenna? And Sim and Agnes? I miss that young devil, I'll admit that, but he is none too anxious to take Agnes from you just yet."

"They are both well, as is my mother. Davon, please, the news?"

He looked down at her where she sat on the hearth rug before the pale, flickering fire and sighed. "It's about John," he admitted. "After I left here in August, I sent a man with a letter to Ralph Eure, Rufenna. In the letter I advised him that I was acting on your mother's behalf and wished to ransom the boy. No," he said quickly, raising his hand, "don't scold me. I knew you wished to handle the matter but I was uneasy about the length of time it was taking Eure to notify you. I did not wish to upset you or your mother by saying so, however, so I decided to do what I could to let Eure know that you were not alone in this matter That he would deal with me and the force of the combined Hammond and Lyall men. I hoped it would carry some weight with the man, you see. I received a report from my messenger. Lord Eure was there, refused to discuss any ransom of the lad, and would not let my man see John. I didn't like it," he admitted, studying his boots, hating to see the white, stricken look on her face. "I am just back from England myself, lass, and your brother is not there. I suspected it, you see, and went to find out. John *was* there until early September. Then he was taken out under guard and my spy reported that the troop rode west. From the information I could gather, I believe they have taken the boy either to Newcastle or Carlisle. I promise you I will find out."

White-faced, Rufenna stared numbly at him. "Why would they take him away?"

Davon shrugged. "I can't say, Rufenna. Perhaps they felt that he would be more secure at Newcastle or Carlisle. Our new Lieutenant, the Earl of Angus, has been busy this summer, lass. He has led several raids too close to Alnwick for Eure's comfort. They could believe greater security is necessary for the hostages. Some, taken in Edinburgh, are still there. As for Carlisle, if he's been sent there, it will be to Lord Wharton, who is, as you know, the governor of Carlisle and one of the two most hated and feared men on the English Border."

"Eure is the other!" she said.

"Eure is a bastard and a swine," Davon agreed

grimly. "He has clawed his way into power in England over the smoking Scottish border! He leads raiders over here every night. If Eure gave the boy to Lord Wharton, I will be very interested in discovering why! Even though they're on the same side, they're rivals for power in England and I cannot understand why Eure would agree to give up a valuable prisoner."

"We don't know that he has, do we?"

"No," he admitted. "It's more likely he's sent the boy to Newcastle for safety. I intend to find out. I've also sent a message to Angus, Rufenna, telling him of your brother's capture and the fact that he's been removed from Alnwick. I asked him to let me know if he has any information concerning the boy's whereabouts. The more people who know we're looking for the lad, the better chance we'll hear something about him."

She sat before the fire, staring down at her tightly clasped hands. "What do I do, Davon?"

"Nothing!" he said emphatically. "I urge you to do nothing at this time. Let me try to discover his location and then we'll decide the best course of action. Don't even tell your mother; it would only distress her further. I hope to have news for you in a few weeks. Finding the boy will take time, lass. I can't do it overnight. So just be patient and wait until you hear from me. We'll investigate Newcastle and Carlisle and anywhere else that seems likely." Davon looked at the trembling of her mouth and reached down to take her cold hands in a warm, firm grasp. "Try not to fret about it, lass. At least we know now that John was removed safely from Edinburgh and has been at Alnwick these last months. We'll find him; I give you my word."

It was precious consolation for Rufenna during the long autumn weeks that crept past. Davon left immediately that day to begin his inquiries and had twice sent her messages to say he was pursuing it. No word or sight of John had been found at Newcastle when Davon and his men penetrated that ancient English city. Rufenna wondered if the news from Carlisle would be as bad. She pushed the thought from her mind that she had no way of ransoming John if—when!—Davon found him. She was even bereft of Sim's cheerful company at supper, since Sim insisted he should be with Davon to aid in the search for John. Agnes, now large with child, moped and cried with loneliness and was no consolation to Rufenna. Rather the other way around. To comfort her maid, Rufenna encouraged her to sew for the baby and even found herself picking up the detested needle occasionally.

Rufenna went through the cold days, always weary, often hungry, and wondered sometimes why she had thought life was hard this time last year, when she was safely tucked away at the Abbey. Christmas came and went with heavy snows and freezing temperatures, blanketing the scorched land, covering her scars. There was little to celebrate at Lyall since both food and supplies were tightly rationed to last out the cold winter. All hope now lay in a good early spring harvest to replenish the shelves in the storeroom that were emptying much too fast. More and more of the soldiers of the garrison at Lyall were riding out hunting, trying to supplement the scanty meat stores with fresh carcasses of deer, scrawny hares, and fish from the nearby river.

All the while Rufenna held Lyall together. She kept a cheerful smile on her face for her mother, assuring her that a ransom demand would come soon from Lord Eure. She did what she could to alleviate suffering in the village, parting with some of the precious stores from Lyall to assure that the aged and infirm would last out the cruel winter. The effort it cost her only Walter could guess at. They could not know of the tears of weariness, discouragement, and helpless pity for her people that she shed in the safety of her bed. No word had come from Cessford, either. She had no way of knowing if Neville told his uncle the truth or if he was still hoping Rufenna would change her mind. Not once had they had an offer of assistance from Sir Robert or even an inquiry into whether they needed any help. Cold silence from Cessford prompted Rufenna into deciding that Neville *had* told his uncle the truth and they were being punished. She shrugged it away, not caring a whit about Sir Robert's anger or neglect of them. She had never wanted his help and would not have taken it if it had been offered.

By January, Rufenna was so frantic for news from Davon that she would have fallen at his feet with gratitude if he had appeared—but he did not. From Hammond, too, came silence, until the cold, bleak day Walter came hurrying up the stairs to fetch her.

" 'Tis Master Sim, mistress. Wounded and asking for you. We have him in the hall."

"Bring him up immediately, Walter. We must not leave him in the hall! It's very chilly there. I'll try to prepare Agnes and meet you in their chamber."

As she sped down the hall to find Agnes and warn her to get the chamber ready for her husband, Rufenna wondered desperately what could have happened. She watched them carry the big Borderer into the room and helped Walter get him settled in the bed. Agnes burst into tears at the sight of her wounded husband and collapsed on his body. When Rufenna attempted to drag her off, the maid promptly clutched her belly and moaned that the pains were starting. Just then Lady Lyall came into the room.

"What's to do here?" she demanded.

Rufenna hardly knew what to tell her first. "Sim has just arrived, wounded, and now Agnes says the babe will arrive soon."

"Take Agnes to the birthing room, Mary," Lady Lyall said to her maid. "Rufenna, you attend to Sim and I will take care of Agnes."

As the moaning Agnes was led away by Mary and Lady Lyall, Rufenna turned her attention to the man on the bed. His arm was clumsily bound in a bloody bandage and before she would let him tell her a thing, Rufenna set about getting his arm cared for and seeing him more comfortable. When this was done and he ate a little, she sank down on the side of the bed and stared anxiously at him.

Sim forced open heavy lids and grasped her wrist with his uninjured hand. "Mistress," he gasped, "I've come from m'lord. He found that young John had been taken to Carlisle and so we went to get the boy back." Sim stopped to catch his breath and allowed Rufenna to give him a drink of the mulled wine.

"He raided Carlisle?" Rufenna asked weakly, staggered by this news.

Sim nodded painfully. "Aye, lass, and the boy is not there! He *was* there; we found someone who saw him taken inside! M'lord has been taken, lass, and you must send word to Luke. We must get him back!"

"D-Davon was captured? At Carlisle?"

"Aye. He isn't hurt but they have him. Lass . . ."

"Oh, Sim! No, don't worry. I'll send to Captain Daniels immediately."

"Tell Luke that m'lord is not the only prisoner there. I saw Buccleuch and several others, taken in Edinburgh in the spring. How the Governor got them, I don't know, but they're there. We raided the dungeon but couldn't release them. I've brought back as many of our men as got away. M'lord, when he saw we were hard pressed, he covered our retreat and they got him. Lass, it was a trap! They knew we were coming and made it easy for us to get in. M'lord was suspicious but we had to go on and try to find the boy. They let us come in and then surrounded us. Like rats in a trap," he muttered, still angry. "Someone betrayed us, lass. Tell Luke that."

"I will, Sim. No, no more now. You can tell me more about it later. Right now you must rest. I'll go and send word to Captain Daniels."

"Wait, lass. Before that, go and see how Agnes does."

Rufenna obediently went down the hall to the birthing chamber and her mother ordered her away.

"There is nothing you can do here, daughter. Mary and I will deal with it."

She heard little cries and moans from Agnes before her mother closed the door. Too tense to occupy herself with anything, Rufenna found herself pacing the drafty hall.

Some time later she heard a baby's cry and when she was allowed in the room, she found Agnes asleep and the baby boy, husky and bearing a remarkable resemblance to Sim, tucked in by his mother's side. Rufenna left to tell Sim the news and promised him a look at his baby son.

Exhausted, Rufenna then went to her withdrawing room, her mind seething with questions. Who could have betrayed Davon's plans? How had the English known they were coming? It didn't make sense! Or did it? If one knew Davon Hammond, one could guess quite accurately what he would do if he found where the boy was held. First he would attempt to take him by force, since negotiations would be of little use with Lord Wharton! Lord Wharton never negotiated with anyone if he could avoid it. Wharton would not have gone to the trouble to collect John from Lord Eure unless he had plans, more serious plans, for him other than the ransom. So if Wharton had John, it was for a special reason, Rufenna was certain of that! But why? Why would

Wharton want the heir to Lyall? Not for the ransom, obviously. So what did Wharton want with John? The glimmering of an idea, frightening, outrageous, came to her. That couldn't possibly be it! Could it? Moving with decision, Rufenna sent for David Shelby.

David frowned over his orders. "Rufenna? You wish me to ride to Torrey immediately, see Captain Daniels, and deliver a verbal message?"

"That is correct, David. I don't want anyone to go with you, nor do I want the message written down. I want you to see Luke Daniels alone, out of earshot of anyone. I want you to tell him what has befallen m'lord and that I am in urgent need of help. I wish to see him personally, away from both Torrey and Lyall. I will ride to . . . let me see. The valley with the small stream, David, that is halfway between Lyall and Torrey. You know the place?"

Reluctantly he nodded, not liking the sound of this. "Rufenna, I don't know what you're planning to do . . ."

"I will tell you later, David. If Luke Daniels is there, and he must be, bring him to the place tomorrow at midday. I will meet him there. If he is not there, come back here and tell me. But send someone to find him and deliver the message. What is the name of the man who always rides with Davon? Wat! That's it!"

"Lass, Master Wat is here, with the other Hammond men. They are wounded, some of them, and anxious to ride to Torrey."

She frowned. "No, not yet. Get Master Wat aside, before you leave, and tell him he is to keep the men here until I can talk to Captain Daniels. I must see Luke Daniels quickly, David! If Luke is not there, make sure the message goes out immediately. Also privately. Tell no one where you are going but Wat. Tell *him* not to tell his men."

"But, lass, Captain Kincaid . . ."

"I'll see the captain myself. I have another task for him. Just . . . go, David. It's of the utmost importance."

"Very well, lass, I'll go now. If he's there, he's to meet you at the stream in the valley tomorrow at midday. If he's not there, I'm to send someone after him and bring him here."

"No," she corrected swiftly, "not here. He's to send a man to me, appointing a time and place for us to meet. I do not want to talk to him here."

"As you wish. What, exactly, do I tell Captain Kincaid? I can't just ride out without a word, lass!"

She smiled at David. "Tell him to saddle three horses, one for me, one for Walter, and one for himself, and we are going out in an hour. Tell him nothing more than that. Not inside these walls, you see. That's important."

Perplexed, he agreed and went off to do her bidding.

It was bitterly cold on the hills. Rufenna tugged her cloak tightly around her body and tucked the ends under. She led the two puzzled men down the hill from the castle and unerringly made her way to the gaunt remains of a burnt-out tower, which stood blindly on the top of a crest, no longer guarding the valley below. It was a cold ride and she wondered if she should have insisted upon it. Still, she had to be *sure* and the old, forgotten peel tower was not more than a half hour's ride from Lyall. To the further confusion of the two men, she had ordered several stout lengths of wood strapped behind each of the three saddles and had rolled a woolen blanket and tied it over the front of her own.

They rode up to the ruined tower and skirted the fallen stone. Rufenna led the way to the gaping doorway and dismounted. Noticing her horse stamping on the frosty ground, she turned to Captain Kincaid.

"I think we should take the horses in with us, Captain. It is too cold out here to let them stand about."

He nodded and dismounted, walking forward to take her reins and lead the two horses up the scarred stone steps into the remains of the tower's hall. Rufenna let Walter go past and then hurried up the steps, anxious to be out of the biting wind. She paused inside the doorway, letting her eyes adjust to the dimmer light. One side of the hall gaped blankly, part of the upper wall being gone, and she moved quickly across the hall to the arched doorway behind it. With glances of curiosity and unease the two men followed her, still leading the horses. Rufenna looked through the doorway and sighed in relief. It had barely changed at all since she was last here, nearly six years ago. She and David had often explored the ruins when they could escape their nurse's eye and wander the hills around Lyall.

"Captain, this room is intact, as you can see. Tether the horses in the hall and bring the wood in here. My blanket, also," she added, shivering in her cloak.

Suppressing their growing curiosity, the captain and Walter tied up the horses and piled the wood in the cold stone fireplace and started a fire. Rufenna found an old, half-rotten bench in the shadows of the far wall and dragged it close to the leaping firelight. Scraps of splintered, dry wood found in the far corners of the room fed the fire and she wrapped her blanket around her and settled cautiously down on the bench, wondering if it would collapse under her weight. It groaned but held and she waited until the two men had moved in close to the fire.

"I know it seems most peculiar of me to talk to you here but I think I can explain why I felt it was necessary. There is no place at Lyall now that I believe is secure. I had to consult with you and yet I dared not speak openly with you inside our own walls! Please, Captain, sit down and give me your advice, for I am badly in need of counsel. You both know," she began, when they had taken up a position by the fire on either side of her, "that m'Lord Hammond was searching for John. He went to Carlisle, discovered John had been there and now was gone again, and m'lord was captured."

There was a gasp of surprise from the captain, and Walter stared at her with shocked eyes. "Aye, my friends, he was taken during the raid on Carlisle, a raid intended to find and free my brother. Sim was wounded but managed to get as far as Lyall to warn us. He said that it had been a trap, Captain. That the English garrison knew they were coming, let them get in, and then surrounded them. Davon was taken as he tried to cover their retreat. He was not injured, Sim said. Sim also said that there were other prisoners there. Scott of Buccleuch and others, all taken at Edinburgh and once in the custody of Lord Eure. Why should Lord Wharton now have them? Why did he get John from Lord Eure and where is John now? Who betrayed the raid to the English? Only the men of Hammond and Lyall knew that m'lord was intending to investigate Carlisle. The men at Lyall knew, didn't they, Captain?"

Frowning at her, Captain Kincaid nodded slowly. "Aye, mistress, they knew. They knew the boy was not at Alnwick; they knew no sign of him had been found at Newcastle and that Carlisle would be investigated. I heard them discuss it more than once. The boy is well liked, mistress, and they were worried about it and discussed ways they could help to find him. Since m'lord ordered us not to interfere, to let him conduct the investigation, we could do naught. But they knew of it."

"You say John is well liked by his men? I think that is not true of someone. Someone, Captain, is betraying Lyall. I cannot believe it came from Torrey. I think the traitor is inside of Lyall."

Walter shot a shrewd, quick glance at her. "Why?" he asked bluntly.

"Because anyone who knows Davon Hammond would know that if he found John, he would try to get him back. Is that not so, Captain?"

Kincaid nodded. "And we knew, lass. We knew he thought the boy was at Carlisle. He sent a messenger, remember, a messenger who stayed the night at Lyall and talked to our men of it."

"I thought of that. So it is someone at Lyall because all spring, summer, fall, it has been *Lyall* which has repeatedly been struck by raiders. They know where our patrols are going, where the guards are, what is vulnerable. I think a man, or men, inside of Lyall has been sending information constantly to the English. Telling them where the patrols would be, telling them of the search that had narrowed upon Carlisle. Any one of our men could guess what m'Lord Hammond would do about it, don't you agree?"

"I agree, lass, but who? It's not that I haven't thought of this before! M'lord spoke to me and we wondered then, when he was here for the handfasting. It was too much of a coincidence that our patrols were never in the same area as the raiders. They always knew too much. But who? And why, lass?"

She shifted closer to the warmth of the fire and gravely considered them. "My cousin Murdoch. It has to be. Who else has an interest in Lyall? Who else would be in a position to plant a spy in our own garrison? It *has* to be Murdoch! Besides that, I'm thinking of John. M'lord said that if Wharton had John, if Lord Eure had been pressured to give him up to the Governor, it would be for a specific reason. Not the ransom. There could not be enough money in it to make Lord Wharton force Eure to hand over John." Rufenna looked pleadingly from one man to the other as she explained her reasoning of the situation. "Can you see it?" she went on when neither man spoke. "He can't want John for the money. Lyall could not give enough money to make it worth Lord Wharton's time to do this. It has to be for another reason."

"What reason think ye?" Walter asked, increasingly uneasy.

"He wants something from someone and is planning to barter John for it. I think he has already bartered him. To Murdoch. He wants something from Murdoch; he gets his hands on John, offers Murdoch the one thing—the heir to Lyall—that Murdoch cannot refuse. I don't know what Wharton wants in return but probably assistance to the English. But I feel sure that it is someone in Lyall, bribed by Murdoch, who has kept my cousin informed; someone who told him where to strike, to weaken us; someone who told him m'Lord Hammond suspected John was at Carlisle and would attempt to get him back. They had only to post a watch at Carlisle and be ready for them. If all this is true, and I think it must be, then we are helpless! Or rather, we would be if we had not found out what is happening. If we attempted to do anything to find John or to aid m'lord, they would soon know of it and we would also walk into a neatly laid trap."

"What think you to do?" Captain Kincaid asked, feeling sure she had already planned a course of action. He was right.

"I have sent David Shelby secretly to Torrey and he is to bring Luke Daniels, the captain of Torrey, to me tomorrow at a secret meeting place. If Captain Daniels agrees, and I think he will, then I have a plan to solve our problems. I brought you here because I did not dare discuss it inside our own walls! We cannot know whom to trust. Now, I trust only my mother, both of you, and David. I cannot believe any of you would betray Lyall. So I will tell you my plan and see if you can think of a way to better it. But whatever we decide here, not a word will be said to anyone else, not even my maid or my mother. Is that agreed?"

"Aye, and very wise, too," the Captain said and Walter agreed. They moved in closer and listened in astonishment to her firm, young voice as she outlined her plan of action.

At noon the next day, Rufenna rode down the frozen bank of the little stream where Luke Daniels waited for her. If she could wring an agreement out of the Hammond captain to assist her in her plan, they would soon see action. An hour later she rode away from the small campfire, leaving an uneasy Luke Daniels behind her, wondering what m'lord would say if he knew just what Luke had agreed to do. He would probably skin him alive, Luke decided, riding back to Torrey. Still, it would be worth it! Lord, the lass had courage! And brains, too. That was no half-baked plan she had presented. It was all figured out and decided on and Luke had very little alteration to suggest. Still, he admitted to himself, if left to his own devices he could not have bettered it! It was clever, bold, and highly dangerous, but she was just stubborn enough to make it work. But, my God, what would m'lord say? Luke straightened his back and kicked his horse into a canter. He would worry about that when he faced m'lord.

CHAPTER TWENTY-SIX

Back again at Lyall, Rufenna called Captain Kincaid in and gave him his orders. Soon the word had carefully gone out through the castle: the mistress was taking a large troop of Lyall men with her to Edinburgh, to request aid from the Queen in securing the release of her brother from Lord Wharton in Carlisle. They would escort the Hammond men as far as Torrey, before riding north to the capital. Rufenna and Captain Kincaid had been very careful to keep anyone inside Lyall from knowing that John was *not* at Carlisle; their entire plan hinged upon the castle believing the boy was there. Neither did they admit, nor did Wat tell what he knew, about Lord Hammond's capture. At midafternoon on the following day Rufenna, accompanied by Wat and David Shelby, rode out the gates of Lyall, leading the combined troops of Lyall and Hammond men. They rode east, to the sheltered valley where Luke Daniels had met Rufenna and, to the surprise of the men, David called a halt there by the stream. He directed the men to set up camp among the overhanging trees that would offer them shelter from any marauding bands of English raiders. Then, following his orders, the troop was called together by David.

Rufenna stood at David's side, her gaze going over the fifty Lyall men clustered tightly around the two big campfires, their alert eyes resting on David as they waited to hear what their orders were. The Hammond men were seated among the Lyall men, as curious as their fellow troopers.

David's voice rang out clearly over the camp, echoing on the cold, still air. The sun was getting low behind the trees, casting a bright but chilly glow over the clearing. "I've no doubt that you are wondering why we have stopped for the night when Torrey is another hour's ride away. We are not going to Torrey; neither are we going to Edinburgh." David waited for a moment but no one spoke, or even moved. He continued. "Your mistress thinks you should be told the truth, should be told why you were brought from Lyall in this fashion and deceived about your intended destination. The truth is, we have a traitor within our walls. A man, in English pay, who has been reporting on our every move. Have ye not wondered why the English raiders seem to know just where our patrols were and how carefully they avoided them? Surely you realized, as we have, that this is not merely a coincidence. No, we have a traitor in our midst. A man, who, for pay, has betrayed m'Lord Hammond and his men. Yes, Lord Hammond went to Carlisle to rescue your master, young John, and the garrison there knew they were coming. They have captured Lord Hammond and some of his men and we also know the boy isn't there. Your mistress believes she knows where John is being held and we will attend to that too. Tonight, after the remainder of the Hammond men arrive to join us, we will ride to Carlisle."

A loud, angry murmur, resembling an outraged beehive, had been rising steadily from the men as

they listened to David and realized that they had
been betrayed by one of themselves. Each man turned
and looked sharply at his neighbor and the mutters
of rage increased. David held up his hand and made
a motion for silence.

"Aye, you're angry! So are we! But we intend to
do something about it. The traitor, if he is at Lyall,
will not know where we are heading and cannot betray us this night. If he is *here*, among you, you must
make very sure he cannot get away and alert the
English. I will assign men for guard duty on the
edges of the camp. You will patrol in pairs tonight
and no one, under any circumstances, will leave this
camp. Do ye understand?"

There were cries of assent from the men.

"Good," David said. "If any man attempts to leave
camp, he is to be stopped." David paused for a moment and then added, "Stopped by whatever means
is necessary. We cannot afford to be betrayed this
night. When the Hammond men arrive, an escort
comes with them who will take the injured men back
to Torrey. We will then ride to Carlisle. Jem, pick
double guards for the camp and post them. Use this
time to rest, lads, for we will travel fast and hard
when darkness comes."

Veteran campaigners that they were, the men rose
immediately and set about preparing an evening
meal over the fires. Angry tones echoed across the
clearing as the men discussed what they had been
told. David, standing quietly beside Rufenna, correctly judged the soldiers' wrath. "If any man tries to
leave this camp tonight," he said soberly to Rufenna,
"he will not make it out alive."

Rufenna, shivering in the cold, biting wind, nodded and moved closer to the fire. The die was cast
now and a long, hard ride lay ahead of them. Who
knew what lay at the end of it?

Rufenna lay curled in a thick, oiled woolen blanket, tucked up close to the fire. She had eaten and rested and they waited now for the arrival of the men from Torrey. David stirred beside her, where he sat wrapped in a blanket. He listened intently. "Someone's coming," he whispered, throwing off the blanket just as a dark, shadowy shape slipped through camp and up to the fire.

"Sir, a large troop of men is approaching from the east."

"Remain on guard, Jem. It should be the Hammond men, but be watchful, in case it is not."

Jem nodded and vanished into the dark trees. The loud hoot of an owl rang out and was answered faintly from the direction of the approaching troop. "It's the Hammond men," David said with a quick smile of relief. He rose and waited by the fire. Luke Daniels rode into the camp, followed by Davon's men.

As the men crowded around the campfire, a sudden commotion erupted on the western side of the camp. A loud shout broke the quiet and David ran in that direction, followed, after a moment of hesitation, by Luke Daniels. Rufenna fought to untangle herself from the tightly wrapped blanket and large, capable hands reached down and freed her. She looked up into Wat's grim face and breathlessly thanked him.

"What is it, Wat?"

"I do not know, mistress. Wait here and I will see." He too ran off into the darkness and Rufenna, ignoring his suggestion, followed him. She reached the edge of the stream to see an angry crowd surging around a figure on horseback, reaching up to drag the man from the saddle. They grabbed and held the horse's bridle and held it hard. She could hear David's voice ring out in command and the crowd moved back a little. Rufenna seized an opening and darted through to see one of the Lyall men being held now by two men.

"Jem?" David questioned, his gaze roving over the imprisoned man.

"He was trying to leave the camp. He knocked out the other guard, grabbed one of the horses, and was trying to get away."

"Someone tether that horse and bring the man back to the fire." David strode away, pausing only to take Rufenna's arm in a light grasp and lead her back toward the flickering campfire. There he turned, standing tautly beside her, with Luke on her other side. Both men's faces were grim and angry and Rufenna realized that they had caught their traitor.

"What is your name?" David demanded.

The man stood in sullen silence and refused to answer.

"Jem?"

"His name is Jack Graham, sir."

"Graham, why were you trying to leave camp?"

Still the man did not answer, or look up.

"Who do you report to, Graham?"

Sharp silence spread over the camp as the men waited grimly to hear from this man. David, realizing his captive was not going to say anything at all, looked at Jem.

"Jem, he is to be questioned. We must know who he reports to and how it is done. See to it."

Jem signaled to the two men holding Graham to follow him and the prisoner was dragged away. One of the men thrust a stick of firewood into the fire and carried it along, for light or . . . Rufenna bit her lip as she saw a flash of steel as one of the guards bringing up the rear of the little procession slid his dirk from his belt and grasped it firmly.

"David," she appealed, "what w-will they do?"

David glanced down at her and then looked at Luke.

"Lass, you would prefer not to know. They will get the information from him. It is vital that we do so. I remember this man," David added, thinking back. "I doubt that much persuasion will be necessary."

Rufenna felt Luke's hard, consoling hand on her shoulder and gazed mutely at him, distressed.

"We have to know," Luke murmured.

A cry of pain or perhaps of fear rang out and echoed eerily across the woods, splintering into taut silence among the icy trees. Rufenna gasped and sat down suddenly on her blanket and allowed Luke to pull the warm wool around her shoulders. They waited in a dreadful little silence and then snapped to attention as the sounds of men approaching reached them. Luke and David rose, facing Jem as he hauled the prisoner up to the fire. David flicked an indifferent glance at the man's white, strained face and ignored the tightly bound hands held awkwardly in front of him.

"Jem?"

"He talked," the little Borderer said cheerfully. "He's one of Master Murdoch's men, sir, and reports directly to him. He has a helper in the village, one Thomas Grimes, an odd-job man. He meets Grimes at the village tavern and reports on where the patrols are going. Then Grimes sends word to Galzean. If Graham doesn't come to the tavern, Grimes rides up to the castle and meets him outside. He has been pretending that he is sending a message to a lass in the village. That's what he told me."

"Did he admit that he told Grimes about Lord Hammond's ride to Carlisle?" Luke demanded.

"Aye, sir, he did. That's how they knew. He sent word to Master Murdoch and the news was passed on by him."

"How long has he been spying on Lyall?" Rufenna asked, rising and facing the men.

"Mistress, he was brought by Master Murdoch when your father, Sir Ewen, first fell ill. He spied on Sir

Ewen and Master Alexander. He sent word to his master at Galzean when Sir Ewen died."

So that's how Murdoch knew about her father's death so quickly, Rufenna thought. John had been right.

"Do we take him back to Lyall?" asked Jem. "Or do we . . . ?"

There was a long silence, broken only by an occasional shuffle of feet or movement among the men. Rufenna glanced at David and Luke Daniels and then she realized that all eyes were on her. The traitor and her men and the Hammond men were waiting patiently for her to make a decision. She looked back at David imploringly, but he frowned slightly and shook his head. His frown told her that she was the leader of these men and the responsibility was hers. No one could give the orders for her. Rufenna returned the looks of the men, swallowed nervously, and straightened her slender shoulders. These were her men, she thought proudly. By their waiting they had acknowledged her. She could not let them down or make them ashamed of her. She cleared her throat and spoke to Jack Graham, the traitor.

"You have been responsible for the deaths of not only Lyall men, but of your fellow countrymen. Therefore, I have no choice but to condemn you to death." She turned to David. "Lieutenant Shelby, see to it."

Her men immediately leapt into action and, with shouts, seized the condemned man and dragged him away. Rufenna's voice deserted her and nobody heard her say, "Make it swift."

Although not known for his bravery, Jack Graham did not beg for mercy. He had lived on the Border all his life and knew when he agreed to spy on Lyall that he was taking a chance. If captured and found out he knew that Border justice would be swift and sure. He said nothing as he was dragged away. Luke

Daniels took Rufenna by the arm and led her in the opposite direction. "It won't take long," he promised.

The execution did not take long but it seemed forever to Rufenna. There was no way to get far enough so she could not hear Graham's involuntary cry as the rope was put around his neck and he was strung up. She put her hands over her ears to shut out the horrible, choking, strangling noises that seemed to go on and on. The men had made little effort to hang him properly, with a quick snap of the neck. They just strung him up and let him choke to death. Even that, some murmured, was too good for him. At last Luke Daniels touched her on the shoulder.

"It's all over, lass."

The dead man was cut down and every man took a stone and covered the body. They knew it would not be well if the English or Murdoch's men discovered their traitor, at least until they had accomplished their mission at Carlisle. Beyond that the scavengers could have him, the troopers thought, as they placed their stones and turned to spit deliberately on the ground.

Rufenna fought back nausea as this was being done. She could not be sick now. She needed all of her energy to lead these men. They trusted her and if she showed weakness now, she would never regain their trust. So she walked about in the cold and tried to fasten her thoughts on something else, anything, rather than the events of the last half hour. She consoled herself with the thought that there had been nothing else she could do. She had given the only command possible. In the Border, where one's life often depended on trusting and relying on one's fellow trooper, a traitor, one self-confessed and caught in the act, could not be allowed to escape.

Soon David and Luke had the combined troop mounted and the long ride to Carlisle began. It was more than sixty miles to Carlisle, as the crow flies, and Rufenna wondered how long it would take them to cover the distance. She knew the ride would be fast and difficult, and it was. The frosty ground, crunching beneath the horses' hooves, was rough and slippery with ice in places. They lost precious time skirting hills, circling around clear of Lyall, and avoiding the villages. When they neared the village of Lyall, David sent two men to silence Tom Grimes and then catch up with the rest of the troop, if possible. It would not do for Tom to find out what was happening. On they rode, passing Riccarton during the hour before midnight. Rufenna was bundled in her blanket, intent only in staying in the saddle and not causing the men to slow their pace for her benefit. She was too proud to show her fatigue.

Icy wind swept across the valleys and blasted them in the face as they passed out of the rolling hills west of Riccarton and entered the marshy plain near Hermitage Castle. Rufenna was thankful she was so warmly clothed, wearing a woolen shirt, a leather jerkin lined with lamb's wool under her leather jacket, and the dense, oiled woolen cloak. Walter had found her a pair of woolen hose, ones belonging to young John and worn on hunting days in the winter. They cut the chill on her legs but her leather breeches clung damply to her thighs. When David, riding in front of her, stopped suddenly, she nearly rode into him and her horse danced about for several seconds before settling down. The men halted instantly, waiting in silence as they saw that upraised hand. A scout rounded the slight rise ahead of them and rode up to David and Luke. Rufenna urged her horse forward to hear what the man said.

"Sir, there's a horseman on the other side of the hill."

"A single horseman?"

"Aye. We spotted him leaving a copse of trees and watched him head for the valley. He has not yet seen us but he came from England."

Luke and David exchanged puzzled glances. "What," wondered David, "would a lone horseman be doing out here on a night like this? I think we'd better challenge him. His errand must be urgent. If he's seen us, he could alert a nearby troop of English raiders. Where did you see him going, Jem?"

"He's just entering the valley on the other side of the rise. It's a bit steep there, sir. If we blocked both ends, he could not get up the slope to get away. Narrow, ye ken, and rocky."

"See to it," David ordered, motioning Jem forward and giving low-toned orders. A handful of men silently left the line and went to the far end of the valley, while others returned to the mouth of the narrow valley and signaled other men to come with them. Within minutes they had the rider trapped neatly in the valley and wasted no time in moving in on him. Luke and David waited impatiently, chafing at the time being wasted by this necessary precaution. The struggling form was driven forward by the big Border troopers and held, squirming, before Luke and David.

"State your name and purpose," David commanded. There was something in that young man's voice that stated clearly that no nonsense would be tolerated.

"Lem Robson, m'lord," the captive answered promptly.

"And your purpose, Master Robson?"

"I-I was with a party of raiders, sir, Scottish raiders," he added, swiftly sizing up the unexpected troop of men. "I became separated from them."

"Jem?" David had noticed Jem frown and start to speak.

"I think he's English, Master Shelby. There are

Robsons on both sides of the Border, of course, but I don't think he was with a raiding party. We found this on him." Jem handed David a small package. "It was sewed in the lining of his coat and we found it when we searched him."

The package was a square of oiled silk, firmly sewn shut. David could hear the crinkle of paper inside, and pulled out his dirk and slit the package open. The man struggled suddenly, fighting to get free from his guards, and Jem reached over and tapped him firmly on the back of the head with the hilt of his dirk. The man collapsed onto the frozen ground and two troopers heaved him back upright. David slid the letters from the package and held them up to catch the fitful rays of the moon, and tried to read them. He gave up and silently handed them to Rufenna, knowing she could read and write much better than he. Rufenna held the crisp paper and slanted them to throw light on the superscription. She gasped, reread the name written in a bold, firm hand, and quickly looked at the other letters. Then she went back to the first letter and opened it. Her mouth tightened as she read the slashing, bold words on the page and she looked up at the waiting men.

"He is indeed English, David! These are letters from Lord Wharton, Governor of Carlisle. One is addressed to my cousin Murdoch, one is addressed to the Earl of Glencairn, one to Lord Fleming, and the fourth one is to John Maxwell, Lord Maxwell's son!"

Luke looked keenly at her. "Is there anything in them that would jeopardize our ride tonight? If so . . ."

"No, these concern other matters, I think. I've only read the one to my cousin."

"Then let us go on," Luke said impatiently. "We can deal with those later."

"Jem, gag the man and tie him up." David looked

past Jem and nodded. "You caught his horse, too? Good. Let's ride."

They rode on, passing Mangerton Tower, stronghold of the Armstrongs, and skirted the edges of Solway Moss, and crossed into England. The sharp scent of the salty marsh assailed Rufenna's nostrils as they edged around the treacherous boggy land beside Solway Moss. They skirted the village of Longtown and soon could make out the towers and church spires of the town of Carlisle in the distance.

On the fringe of the town David called a halt in a thick grove of trees. "Jem, assign several men to keep the prisoner here and if you're surprised, kill him. He must not tell them about us. Men, we're on the edge of Carlisle. You know what to do. Captain Daniels will lead the attack on the castle, taking you in by the route used by Lord Hammond. It's an old, disused entry and they will not be expecting us this time. I am taking twenty men and we will take the castle stables. We will need mounts for the lords and their men. Mistress, you will ride with me. Unless," David added, with a swift grin, "you would prefer to remain here with the prisoner?"

Rufenna straightened her back, throwing off her weariness at the long, cold ride, and met David's gaze with determination. "I think I should go with Luke to free m'lord."

Both Luke and David looked at her in consternation. "Mistress," Luke said swiftly, "your supervision is more greatly needed in the stables, covering our line of retreat." He didn't dare suggest that m'lord would have his hide if he let the lass go into the dungeon with them. God only knew what kind of opposition they'd find and if the lass was hurt . . .

"Very well," Rufenna agreed, knowing perfectly well what he was thinking. "I will go with David." She returned David's relieved smile and knew he, too, preferred to keep her out of the heavy fighting.

"Luke, are your men ready?" David asked.

"Aye, ready."

Moving in a double file, the men silently penetrated the enemy city.

CHAPTER TWENTY-SEVEN

The walled city of Carlisle lay bathed feebly in the dim moonlight. The castle stood firmly on its mound, washed on two sides by the Eden River and the little river, Caldew. It was a formidable sight even in this light and Rufenna paused at the edge of the river, wondering if they could ever get safely inside that fortress. She thanked God that the river was low at this time of year, since a soaking in the freezing weather could be fatal. Moving silently across the river, their harnesses wrapped in rags to prevent them from clinking and betraying their presence, the small army of men crossed and gathered against the tall, sheltering walls. They knew from their last trip here with Davon that their scaling ladders would be too short, but a small, disused postern gate had been discovered last time and this was forced without much effort. Two or three men squeezed in, by removing several stones below the gate, and forced open the blocked gate to admit their comrades.

The men dismounted and Luke left a few men to guard the horses and the postern gate, to secure their retreat. The towering walls of the ancient fortress surrounded them and the men flitted as silently as ghosts across the rough, cobbled courtyard, mere wraiths in the dim light as they moved toward the main castle block. Rufenna went quietly with David to the stables, where they would seize and hold the mounts needed for the imprisoned men waiting below in the dungeon.

The warm, comforting smell of horses filled Rufenna's nostrils as she followed David into the dark stables. A shadow loomed up in front of them and there was a quick, silent struggle before quiet again filled the echoing rooms. Several horses, scenting unrest and picking up the sounds of movement, began to move about uneasily. They resented their rest being disturbed by the stealthy movements in the dark old building. One by one the sleepy stableboys were dealt with and David quickly and silently secured the stables. Rufenna, waiting near the door, heard the rest of the men force the gate of the keep and open the massive doors of the outer dungeon. Luke took his men down the dark stairs to where they tore away the door of the noisome inner prison, a rough vaulted chamber to which no ray of light ever penetrated even on the brightest day.

At the same time, Rufenna perched herself on a stack of hay in a corner of the stables and pulled the letters from her pocket. She held them up to the window and read them all, marveling at the luck that had made them cross that courier's path this night. Davon would be very interested in these letters, she knew. As she studied them again, before returning them to her jacket, she was aware of men moving soft-footed about the horses. A clink of a bridle reached her ears and she looked up to see her troopers bringing out the horses and saddling them. To her sudden amusement, she realized they were saddling every horse in the stables! David passed near her and she touched his arm.

"Why so many horses?"

"Now, lass, think a bit! Why should we leave good horseflesh for the Governor? We don't know how many prisoners Luke will free, now do we? And we certainly don't want to leave mounts for Lord Wharton's troopers to pursue us, do we? It will take them a bit longer if they have to go out and find other mounts."

She smiled affectionately at David, not noticing the warm gleam in his eyes as he looked at her, sitting there on the pile of hay. He touched her shoulder softly and turned away, returning to supervision of the men in their tasks. He tried not to think of Rufenna, looking so warm and beautiful in the shadows.

He had always been fond of the lass, as he watched her grow from a tousle-headed toddler to a gangling little girl. They had played together, ridden together, and now were fighting together. He had known all his life that the daughter of Lyall was not for him. What could he, although of good family, offer such a one?

He had told himself repeatedly, since her return to Lyall from the Abbey, that she would wed someone of her own station. He had even half persuaded himself that he had only a brotherly affection for her. But now, under the stress and danger of the situation, he knew it was not so. She was not for him, but he did not look upon her as a sister! He had violently disliked Neville Kerr and loathed Sir Robert. She was well advised to be shut of that pair! But Lord Hammond? What did she really feel for Davon Hammond? If she hated him, why had she stayed at Hammond Tower to nurse him? Why was she here now, rescuing him from the English? In his bones David knew, and he hoped he had judged m'lord correctly also. Davon Hammond was indeed the man for her, David grudgingly admitted, but did his lordship know it? If he did, would the lass ever admit it? David smiled softly to himself, knowing the lass would fight to the end. She did not lack for spirit or intelligence. But she was stubborn. Lord, the lass was stubborn!

In the bowels of the dank dungeon the Hammond and Lyall men were opening the doors with the large brass key taken from the keeper they had surprised. The instant the door was unlocked, Davon strode out of the small cell, his hand going to Luke's shoulder and gripping it tightly. "Thanks, Luke. You're a welcome sight."

Luke grinned. "The lass brought us, m'lord. Her men are holding the stables."

"Let me have that key a moment," Davon said, taking it and going swiftly down the hallway to a cell. "Buccleuch?"

"Thank God," the big, middle-aged man said as Davon unlocked the cell door. He stepped out into the passageway, accepted the sword that Luke handed him from the armament room they had broken into, and he turned, following Davon to the twisting stone stairs. Luke's men were rapidly releasing all the men in the cells and arming them, and a growing crowd of armed men formed behind Davon and Buccleuch. Davon went lightly up the stairs, his sword ready, and burst into the keep to find part of his men engaged in a spirited fight with a dozen or more of the castle garrison. He and Buccleuch eagerly entered the fray, forcing a path through the hard-pressed castle guards to the doorway that led to the courtyard. "Luke!" Davon yelled, beating aside the sword of a castle guard and spitting the man neatly. "Get the prisoners out!"

While the Hammond men forced the guards back against the far wall, Luke urged the prisoners toward the courtyard door, followed by Davon and Buccleuch. There were scattered groups of fighting men in the courtyard but they managed to avoid them and reach the stables.

Rufenna, still half listening to the swelling noise

outside, put the letters away safely inside her shirt.
The clear sounds of fighting were definitely heading
this way, echoing across the cobbled stones of the
courtyard that separated the stables from the main
castle buildings. She sensed movement outside and
slipped David's dirk from her belt, ready to help if
she should be needed. The men, keeping the horses
quiet, were alert now and waiting in strained silence.
Men were moving around near the door which had
been opened just wide enough to admit a single man.
Rufenna tried to listen at the window to the swelling noise and still peer into the dark area about the
door. Suddenly, startling her, a hand touched her
shoulder and she spun around, the dirk flashing up.
A firm hand gripped her wrist and removed the dirk.

Rufenna flung herself into Davon's arms and held
him close in the first embrace that she had ever
given him without reservation or restraint. For a
long moment he held her, straining her body close
to his, unaware that David saw and turned away.
Then she remembered herself and pulled away.

"Easy, lass, I'm a friend," Davon said quietly,
amused, slipping the dirk back into her belt.

"Are you indeed?" Rufenna asked breathlessly, her
emotions still scrambled with fear and joy.

He looked straight at her and frowned. "Do you
doubt it still?"

She swallowed. "No," she whispered. "Are all the
men out?"

"Aye, and a few choice prisoners of the Governor's
as well. We've got to move now. The entire castle
is roused. Come with me."

As he spoke, he led her to a waiting mount and
threw her up into the saddle. Before she could protest, he had mounted behind her, signaling David to
start mounting the men who were slipping quickly
through the door. She saw Luke rush in, followed
by the rest of the men, and they were half carrying

some of the released prisoners. Davon didn't wait for all of the men to get mounted. He saw Luke guide his horse out the door and followed, plunging out into the dimly lit courtyard.

Soldiers, strapping on their swords as they ran, were pouring out of the castle into the courtyard. A man ran at Davon, his sword swinging wildly at the horse, and Davon neatly pulled his mount aside and delivered a slashing blow. The man crumpled and sprawled untidily across the cobbles. Luke was herding the now-mounted prisoners toward the open postern gate, and Davon joined him near the gate. A handful of Hammond and Lyall men were holding off the soldiers in the courtyard as all of the prisoners escaped out the gate and fled down the slope toward the river. Davon signaled Luke to go with them and turned to deal with several soldiers who had broken past the rear guard and were heading for the gate.

Rufenna, held tightly against him, watched him drive the soldiers back into the tightly pressed group of Hammond men and helped cover his men's retreat out the gate to where troopers waited with their horses. When the last man cleared the gate, Davon took his mount through and turned, sword at the ready, as his men mounted and rode quickly down the hill to the river's edge. The milling soldiers in the courtyard re-formed and began to advance on the gate and one of them, just ahead of the rest, raised a weapon, glinting dully in the dying moonlight, and there was a terrible explosion. Davon pulled the dancing horse sideways and the ball whistled harmlessly past them.

"W-what was that?" Rufenna demanded breathlessly, clinging to the pommel.

He chuckled in her ear as he turned the horse and raced down the slope. "One of the new handguns. You needn't worry. They can't hit anything with them. Grossly inaccurate, lass, and much more dangerous for him than for us. They usually explode, you see. Have you enjoyed yourself tonight?"

"Of course," she said stoutly, trying to ignore the ribbons of pain that were beginning to sear up her thighs and buttocks. She had been too long in the saddle before they reached Carlisle and the short rest in the stable had been inadequate. Now, ride again they must or perish.

They splashed through the river and followed the main body of men surging up the hill ahead. "Is there some reason that Luke is taking the men to those trees?" Davon asked.

She nodded breathlessly.

Davon guided the horse up the hill and entered the trees, his eyebrows going up at the sight of the man neatly trussed up and gagged, waiting in the clearing in the trees, surrounded by a group of Lyall men. "Who is he?"

"A prisoner we collected on the way. I'll tell you about it later."

Luke approached them, smiling companionably at the girl mounted before his master. "We mustn't tarry here, m'lord. They'll find horses somewhere but we've taken all we could find in the stables so that should slow down the pursuit."

"Good. Give the word to move out."

Davon guided the horse across the clearing and, assured that the men were following him closely, set a fast pace for the Border.

Rufenna could feel his chin brushing her hair and she relaxed against him. "Did you enjoy your visit with the Governor?"

"Not much. What took you so long? I expected you yesterday."

She framed an indignant retort, then became aware of the silent laughter shaking the warm, lean body pressed so closely behind her. "We had a few things

to deal with first," she said, deliberately calm, and
he chuckled in her ear.

"You must be weary," he murmured, his arms
tightening around her.

"I am. The men are, too."

"Who's your prisoner?"

"An English courier we collected along the way.
He was carrying some very interesting letters. I'll tell
you about them when we stop."

David and Luke pulled alongside and Davon
glanced back at the double line of troopers behind
him.

"Luke, the men have ridden hard and will have
to rest once we're across the Border. Shall we stop
near Riccarton?"

Luke shot a glance at the girl before his master
on the horse. "Aye, sir, we should. The lass is tired,
too. Buccleuch is riding with his own lads at the
rear and says he'll leave us at Hermitage. He sends
his gratitude for his rescue from Wharton and says
to thank the lass."

Davon nodded and looked down at the fiery red
head nestled against his chest. The lass could be
thanked later. She was fast asleep.

Rufenna, held firmly in Davon's arms, slept the
entire ride to Riccarton. They had ridden fast, expecting pursuit, and had not been surprised to have
the rear scouts ride up with news of a fast-moving
troop behind them. Taking to side paths, they eluded
their pursuers, and reached the foothills past Riccarton without incident. Safely in the mountains just
as a cold dawn began to lighten the sky, Davon
called a halt on a thickly wooded slope. A small
stream ran at the base, and although edged with ice,
was not frozen. Both horses and men needed water
and the trees would offer protection from the English
pursuers.

Lifted gently to the ground, Rufenna was wrapped snugly in her blanket and eased down next to the fire. Her disheveled hair, framing her pale face, glinted in the warmth and leaping light of the fire, and Davon, glancing up suddenly, surprised an expression on David's face that knitted his brows thoughtfully. David, unaware of the silent watcher, gazed at the sleeping girl for a long time before turning away. Davon watched him go and sat down thoughtfully. David was in love with her, Davon thought, surprised at the surge of jealousy that ran through him. His frowning gaze shifted to Rufenna's face and his lips tightened. David Shelby was a good soldier and a fine man—but he was not the man for Rufenna. Perhaps, Davon thought with compassion, David knew it. There had been sorrow in his eyes as well as love.

Sometime later, awake and refreshed by a hot meal, Rufenna faced Davon by the fire. She had told him of the night's adventures, beginning with Sim's arrival at Lyall, unaware that he had already received the entire tale from Luke and David, and finished with the capture of the English courier. Now she reached inside her shirt and removed the package of letters and held them out. Davon took them, his fingers tightening on them as he felt the warmth of the silk, warmth retained from contact with Rufenna's body.

"There's a letter to Murdoch, Davon. Lord Wharton says that Murdoch is to do his utmost to persuade Sir William Douglass of Drumlanrig into the English fold. If Sir William refuses to be persuaded, Murdoch is to retaliate with force. He also reminds Murdoch of his promises. Davon, I feel sure that Murdoch has John! That Lord Wharton bartered John to Murdoch in return for this. Now, having handed over John, Wharton is telling Murdoch what he has to do to keep his part of the bargain."

Davon, reading the letter swiftly, agreed. He then turned to the next letter. "Glencairn? A letter to the Earl of Glencairn from the Governor?"

"Yes, and he reminds him of his promises to King Henry and demands men to accompany Lord Eure on a raid on the Douglass properties. The letters to Lord Fleming and John Maxwell say the same thing."

"Mother of God!" Davon muttered, reading the rest of the letters. " 'Tis fiendishly clever, Rufenna. All are to give men and aid for attacks on the Douglass properties. Now, why are they so intent on harming the Douglasses? Could it be because of Angus—he is head of the family—striking so recently against England? Henry doesn't like his brother-in-law and you remember when Angus was married to Henry's sister, Margaret, he was Lieutenant of Scotland for years. Now he's making life merry for the English on the Border and I hear Wharton is furious about Angus's activities. Angus has certainly left the English fold with a vengeance. Well, they seem to be planning a raid on Douglass of Drumlanrig and on the Douglass properties in the East and Middle Marches. You realize why, I'm sure; they are striking at Angus! He's the one man in the Scottish border who could raise the Border against England, and they know it. If they can shatter the Douglass might first, then there would be little organized opposition to their invasion of the Scottish border. Hell and damnation, Rufenna! This is a very serious affair. Without Angus to raise the Border, we can expect to see the damned English camped outside our gates! Eure will, no doubt, strike against Angus in the east and Wharton against Drumlanrig in the west. We've gotten the forewarning and we have to make sure that their plan doesn't work! Otherwise, the entire Border will be engulfed in flames! We'll have to get a warning to Drumlanrig. In fact, we could send the letter to Sir William Douglass."

Rufenna reached over and her hand closed on the letter addressed to Murdoch. "No, not yet. We must get John first! Davon, Murdoch has him." She shivered, remembering Murdoch's uncontrollable temper and his sadistic streak. "Why can't we use that letter to get him back?"

He frowned thoughtfully at her. "Trade it, you mean? He'd never trade the boy for this, Rufenna. He could swear he didn't have the boy, knew nothing of any agreement with Lord Wharton, and that you had forged the letter to implicate him."

"Oh," she gasped. "Then how . . ."

A gleam lit Davon's eye. "Still, we might use the letter. He's expecting a courier bringing a letter, you see. So, a courier will bring one. This one!"

"You'd let Murdoch have the letter?"

"Aye, it's the only way. If we sent a man inside Galzean with the letter, he would naturally spend the night there if he arrived nearly at dusk. Then we'd have a man inside."

"T-that is very clever, Davon. How do the rest of us get inside?"

He grinned at her. "Leave that to me. We'll get in."

Davon picked one of his own men, whom he felt sure Murdoch could never have seen, and briefed him carefully. The letters were craftily hidden inside the man's boot and he jauntily rode up the hill toward the towers commanding the entrance to Galzean. The sun, sinking quickly behind the castle walls, lent a glow to the old stone, turning it softly pink and then deeper mauve. Rufenna wondered how such beauty could contain such corruption. Davon held the men in the thick trees at tht far side of the valley, out of sight and sound of Galzean. They watched the spurious courier approach the gates, exchange words with the guards, and be admitted. Davon gave a sigh of relief and turned to the business at hand.

"When it is dark, we will move closer to the castle walls. Toby will deliver the letter addressed to Murdoch Lyall, letting him see the other three, but too quickly to be sure of the addresses. It will add credibility to Toby as the English courier. Once the castle is asleep, Toby will gain the walls and silence the guard on the back wall. He will then assist us to come in over the walls. We have the ropes that you brought with you to Carlisle. If the boy is there, we will get him out. Any questions?"

The men asked a few and then, one by one, began sharpening their swords and dirks on soft stones. Time inched along toward full dark.

The men massed slowly, stealthily, beneath the back wall of the castle. Davon frowned up at the bright moon, wishing for a little less light. They did not want to be discovered too soon. All watched the wall, hearing the measured pace of the guard, listening to his quick exchanges with the guards on either side who were pacing the side walls. Straining intently to hear, Rufenna listened to the quiet pacing of the guard, and suddenly it stopped. There was a soft sound of a foot scraping on stone and then nothing. From the top of the wall a bright head appeared, the blond locks of Toby! A dark shape moved, wiggled, and uncoiled over the wall. A rope! Where had Toby found a rope? Davon leapt forward and grabbed it, using it to feed their ropes to the top. The heavy hemp ropes were quickly tied on and slowly the rope was pulled up. Again the head appeared and a hand waved and then Toby had ducked down and they could hear him pacing quietly, just as the guard had done, toward the nearest corner. Rufenna drew in her breath and waited, knowing the guard on that wall would be silenced quickly by the lithe Borderer. Davon signaled several men and Luke and David came forward, grasping the ropes and tying great knots at the bottom. Then they were going up the wall, using their feet against the cold stones and hauling themselves up with their hands. Something dangled around their waists and Rufenna realized in amazement that it was their boots! They had taken them off and tied them to their belts and were going up the wall in their stockings. Without a word she sat down and took off her boots, wondering what to use to tie them together. She flashed a smile of thanks to a trooper sitting beside her, taking off his own boots, as he handed her a short length of rawhide.

"Put them back on," a low voice commanded. "You're remaining below."

She looked up defiantly at Davon. "I'm not. If you can get up that wall, so can I! It's my cousin in there and my brother who is being held prisoner. Most of these men belong to me, Davon, so I'm going."

He squatted down beside her and put a gentle but restraining hand on her shoulder. "Rufenna, it's not as easy as it looks. Some of our men couldn't make it up the wall. My dear, it's nearly a hundred feet to the top! If you fell . . ."

"I won't fall," she said firmly, not sure herself but determined to try. "Davon, please; I want to go with you."

He considered her a moment. "Very well, but only if you'll do it my way."

She wondered briefly how long she had been ordered to do things Davon Hammond's way. Since the moment they met. She wondered if it would ever end!

"I promise. Just let me go," she said quietly, as close to pleading as she could bring herself to do.

"Will," he called softly, signaling to the enormous Borderer whom Rufenna was beginning to know well. "Will, Mistress Rufenna is going up with us. I want you to take a rope parallel to her and I'll secure her to you." As he spoke, Davon uncoiled an extra rope and knotted it firmly around the big Borderer's waist. He then removed his cloak, quickly folded it lengthwise, and wrapped it around her slim waist. Over this he wrapped the rope, testing the knot. "This will keep the rope from chafing you, Rufenna. You will go up slowly, feeling with your stockinged feet for footholds in the stone walls. The wall is rough and does offer many good footholds, so look for them. It will take some of the strain off your arms and rest you. Pause to rest whenever you feel you need it. I will be just below you on the rope so don't try to hurry. I can hold on all night if need be."

Rufenna nodded and followed the two silent men to the base of the wall. She leaned back her head and gazed up at the sheer wall rising above her and swallowed hard. Could she possibly climb that wall? It looked so enormously high! A shiver of fear went down her spine, the first real fear she had felt since the beginning of this adventure. Perhaps she should have stayed at the bottom and waited until the men had captured the castle and let her in the gate. But no, she hadn't flinched yet. Then Davon was lifting her up onto the rope and she took the rough hemp in a firm grasp.

To Rufenna, the wall seemed endless. Inch by inch she went up, aware of the silent figure below her and the massive bulk of Will on her right side. They paced her steadily, not letting her rush or falter. Her hands were starting to slip on the rope and Rufenna realized that her arms ached unbearably from the strain. Davon had been right; she couldn't make it! Panicky, she tried to move faster, knowing her palms were sweating with fear at the thought of the awful drop beneath her. If she fell, she could take Davon down with her! Her damp hands slipped again on the rope and she slid downward for several feet before her scrambling toes found a foothold.

"Will," whispered Davon. "Go on up. I'll move

her up as quickly as I can and as soon as you have enough slack in the rope to get over the top, haul her up."

Will nodded and swarmed up the rope, stretching the rope tied around Rufenna's waist painfully tight. Then she felt Davon close behind her, quietly easing her back against his chest, making her relax the strain on her arms by leaning against him. Using his strong arm and leg muscles, he began inching up the rope, carrying her with him. As some of the intense pain left her shoulders, Rufenna began using her hands again, helping him. Then, ten feet from the top, she felt the rope tighten around her waist and realized that Davon was easing back, away from her. Slowly, letting her use her feet as guides, so that she would not dangle helplessly at the end of the rope tied around her middle, Will began pulling her up. Then the top of the wall was scratching her palms and strong hands lifted her up and over the wall. She stood panting, hugging her aching arms to her chest, as Davon came up and climbed over the wall. The men had already silenced the guards on all four walls and were waiting quietly for the rest of the men to reach the top. This was done in such silence that Rufenna could hear her heart pounding.

Davon rested for a brief moment and looked down at Rufenna. She knew that look. He didn't speak, just gave her a quick "I told you so" look before he turned to lead the men away. Following Davon, they made their way to the tower door in the corner. Davon made sure they understood that, whatever else happened, they were to search first for the boy and secure him. John was to be taken out of the castle immediately and delivered to Jem and his men waiting with the horses. Toby, who had used his time well, had discovered the floor where Murdoch's chamber was and where he suspected the boy was being kept. He had seen a tray leave the kitchen and noticed that the servant carried it up to the main residence floor. Now he led them to that entrance from the stairwell and Davon hesitated before the great wooden door. He loosened the sword in his scabbard and slid his dirk into his left hand. Will, obviously following orders, moved back and restrained Rufenna, holding her gently against the wall of the landing until most of the men had followed Davon through the door. Then he led her through and she recognized this passage. It was where Murdoch had brought her! She began trembling and felt the blood leave her face. Davon looked back, saw her white, strained face, and his eyes hardened. He had not forgotten what she had endured here either. He had waited patiently to settle this debt! Well, it would be settled tonight! Relying on instinct, he went straight to the door where Murdoch had imprisoned Rufenna and tried the knob of the clumsily repaired door. It was locked. Standing back, he kicked the lock furiously, sending it flying back and crashing into the wall. A frightened, pale face peered at him behind the door. There was John, bedpost clutched to use as a weapon, ready to fight. Davon let Rufenna go past him for a quick hug for her brother and then met David Shelby's eyes.

"David, get them out, now. Take Will and however many men you need but take them back up to the wall and lower them down. Jem is waiting with the horses. Hurry!"

David rushed in and hustled the bright-eyed but bewildered boy from the room and threw his own cloak around the boy's shirt-sleeved body.

"I knew somebody would come," John said unsteadily.

"Of course. We just had to find you," Rufenna said, trying to stem the hot tears burning at the back of her lids.

"Later," said Davon.

"Come," David said, grasping them both by the

arms and urging them to the door. "We have to get him away now, Rufenna."

"But what about Davon?"

"He'll cover our retreat," David said smoothly. He knew perfectly well that Davon, even now, would be looking for the master of Galzean, with murder in his heart. What a pity to miss that!

John peered down over the wall and looked at Rufenna. "I'm not sure that I can climb down that."

"You won't have to. David says they'll send us both down the way I came up. Do just as he says, John."

"Rufenna, we'll send you down together, one on each rope. All you have to do is try to keep your feet sliding down the wall, to brace yourself. Otherwise, if you just hang there, you'll slam into the wall too many times for comfort."

Ropes were tied firmly around their waists, ropes padded with cloaks from the men at the top of the wall. Then Will and another man were easing Rufenna over the top while David and Toby lifted John over. Trying not to look down, Rufenna made the nearly impossible attempt to keep her feet braced on the wall as she was slowly lowered. The rope cut painfully into her flesh, making itself felt through the padding, and the icy wind swirled around them, numbing hands and feet. At last, to her intense relief, she felt hands reach up and grasp her ankles and steady her.

Then the men were untying the ropes and hurrying them into the trees where the horses waited. Rufenna sank down on the ground, wrapped again in her blanket, and another blanket was bundled gently around the shaking form of the boy. She felt so tired she wanted nothing more than to lie down on the frosty ground and close her eyes. A silver flask was pressed into her hands and a large, firm hand tilted it up toward her mouth. She swallowed the burning liquid that raged down her throat and into her stom-

ach like a fiery comet and shut off her breath for
a long second. She gasped, sputtered, and then relaxed as she felt a warm glow begin to spread through
her stomach. She obediently drank another big swallow and then another of the raw Scots whiskey and
sighed happily. It had warmed and relaxed her and
she was grateful for the comfort. Then the man was
persuading John to drink a few more swallows and
she could dimly hear John's protests and sputterings.
She forced herself to try and stay awake.

"Rufenna, what is m'lord Hammond going to do
about Cousin Murdoch?" John was asking her as he
shook her arm roughly. "Rufenna!"

"I don't know," she murmured.

"I hope he kills him!" her brother growled, his
voice deeper than she remembered.

"He probably will," she whispered, not caring at
all what Davon did to Murdoch. She only wanted to
close her eyes for a little while, just to rest.

While the men who waited with the horses brought
John up to date on the night's adventures, Davon
was stalking through the main sleeping wing, looking
for his quarry. The entire operation had been con-
ducted with such stealth, the sentries on the walls
silenced with such expertise, neither the servants nor
the guards yet knew that an enemy force had invaded
the halls, so no one appeared to deter Davon in his
search. He reached the door at the end of the hall
and entered a large corner chamber. As he turned
the knob and thrust the door open, a sleepy voice inquired, "Who is it?"

Davon strode into the room and to the side of the
bed. With his drawn sword he pushed back the heavy
bed hangings. Murdoch blinked against the sudden
intrusion and his eyes widened at the sight of the
coldly furious man standing there, holding a bared
sword to his throat.

"W-who are you?" he bleated.

"You miserable whoreson! Make war on women and children, will you? Get your worthless body out of that bed before I skewer you where you lie!"

Murdoch, keeping a wary eye on the sword, cautiously sat up. "Hammond? I thought it was you! What are you doing here?"

"I have retrieved the boy, Lyall, and now I intend to kill you. Do you choose to die with your sword in your hand or shall I spare us both the effort and kill you now?"

Murdoch swallowed the rising fear in his throat. "I-I'll fight."

Davon stood back and allowed his enemy to slide from the bed. He watched Murdoch's nervous gaze rove around the room as he noticed the cluster of men in the doorway and filling the hall. The narrowed eyes slid sideways to the bellpull but Davon had seen the movement. In a swift motion Davon reached it and neatly sliced the bellpull off above Murdoch's reach.

"Your sword, Lyall! I don't intend to tarry here all night!"

One of Davon's men stepped forward, picked up Murdoch's scabbard where it lay across a chair, and withdrew the sword, tossing it across the room to the man standing uncertainly, clad only in a long nightshirt and bedsocks.

Davon, whose boots were still tied around his belt, quickly undid the knot and handed them to the man nearest him. Then he raised his sword. "Now, Master Lyall, let us put an end to this," he said between his teeth, moving in on his foe. The clash of steel upon steel rang out in the room and the fight began in earnest. David, arriving in the doorway, stopped abruptly and surveyed the two duelists. Davon had the height and reach to his advantage but he was weary from the long ride and the added exertion of getting the lass up the wall. Murdoch Lyall, shorter and plumper than Davon, was well rested and was also a skilled swordsman. David watched the duelists close up, the two swords glinting in the dying fire-light. Davon was fighting coolly but fiercely, pressing his opponent as hard as he could. Murdoch, aware that his foe was tired and angry as well, carefully fought a defensive fight until Davon should wear him-self out. David looked sharply at Davon, hoping that Murdoch was not going to be right. Then he sighed, for Davon's tall, strong figure was moving easily with no sign of distress, as he wielded his thirty-pound broadsword as if it were a toy. Back and forth they went, pacing the long room, their stockinged feet stamping quietly on the floor.

Below in the Great Hall the alarm had been given. A trooper posted on the stairs came rushing down the hall to the corner room and caught David's eye.

"Sir," he whispered urgently, "men are awake down-stairs and will soon be coming up the stairs."

David nodded. "Take enough men down to the next landing and wait for them. They must be held there and our line of retreat kept open. We will join you as soon as this business is done," he added, ges-turing toward the two swordsmen who were oblivious to the interruption.

The trooper nodded and scurried back to the heavy door that opened onto the stairs.

The fight was moving more quickly now. Davon knew that if the castle garrison was not yet aroused it soon would be and there would have to be a swift end to this fight if he were to get his men safely out of the castle. Murdoch had also realized it and now admitted to himself that his strategy was not going to work. He was also stirred to fear by the deadly purpose he read in Davon's eyes. He barely parried a slashing blow and pulled back for a space before launching himself forward in a savage attack at Da-von's head. The shining blade drove straight for Da-

von's face, and with a steady arm Davon took the
blade close to the hilt of his sword and forced it
aside. Beads of sweat were beginning to form on Murdoch's brow and the heavy hilt was feeling slippery
in his grasp. He was panting with the effort now,
and stumbled, badly parrying a lunge before side-
stepping to safety. But it didn't last. He had scarcely
caught his breath before Davon was on him again,
pressing hard against his guard, his sword moving
like a living being.

"So you thought you'd betray Scotland to the English, Lyall? Lord Wharton will be saddened to lose
such an enthusiastic ally," Davon mocked, not even
out of breath.

"I don't know what you mean," Murdoch panted,
darting away from Davon's dancing blade.

"Don't you?" Davon deliberately baited him again.
"Haven't you realized yet that it was *my* man who
brought you that letter? We intercepted the real messenger. Well, if I kill you now, I will at least save
Scotland the expense of hanging you for treason!"

"Damn you, Hammond! You've interfered once too
often!" Murdoch cried, his rage brought to the boil-
ing point by this insolent statement and the terrible
realization that Davon could have killed him at
least twice already and was toying with him, as a
cat does a mouse before she moves in for the kill.
He flung himself forward, cutting and slashing wildly
with his sword, growing more and more furious as
Davon parried every blow. He tried to break through
Davon's guard again and again but each time his
blade was caught and turned aside. Sweat trickled
down his face, blinding him, but he dared not raise
his free hand to wipe it away for fear of beating aside
that wickedly glinting blade one second too late. He
circled, growing more cautious as he realized his own
danger, but his breath was coming in painful gasps
and his face was nearly as white as his shirt. It added

greatly to his fury that his opponent was showing no signs of distress. Davon's face mirrored his confidence in the outcome; his eyes were clear and intent, his hand steady. He pursued his grim purpose with measured coolness and skill, not showing by the flicker of an eyelash his awareness of his opponent's growing panic.

He slipped under Murdoch's guard and left a slashing cut across Murdoch's chest, ignoring the murmur of approval of the men as the red stains spread across the white nightshirt. The room resounded with the muted stamping of stockinged feet and the scrape and clang of the blades while Davon easily held Murdoch off as he fought to find a weakness in Davon's guard, to find one small opening. . . .

The muscles were standing out on Murdoch's face and neck like cords but Davon still moved easily, his wrist like flexible steel, his hand and arm steady. The strain and effort were still scarcely showing on him and his men wondered at his stamina.

The sounds from the stairs began to penetrate the hall and Davon, beating aside Murdoch's badly aimed thrust, glanced back at the doorway. His eyes met Luke's for a fleeting instant and he turned back, knowing he must end this now and get his men away. His jaw tight with determination, he rounded on his faltering opponent. His blade danced right, left, under . . . It slid under Murdoch's blade, beating it aside, and went through the chest wall as smoothly as it would penetrate butter. A sigh of approval for such a neat thrust rose from the watching men as Davon gently withdrew his blade. Murdoch's sword fell from suddenly nerveless hands, clattered loudly on the stone floor, and his eyes widened in shock. As if in slow motion his hands came up to the wound in his chest just as his knees began to buckle. He was dead as he fell to the floor in a heap.

Luke stepped forward and knelt by the fallen figure and looked up. "Dead. A clean thrust through the heart."

Davon wiped his blade on the nearby bed hangings and turned from the sight of his fallen enemy. As he tied his boots to his belt, he could clearly hear the sounds of fighting on the stairs, and he took his men swiftly down the hall and pulled open the heavy door. Half a dozen of his men blocked the stairs just below the landing, holding off a group of Murdoch's troopers. At Davon's signal David took the rest of the men up the stairs at a run, while Davon and Luke went down to help cover their retreat. Step by step they yielded ground, moving steadily toward the stout door at the top of the stairs. The sharp turn of the stairs just below the tower door gave them the narrow place they needed to release the rest of the men. The tightly packed Lyall men, finding their way barred now by only two men, surged forward. Davon lunged down a step, his deadly blade cutting a swath through the ranks of men closest to him, and they fell back a few steps in confusion.

"Now!" he said to Luke and they turned and ran through the open tower door, slamming it shut behind them. Davon sent a quick glance around the walls, breathing more easily as he realized that they had been successful in gaining time for all of the men to get over the wall and reach the safety of the trees. Even as he braced his weight against the heavy door, ignoring the loud hammering coming from the other side, Luke swung his legs over the wall and disappeared down the nearest rope. With a grin, Davon abandoned the door and ran for a rope, aware of the door bursting open and the furious soldiers surging through. He went down fast, letting his hands slide on the heavy rope, bracing himself lightly with his stockinged feet.

"There's one!" someone shouted from above as Davon reached the bottom and ran for the woods.

"Where's an archer? Damnit, man, get one! They're getting away!"

When Davon reached the trees, most of the men were holding their horses and waiting for him. Rufenna lay curled up in her blanket, sleeping peacefully. After a startled look, Davon knelt by her, ignoring John's eager questions.

"Did you kill him, m'lord?"

Davon nodded absentmindedly.

"Did he beg for mercy, m'lord? Do tell me about it!"

"Later, son. There will be plenty of time for you to hear everything."

John, impatient to hear of Murdoch's fate, missed the implication entirely. "Can't you tell me now?"

Davon grinned, a little amused by John's bloodthirsty curiosity. Then he turned Rufenna's flushed face toward him. He could smell the reek of whiskey and, sitting back on his heels, looked at Jem. "Jem, I told you to give her the whiskey when she came back down to revive her! I didn't tell you to get her drunk!"

Jem stammered an apology, saying he hadn't meant to give her so much. "She had only a few swallows, m'lord, and then she just went to sleep. Tired, I warrant."

"Drunk," Davon said firmly. "That was strong whiskey. Hell and damnation! Very well, Jem, you didn't mean to, but it's done now. Get the boy on his horse and hand her up to me."

He led his small army of men from the trees and down the slope. The still night air clearly carried the confused sounds of men and horses in the castle's courtyard and the rasping of the portcullis as it was raised. Davon turned to Luke. "Pass the word that we'll have some pursuit. Have ten men fall back to delay them if necessary and tell the rest to set a fair pace."

Luke nodded and vanished down the double line of men.

Before Murdoch's captain could mount and lead his men out of the castle, the troop of hard-riding Hammond and Lyall men had vanished into the darkness. Cursing, the captain scouted around, finally picking up their trail but already too well aware that pursuit would now be useless. They had too great a head start and tracking them would be a slow, laborious business. Shrugging in resignation, he turned about and led his hastily assembled force back to Galzean.

As the first streaks of dawn lighted the sky, the weary troop of men were riding toward the high towers of Torrey. Rufenna still slept quietly in Davon's arms and David Shelby had taken the lad, now exhausted with hard riding and excitement. First a pearly pink light streaked across the sky, followed by a warmer rose as the sun came up over the trees. It glimmered on the girl's burnished head as she was lifted tenderly from the saddle and carried into the castle. The night's work was over and a new day had begun.

CHAPTER TWENTY-EIGHT

Disturbed by the clamor of men and arms in the courtyard and the castle's hall, Elizabeth Hammond threw back the covers and ran lightly to the high window. She pulled a chair into place and, climbing on it, threw wide the wooden shutters barring the dawn light.

"Davon!" she cried, waving madly to the tall, black-haired man in the center of the men milling around the courtyard. Then, catching sight of the slim burden he carried, she frowned. She knew that tumbling mass of flaming hair! Rufenna Lyall! Elizabeth abandoned the window and began pulling on the first clothing to come to her impatient hand. What could have happened to Rufenna? How had Davon caught her again? Her brain seething with questions, Elizabeth buttoned up the woolen dress and grabbed her warmest cloak and hurried down the stone steps. She pushed her way through the men surging into the warmth of the hall from the freezing wind outside and caught Davon with Rufenna in his arms, just as he entered the castle.

He frowned down at her. "History repeats itself, dear sister. May I ask what you're doing here?"

"I came for a visit," Elizabeth said hastily, her gaze on the girl in his arms. "Davon, what happened to her?"

Davon turned, saw Elizabeth's frightened face, and smiled. "I have not harmed her, lass. She's drunk."

Elizabeth stared at him in disbelief. "Drunk! I don't believe it!"

"Well, 'tis true. Jem gave her too much whiskey and the next thing I knew, the lass was drunk. Can you see that a chamber is prepared for her? Her young brother also."

"Bring her up to my chamber," Elizabeth said quickly, remembering only too well Rufenna's last visit to Torrey and Davon's intentions. "Her brother? Young John? Oh, Davon, you got him back?"

"We did indeed. The boy is cold and hungry, Elizabeth. Will you see to him?"

"Aye, but bring Rufenna to my chamber first. Then I'll see that John is cared for. Davon, tell me what happened!"

"Later, lass. There's much to attend to first. Get Rufenna and the boy settled and then join me for breakfast in my rooms. We're all weary and hungry."

At Elizabeth's urging, Davon handed his light burden over to Will, grinning in amusement at his sister's obvious plotting to remove Rufenna from his reach. The big Borderer, Will, took the sleeping girl and carried her up to Elizabeth's room. When both Rufenna and John were tucked up, Elizabeth went directly to Davon's chamber, determined to get the entire story from him.

Over the generously filled table Elizabeth surveyed her brother. His dark, crisp hair was damp from his hasty wash and he looked tired but content. Before she could begin her questioning, he abruptly restated his question.

"What are you doing at Torrey, Elizabeth?"

She flushed slightly, remembering her last trip home

and the scene that ensued. "A messenger was coming this way from the Queen and I asked for escort. I just wanted to come home for a time."

"Oh? For what purpose?" His dark eyes glinted in amusement, since he knew perfectly well why she wanted to come home.

"Davon, Patrick Douglass brought me," she said quickly, bringing out the truth in a rush. "He was bringing messages to his uncle, Lord Angus, at Blackhouse Tower. I asked him to escort me here first. Davon . . ."

"Messages?" Davon interrupted her sharply. "Did young Douglass say what the messages were about?"

She looked at him, puzzled. "No, only that they were orders from the Queen."

"Is he coming back here from Blackhouse Tower? When did he leave here, Elizabeth?"

"Davon, what is the matter? Why is it important . . . ?"

"Just tell me, lass, and then I'll explain."

"He left yesterday afternoon. I suppose he reached Lord Angus by supper. No, he's not coming directly back here. He was going on to Drumlanrig to see his father for a few days and then come back to Torrey for me. Davon, where have you been? Luke wasn't here, you weren't here. I didn't know what was happening."

"We've had quite a time of it for the last few days, Elizabeth, and I've urgent information for Angus. For Sir William at Drumlanrig, also. Did young Patrick know for a certainty that Angus was at Blackhouse Tower?"

"He said so. Davon, do tell me what this is about."

"As you know, we were trying to find young John and I discovered that Eure had given him over to Lord Wharton at Carlisle. I went after the boy and we were betrayed. I was taken by Wharton's men. Sim made it back to Lyall Castle and told Rufenna and she sent for Luke. Not only did she find the man who had betrayed us—she's a clever lass!—but she persuaded Luke to go with her to Carlisle and free me. Aye, you might stare! She did it, too!"

Elizabeth was staring at her brother in astonishment. "Rufenna? Rufenna rescued you from Carlisle? Davon, how could she do that? I mean . . ."

He grinned boyishly. "I know what you mean, lass. She brought the Lyall and Hammond men and got me out. Then, from some letters they intercepted on the way, we discovered the lad was at Galzean. Her cousin Murdoch's castle. I felt it was time that bastard was dealt with," Davon said lightly, pouring himself more ale. "So, we went to Galzean and got the lad back."

"And Murdoch Lyall?" she asked curiously, wondering just what her brother had done to him.

"Dead," he said briefly. "Elizabeth, most of the letters Luke and Rufenna intercepted were concerned with the Douglasses. I need to see Angus as soon as possible."

"You're not leaving for Blackhouse Tower now!" she cried, looking at the deep lines of fatigue around his mouth and eyes. "Davon!"

"No, the men are weary and so are the horses. I intend to let them rest first. We'll leave later this afternoon."

"And Rufenna? Does she stay at Torrey?"

He met her curious stare and nodded. "I'll leave her and the boy with you until I return. Then I'll see them to Lyall myself."

I bet you will, Elizabeth thought to herself. You're not about to let her leave Torrey without you! Once again she wondered what game her brother was playing and then she shrugged. The longer she knew Rufenna Lyall, the more convinced she was that the redhaired daughter of Lyall could more than handle her brother!

* * *

Rufenna awoke to a loud knock on the door. She rolled over in the bed, unconsciously pulling the heavy blankets higher up on her shoulders, and turned her head to see what the noise was. Elizabeth, slipping quietly across the room to the door, saw the green eyes open, blink, and slowly close again. Then they were wide open as Rufenna sat up, clutching the covers to her throat, as she recognized the deep voice speaking to Elizabeth at the door.

"Davon?" she called. Elizabeth turned and Rufenna saw Davon standing in the doorway. Her gaze went to his boots and spurs. "What is it?"

Davon stepped around Elizabeth and strolled to the side of the bed. His dark eyes brushed across her, taking in the tumbled red curtain of hair, the slim, white shoulders, and he smiled. "How do you feel?"

"Very well," Rufenna said, wondering why he asked.

His brows shot up. "You don't remember? I was sure you would be cursing Jem this afternoon."

Rufenna frowned as she tried and failed to remember why she should be angry with Jem. "What did Jem do to make me angry with him, m'lord?" she asked, stifling a sudden yawn. "What time is it?"

"Jem gave you too much whiskey, lass, and you slept all the way back to Torrey. It's late afternoon and your brother is still asleep." Rufenna thought to herself that if she had been awake and sober, she would have insisted that she and John be taken home to Lyall instead of to Torrey Castle.

Her gaze went back to his boots and spurs. Davon was obviously dressed for riding. Where was he going? A suspicion crossed her mind and she raised alert green eyes to his. "You're leaving?"

"For a short while. Elizabeth is here and will keep you company until I return. Lass, I need those letters. Jem says Toby returned them to you."

She knew exactly why he wanted them. "You're going to warn Lord Angus," she accused.

"As soon as you give me the letters, lass, we're leaving," he admitted, scenting what was to come.

"I'll go with you," she said briskly, meeting his bland gaze with challenging eyes.

"No, not this time. You'll stay with Elizabeth. We'll be riding hard, girl, and you need some rest. The letters?"

"You are taking my men with you? If so, you'll take me too."

"The Lyall men will remain with you," he said firmly, having known she would try this. He swung away from the bed, saw her clothes tumbled on a chair, and went straight to them. Ignoring her indignant protests, Davon calmly searched her clothing until the bundle of letters slid into his hand. He turned, grinned at her, and went back to the door. "Have a pleasant rest, lass, and we'll soon be back."

"Davon!" she cried, but he was already out the door. "Hell and damnation!" she swore as the heavy door quietly closed.

"Rufenna!" Elizabeth gasped.

Rufenna blushed guiltily but thrust the covers from her with a determined hand. "May I have something to eat, Elizabeth? I'm terribly hungry. Also, could you send for David Shelby? I need to speak with him."

Elizabeth looked at her with suspicion in her eyes. Could Rufenna be planning something? Something Davon wouldn't like? "Very well. I'll send for some food," she agreed warily.

"And David," Rufenna insisted. "I must see if all my men are well. I slept through the journey last night."

As soon as Elizabeth was out the door, Rufenna leapt from the bed and began pulling on her clothing.

"You don't have to wear those clothes," Elizabeth said, some moments later, bringing in the loaded tray. "Marie will bring a dress for you."

"That will be kind of you," Rufenna said, wolfing down the food. She was starving! She kept her face innocent as she asked: "What brought you to Torrey, Elizabeth?" Rufenna listened intently to Elizabeth's tale and gleefully seized on the information that Lord Angus was at Blackhouse Tower. She also pried the story from the unsuspecting Elizabeth as to what had happened at Galzean after she had been sent back over the wall with John. Warmth flooded her at the tale of the duel, which Elizabeth had obtained from Luke Daniels while Rufenna slept. Murdoch was dead! They would be troubled by him no more. Now his castle and lands would revert back to the main branch of the Lyall family. She admitted to herself that she had hoped Davon would kill him. Perhaps she would be able to get more details out of David.

"M'lady," Marie said, putting her head around the door. "Master Shelby is here to see Mistress Lyall."

"Send him in," Elizabeth said reluctantly, not liking the glint in those green eyes. If Rufenna did anything foolish, Davon would blame her!

"David!" Rufenna gave him a warm smile and beckoned to an extra chair.

David bowed over Elizabeth's hand and seated himself, his affectionate gaze going to Rufenna's fresh face. "Are you rested, Rufenna? You look much better."

She flushed slightly. "Tell Jem I will talk to him about that whiskey," she teased, "when I see him! I don't remember a thing about the trip back. David, will you have my men get ready to ride? We're leaving shortly."

Elizabeth gasped and looked imploringly at Rufenna. David gazed steadily at her and met those mischievous green eyes. "Where shall I tell them we are going, lass? Home to Lyall?"

She shook her head. "Blackhouse Tower. We have business with Lord Angus first, and then we'll return home."

"My lord has already gone to warn Lord Angus, Rufenna."

"I know. He told me he was going. So are we."

David suppressed a grin and tried to look severe. "Why?"

"We will finish what we began before riding for home, David."

"In other words," he said ruefully, "you're going because m'lord told you to stay here and you must show him you will do as you please. Lass, this is foolhardy. M'lord can carry the warning! We have no business there."

Her mouth tightened. "Indeed we do! Have you forgotten, David, what those letters said? The English are mounting a large raid against the Douglass property and you can be sure it will be directed mainly against Lord Angus. Lord Hammond took most of the Hammond men, didn't he?"

David nodded.

"Then he knows and I know that Lord Angus will need all the men he can raise and we will take the Lyall men to him. M'lord knew how important this was or he would have sent a messenger bearing the letters to warn Angus. No, they need men and we'll not sit here in safety while they face an English army! Would you have that English army on our lands? If Lord Angus fails to stop them, David, who can?"

David frowned, knowing every word the lass said was the truth and yet hating to admit it. He also knew how tempted Lord Hammond had been to take the Lyall men with him and how eager they were to go. M'lord had left them because he knew

Rufenna would insist on accompanying her men. He sighed, foreseeing the inevitable.

"I'll get the men ready," he said, "We'll have to ride fast to reach Blackhouse before dark."

Rufenna pushed back her plate and ignored Elizabeth's pleading. "I'll be ready shortly, David, and meet you in the courtyard."

"Rufenna," Elizabeth begged, as David went to carry out his orders. "Please, don't do this! Davon will be furiously angry. He'll say I should have stopped you," she cried, wringing her hands. "If something happens to you or your brother, he'll blame me."

Rufenna took the agitated hands in a firm grip. "Elizabeth, listen to me. This is a serious affair. Think of Lord Angus's danger. And Patrick! He is there with his uncle. They are going to move against Angus and Drumlanrig both! Elizabeth, my dear friend, Davon won't blame you. He will know you could not prevent me from leaving here. I will ask you a favor, though. Will you keep my brother safe until I return? I would not like to take him to Blackhouse Tower. If the English manage to capture John again, I think it would kill my mother. He is the heir, you know, and now that Murdoch is dead, there is no one else. John must be kept safe. Will you do this for me?"

"You know I will, but, Rufenna, let David take your men. There is no need for you to go yourself."

"You think I should ask my men to face danger I am unwilling to face? Nay, Elizabeth. I represent Lyall and I'll be safe with my men. They will care for me, you know they will. I cannot send them off leaderless."

Elizabeth acknowledged defeat, said a tearful farewell to Rufenna, and watched the troop ride through Torrey's gate. What *would* Davon say, she worried.

Rufenna, riding hard at the head of her men, wondered the same thing. He would be very angry. The lordly leader of the Hammonds was unaccustomed to having his orders challenged, much less blatantly disobeyed. He would doubtless try to send her back but she would not go. Everything she had said to Elizabeth was the truth. Angus was desperate for all the help he could get and Davon was convinced the attack would take place very soon. It might already be beginning, she thought, pressing her horse to the fastest pace she dared set. Wharton was determined to smash the Douglass rise to power and what he considered a betrayal to England. He would stop at nothing to punish Angus and the rest of the Douglass family as severely as he could. If he did not accomplish this punishment, then he would lose his control over the other Border families under his thumb. If Angus threw off the yoke of England and stood firmly for Scotland and succeeded in his rebellion, then he would be joined by other Scottish families whom King Henry was now pressuring and threatening. Rufenna could clearly see the danger of Wharton's position and knew he would have to send everything he had against the Douglasses. No other man could hope to rally the Border like Archibald Douglass, Earl of Angus. No other family held the power, the influence, the stature to raise the Border against Henry. Only the Douglasses, and they could only be raised by Angus. So the coming battle—and Davon was convinced it would be a large-scale maneuver by the English—would greatly help in deciding Scotland's fate. Rufenna could not withhold her men. She knew her position was unassailable and that Davon could not refuse her men.

She even admitted, as they pounded furiously over the hills toward Blackhouse, that she had another, more compelling reason to go. Davon was there. If there were a battle, Davon Hammond would be at the front, leading the charge! She tried to convince herself that all would be well. He seemed to lead a charmed life, but even Davon's luck could not hold forever. If he fell, she wanted to be there. Grimly, Rufenna knew she would have to face his anger, stand against his orders to return to Torrey, and yet conceal her real reason for joining him at Blackhouse Tower. He must not suspect! She could not bear his mockery or pity. Would it amuse him to know that she loved him more than anything in the world? Or would he pity her, knowing he could not return her love? He desired her, that she knew, but love? It was more than she dared ask of him.

When the last valley was reached and they could see the bulk of Blackhouse Tower looming above them on the darkened hill, Rufenna began to grow afraid. Davon's wrath would be dreadful. Could she bear it? Could she stand against him without weeping? Her mouth tightened and her chin lifted as she braced herself for the ordeal to come. Mutely she listened to David answer the sentry's challenge and saw the gates swing open to admit them. Rufenna sat very straight in her saddle, ignoring her weariness. She rode forward to meet her host, determined not to disgrace herself before the great Lord Angus.

Moments later she rose from a curtsy and peeped at the mighty Lord of Angus, who watched her closely in the echoing stone hall. His lips twitched with amusement at the sight of the beautiful lass, garbed in men's dirty leather breeches and jacket, sinking deep into a formal curtsy He smothered a grin and lifted her to her feet.

"Blackhouse Tower is honored by your presence, Mistress Lyall. May I ask the reason for your visit? Is there some service we could render you?"

Rufenna swallowed hard and met his piercing eyes. She felt this man could see through her, straight to her soul. "My lord," she said, trying to sound calm. "There is no service I ask of you. I come to offer you the Lyall men, who are eager to place themselves

in your service. Has m'Lord Hammond arrived? You
have spoken with him?"

Archibald Douglass smiled down at her and nodded. "He arrived an hour ago and acquainted me with
his news. Is this why you are come, Mistress Lyall?
I did not understand from m'lord that you were expected."

Rufenna gave him an uncertain smile. "He does
not expect me, my lord, but it was my men who
caught that English courier and seized the letters. We
wish to offer our help against the English."

"I see."

Rufenna, aware of that assessing gaze, had the sinking feeling that he did indeed see more than she
wished him to see. He knew, she realized, that Davon
was not only not expecting her here but that Davon
would be displeased to find she had arrived.

As Lord Angus ushered her up the stairs to the
private room where he was dining with Davon, Rufenna studied him, hoping for an ally. He was a big
man, as most of the Douglass men were. Tall, solidly
built, flaming red hair that matched her own. He
had a grace, an ease about him that impressed her.
Here was no rough soldier! He had spent too many
years in exile from Scotland, years spent at the English Court, to be less than a polished gentleman now.
Gone was the brash young head of the House of
Douglass, who had once been married to Margaret
Tudor, widow of James IV. Gone was the eager but
rough soldier who had been Chancellor of Scotland
and guardian of the infant king, James V. Twenty
years in England in exile had mellowed him, polished
the edges, taught him restraint, added to his wisdom.
For his age—and Rufenna knew he must be in his
mid-fifties—he was in splendid condition and looked
capable of facing and beating the worst England could
send against him. Insensibly her spirits rose and she
smiled charmingly at him. His eyes twinkled and he

halted her just outside the door. He lowered his voice and whispered, "I gather m'lord is going to be angry?"

She nodded, her gaze appealing, not trusting herself to speak.

"He forbade you to come?"

Again a nod and an unmistakable glance of pleading.

"Well, lass, if m'lord is correct in his estimate of Eure's plans, and I'll wager he is, then I need those gallant laddies of yours and I will happily accept you in my service. I'll not let him eat you, lass," Angus ended with a grin, wondering how Davon Hammond could ever resist those bright green eyes. Sternly he reminded himself of his own young bride awaiting him at Tantallon and he sighed. "I'll give you what support I can, lass, so come on in. We may as well get it over with."

He opened the door and ushered her in and as quietly closed it behind her, leaving her standing alone in front of the door. He would give Davon a few minutes to spend his wrath and then go in and rescue the lass.

Rufenna's frightened eyes found and clung to the tall figure standing before the roaring fire and she waited silently for him to turn and see her. Slowly he sensed her presence, turned, and their eyes met. His black gaze sharpened.

"What in hell are you doing here?" he demanded. "Did I not tell you plainly to remain at Torrey?"

"Davon," she said quietly, hoping to interrupt his tirade, "I brought the Lyall men to Lord Angus and he is grateful for them. I could not see denying him my men and remaining in the safety of Torrey."

Davon strode furiously across the room, catching her shoulders in a hard grip. "I could shake you," he said, his teeth clenched in rage. "One day you will try me too far, my lass, and I'll teach you obedience so that you will cry for mercy! I will not have you here! You will return at daybreak to Torrey and stay there!"

Rufenna met his gaze fearlessly, her fright dissolving in the face of his anger. He couldn't eat her, after all, and once his wrath was spent . . .

"You have no right, Davon, to order me to go anywhere. I have never seen a contract saying that you own me. I will lead my men where I see fit and I felt they were needed here. I am very sorry that you don't like it, but we are here and we intend to stay here."

"We'll see about that! Where's Shelby? I should take a strip off his hide for allowing you to come here."

"David," she said evenly, aware of the warmth of those iron hands gripping her so tightly, "takes his orders from me, Davon. If he refused to follow an express order, he would answer to Captain Kincaid. You presume too much, m'lord," she went on, retreating into formality. "I have been accepted by Lord Angus and we remain at Blackhouse."

Whatever retort Davon was about to make to that open defiance was hastily swallowed as the door opened and Angus came in, his bright, intelligent gaze traveling from a grim face to a determined one.

"I see you are welcoming Mistress Lyall and her men, m'lord," he said smoothly, ignoring the fact that Davon was holding the lass in a painful grip. "My page says that our supper is ready. Shall we sit down?"

Slowly, reluctantly, Davon released Rufenna and allowed her to move to the chair Lord Angus was indicating. Damn Angus, he thought furiously. He is enjoying this. Rufenna cast a swift glance at her host and thought so too. My Lord Angus was greatly amused by their quarrel and was clearly wondering what the outcome would be. She knew that she only had to stand firm and Davon could not make her leave. It was, after all, Lord Angus's castle, not Davon's. He had no authority here. She was also aware that Davon knew it and was seething at her daring. As she took her place at the table, Davon bent over her briefly as Angus turned away to speak to the page.

"I am not finished with you, my lass, so do not think it. I will deal with you later."

With a trembling hand Rufenna took her glass of wine and swallowed some of the fine French vintage. She needed the courage it might give her to get through the rest of this evening.

"If Mistress Rufenna would not be bored, m'lord, I would like to discuss this matter a bit," Lord Angus said as the servant finished serving them and quietly returned to the hallway to wait. Rufenna met his gaze, smiled, and admitted to curiosity concerning their plans, and Angus turned to Davon. "What are you expecting Eure to do, m'lord?"

Davon leaned back in his chair and met the alert gaze of his host. "I think he will raise as many men as possible and attack the Douglass lands. Lord Wharton, aided by John Maxwell and others we may know nothing about, will move against Sir William of Drumlanrig. Has Sir William been warned?"

"Aye. After I first talked to you, I sent young Patrick to him to carry the warning. I agree," he added thoughtfully, "that Eure will attempt a raid on a larger scale than we have usually had. Henry Tudor is *very* displeased with me, you understand." Angus smiled and then shrugged. "I am fully aware of the depth of his rage and am not surprised at this latest move. I have had a letter from Lennox, sent from Carlisle recently, urging, nay, imploring me to reconsider my position. What Henry has to offer does not tempt me, for they will menace Scotland at their peril. I owe nothing to Henry."

Davon shot a glance at him. "He must be very angry about your change of allegiance."

Angus's head came up and his normally mild expression vanished. "I owe England no allegiance and never have done," he flashed. "I am a Scot and will remind you of the fact."

Davon met his host's flashing eyes and said quietly, "You spent many years in England, my lord, at the Court of your brother-in-law. You cannot blame the Scots for doubting your allegiance."

Rufenna swallowed nervously at Davon's daring at so addressing the new Lieutenant of Scotland.

"My Lord Hammond, you misunderstand the situation. I did not leave Scotland by any desire or wish of my own. I was driven from my home by the rapacious greed and the fear of James Stuart! My quarrel has never been with Scotland. It was with James. When I married his mother, he was a wee babe, in urgent need of protection. I gave him that protection to the best of my ability and I dare ye to deny that. Did the lad appreciate it? Nay, he was a Stuart and they have ever been thus. For centuries the Stuarts— a family of Johnnies-come-lately—have held onto their throne with frightened hands. My ain family," he added, his Scottish brogue deepening as he warmed to his subject, "has its roots back into the mists of time. You know the saying about my family? 'Men have seen the stream but what eye ever beheld its source.' We have been here so long, no one remembers from where we came but the Stuarts would see us dead, to the last Douglass. Ah, the Stuarts!" he said scornfully. "Bred from an upstart steward of Rabbie Bruce's, claiming all to cover their ain lack of heritage. Nay, I'll never bend a knee to a Stuart king, not knowing that he would place the sword in my back if I bent it to him. Aye, ye know, my lord. They are greedy, jealous, and grasping, frightened of any shadow, knowing their claim to the throne to be so weak as to affright them into rash actions. For centuries it has been thus."

Davon knew what Angus was saying was not only true but a fair and succinct appraisal of the centuries-old feud between the most powerful family in Scotland and the Stuart kings.

"There is truth in what you say, m'lord," agreed Davon, "and the Stuarts have ever feared the Douglass power. James, perhaps, more than most."

"Aye, James Stuart, greedy bastard that he was. Sit you there and tell *me* he feared us? Hell, man, he feared all of the Border families. Have ye forgotten that your ain father, brave soldier that he was, was imprisoned for a time by our good James Stuart? And why? Because your father was respected, powerful, and did too fair a job of keeping his section of the Border under control! Twenty-seven Border lords did he imprison that year, for much the same offense. If they were powerful enough to control their districts, James feared them and determined to break their power. And the Douglasses have ever been at the top of that list! Nay, man, do not talk to me of allegiance. I have ever been a Scot and loyal to my country but swear loyalty to James I would not. He drove us from our homes, our lands, and I'll not forget that. When he died, we returned and have been reinstated by the Queen. As for Henry, that sly fox, he knows well I owe him naught. He thinks to use me, and the Douglass family, to take Scotland for his own but it will not succeed. He cannot crush us, or frighten us. He sends vermin like Ralph Eure to take Scotland for him? Mother of God, Eure take Scotland? He couldn't take hell if Henry gave him the keys!"

Davon grinned suddenly; the tension that had built between the two men was broken by that amused grin. Their eyes met and locked and a silent understanding was reached. Rufenna let out a little sigh and relaxed.

"We'll have to see that Eure doesn't get the keys,"

Davon said calmly, relieved now that he had found out what he wanted to know. Angus would not change his coat and betray them. Of that he was sure. Henry, his judgment warped by age and illness, had made a grave mistake in encouraging Wharton and Eure to attack the Douglasses. They would soon learn of that mistake.

"What do you think Eure will do?" Davon asked of his host.

"If his orders are to strike Douglass land, he has a vast amount of choice," Angus said, frowning. "He could take his force and ride east, to Tantallon, but I don't think he will try that. He doesn't have siege guns, I understand, and Tantallon Castle cannot be taken without them. He knows that. Hertford tried in May and failed. So that leaves, in the east, Cavers House, which belongs to my cousin, Lord Cavers; and the Douglass lands around Melrose. If he goes west, he could join Wharton to hit Drumlanrig, Lochmaben, Threave, Douglass . . . there's a deal of choice. I think he'll strike east, since the letters to Fleming and Glencairn, that treacherous bastard, said to assist Eure. If they were going to strike west, Fleming and Glencairn would have been told to send their men to Wharton. You agree with this?"

Davon had also been thinking it through. "I do. I don't believe they'll even try to take Tantallon, which leaves Blackhouse, Cavers, and Melrose. Since they must know you are here at Blackhouse, I think it will be Cavers or Melrose."

Rufenna, trying to follow this geographical hopscotch, was frowning.

"Lass?" Angus questioned, seeing the frown.

"Why Melrose?" she asked, looking at him. "I was not aware that you had a castle there."

"We don't, lass, but we own farms there and endowed the Abbey. Douglasses have ever been patrons of Melrose Abbey. Most of our sainted ancestors are buried there."

"You don't think the English would attack an abbey?" she demanded, astonished.

The men exchanged glances. "Why not?" Davon asked. "Henry is no longer Catholic. Surely you know that after he broke with the Mother Church, he took a terrible revenge on the religious houses in England. Stripped them, burnt them, oh, yes, lass. He's a Protestant now with no respect for Catholic abbeys. And his henchmen follow in his bloodied footsteps."

Dimly Rufenna remembered hearing about Henry's infamous desecration of England's religious houses and the revulsion that swept Europe. She remembered hearing the Abbess at St. Whitby's speak of it in hushed tones to the other nuns. They had stopped abruptly when she came into the room. Now she nodded numbly at Davon, still shocked at the idea that a house of God would not be safe from intruders.

"I think it will be the Melrose farms and Cavers House," Angus said thoughtfully. "At first light, I will send a warning to Cavers and the adjacent farms. We can send out scouts and hope to have news of their coming in time to intercept them. Until the English cross the Border, there is little we can do but wait. I have sent word to Scott at Tushielaw and at Branxholm, asking for their men. We will need more than we have here, I warrant. Lass, it has been a long day for you. Your eyes look heavy with fatigue. My page will show you to your chambers and I hope you rest comfortably there."

He rose and bowed over her hand and Rufenna stifled a yawn that had been threatening her. The food, the long ride, and even the quarrel with Davon had combined to induce weariness and drowsiness.

" 'Tis not a residence for ladies," Angus added with a smile, "as it's only a rough tower fortress, lass, but you are welcome to what comfort we can offer you."

The page appeared at her elbow, obviously waiting to show her to the room assigned to her, and Rufenna turned to Davon. "I bid you good night," she murmured, refusing to catch his eye. "M'Lord Angus," she said, whisking herself out the door and hastening down the hall before Davon could insist on having private words with her. She had not forgotten his threat to finish their discussion and she instinctively knew she would be on the losing end of any argument with Davon Hammond. She felt she had come out of the ordeal quite well so far. Quickly she followed the page down the chilly stone corridor.

Davon would not get the interview he wanted, she thought . . . if she were sufficiently careful. Rufenna said a smiling good night to the page, locked the door, and went straight to the glowing fire to tear off her travel-stained clothing.

She would have been less confident and relaxed had she witnessed Davon's rapid departure from his host. Pleading weariness, he left the dining room and swiftly questioned the page. A silver coin in his pocket, a knowing smile on his face, the page trotted happily to the far end of the corridor and went up the winding staircase to m'Lord Angus's rooms. Quiet lay on the corridor he had left, unbroken by the only two occupants of the entire floor.

CHAPTER TWENTY-NINE

The lower floor of Blackhouse Tower, containing the kitchens and Great Hall, lay in silence. Troopers lay sleeping on the straw pallets on the stone floor, warmed by the fires kept going in the vast fireplace. The floor was tightly packed with men's bodies as they rested heavily after their long, cold ride. In the kitchen area the tower servants lay sleeping, catching what rest they could before dawn drove them from their beds to attend to the needs of the quartered soldiers.

At that moment the Earl of Angus's still-angry guest was striding down the stone corridor toward the door of Rufenna's room. In his hand glinted the large brass key that fitted his door. If the page had been correct in his information, that same brass key would also fit Rufenna's door!

The first indication that Rufenna had that her chamber was in danger of imminent invasion was when her door key, pushed firmly by some object from outside the door, fell to the floor and clattered on the stone. Puzzled, she stared at the key and wondered how it had fallen from the lock. Then her startled eyes flew to the door as the unmistakable sound of a key being fitted into the lock reached her ears. Unconsciously she shrank farther under the heavy covers and stared in horrified fascination at the door. The key grated in the lock, the door swung open, and Davon walked into the room. Without a word he turned and relocked the door and slid the key into his pocket. Swiftly he stooped and collected her key. It also disappeared into his pocket.

"W-what do you want?" she demanded, half angry and half frightened.

He surveyed her coldly. "I told you I would deal with you later, Rufenna. Get out of that bed and come here. I am going to give you a hiding you won't soon forget."

Rufenna looked at him in disbelief and slid deeper under the covers. She was painfully conscious of the fact that she wore nothing but a thin linen shirt which only reached to her thighs. "Y-you wouldn't, Davon!"

He strode to the bed. "I would," he said grimly. "You are going to learn that you disobey me at your peril, my lass! I could *beat* you!" he said furiously, jerking back the covers and dragging out her shrinking form. His hands gripped her shoulders painfully, forcing a sob from her. His flashing eyes searched her face, seeing the fright and anguish there, and he crushed her against him. His mouth took hers with a punishing, unrestrained violence. The salt of her tears mingled with the warmth of their lips, and with a curse Davon drew back and looked down into her face. She lay quietly in his arms. Her eyes were tightly closed and her mouth was soft and tremulous. The resistance had gone out of her and she was soft and pliant in his arms. He glowered at her.

"Merciful Savior! One of these days, Rufenna, you are going to drive me to—" He broke off and thrust her from him. Then he moved from the bed and stood facing the fire, his lean hard back toward her.

She stared at that rigid back in uncomprehending bewilderment.

After a minute she sat up and pulled down her inadequate shirt with unsteady hands. "D-Davon, I'm sorry."

"So you should be. You have no business here," he said shortly, refusing to turn around.

"I felt I h-had to come," she cried, trying to soften his anger and justify her actions.

He turned slowly and stood, feet planted apart, before the glowing fire. His black gaze went over her, from her tousled hair to her long, bare, slim legs, and his mouth tightened. "You had to show me you could do whatever you wished, Rufenna. That I have no authority over you, that you have no respect for my wishes, and that you can use your damned wiles on me and bend me to *your* will. Since you are Lord Angus's guest, I cannot send you home. But, Rufenna, now is a good time for us to have a clear understanding. You may charm and cajole me but you will not bring *me* to my knees! God knows that I want you. You know it and have known it from the first. Neither can you deny what is between us."

His words, clipped with passion and determination, rang out in the quiet room.

"This time it will be different. You harp on the fact, girl, that I have forced you into my arms and taken you against your will. That I have left you no choice, that I have taken what you would not willingly give. There is, perhaps, some truth in that. I admit it. But you also deny the pleasure, the joy you've found in my arms, Rufenna. You deny what is between us; you protest that I am a ruffian, one who callously takes you on my whim. Well then, never again will I force my attentions on you. If you're as unwilling as you claim, you need never again fear that I'll take advantage of you. So we'll have this clear, *now*. Come here."

As if in a trance she rose and walked on trembling legs to him and waited, white-faced and silent, in front of him. He looked down on her, searching her face. She could see a hard nerve twitching at the corner of his mouth, a mouth sternly held in check by his determination.

"If you care so little, Rufenna, if you wish to be free of my attentions, say so now," he continued softly. "I will have a straight answer from you tonight and we will settle this. If you want me to stay, you will *say so*. If you do not want me, I will walk out of this room and never trouble you again. The decision is yours."

Rufenna swallowed and with great concentration tried to stop the trembling of her white lips. She was dazed by the dangerous pit yawning at her feet. Holy Virgin, she thought wildly, gazing up at that stern face. How could she admit to him what he meant to her? *He* had carefully admitted nothing! Yet if she let him go, could she bear to watch him walk out of her life? With a cold certainty she felt he meant what he said. No longer would he allow her the pretense of resistance. He was demanding total surrender. She would humble herself, accept what he offered as his mistress or lose him forever. He waited in taut silence for the words that would not pass through her stricken throat. The tension between them grew, reaching unbearable proportions, and he savagely resisted the temptation to seize her and force the words from her lips. Bleakly he saw her trembling hands cover her face and without a word he walked past her to the door, burying his pain and frustration behind a cold armor that had never before been so mercilessly pierced.

Rufenna watched with anguished eyes that tall, rigid back cross the room, the hand slip the keys from his pocket and unlock the door. His hand resting on the doorknob, he turned and two brass keys were thrown on the floor, to lie there glittering at her. Her lips cried his name soundlessly as he opened the door.

"Davon!" she gasped, forcing the word through her tight throat.

He froze where he stood, not turning, waiting.

"Please!" She couldn't say it; the words stuck in her throat, refusing to pass. *Oh God!* her heart cried. *Don't let him go!*

He turned and the black eyes met hers in a painfully intense glance. He saw through her pitiful defenses, saw the helpless trembling of her hands and lips, saw the agonized appeal of her eyes. But he waited. It had to be this way, he knew. A total surrender that even she could not retract come dawn's light.

"I . . ." She swayed toward him, her hand going out in an appeal. Then she was in his arms, held tightly to his hard body and clinging shakily.

His mouth found hers and his tightly controlled passion poured over her, as a dammed stream suddenly released. She pressed against him, molding her body to his, holding him tightly around the neck. He kissed her with a haunting passion, a wild hunger that sent the blood singing through her veins, that lit a warm throbbing ache within her.

"Say it," he said softly, forcing up her chin with a firm hand.

She saw the need in his eyes and swallowed the tears gathering in her throat. She couldn't ask for love but she would settle for what he offered. "P-please stay," she whispered.

The linen shirt slid down her shoulders and dropped soundlessly to the floor as Davon gathered her up in his arms and carried her to the bed.

banged on the door, to the three glittering keys.
Lisa lips cried his name soundlessly in the repeat of the
door.

"Johnny!" she gasped, forcing the word through her
rigid throat.

He froze where he stood, not turning, waiting.

"Please?" She couldn't say it. She didn't dare. In
her throat, refusing to pass. Oh God! her mind cried.
Don't let him go!

He turned and she shut her eyes met hers in a painfully intense glance. He saw through her, gained defense, saw the helpless trembling of her hands and
lips, saw the agonized appeal of her face. But he
waited. It had to be this way, he knew. A total surrender that even she could not refuse came drawn to
him.

Then she moved toward him, and liquid pains
burst in an appeal. Then she was in his arms, held
tightly to his hard body and clinging sharply.

His mouth found hers and his thirsty controlled
passion poured over her, as a dammed stream suddenly released. She pressed against him, molding her
body to his, holding him tightly around the neck.
He moved her with a thought so ample would burst
that sent the blood racing through her veins, that
set a warm unbinding ache within her.

"Say it," he said softly, forcing up her chin with
a firm hand.

The say the need in his eyes and swallowed the
tears softening into her throat. She couldn't ask for
love, but she would work for what he offered. "Please,"
she said whispered.

He pulled her, she down, her shoulders and
dropped compliantly to the floor as Devon reached
her up in his arms and carried her to the bed.

CHAPTER THIRTY

Davon rolled over and lay watching the sleeping girl by his side, and a tender smile curved his mouth. Her burnished hair, glimmering now in the pale, wan light of the winter sun, spilled across the pillow in a russet cloud. He stroked the tumbled locks from her brow and saw her eyelids flutter open.

"Good morning, sweetheart. It's time to get up, I'm afraid."

Rufenna stretched leisurely and smiled up at him. "Are the men up yet?"

"I believe so. It's well past dawn and I've been hearing movement on the stairs for the last half hour. We may spend the day waiting or we may see some action. Whichever, I think we should be up and ready to move."

"Do you think the English will come here?"

"No, I don't. I don't think they'll attack Angus directly and they must know he is here by now. We've got scouts out."

"Davon, you should not have made him so angry last night! It was a terrible risk to take."

Davon gave her a boyish grin. "What! Do you think I'm afraid of Angus? My dear child, he may be the new Lieutenant of Scotland but he is a Douglass and the Douglass power has been waning in Scotland. I'll not deny that they're still a powerful family, particularly in the Border, but if it came to trouble, my standing with the Queen is better than his, I'll warrant! Also with Arran. Good God, child, Arran hates Archibald Douglass! He is forced to cooperate with him because he needs him to hold the English at bay. He can't like it but I have little sympathy with him. No, I'll not have any trouble with Angus. He is only too anxious for our help so he can send Eure dashing for home. You know Angus's new bride is waiting for him at Tantallon? He'll not want to tarry here all winter!"

"Who is she, Davon?"

"A lovely young lass by name of Margaret Maxwell. Aye, Lord Maxwell's daughter. You can see why Henry believed he could bring Angus back to the English cause. Henry holds the bride's father and brother securely in London and undoubtedly is trying to use that to force Angus's hand. It will not work, as you'll see. Henry has never been the judge of character that his father was and he has badly misjudged Angus. If Henry thinks Angus can be stirred to loyalty at the point of the sword, he'll discover differently to his sorrow. Come, we must get up. The reports from our scouts should be coming in very soon."

Davon kissed her lightly and resisted the temptation to delay their arising. He resolutely rolled out of bed, reaching for his leather breeches and shirt. He retrieved Rufenna's shirt from the floor, tossed it to her, and stamped into his boots.

"By the way, did you leave young John at Torrey?"

"With Elizabeth, yes. I thought it would be safer for him there. When this is over, I'll ride back with you to fetch him and take him home."

Davon turned abruptly and pinned her to the bed

with an eagle glance. "Home? I'll see that the lad is safely escorted to Lyall. You'll remain at Torrey with me," he said quietly.

Rufenna slid from the bed, pushed her heavy hair from her face, and met his eyes. "Davon, I c-can't! I must return to Lyall!" she said desperately as she saw the growing shadows in his eyes. "My mother, Davon. She has suffered enough," she added painfully, saying as clearly as she could that she could not bring shame and grief on her mother by living openly with Davon at Torrey. "After she's better, I could perhaps visit Elizabeth or you could come to Lyall . . ." She trailed off, and watched the tightening of his face.

"So you've made your choice?" His voice was flat and cool.

"No, it's not a question of choices, Davon! I have no choice in this, you know I don't. I could not abandon my family."

"Neither can you trust me to arrange it? I thought we had come to a better understanding than this, Rufenna. I—"

The loud knock on the door brought him around and striding across the room.

"M'lord, Lord Angus asks your presence at breakfast. There is news."

"We'll come immediately," Davon said to the page, shutting the door and turning back to her. "Are you ready? The scouts must have come in with their report."

Rufenna tucked her shirt into her breeches hastily and grabbed her jacket. "I'm ready," she said breathlessly, glad of the timely interruption. They could argue this out at Torrey, she thought, as she followed Davon down the corridor and up the stairs to Angus's private rooms.

Angus was already at the table and making short work of the plentiful breakfast spread on the table. They took their places and served their plates from the platters offered by the page. In one quick glance she saw her host was dressed for riding and was wasting little time over his meal.

"What news, m'lord?" asked Davon as he accepted a cup of ale.

"The scouts report a large body of men moving east toward Kelso. I suggest we go along and see who they are."

Davon chuckled. "I agree. They might be the ones we are expecting, at that."

Rufenna ate quickly, knowing she would need the food during the long day ahead and realizing it might be many hours before they ate again. When Davon rose from the table with his host, she too was ready. Angus, his face already preoccupied with the day's work ahead, shot a glance at her.

"The lass?" he asked Davon.

"I go with you," Rufenna said quickly, looking hopefully at him.

He studied her for a long moment. "She's a gallant lass, Hammond. She has my permission if it pleases you. I will not interfere in this. It is to be your decision." Picking up his cloak and sword, he walked to the door. "I will wait in the courtyard."

Rufenna turned to Davon, her gaze wide and serious. "I must go with my men, Davon."

He stared down at her, his hands grasping her slender shoulders. "Your men will ride with the Hammonds, Rufenna. It is no place for you."

Her chin came up. "My place is with them, you know it is. I have brought them this far; I must go with them."

She saw the denial in his eyes and her own gaze softened.

"Besides, I want to be with you. 'Twill be safe enough, Davon!"

The firm curve of his mouth softened and his arms went around her. " 'Tis very dangerous, sweetheart, but . . . Hell, you'll not be much safer here! If Eure finds that Angus is gone, he may try to take Blackhouse Tower. Still . . ."

She stood very straight in his hold and he was touched by her earnestness and youthful dignity.

"Very well, but you must do exactly as I say, Rufenna. You'll obey my orders instantly, without arguing!"

"I promise." Rufenna knew he was right; she lacked experience for this type of fight and would be safe if she did as he bid her.

He tightened his grip on her and kissed her long and passionately. Rufenna clung to him, feeling the warmth of his body through her leather breeches and jacket.

"We must go. Angus is waiting for us. I shouldn't take you, but . . ."

"But you want me to go with you," she whispered, touching his cheek softly. "I'll be good, Davon, and do as you say."

He sighed. "I've heard that before. Come, we mustn't tarry. The men are waiting to ride. Why do I let you talk me into these crazy things?" he asked aloud, wrapping her cloak around her shoulders and leading her to the door. "You're a bad influence, Rufenna Lyall."

The ride to Kelso was silent and fast. The men were grimly intent on finding the army of men reported by the scouts and determining if they were Eure's men or not. Rufenna rode between David Shelby and Davon's man, Will, and watched the tall, black-haired man riding in front of her sit so proudly in the saddle. Something about the strength and purpose of that figure ahead reassured her. It would be all right.

They could smell the acrid smoke long before they reached Kelso Abbey and their pace quickened. The troops rode only a little way up the road before they reached the bridge over the River Tweed. There, bowered in the trees, was the smoking tower and, high over everything in the little village, the pink sandstone Norman tower of the smoldering ruins of the Abbey. Rufenna had no idea what to expect and gazed with shocked eyes at the ruins. As they reached the Abbey, Angus stopped the troop and sat looking around, his face closed and grim. Devastation lay everywhere, surrounding them like an angry wasteland. Men spurred forward toward the still-smoking ruins of the Abbey building, and David Shelby, his own face tight with control, reached out and took her bridle, holding her where she was.

"Wait," he said briefly, watching the men ride cautiously up to the Abbey.

Rufenna swallowed the painful lump in her throat, wanting to cry out at the carnage and destruction spread before her. Kelso Abbey had been so quiet, so serene. Now it lay blackened and ruined, fired by greedy, vengeful hands. With bemused eyes she saw David dismount and join the group of men, including Davon and Angus, who had gathered around the black-robed figure sprawled on the ground.

"David?" she whispered as he returned to his horse. He stared unseeingly at her, shocked by such savagery. "They were here," he muttered unnecessarily. "Eure and his men. Arran had left a hundred men here to watch the Border and guard the abbeys. Eure caught them last night and you see what happened. That is a monk over there, Rufenna, dying of wounds. They tried to hold the Abbey and fought until they were penned up in the Abbey tower." He stopped suddenly and wiped his face with a nerveless hand. David was sickened by such murdering. "The English fired the building, driving them out. Angus's men have combed the Abbey. The hundred men of Arran's are dead, slaughtered without mercy where they fled from the flames of the burning buildings. Twelve monks, hacked to pieces; how many more burned alive or dying from their wounds . . . God, even Henry of England should not be capable of such as this!"

Davon strode forward, his brow thunderous with rage. "We ride for Melrose, Rufenna. Help is coming from the village for the wounded here. Do you want to go back to Torrey?" he asked, his voice clipped with fury.

Dumbly she shook her head, determined to continue.

"M'lord," David called as Davon stalked away. "Any word of where the army went from here?"

"Melrose, the monk says. He remembers hearing the order given. He was left for dead," Davon added, going over to his waiting horse.

Rufenna wiped tears from eyes smarting from the smoke that continued to rise from the smoldering Abbey and was blown directly toward them now by the rising breeze. The wan winter sunlight poured over the blackened ruins as they turned and followed the River Tweed toward Melrose. Rufenna could feel, all around her, the temper of the men changing. They had left Blackhouse Tower in a mood to find and send Eure fleeing for home with his tail between his legs, to show the invading English that their trespass on Scottish soil would not be allowed. Now, from the murderous expressions on their faces, Rufenna realized that they would not settle for that. They wanted blood and intended to have it.

It was midafternoon when the bulk of Melrose Abbey came into view. Rufenna breathed a deep sigh of relief as she realized that the rising columns of smoke were not coming from the Abbey, but from the village of Melrose, which lay beyond. The Abbot, his face pale and bruised, rushed out to meet Davon and Lord Angus in the Abbey courtyard, his distress clear to Rufenna where she waited. The men dismounted and followed the Abbot into the building, and with a swift decision Rufenna slid from her horse and hurried after them. Her eyes widened at the sight of the Abbey's interior.

They had not sacked and burned Melrose, as they had Kelso, but it had been ruthlessly plundered. Chalices and goblets had been snatched from the altar; chairs and benches were overturned and smashed; windows had been wantonly broken, leaving glittering piles of shattered stained glass spread over the floor. The hand of willful destruction was obvious through the Abbey's chapel. Without a word the Abbot led Angus and Davon through the ruined nave and around the monk's choir, to the imposing Douglass tombs lying on the back wall behind the Abbey Tower. They stared silently at the broken tombs, defaced cruelly, deliberately. Near them, under the east window, was the place where Robert Bruce's heart had been interred. Sir James Douglass had tried to take it to the Holy Land as Bruce had requested. When he was killed in Spain, the heart had been returned to Scotland. Here, too, was malicious damage as the raiders had attempted to pry up the stones and either remove or destroy the golden casket. The smell of horse dung and human feces surrounded them. Angus's bleak gaze roved over the broken stone and shattered stone effigies that commemorated his dead ancestors.

"Henry's henchman hopes to take the Border country of Scotland by this method? I will write the instrument of possession on their own bodies, with sharp pens, and in blood-red ink. So Eure, that puling jackal, would deface the tombs of my ancestors?" Angus said softly, his deep, angry voice carrying clearly across the open spaces of the crypts. "That ill-begotten whoreson, when I finish with him, he will plead for God's mercy! I will string him up by his limbs and cut his bowels from his quivering body! I will . . ."

Rufenna, averting her eyes from the shambles lying about them, and trying not to breathe the befouled air, tried to avoid listening to the curses pouring from Angus. Gone was the mild-mannered man who had teased her so gallantly last night. In his place stood a towering Scot, enraged beyond his tolerance, flaming with fury and vengeance at the blow that had been struck against him and his family. Never had Rufenna seen so angry a man. His eyes flashed with a fire that sent nervous tremors down her spine, and his very vivid description of the hanging, drawing, and quartering he intended to inflict on the hapless Eure made her shudder in revulsion. Killing, it was clear, was much too good for Ralph Eure. Angus would settle this score, in the old ways, the ways of the Border If Eure had been present, she realized, Angus would have ripped him limb from limb with his bare hands. Obedient to Davon's hand on her arm, they quietly left the crypt, their boots crunching on the broken glass, and went out through the nave to the frosty sunlight. Without speaking they returned to their horses, held by the rest of the silent, angry troopers. Rufenna cast a quick glance at Davon's face and discovered that in his own way he was nearly as angry as Angus. It showed in the narrowed eyes, the tight control of the mouth, the jut of his chin. She hoped with all her being that she would not have to witness the punishment of Eure for, when they caught up with him, their vengeance would be terrible.

The Douglass lands around Melrose lay in smoking ruins. The rude huts of the tenants were mere blackened heaps on the ground. They spent some time questioning the farmers as to the route of Eure's army, and saw to the immediate needs of the stricken families as best they could. Rufenna's tender heart went out to the women and children, huddled miserably under the bare trees for their only shelter from the biting winter wind. She saw the flash of gold coins change hands as Lord Angus talked to his tenants. He saw to their most pressing needs of food and shelter and directed them to the nearest village left untouched by the army. Money was provided for the care of the women and children. Then he was leading the troop away, up toward the rising hills. They camped for the night in a sheltered vale which lay snugly between two rounded hills. Rufenna sat beside Davon before the fire and listened to the conversation.

"The scouts report that Arran and a small force are not far away, Hammond. I've sent a messenger after them, requesting that they come to our aid. In the morning we must locate Eure and try to discover the size of his force. Our scouts are out now, hoping to locate them by the light of their fires."

"It's no small force, we know that," Davon said thoughtfully. "If the monk at Kelso and the Abbot at Melrose are correct in their estimates, Eure must have well over two thousand men, perhaps nearer three thousand. We have scarcely three hundred lances, m'lord, and I doubt that Lord Arran has enough men to even the odds."

"We'll be outnumbered, Hammond, ye can count on it." Angus gazed fiercely into the firelight. "We will just have to outthink them and outfight them," he said more cheerfully. "I want Eure and I will have him. We'll contrive; never fear."

Rufenna was awakened after midnight by the arrival of two scouts. She stirred under the woolen blanket, feeling the sudden chilly air against her as Davon eased her out of his arms and down onto the pile of straw he had found to cushion her from the frozen ground. She struggled up on one elbow and listened.

"My lord," the first scout said quietly, "I have located Lord Arran and given him your message. He swears he will ride immediately after dawn and join you with his men."

"Thank you, Tim. Go to the fire and warm yourself. It's a bitter night for scouting. Now, Gregor, what news have you of the English?"

"M'lord, we located them to the southwest. They have scouts out too, and seem to be searching for us. I think they have learned we are here and intend to attack us tonight."

Angus swore and turned to Davon. "Did you hear that?"

"Aye. We'd best be on the alert, m'lord. Shall I see to it?"

Angus sat down wearily after dismissing Gregor with a wave of the hand. "Aye, Hammond, we may have to move at short notice."

Davon moved away from the fire and called for Wat and David. "Have the fires doused," Rufenna heard him order. "Tell the men to be prepared to ride on the order. The English are scouting for us and we may have to move quickly."

The early hours of the morning brought about their swift departure from the camp and a move into the concealing hills. For the rest of that weary day they played hide and seek with Eure's army. Eure was determined to force Angus to stand and fight; Angus was equally determined not to face his enemy on a field of battle until his reinforcements arrived and he could pick a location of his own choosing. In the daylight a double number of scouts rode out, trickling back to their constantly moving camp with news of Eure's activities. The English had made a raid on Broomhouse Tower, firing it and burning an old woman and her family alive. The mood of the men, on receipt of this news, darkened, and they were becoming weary of this cat-and-mouse game with Eure. They, too, were anxious to come to grips with the

English. But Angus stood firm. He would fight on ground of *his* choosing and wait for his reinforcements. Davon agreed with him and quieted the mutterings of the impatient men. Midday brought Lord Arran with a detachment of cavalry and a troop of Scott of Buccleuch's riders and the latest reports of the scouts. Eure had again plundered the area around Melrose and sacked the farms and villages he had missed the day before. Now he had turned west, riding for Ancrum Moor. It was not difficult for Angus to guess Eure's route: across Ancrum Moor to Cavers House, hitting William Douglass, Lord Cavers, before riding to Blackhouse Tower, which was now only lightly guarded by Douglass men. When this news was relayed to Angus, a quiet smile touched his mobile mouth and he nodded.

"Now, I'll have him where I want him," he said to a puzzled Lord Arran. Davon flicked a quick look at Arran, wishing they were not burdened by his unmilitary presence at such a time, and went off to tell the men to prepare to ride.

Rufenna, feeling as if she had spent weeks instead of days in the saddle, wearily fell into line. The men's fatigue slipped from them like magic at the news that they were going to catch and attack the English army. They rode straight in the saddle, whistling cheerful tunes and checking swords, lances, and daggers. Rufenna, after a while, became infected with some of their spirit. She checked the dagger Davon had put in her belt that morning to make sure it was easily reached. As the February sun spread over the rolling brown hills and shimmered on lingering patches of frost, they rode hard, following Angus in a move to outflank the English army. He knew where and how he wanted them and wasted no time in driving his men hard to get them into place in time. Taking his little force in a fast, curving line around the slower English army, Angus reached his destination well ahead of the English. He placed them on the moor, just north of Ancrum, five miles from Jedburgh. Using the broken ground on the edge of the moor to hide some of his army, Angus and his men waited for the army to come into view. The men were dismounted. Their horses were taken to the rear by a troop of men and they sought cover where the rough ground provided it. Davon, after positioning his men in the van, took Rufenna's horse by the bridle and firmly led her away. Behind Angus's force was a slight rise, crowned by a copse of trees. Davon trotted up the slope and into the copse and turned to the five hand-picked men.

"Will, I am entrusting you with her safety," he said. "I want two archers sent up those front trees to cover the approach. You, Jem, and Ned are to stay close by Mistress Lyall. You can see the moor clearly from here and if enemy horsemen approach, the archers are to delay them while you get her away. If that happens, take her straight to Torrey and see to her safety there."

Davon moved his horse close to hers and touched her cheek. "Rufenna, you are to do exactly what Will and Jem tell you to. They're responsible for your safety and if you do anything foolish, they will pay for it. Is that clear?"

"I should be accustomed to taking orders from you, my lord," she said smartly, concealing her fear for his safety.

"That I doubt. You'll have a good view from here and if the battle goes against us, and I do not think it will, you're to leave with Will and Jem immediately and await me at Torrey. I have your promise, remember?"

She nodded, her throat tight with fear for him. She watched him canter down the hill, his steel helmet glinting in the fading light. Tears swam in her eyes as she wondered if she would ever see him again.

Will realized her agitation and moved his horse in close to her.

"He'll be fine, lass. He's a devil with that sword, you know," murmured the big Borderer reassuringly. "Look! There are the English."

The English army came into view across the moor and Rufenna gasped in dismay. To Angus's three hundred lances had been added nearly two hundred men, giving him no more than five hundred soldiers. Eure, on the other hand, had three thousand men. The dying sun sparkled on their steel-tipped lances, on their helmets, on the white sashes bearing the red cross of St. George, which were shaded to a deep crimson. Forward they rode in perfect precision, and it was Rufenna's first look at an advancing army. They rode in orderly rows, with the archers marching in front. From the rise she could see that Eure had two small field cannon and many of his riders were carrying the new handguns, gleaming blue in the wavering light. Rufenna knew nothing of organized battle, for her only experience had been in lightning raids carried out in moonlight. She felt a tremor of fear run through her at the sight of that massed row of men, bearing down with determination on Angus's scattered force.

"Lass, don't look so stricken," Will said quietly. " 'Tis not nearly as bad as you're thinking. Look ye, they may be many but they're tired and heavy with plunder. Also, that crafty devil Angus has flanked them, so that the setting sun will be in their eyes. See?"

Rufenna saw and also saw that the guns, now firing at the broken line of Scottish soldiers, were doing no damage. She didn't know if the English gunners were poorly trained or if they were having difficulty in judging their target because of the blinding sun in their eyes. A brisk breeze had come up and was also hampering the gunners and archers by blowing the

smoke right back in their faces. Will grinned cheerfully and settled down comfortably in his saddle to
watch. With the wind blowing the sound of the
trumpets away from them, the Scots did not hear
the English order to charge and only realized the
order had been given when the archers opened ranks
to let the lancers through. The Scots braced themselves, ready for the charge, and a short stillness hung
over the field. Then, with a cry, the English lancers
started up the slope.

Davon had positioned his men in the front rank
with ample space between them, and now he leapt
to his feet and waved them forward with a ringing
cry. The Scots poured down the slope, their claymores swinging widely from side to side. Those two-
handed, six-foot-long blades, in the proper hands,
could cut a swath through any army. Now they were
using them in the old way, whipping the mighty
blades right and left, like a scythe, leaving wide paths
behind them littered with bloody men. Behind Davon's men were the Lyalls, using their swords to take
care of any Englishmen who had escaped the Hammond punishment, and they were solidly backed by
Angus and the lancers. On the right, Scott of Buccleuch led his cavalry in a stinging strike against the
English flank, while the Douglass men pressed hard
on the other enemy flank. In the face of the savage,
relentless attack by the small Scots army the English
fell back in disorder, stumbling around to flee from
those murderous blades that swung like silver death
around their heads. Their own more conventional
swords were useless against the two-handed claymores
and they were not given the chance to use their
lances.

Deeper into the press of men Davon went, taking
his lads forward in a murderous charge. The ranks
of English troopers had broken, turned back on their
flanks, helpless to halt the swift passage of the Scots.

Eure was moving forward, trying to force his men to advance against the Scots, but they were breaking and melting all around him, backing away from that relentless advance. Angus, towering on his horse above the press of men, saw Eure and began to fight his way toward him. Davon, on foot, also began closing in on the English leader. Around the luckless Eure, the Scottish raiders who were riding with him, plundering their own country and neighbors, began to realize the English were losing. The large group of Nixons and Crosers and their followers who had sided with the English in order to enjoy the advantages of raid and plunder, began tearing off their white sashes bearing the red cross of St. George. Falling on the trapped English soldiers beside them in the press, they joined the melee, well aware that Angus would not refuse their services at a time like this and would ignore, for the present, their convenient and actual change of coat.

Up on the hill Rufenna and her escort watched the terrible slaughter of the English troops, who were now so disorganized and panic-stricken that they were throwing down their weapons and trying to flee. But the furious Scots, bent on avenging Kelso and Melrose and hundreds of other cowardly and cruel acts by Eure and his men, caught them and forced them to stand and fight. Rufenna, sickened by the carnage below, covered her eyes with her hands and refused to watch. A complete victory for the Scots was essential now but this was her first experience in the terrible sights and sounds of an actual battle and she was repelled by the blood and slaughter.

The air was heavy with the reek of gunpowder and the sweat of men and horses. Even where she was, she could hear the terrible din on the moor, of steel against steel, of anguished cries of the dying and wounded, and the scream of injured horses. She made a move to try and help, to get to some of the staggering wounded so she could deal with them, stanch their bleeding, something. But Will held her in a firm grasp and said nothing could be done until the battle was over. He had been commissioned to keep her safe and she must obey and stay out of danger.

Davon parried the blow of a mounted English rider, swinging his sword up and down in an arch, and brought down both man and horse. Then he was shoved roughly aside, just as he heard a cry muted by the sounds of battle around him.

"Hammond! Watch out!"

Staggering and trying to regain his balance, Davon looked around to see that it was David Shelby who had pushed him aside, David who even now was trying desperately to evade the steel-tipped lance expertly thrown by the English soldier who had aimed it for Davon's heart. Davon watched in helpless silence, during a long, stricken second, as the flying lance crossed the space and plunged into David's chest. David went down heavily, pinned to the ground by the force of the lance. Davon turned furiously. Two Lyall men, seeing the lance hit its target, fell on the English soldier and he was dead before he hit the ground. Davon knelt by David, easing his shoulders up from the ground, pulling the lance free of the clinging earth.

"Lie still, lad, we'll get you out of here," he said soothingly, his glance on the spreading circle of blood around the shaft of the lance. The two Lyall men moved forward to stand over them, and cleared a path around the fallen man and his leader.

"No," David gasped, his hand coming up to grope for Davon's arm. "It's no use, m'lord."

"That was meant for me," Davon murmured, looking at the lethal shaft of polished wood. "You saved my life, David."

David's breath was coming in sobbing gasps as he tried to speak. Davon leaned over him, straining to hear the words that were costing the young man such terrible effort. "It was for her. She loves you. Take care of her."

"I'll take care of her," Davon promised gently, his eyes filled with understanding and compassion. "She'll miss you, lad."

"She's so beautiful . . ." the lad gasped, blood bubbling at the corners of his young lips. Then he sighed quietly and his head fell sideways against Davon's supporting arm. Gently Davon lowered him to the ground and turned him onto his side. He pulled free the bloody lance and threw it aside with a savage hand. Then he looked up at the two waiting men and rose to his feet.

"Mark this location well, lads, since his mistress will wish to bury him at Lyall."

The two men nodded wordlessly.

Davon grasped his sword firmly and moved into the struggling, fighting men, heading directly toward the embattled figure of the English leader. He, too, had a few scores to settle with Eure. Angus, he saw, had been carried by the milling press of men to the side of the field, and was directing a hard attack against the core of English veterans trying to hold their ground. On Davon went, his arm aching from the weight of the sword, half numbed by the force of the jarring blows as he parried and struck at the men between him and Eure. He saw Brian Laiton, Eure's second in command, go down beneath the hammer blows of a tall, red-haired Douglass and then Davon was facing Eure.

He brought his sword up and thrust hard at the English leader. Eure, nearly as tall as Davon, and with as good a reach, moved swiftly and let the Scot's blade slide harmlessly down the length of his sword. Eure, a well-known swordsman, brought his dagger up to chest height so as to parry any blows that got past his sword. Davon did the same. He was tired, his arm felt almost numb now, but his spirit had not flagged and he knew he could outfight the Englishman. He had seen the flash of recognition in Eure's eyes, knew Eure was determined to buy his life at the highest possible price. Slowly the men moved away from them as the Douglass men threw a tight circle around the two fighting men to give them elbow room. The trampled earth of the moor was slippery underfoot as Davon thrust and parried with his great sword. He moved steadily around until his back was to the blazing sun, sinking behind the hills in a crimson glow. He saw Eure's eyes narrow against the bright light, saw the sweat glistening on his brow and knew he was pressing the Englishman hard. Once Davon slipped in the mud, going down on one knee. The groan of the watching Scots was not heard by either man as they concentrated intently on each other. Just in time Davon got his sword point up, parrying the thrust with which Eure meant to finish him. Davon quickly regained his feet. Then he moved from a defensive position to a fierce attack, as he swung the big sword furiously close to Eure's head. Eure tried desperately to escape that razor edge. He fell back a pace, trying to break through Davon's guard, but found himself so hard pressed to defend his head and throat from the wicked blade that he couldn't press his own attack. Sweat was running down his face, stinging his eyes and covering his lips in a salty tang. He was nearly done and knew it. He made one last thrust at Davon, his hand unsteady now, and it slithered noisily along the side of Davon's blade. Then it had been flicked aside by the broad blade and the opening to Eure's heart was clear.

Davon did not hesitate. His hand rock-steady, he threw his weight forward, driving hard at the exposed chest. His blade, accurately aimed, slid between the inch-wide gap between the edges of Eure's vest of

mail, driving through until the hilt was stopped by
the chest wall. Eure staggered; his hand closed spas-
modically over the filigreed hilt of his sword and
then it slid noiselessly to the ground. There was a
roaring in his ears as he lurched backward, a fiery
hot path where six feet of cold steel had penetrated
his body. His knees sagged, and with a look of utter
astonishment on his face he pitched forward, falling
heavily to the ground. Without expression or words
Davon withdrew his sword and glanced around at
the tight circle of Douglass men. They had prevented
any interference in the duel and now broke their
ranks to surge forward, yelling cheerfully. Before the
sun had finally set, the last cluster of fighting men
had surrendered their swords.

Lord Arran and Lord Angus walked over the field
and stopped by the fallen body of Ralph Eure. Arran gazed down at the tumbled body, at the white
tunic with its red cross nearly obliterated by the
wearer's blood. At their feet lay one of the toughest
of the English raiders and the most hated man on
the eastern Scottish border.

"I had hoped to do this myself," Angus muttered,
bending to pick up the dead enemy's sword. "I would
like to congratulate the man who did do it."

A voice murmured beside him, one of his men
who had witnessed the fight.

"Lord Hammond, was it?" exclaimed Angus. "I
should have guessed. That's a beautiful, clean thrust,
Arran."

Arran stepped back fastidiously from the pool of
blood resting near his boot. "May God have mercy
on his soul," he said, "for he was a cruel man."

Angus shot the Regent a look of contempt. "He
was past God's mercy," Angus said bitingly, remembering the slaughter at Kelso. "He will have to deal
with the devil now. Well, m'lord, are you satisfied?"

Arran, tears in his eyes as he surveyed the shambles on the moor, nodded. "My lord," he said, embracing the surprised and embarrassed Lieutenant of Scotland, "I am much happier for you and I cry your pardon for ever thinking you might be Henry's man."

Angus muttered gruffly, accepted this belated apology, and thankfully turned to the cleaning-up task at hand.

Sometime later Davon stood by Rufenna on the slight rise and held her hand tightly. She gazed down at David's body wrapped in his own blanket and blinked back tears.

"He saved my life, lass, by giving up his own. We will take him to Lyall for a proper burial. Is that what you'd like?"

She turned into his comforting arms and sobbed against his chest. "Yes, please. It is what my mother would wish, too."

Davon left her side and directed the men to put the body on the waiting horse. "You will take him to Lyall to Captain Kincaid," he told the two silent men standing by the horse. "You can give the captain the details of today's action and tell him to advise Master Walter that the lass goes back to Torrey with me. She will visit for a time with my sister Elizabeth."

Rufenna caught Elizabeth's name and turned quickly to Davon. "Is Patrick Douglass here today, Davon? I did not hear of his return . . ."

Davon shook his head. "He's at Drumlanrig with his father."

Hardly caring that this was not the time to make a plea for Elizabeth and Patrick, she looked up at him mistily. "Davon, Elizabeth loves him so much . . ."

He put his arm around her, pulling her against his warmth in the chill evening air. "I have the feeling," he sighed, "that the Hammonds will be allied with the Douglasses, whether we will or not. Yes, lass, I will withdraw my objections to her Patrick! His uncle has more than proved himself this day. He's a bonny fighter, is Angus, and it might be very handy to have such a one in the family."

The first smile of the day touched her tired and saddened mouth as she turned with him toward the horses.

"Come, lass, it's time to go home."

CHAPTER THIRTY-ONE

They had said their farewells to Lord Angus. Rufenna had been heartily kissed by the stalwart nobleman and thanked sincerely for the help of her men. Then they had gathered up the Lyall and Hammond men and ridden out to find a quiet place to camp for the night, away from the sight and smell of the battlefield. Now she sat cross-legged by the campfire, a blanket draped around her shoulders, and finished eating the hot piece of venison Davon had given her. They had been successful in bringing down a lone deer and Will had skillfully roasted it over the fire. Somewhere they had found some potatoes and a large chunk of dried-out cheese, which still had the faint smell and taste of leather. She wondered from whose saddlebag the cheese had come and smiled fondly in the darkness. They did take good care of her, these big, tough Borderers. The sounds of bits clinking and the low murmur of voices reached her and she peered into the darkness on the other side of the fire. With the firelight in her eyes she could do no more than make out some mounted men moving away from the rocky clearing. They had made their camp in the safety of the hills, picking a spot so like the one where she had first stumbled on Davon and his men that she shivered in recollection. He had built her a fire in a V-shaped crevice in the rock, a snug, sheltered location away from the main group of men.

"Were you posting sentries?" she asked curiously as he came back around the outcropping of rock and settled himself beside her.

"We're well guarded," he said smoothly. "Have some more venison." He offered her the thick, fragrant chunk poised on the end of his dagger and she absently took it.

"Who was leaving the camp, Davon?" she persisted, nearly burning her mouth on the hot meat. There was something evasive in his answer that roused her suspicions.

She had to wait impatiently for his answer as he carefully, deliberately chewed his own venison and swallowed it. "The Lyall men."

Rufenna sat up abruptly. "You can't mean . . ."

He grinned down at her, his white teeth flashing in the firelight. "I do mean the Lyall men. I have just sent them home. They will not be back."

She stared open-mouthed at him. "But *why?*"

He chewed another chunk of venison and said thoughtfully, "I suppose you could say I am abducting you, sweetheart."

"Davon, don't jest about this! Why have you sent my men home without a word to me? You had no right!"

"Didn't I? Well, they went, my love, and never questioned my right to give them their orders." Davon smothered a grin as he remembered the squabble he had had with the Lyall men. Jem had protested stoutly that he took his orders from Mistress Lyall and no other. The men had voted her a share of the booty and tomorrow they would divide it up. As for leaving, well, m'lord . . . Davon had grasped the loyal Lyall man by the arm, taken him a few steps away from the others, and explained. After that, things began to go as he had planned. Now he turned back to the astounded girl at his side. "As for jesting, I am not. You may consider yourself properly abducted, whisked away, whatever."

She looked at him in exasperation and with difficulty resisted the urge to hit him. "Tell me this instant what you're talking about, Davon Hammond!"

"You seemed reluctant to be my guest at Torrey, Rufenna, so I decided to take you to Hammond Tower instead. My men are very fond of you, lass, but they'd never help you escape from me. I'd skin them alive and they know it. No, we're going to Hammond for a lengthy stay."

"You can't do that! I won't go! How *dare* you?"

She attempted to rise but he pulled her firmly back down and wiped his hands on a linen handkerchief. Then with cool deliberation he leaned over and wiped the meat juice from her indignant chin. "I dare, my love. I told you at Blackhouse, Rufenna. I have no intention of letting you ride off to Lyall or anywhere else without me. Think, love, how inconvenient 'twould be to have my wife at Lyall while I'm at Torrey."

"Y-your wife?"

"I have a priest waiting at Hammond. Did you think I intended living in sin with you? It would be delicious, I'm sure, but your mother would never forgive either of us."

"I can't marry you, Davon!"

"Why not?" he asked coolly, not a whit disturbed by her refusal.

"You're betrothed to that girl, the one in Edinburgh. Sim told Agnes."

Davon frowned. "Are you talking about Janet Gordon? God in heaven, I never had any intention of wedding Janet. I've meant to marry you since that first night we spent at Hammond! It took me a time to realize it, of course, but the issue was never really in doubt."

"It is too! I never said I'd marry you, you conceited pig! How dare you blandly inform me that a priest is waiting at Hammond to marry us when you've never said a word about it or about loving me or a-nything!" She choked on an angry sob and pushed his hand away as he reached over to wipe away her tears.

"Did I need to say it, sweetheart? I thought you understood me perfectly the other night at Blackhouse. Well, you know now and arguing won't gain you a thing. When we reach Hammond, we'll be wed and that's that."

"But my mother, Davon! She should be there."

"Later, love. I will not wait for all the time a wedding feast will take to prepare. Later, when the Border is not so unsettled, we will go home to Lyall and have the feast. And it can last for forty days and forty nights if you wish."

"Davon, you have not asked anyone's permission! The banns have not even been cried."

"Ah, now, there you're wrong. The last thing I did before we rode out of Torrey was to awaken your brother and he gave me his permission. He will be quite a man, that boy. And as for your mother, do you think she will be at all surprised?"

"John didn't say a word . . ."

"I swore him to secrecy until I could propose to you properly."

"Oh." She sat in silence for a moment. "I cannot be wed to anyone in these filthy breeches and jacket."

"It will make no difference what you wear. I have always thought you most delectable in nothing at all."

She blushed and tried to get up, but he caught her, pulling her down into his lap.

"Oh, no, you don't run away. I've spent far too much time chasing you around Scotland and not nearly enough time making love to you."

He tumbled her over onto his blanket and pinned her neatly to the ground. His arms went around her and he kissed her tenderly. She tried to resist him but could not.

"Davon . . ." she protested, pulling her mouth free.

"Stop talking."

"But I—we—"

He silenced her feeble protests with his lips and his hunger grew. Rufenna surrendered, allowing the warm tide of passion to wash over her. Her arms went up around his neck. For long minutes they clung together, her own need killing any further protest she might have thought about making. When he allowed her to breathe, she lay back in his arms and searched his beloved face with anxious eyes.

"Davon, do you love me? Really love me?" she asked uncertainly.

He touched her quivering lips with a tender finger and stroked her silken cheek. "More than anything, my darling. Life with you will certainly be interesting but life without you doesn't bear thinking about. You're in my blood, part of me. I couldn't do without you now."

She gave a relieved sob and buried her face against his throat. "I love you, Davon. I always will. Don't ever let me go."

He pushed her back gently and smiled down at her with infinite tenderness. "No chance of that, my love. I told you I've abducted you and I'll never let you escape from me."

His warm lips came down, blotting out the light, sending a stirring thrill through her being. The last vestige of armor around his heart crumbled away as he carried her to the back of the sheltered cleft in the rock. Their love blotted out the cold and the dark and bound them together forever.

Davon's men sat around their campfire, on the other side of the tall buttress of rock, and discussed the day's action. They had scavenged the English baggage train, depleted though it was, and found several intact kegs of wine. Now Will, with a knowing gleam in his eye, lifted his horn cup and proposed a toast.

"To the lass, the new mistress of Torrey."

"To the lass!" the men answered cheerfully, delighted and relieved that their lord had picked such a gallant woman for his wife.

"Do we go to Hammond as he planned or will she persuade him to take her back to Lyall?" Wat demanded, looking around the circle of men. "I'll wager Hammond."

"Nay," cried Will. "I'll put my money on the lass."

"Ha! M'lord must pay you too well, Will, if you'll throw your money away such!" Wat said firmly. "Ten shillings you'll owe me when we reach Hammond."

"We'll see," Will retorted, thinking they were underestimating Mistress Rufenna. "She has a way with her," he added, grinning at Wat.

"So," said Wat, "does m'lord. Ten shillings, Will."

When the towers of Hammond could be seen through the clinging morning mist, Will sighed and handed over the ten shillings to Wat. Well, he'd lost that bet, but he didn't mind. He could still dance with the bride tonight. Whistling cheerfully, Will followed the tall figure of his lord through the gates of Hammond.

Dell Bestsellers